PRAISE FOR *THE PATH OF THORNS*

"*A delightfully sinister fairy ta*
romance, and revenge served bi
Hannah Whitten, *New*
author of *F*

"*In this spellbinding tale, love is a dark and fractured thing.* The
Path of Thorns *dares you to enter a world where there are no heroes,
lies are the currency of the wronged and characters will pay any
price to get their revenge. Slatter spins a mesmerising story, whose
pace never falters and which kept me reading long into the night.
A brilliantly assured modern fairy tale.*"
Lucy Holland, bestselling author of *Sistersong*

"*A gothic masterpiece – rich and dark, with enough twists and turns to
keep you reading late into the night. A spellbinding, memorable novel.*"
Juliet Marillier, author of the *Blackthorn & Grim*
and *Warrior Bards* **series**

"The Path of Thorns *is ferocious and filled with monstrous women
who neither seek forgiveness for what they are, nor want anything
less than what is owed to them. There are no good people here, no
real heroes. Instead, we have people who will not be silenced, not by
the world, not even by death. A glorious, bloody, unflinching book.*"
Cassandra Khaw, *USA Today* **bestselling author of**
Nothing But Blackened Teeth

"*Beautiful and vicious. Although it is a ruthless, Gothic tale, bright
and bitter as poison, cold as a crypt, its chinks are stopped against
the bleakest winds with deft, jewel-toned tales, and at its bruised
heart, it is as loving and warm as a wolf curled around her cubs.*"
**Kathleen Jennings, British Fantasy Award-winning author
of** *Flyaway* **and World Fantasy Award-winning illustrator**

...le full of dark rituals, reluctant
... arly cold ... a modern classic."
... the New York Times bestselling
... or The Wolf

Also from A.G. Slatter and Titan Books

ALL THE MURMURING BONES

THE
PATH
OF
THORNS

A.G. SLATTER

TITAN BOOKS

The Path of Thorns
Print edition ISBN: 9781789094374
E-book edition ISBN: 9781789094381

Published by Titan Books
A division of Titan Publishing Group Ltd.
144 Southwark Street, London SE1 0UP
www.titanbooks.com

First edition: June 2022
10 9 8 7 6 5 4 3 2 1

This is a work of fiction. All of the characters, organizations,
and events portrayed in this novel are either products of the author's
imagination or are used fictitiously.

Copyright © A.G. Slatter 2022. All rights reserved.

A.G. Slatter asserts the moral right to be identified as the author of this work.

No part of this publication may be reproduced, stored in a retrieval system,
or transmitted, in any form or by any means without the prior written
permission of the publisher, nor be otherwise circulated in any form of
binding or cover other than that in which it is published and without a
similar condition being imposed on the subsequent purchaser.

A CIP catalogue record for this title is available
from the British Library.

Printed and bound by CPI Group (UK) Ltd, Croydon, CR0 4YY.

All darkness is a gift, but you must find the light in it.

—Murcianus' Book of Oddities

1

At last, an ending.

Or a beginning.

Who can say?

My previous three weeks have featured a long series of carriages; conveyances of varied age, cleanliness and distinction, much like my fellow passengers. From Whitebarrow to Briarton, from Lelant's Bridge to Angharad's Breach, from decaying Lodellan where fires still smoulder to Cwen's Ruin, from Bellsholm to Ceridwen's Landing, and all the tiny loveless places in between. A circuitous route, certainly, but then I have my reasons. And this afternoon, the very last of those vehicles finally deposited me at my goal before trundling off to the village of Morwood Tarn with its few remaining travellers – three brittle blondes, sisters, with not a good thing to say about anyone, nor a word addressed to me in several hours – and despatches to deliver.

Or rather, at the gateway to my goal, and there now remains a rather longer walk than I would have wished at such a late hour and with such luggage as I have. Yet, having waited some considerable while with foolish hope for someone to come collect me, in the end I accept that I've no better choice than Shanks's pony. My steamer case I push beneath bushes just inside the tall black iron gates with the curlicued *M* at their apex – as if anyone might wander past this remote spot and take it into their heads to rifle through my meagre possessions. The satchel with my notebooks is draped across my back, and the carpet bag with its precious cargo I carry by turns in one hand then the other, for it weighs more than is comfortable. I'm heartily sick of hefting it, but am careful as always, solicitous of the thing that has kept me going for the better part of two years.

The rough and rutted track leads off between trees, oak and yew and ash, so tall and old that they meet above me. I might have appreciated their beauty more had it been earlier in the day, had there been more light, had it been summer rather than autumn and my magenta coat been of thicker fabric, and had my nerves not already been frayed by the tasks before me. And certainly if I'd not, soon after setting off deeper into the estate, begun to hear noises in the undergrowth by the side of the drive.

I do not walk faster, though it almost kills me to maintain the same steady pace. I do not call out in dread, demanding to know who is there. I do, however, pat the deep right-hand pocket of my skirt to check for the long knife. I have walked sufficient darkened streets to know that fear will kill you faster than a blade to the gut or a garrotte to the throat because it will make you foolish, panicky.

Whatever it is has stealth, but somehow I sense it creates just enough noise on purpose that I might be aware of its presence. Occasional snuffles and wuffles that must seem quite benign, but which are not when their source is defiantly out of sight. Some moments I catch a scent on the breeze – a musky rich odour like an animal given to feeding on young meat and sleeping in dens –

and that threatens to turn my belly to water. I lift my chin as if the sky beyond the branches is not darkening with storm clouds, as if I am not being stalked, as if my heart is not pounding so hard it almost drowns the close-rolling thunder. But I keep my steady, steady pace.

Eventually, I step from beneath the twisting, turning canopied road and get my first sight of the manor house spread out below. I pause and stare, despite the knowledge that something still lurks behind me. I take a deep breath, give a sigh I didn't know was waiting in me. There is a tremble to it, a quaver I'd not want anyone to hear.

Courage, Asher. There is no one else to have it for you.

It might have appeared quite simple, the structure, if approached from the front: almost slender-looking, two storeys of pale grey stone – silvery – and an attic, but I'm coming at it on an angle and can see that the building is deeper than it is wide. It digs back into the landscape and I wonder how many rooms there might be. In front are flowering tiered gardens, three, leading up to ten steps and a small porch, and thence to a door of honey-coloured wood set beneath a pointed stone arch. A duck pond lies to the left, and to the right flows a stream, too broad to jump but too narrow to count as a river. I wonder if it ever floods.

Lightning flashes, great white streaks of fire casting themselves across the vault of the world. The crack of it seems to echo in my chest. I blink hard to rid myself of the strange effect it has on my sight. The colours leached to black and white like an engraving in a book are discombobulating.

Behind the house itself is a smallish structure, dark wood and white plaster, of such a size as might contain four rooms. It has a tall chimney and a waterwheel is attached to the side, fed by the not-quite-stream-not-quite-river.

Once again, the lightning flashes, striking the ground in two places in front of me in quick succession and a third time hitting an old yew not far away. It stands, a lone sentinel by the side of the drive, and it burns so quickly that I'm astonished rather than afraid. I'd stay to watch, too, except the heavens open and thick angry drops fall hard and inescapable; they will extinguish the tree. In spite of everything, I smile. From the undergrowth behind me there comes a definite growl, all trace of sneakery and concealment gone.

Finally, I run.

I leave the path, which meanders back and forth down a gentle slope to the manor, and take the shortest route over the rolling lawn. The journey would be less fraught were I not concerned with twisting an ankle and clutching the carpet bag so tightly that my ribs bruise against its contents. I arrive at the entrance no less wet than if I'd simply strolled. My progress has obviously been noted as the door is pulled open before I set foot on the first step.

Inside that door, a blaze of light and a tall man waiting, attired in black, a long pale face, thinning grey hair scraped back over his scalp. For all his skeletal demeanour he wears a gentle smile and his eyes, deep-set, are kind. His hands are raised, gesturing for me to *hurry, hurry*.

Just before I pass beneath the archway, I glance over my shoulder, at the lawn and gardens across which I've come. Lightning flares once more and illuminates the grounds, silvering a strange, hunched silhouette back up on the curve of the drive, and I think of... something. Something large but of indeterminate shape, something I cannot quite place, nor does its colour even remain in my memory; there's only the recollection of red eyes. Resolute though shivering with more than cold, I cross the threshold and the door is swiftly shut.

The entry hall is surprisingly small, not grand at all, but well-lit; a silken rug like a field of flowers takes up part of the floor space and I make a point not to step on it with my muddy boots. There are compact pieces of furniture: plain occasional tables, a single cherry-wood chair, an umbrella stand hollowed from a sparkling rock of some sort, a rosewood hallstand bearing scarves and a parasol, but little else. Closed doors with ornate brass knobs lead left and right. The burnished staircase to the upper levels is quite narrow; its carved newel posts are the heads of girls with nascent antlers on their foreheads; hind-girls. I wonder if they come by here on their migrations. On the landing partway up there are tall windows that show the dark grey of the clouds, the play of the lightning.

'Miss Todd,' says the man with certainty; no surprise, really, unless this place is frequented by random young women. Or not so young in my case; not old, but I'm certainly *older* than the last governess. His gaze travels up and down me – not in a sexual fashion, merely curious: I'm a little taller than he, broader across the shoulders. *Statuesque*, my mother said on good days; *hefty* on the bad ones. He waves his hands as if doing so might squeeze the moisture from my thin jacket and thick black skirt. I catch sight of my reflection in the enormous mirror that is the centrepiece of the hallstand; almost unrecognisable. The tiny green silk hat appears to have melted, and I can feel the extra weight of the rain in the tight braided bun of my mousy hair. It will take hours to dry. My face is pale and I appear ghostly, although I've never felt so solid in my life. I glance away before I can examine too closely the look in my eyes, and blink, hold it for a few moments to compose myself so the man cannot see inside me either.

'Yes,' I say and it feels not enough. 'I'm Asher Todd.'

'I am Burdon. We did not expect you until tomorrow, my dear Miss Todd.' His hands clasp together like penitent wings. From behind the door to the left I hear cursing and scurrying but no one appears. 'I do apologise; we'd have had Eli meet you with the caleche. Although given the current weather perhaps the caleche would not have offered much protection.'

'Ah, the walk was refreshing, Mr Burdon; I've been trapped in coaches and carriages for days' – weeks, but he does not need to know that – 'the open air did me good.' There's a rose-gold mourning ring on the middle finger of my right hand; it's slippery from the rain and I try to dab it dry with the least soaked part of my skirt for I cannot allow it to slip off.

'Just Burdon, Miss Todd. Well, I hope you don't take a chill; the family would not be best pleased were you to fall ill from our neglect.' He gives a little bow, strangely sweet. 'Come along, I shall take you to your room.' He eyes the carpet bag clutched to my side, the satchel dripping noisily on the flagstones. 'Is *that* everything?'

'Oh no. My trunk.' I frown. 'I left it by the gate.'

Burdon looks over my shoulder and juts his chin. I turn to see a figure stoop to pass beneath the stone arch of the door, my steamer trunk nestled on a broad shoulder.

The figure gently puts the trunk on the fine rug as if it – and he – weren't gushing with raindrops, then shakes himself like a dog. An oilskin cloak and a broad-brimmed hat are removed with a great cascade of droplets, and the shape resolves into a tall young man with black hair, green eyes and stubbled chin. He glances at me, then away as if I hold no interest.

'Eli Bligh,' Burdon says and at first I think it's an introduction, but no: a reprimand. 'Mrs Charlton'll not be pleased at that.' The butler nods meaningfully at the small lake that has collected on the floor, soaking into its covering.

Eli shrugs. 'To the lilac room?'

'If you please.'

Eli hefts my luggage once more, as if it contains nothing more burdensome than feathers, not books and boots, frocks and carefully wrapped bottles, as well as a basalt mortar and pestle blessed by the Witches of Whitebarrow. He turns and is gone up the polished staircase before Burdon and I even take a step to follow. As he passes I catch a scent of port-wine pipe smoke and something I cannot quite place. The butler touches my shoulder but lightly, to direct me upwards.

'It's a good thing you got to us before evening fell; the estate can be a dangerous place for those unfamiliar with the lay of the land. There's a disused quarry you'd not want to discover by accident.' He smiles to take away any suggestion of fearmongering. 'I daresay you'll learn our ways soon enough.'

'Thank you, Burdon.' Using a person's last name thus, speaking as if I were his better, is not natural to me; in my life I've often sought refuge with servants. 'And the family…?'

'At a fete in Morwood Tarn,' he says, then glances through the great windows as we step onto the landing. 'Although I daresay they'll have taken shelter somewhere to avoid the storm.'

'Ah.'

'Just between me and thee, Miss Todd, if I were you I would take the opportunity to rest this evening. You'll be earning your coin soon enough with those three children, and you might be a day early, but you'll be expected to begin work on the morrow.' He smiles fondly to let me know they're not entirely monsters, then the expression stales. 'And I've no doubt the elder Mrs Morwood will put you through your paces as well.'

I look askance at him, but he merely smiles again and presses my elbow: *Go left*.

Along the first-floor corridor, to a pretty room (so, no servants' hideaway in the attic for me). I don't enter quite yet, but survey the space: a fire fresh in the grate but no sign of who set it; an armoire, dressing table and secretaire all in a pale, honey wood. By the hearth are an armchair and a small table with a tray on it: a bowl of steaming stew, a plate of bread, a single cake, and a glass of what looks like tokay await. My stomach rumbles. I can only assume my progress was noted well before Burdon went to the front door. The curtains are a washed-out purple, as are the draperies around the bed. On the bedside table with mother-of-pearl inlay there is a small crystal bowl of dried lilac, so the air is lightly scented. My trunk sits at the foot of the bed, and Eli is gone but for that hint of pipe smoke and a trail of wet footprints on the silk rug.

'Are there other staff, Burdon? Apart from yourself and Mrs Charlton and Eli Bligh?'

He snorts a laugh. 'I don't think Eli would like to hear himself called "staff". He's got a cottage in the grounds; Enora Charlton's the housekeeper, then there's Luned, the maid – we three live in. There are twenty tenant families scattered across the estate; part of their contract is to pitch in to keep us running – Owen Reiver

14

doubles as coachman and his boy Tew as footman when required. Tib Postlethwaite brings the milk every morning, and her eight sons work the fields. Two of the Binion girls come in to help clean once a week – it's a big place – now, they're twins, impossible to tell apart; don't even bother. There's the coppice-worker out in the woods. But I daresay we're a bit different from grand houses in cities. We make do.'

I enter the room; Burdon does not follow. I face him and he bows, a courtly gesture.

'I trust you will be comfortable here, and perhaps even happy with us.' He smiles again. 'Should you need anything, the cord by the fireplace will bring myself or Luned or Mrs Charlton. Sleep well, Miss Todd.'

'Thank you, Burdon,' I say, thinking I won't retire for an age; then I glance out the windows and see that night has fallen whilst I paid no attention. I'm aware of the door closing as I stare at the rain throwing itself against the glass as if it would burst in. As I hear the *click* of the snib I'm overcome with exhaustion. I stumble to the armchair, tremors overtaking my entire body and I think I will be sick, right here in this pretty, pretty room. I let the carpet bag slide to the floor; there's the gentle thud of the contents on the rug (not too much of a protest), the satchel follows it, and I slump.

After a while, the shaking subsides, as does the roar in my head, but my stomach is still all-at-sea, so I break off a piece of bread and stuff it into my mouth like I wasn't brought up better than that. It's salty and sweet, and soon I've eaten it all too quickly. Then the stew, which is delicious, meaty and rich with red wine. The tokay and the cake I leave for later so as not to make myself ill.

I'm drowsing in the chair, one side of me dried by the fire, the other still sodden and cold, when there's a knock. I call out, 'Yes?' but receive no reply, so I heave myself upwards and go to answer the door.

No one is there.

I step into the long, dimly lit corridor, and look around. To the right another door is open, partway along, so I tiptoe towards it. Inside there's a bathtub, clawfooted, rose-scented steam rising from it. Two thick towels are folded neatly on the corner of a dark wood cabinet, a bar of soap perched on top.

But again, no sign of who drew it.

I shrug; I will take it.

Such a beginning is mine at Morwood Grange.

2

I know I'm dreaming but cannot shed the sensation that the moment is being lived yet again.

It's the day my mother realised what I could do. The morning is cold, icy and we are in one of the small rented rooms that peppered my childhood. I'm five, no, six; we have not been here long. Mother's made a deal for some firewood and bread with the landlord, whose wife doesn't like her. We're sitting in front of a tiny fire eating stale bread, she on the only seat in the place, me on the floor, cross-legged on one of the thick coats she managed to smuggle out of the last household we joined, however briefly. When night falls, we'll spread it over the thin bed we share to keep the cold at bay.

There's not much kindling and we must eke it out. The flames in the hearth are feeble, barely any heat coming from them, and hardly a gleam of light to spark off Heloise's glorious red hair. I'm staring at the fingers of pallid orange with their occasional flicker of blue and I'm wishing, oh how I am wishing they were larger. Higher. Hotter. I don't know when the fire grows, all I'm aware of is that I'm warmer, the flames are leaping.

'Asher!'

I don't know how long my mother is calling me, either, but I know when her fingers close over my shoulder. I'm still well-fed from the last house, there's fat on me, but her nails dig in and hurt. 'Mama! What did I do wrong?'

'What did you do? What are you doing?' Her face is so close, her eyes fair burning. 'I've been watching you, watching that fire.' She loosens her grip on me and I want to cry out with relief. 'You can't do that again, Asher.'

'But, Mama, I only wished.'

And the look she gives me… I couldn't recognise it then, but I would see it again in the years that followed. Oh, I could see fear. Fear for herself, for me. But I came to realise as I grew that there was also a sort of hope, a kind of ambition. The beginnings of a plan, even then.

Heloise kneels beside me, gathers me up and says, 'My dove, you must not do such things. You must not ever let people see that. You can't let them know you're different. They'll burn you, my heart, or drown you in the cold depths.' She strokes my hair, crooning that I must learn to keep secrets, and I do not sleep that night for the terror sinks into my bones and makes me shiver.

I've never played with fire since.

* * *

I wake with a sudden weight on my stomach, painful, the violence of it at odds with the high giggling that accompanies it. For long moments I'm disoriented – as I have been every night and day for the past few weeks since leaving the house that is not mine in Whitebarrow – then I smell the lilac and remember where I am. Opening my eyes, I find two faces, small and round and pleasing, girls of about five and ten. The littlest is right on top of me, red-haired, blue-eyed, striking. The elder reclines beside me, brown curls tumbling, pale skin, eyes that match her sister's. They both wear dresses of red plaid. I smile in spite of the discomfort and irritation at such an incursion. 'Good morning. You will be Sarai and Albertine.'

I gently dislodge Sarai and sit up, prepared to play, but then I see the boy, who will be the nine-year-old Connell, in navy trews, a white shirt and a short jacket. He is by the dressing table and has the mouth of the carpet bag – which I'd carelessly left unhidden, thinking this room sacrosanct – in his hands, not quite open. A spear of anger rushes through me as if it's fire and I give a formless cry. The boy startles and steps away – for a moment I think he will pull the bag and make it fall, but the receptacle remains safe.

I push Albertine and she rolls off the bed with a squeak. I follow, kicking her accidentally. The boy's eyes as I lunge are huge; I grab his upper arm. I feel my mother's rage shoot through me as if I'm the conduit for the worst of her. My fingers bite into the softness there and although part of me says *No*, I cannot quite stop. I tighten my grip and shout into his face.

'How dare you?! How dare you?!'

And he begins to cry. Behind me his sisters set up a howling and I at last manage to leash my temper. I let him go, but he's too afraid to move. Straightening, I take deep breaths, then touch his shoulder; he's shuddering. I'm ashamed. This is not a good start.

In my fury, with my height, I must be a giant to him. I crouch so we're eye-to-eye.

'Connell. I am sorry to have shouted, but you must not interfere with other people's effects. This is mine, this is private. This chamber is my own space while I am here, so you will promise me now never to come in again without my permission. Connell?'

Tears spill with the jerky motion of his nod. Mine are not far behind, but I push them away.

'You must speak it aloud, Connell, or it's not a proper promise.'

'I promise. I promise, Miss Todd.' His voice trembles, but he sounds as sincere as he does fearful.

'Good boy. Now,' I gently tap him under the chin and smile, 'we are friends, yes?'

'Yes, Miss Todd.' A shaky smile.

'And because we are friends, you may call me Miss Asher,' I say and he blinks in surprise. I turn to the girls, who've subsided, sitting on the edge of the bed. 'And you, misses both, do you solemnly promise never to enter uninvited?'

'Yes, Miss Asher,' they chorus.

'Then all is well and forgiven. Now, I must prepare.' I glance at the clock on the mantle – still early – I wonder who dressed them. 'We shall meet downstairs in an hour and we shall begin afresh.'

When they are gone, I sink into the armchair, shaking. No matter what my very good reference letter says, I have little experience of children. But I know enough that such a fury will be all they remember of me. Yet I wanted them to like me.

Rising, I check on the carpet bag and its contents; nothing has been disturbed. I notice then that a fresh tray has replaced last night's empty one: a bowl of porridge, a silver pot and cup, two pieces of bread, some jam and butter. So: someone else has entered while I slept so deeply. The lilac room is busy as a market square.

I must find a hiding place. There is a lock on my door, yet a locked room looks like there's something to conceal. My trunk is another matter – a secured chest simply seems like a natural

caution. Still, I will need somewhere else to store my secrets –
locks can be picked all too easily.

* * *

A little less than an hour later, there is a tentative knock. I wear a
deep green baize frock, a still-damp braid hangs down my back,
the tiny seed pearl earrings that belonged to my mother nestle in
my earlobes. The carpet bag is in the locked trunk for now. I pinch
my cheeks and nip at my lips to add a little colour, but otherwise
I am decidedly unadorned. A proper governess, with mud-water
eyes and middling brown hair, nothing more, nothing less.

I open the door to find a young woman, perhaps eighteen – about
ten years my junior – with blonde curls under a white mobcap, a
pale blue frock with a pleated bodice, full skirts and a snowy apron
over the top. She bobs a curtsey, somehow managing to make it
look impertinent.

'Miss Todd, would you come down? Master Luther and
Mistress Jessamine will see you.'

How sweetly phrased yet entirely unrefusable an invitation.
I give a smile which she doesn't return, just turns and clips off,
assuming I'll follow. I do so.

'May I have your name or is it to remain a mystery?' I ask,
teasing. She doesn't look back, but I hear, faintly, the word *Luned*.

'Was it you who ran the bath for me last night, Luned?'

'Aye, and left your dinner, lit the fire,' she says as if it was a
great effort and not simply her duty. 'Mrs Charlton told me to.
You weren't expected so soon.' Just in case I should doubt the
inconvenience caused.

'Thank you. It was very pleasant to find everything prepared
after such a journey. Have you worked here long, Luned?'

21

'Almost two years,' she says, and throws a glance over her shoulder. Her glance is sly, narrowed. 'Longer than the last governess.'

'Indeed?' I say as if untroubled, as if I know nothing about the situation. 'And where did she go?'

'Ah, back where she came from, miss. Didn't find our climate to her liking; a little too fertile, what with all the rain.' And there's a sound that might be a sigh or a snigger, but certainly all nerves.

I tuck that noise away, and her edgy hostility, make a note to keep an eye on her. She might as easily be foe or friend, and anything may tip the balance. Down the stairs, into the small entry hall again, then through the left-hand door, now opened, and along a corridor brightly lit by the sunshine pouring in the row of windows, also to the left. Outside the gardens look fresh and damp and very green, but there's not a flower still on its stem after the violence of the storm: they lie in a carpet on the lawn, brilliant points of colour like gems; red, purple, orange, yellow, pink and violet. She points and calls as we go: 'Parlour, Master Luther's office, Mistress's music room, breakfast room, dining room.'

Luned stops abruptly and I almost run into her as she throws open a door, 'Library,' then moves back so I may enter.

'Thank you, Luned. I hope your day passes well.'

She looks surprised as she leans in to close the door behind me.

The panelling is dark, three leather couches wait in a U-shape before the fireplace where a blaze crackles, and there's a small elaborately carved desk beneath the large window. Most of the walls are covered in shelving and I resist the urge to examine them before I do my new employers. I drag my gaze away from the tomes, fix a prim smile on my lips and peer at Luther and Jessamine Morwood.

I look at her first, sitting on one of the couches, embroidery in her lap. She is tiny, not much taller than her oldest child. Her fall of black hair seems to have had anxious fingers run through it more than once; eyes framed by long lashes, skin sallow. Her red silk dress is intricately made with bows and gold lace, ridiculous for everyday wear but the rich are a law unto themselves I have found. Around her throat is a ruby-encrusted choker, from her earlobes hang matching earrings, her fingers are heavy with rings, her wrists with bracelets. Surely she's not dressed this way for my sake? But then she gives me a tremulous smile and I think that perhaps her husband's the one who wants her to look like this: she's a prize, a sign of his prosperity, an *adorned* wife.

In Whitebarrow, I heard tales of bejewelled cadavers kept in some churches, decorated saints, trapped beneath by bonds of gold, silver and gems all held together by curses and hex-prayers. Jessamine Morwood makes me think of those. I look away from her, the thought of corpses not one I want in my mind.

'Miss Todd,' says Luther Morwood, drawing attention to himself as he stands by the hearth in an ensemble of various shades of charcoal. He offers his hand, which I take, noticing the neatly trimmed nails, the way his shirtsleeve protrudes a uniform inch from the deep grey of his frockcoat. A gold watch chain hangs from a pocket. He is rather tall; his short hair and neat goatee are ruddy. His expression tells me he has no time for my kind.

Then it occurs to me. They are prosperous and I must know how prosperous; I must know what a privilege it is for me to be here even though the estate is so very remote; they need no peers or fancy townhouses in Lodellan or Breakwater or any of the cities ruled by princes and bishops and other stripes of thief. They are very, very wealthy and as long as I realise that, all will be well.

'Mr and Mrs Morwood, it is a delight to meet you both,' I say and let his hand go as quickly as might be polite; his palm is cold and dry, the sensation somehow as unpleasant as one sweaty and hot.

'Your letter of reference was excellent, Miss Todd,' he says, and I simply nod. *I know.* 'Although we hardly need you; my wife is more than capable of ensuring they know their letters and numbers. Next year Connell will be sent to a boarding school, but until then he requires supervision and some tutoring. The girls, whatever you choose to teach them will do well enough.'

A flush rises in my face. His message is clear: I'm not welcome. I note he does not mention the governess before me.

I flick a glance at his wife; she's got a well-trained expression and it's only because I'm paying attention that I see the tightening of her nostrils and lips, the loss of colour. How long have they been married? Ten years at least to have Albertine. Where did Jessamine come from? Is she a Lodellan lady? Or from another estate close by? Or St Sinwin's Harbour or Bellsholm? I wonder what existence Jessamine expected from her marriage.

'I have knowledge of many subjects, including mathematics and some medicine, botany and biology – would you like me to prepare Connell for those? I assume you will wish him to attend a university. It will give him an advantage.' I lower my gaze. 'Your mother, who hired me, was quite clear about that.'

Luther Morwood is silent for a long moment – perhaps it's unwise to show my teeth so soon – before clearing his throat.

'Whitebarrow is a fine town, a fine university. Was your father a doctor or a lecturer there?'

'I did not know my father, sir; he was gone before I was old enough to recall him and my mother did not wish to speak of him. I believe she found it too painful.' Let them make what they will of that, either that it's truth or a lie. That perhaps my parents knew each other no more than a night as a business transaction. That I am yet another bastard left behind by roaming scholars or soldiers, medical students or doctor-professors. It matters not: the letter of recommendation from Mater Hardgrace's Academy is of the highest order, not at all forged, speaking of my intelligence, resourcefulness and determination. It contains but a few small lies, including my attendance at that institution. What learning I do have will be more than sufficient to teach the Morwood children. 'I was simply fortunate that my mother believed in the benefits of learning; she scrimped and saved so I might do better than she had in life.'

'Your mother is also deceased?'

'Yes, sir. Gone almost two years. Her existence had been hard and she was worn out. Glad to go, I daresay.' Another lie.

'I'm sure she's resting in the bosom of the Lord,' chimes Mrs Morwood, and I struggle to keep my expression under control. No god offered Heloise comfort or took her soul in, and no god-hound blessed her passing.

Still, I manage to say, 'Thank you. That is a kind wish.'

'What a lovely ring, Miss Todd, most unusual,' continues Jessamine Morwood, as if jewellery is a safe subject on which women might converse.

Instinctively, I try to hide it, then force a smile, and touch the thing as if it was always my fond intent. It was made for another's

25

hand; a slight glass dome covers a braided lock of mouse-brown hair, the same shade as my own.

'A memento mori,' I say truthfully. 'Tell me, please, Mr Morwood, when shall I meet the elder Mrs Morwood?' The temperature changes, a distinct chill in the air. 'Only she was the one to employ me and I should like to offer my gratitude in person.'

'Was there a problem earlier?' Luther ignores my question, asks one of his own in a low tone, grinning as if about to catch me out. I tilt my head and he continues: 'I heard a raised voice as I took the stairs. I didn't recognise it so assumed it was yours. Perhaps the children were causing trouble?'

'No, sir,' I say, not too quickly. 'Merely a disturbance in my sleep. I have travelled a good many days, and was disoriented upon waking. I think perhaps I cried out. Tomorrow will be better. I shall endeavour not to break the peace of your house again.'

'I have a tincture for sleeping, should you require it,' Jessamine pipes up. Her husband glares at her.

'Thank you so much, Mrs Morwood, that is tremendously kind. I shall let you know.' I smile at them both. 'And now if that is all, shall I attend to the children?'

Luther Morwood nods curtly. 'My mother will wish to see you, Miss Todd, of course. She will call for you this afternoon.'

'Thank you, sir.'

I leave the library and hear a whisper in the corridor, a conspiracy of mice, and am careful to quickly close the door after me. Albertine, Connell and Sarai await; it's clear from their expressions they were listening and heard me lie for them. I offer my hands: Albertine and Connell take them and Sarai moulds herself to my skirts in a hug.

3

The day passes in a rush of morning lessons: geography, mathematics, reading and comprehension, writing. Four subjects seemed enough, and it will take me a while to establish the limits of their learning to date, then after lunch we exercise in the gardens. They are, on this short acquaintance, pleasant children, polite and curious.

They will be, I believe, fine sources of information, but I do not ask them many questions, not today. Not so soon. It wouldn't do for one of them to report back how inquisitive Miss Todd is. In the evening, I dine with the family and make polite conversation with Jessamine, answer Luther's periodic questions – he is mostly disinterested in me, always contemptuous – and keep an eye on the children's table manners. Mrs Morwood senior is not present and I have had no summons, but refrain from asking about her lest it provoke her son.

When the meal is done, I do not have to oversee either baths or bedtimes for Jessamine makes a point of doing that herself. I nod and smile when she tells me: these are the tiny memories children will hang onto in later life, the small tendernesses some mothers bestow. The sort of recollections that will keep one going, will keep one warm, will help one be kind to other children at some point. I have few such memories, but I *do* have them.

In my room, Luned has set the fire as she did the night before, but I doubt she'll draw a bath for me again. I sit in the armchair, staring into the flames, yet careful not to wish for anything. There are matters to which I must attend, promises to keep, but I'm bone-tired and it takes a while before I heave myself upright. First, I roll back the rug, take a small prybar from the satchel, then make my way around the room, tapping at the wooden floorboards with a foot until one gives the right hollow sound, the right amount of shift. It's a simple matter to lever up the board – it's a short one, cut to fit close to the wall – then hold a candle over the void. I realise quickly that I'm not the first person to do this. There are a few cobwebs, some dust – but not a decade's worth, nor a century's, less than a year perhaps. The light washes over a small rectangular object at the bottom of the hole. I reach in, extract it.

It's a bundle of letters tied with a blue ribbon. Two letters to be precise so not quite a bundle, one thicker than the other. My first clue, then, for one of my tasks. I undo the ribbon, open the thinnest one first.

A single piece of paper, thick and white and written in a jagged, rather masculine hand I recognise. The second is the same paper, two sheets, but it's wrapped around an image so carefully and intricately inked that I recognise the faces: Mater Hardgrace of the Academy and a young woman dressed in the plainest of attire that cannot hide how beautiful she is. I saw the large version of this very portrait in an office back in Whitebarrow, that day I made my promise to Mater Hardgrace. The letters are filled with nothing but businesslike chatter, details of weather, of decisions made at the Academy, and final wishes for the young woman to succeed, to remain steadfast and do her aunt proud. A fondness in the tone, yes, and no sense that these words would be the last between them. I take one searching look at that glorious face, then put the letters back where their owner secreted them.

The hollow is big enough for my secrets and theirs; but I shall pursue mine first.

I unlock the trunk, take the jar from the carpet bag, unwrap it and check the wax seal. Still intact. My sigh is equal parts despair and relief as I hold the bottle up to the light and peer at it. The contents seem to move, but that might just be the effect of the fluid it floats in. Once again I swaddle the container in the old shirt, then gently set it in the hidey-hole. I fish another three objects from the bag – my death's assured if they're discovered – and add them. The floorboard slots back in place, and the rug flops over the top. No one will notice, I'm sure.

Tonight, I feel I can sleep soundly without fear of any unexpected visitors finding anything untoward in my possession. Tomorrow evening, I will unpack properly, transfer my things to the armoire and duchess; I'll ask Burdon to have Eli store the trunk wherever it is such things are stored. Then I shall be settled, for however long is required.

Now, though, I find the silver flask in my satchel. I've not touched it in weeks and weeks, kept it, hoarded it like a miser. I check my reflection in the mirror – tidy, unremarkable – then make my way down to the kitchen.

It's a cavernous space, vaulted ceiling so high it's lost in shadows – unusual – with doorless rooms running off it, and stone stairs going down presumably to the cellar. A wide hearth with a fire blazing, sideboards filled with crockery, a large battered table with an assortment of chairs on one side, a bench on the other; a deep double stone sink, copper pots hanging from a ladder suspended from the roof. Flagged floors, warm with radiant heat from the fire.

Mrs Charlton's hair is still quite black but for silver streaks running from each temple and twisted into her loose chignon. She's spare, no fat on her, and large-boned. Her big hands look as if they could easily wring the neck of a chicken but hold instead a delicate piece of embroidery in a hoop frame. She's sitting at the table, its surface scarred from the efforts of cleavers and knives, stained from the tints of food prepared there. Three lanterns are lit for her to see by. A steaming tin mug of tea is within reach. She says without looking up, 'Good evening, Miss Todd.'

'Good evening, Mrs Charlton.' I've not seen her before this, though I've eaten meals prepared by her, noticed the signs of a well-run household. 'It's nice to meet you.'

I don't say *at last* or anything foolish like that.

'What can I do for you, miss?' Still she doesn't look up, just keeps piercing the cambric with her needle, drawing bright crimson thread through to create roses.

'What beautiful work, Mrs Charlton.'

'Can you embroider, Miss Todd?'

'I can barely darn a sock, indeed I'm so clumsy I'd likely pass out from blood loss,' I say, and she snorts. 'May I join you?'

She waves a hand: *go ahead*. 'Would you like a tea? The pot's fresh.'

I sit across from her, hold up the flask, shake it gently. 'I thought perhaps you might like something a little stronger?'

She raises a brow, as if choosing whether to disapprove of me.

30

'It's a raspberry gin,' I say, smiling. 'I've been saving it until a good day.'

'And that was today?'

'The best one I've had in a while.' *Not a lie.*

She puts her embroidery aside and rises. When she's collected two fine-blown glasses from a sideboard, and a small plate of biscuits from a barrel, she returns. I'm generous with my pour, though it's the last of this particular vintage I'm likely to lay hands on. Clinking our glasses, we toast, 'To your health.' The crystal rings sweetly. We sip and sigh.

'Oh my, that's nice.' Mrs Charlton leans back in her chair.

'A gift from an old friend,' I say. *Neither entirely true nor false.*

'Lovely.'

A few moments of silence, companionable. I'll not ask too many questions. But here, this is gossip between women of the same house, a pleasure and a necessity. What better place than a kitchen? How to start though?

She saves me the trouble. 'So, Miss Todd, this is a long way to come from anywhere.'

'The Tarn is a decent size, I think. We seek employment where we may, Mrs Charlton.'

'True, true.'

'There were other positions in towns, bustling places,' I say, 'but this one's remoteness appealed. I've lived in the city, in Whitebarrow, for a long while. Morwood is a nice change.'

'Ah, well. You'll find what you need in the Tarn; it's a self-sufficient spot. You're just far from most things and sometimes that chafes.'

'You're not from hereabouts, Mrs Charlton?' I pour another

measure of the gin for her, keep the last dregs for myself. The biscuits are cheese, sharp and crumbly, delicious.

She shakes her head. 'Been here ten going on eleven years. I came with Miss Jessamine when she married.'

'Ah.'

'I was her nurse when she was little – motherless mite she was.'

'And you couldn't bear to leave her?'

'There was nothing else for me to do in the house in Bellsholm – she's an only child, you see – so I begged her father to send me with her. Called me a lady's maid until the old housekeeper here died, and I just sort of fell into that.'

'So you're from Bellsholm then?' I know it: a decent-sized port-city on the banks of the Bell River, a lot of merchant vessels and land caravans, an intersection where goods are traded and sent off in various directions. There's a small theatre with a marvellous singing automaton that performs every Friday night; I have heard her. People make weekend plans to go and listen, stay for a few days afterwards. It's become something of a spa town too, with pretty inns springing up to accommodate the tourists from near and far – with the usual warnings about not wandering too close to the bend in the river where the *rusalky* swim and try to lure the unwary into the waters with their arias.

'No, no. Born in a tiny place called Tintern and married there for the briefest of times. He died during a plague, along with our newborn daughter; I survived. Made my way to Bellsholm and found work there – Miss Jessamine was a year old. It was like she was meant to be mine.' She smiles fondly.

'I believe I've heard of Tintern...' I frown, trying to dredge the memory.

'Ah, it's tiny, not much of it left now. There was a dollmakers' academy there in the old days.'

'Didn't they used to make toys with tiny pieces of anima inside?' I ask.

'They did! Sliced from their very own souls!'

It was just a semblance of life, but enough to make the things look real. Enough to make the Church disband the dollmakers' guilds, and hunt down any artisans who persisted in their craft, burning them as witches. 'Did you ever see it? The academy?'

'It was destroyed long before I was born. My grandmother used to tell tales about the day it burned, about the men in their purple robes carrying torches and making sure everything was fed to the flames. That included the last dollmaker and all of her apprentices.'

Thinking of my mother's warning about how those who are different are burned or drowned, I simply say, 'A lost art.'

She lowers her voice. 'Miss Jessamine had one of those moppets – it was ancient, passed down from an ever-so-many great grandmother.'

'What happened to it?' I ask. Folk were instructed to surrender them; god-hounds presided over pyres of dolls with tiny souls inside. I've often wondered if their makers felt that burning, wherever they were. If they yet lived.

Mrs Charlton pauses so long I think she will not answer. But then: 'My miss threw it in the hearth. She became… afraid of it.'

So much fire.

'Oh. Well, children can be fanciful,' I say as if I don't know better. As if I don't know that much of the strangeness children see is real, that it peeks from the darkness because it knows adults

33

don't listen to young ones. I don't tell her I've seen one of those dolls in a private collection in Whitebarrow, that it belonged to a dead woman, that I never touched it because it unnerved me. The Church calls them *soul poppets*, but once they were simply toys for the offspring of those rich enough to commission their making. They are rare to find even in university libraries or important museums.

I swallow the last of the gin, too fast to appreciate it. 'I think I'll have that tea now. No, don't get up.' I take a second tin mug from the sideboard – not the one where the fine china's kept – and return to the table, pour myself a drink and top up hers. I've just settled back into my seat when the door at the far end of the kitchen opens. The weak cast of light from the kitchen spills out to show ghostly snatches of the potager, scant rows of herb beds, the last of the summer's vegetables going to seed. Then it's blocked by a hulking shape and Eli Bligh stomps in.

Mrs Charlton glares at him, but all he does is grin. He gently lays a brace of rabbits on the table, polite as a votive offering. He gives me a dismissive look and I stare back bold as brass to let him know I couldn't care less.

'It'll take more than that to make up for all the work on that carpet you ruined, Eli Bligh,' grumbles the housekeeper, but I can tell from her tone she's already halfway there. She's fond of him it seems, and I'm not sure if that should raise my opinion of him, or lower mine of her.

'How many more, Mrs C? Four? Six? Eight?'

'Away with you,' she shoos, and he goes, out into the black. I'd ask more questions, but I think I've learned enough for one night. I'm tired besides.

'What about you, Miss Todd?'

'Asher, please. Call me Asher.'

'Then Enora,' she says.

I smile. 'I don't think I can.' There's just something forbidding about her and I can't imagine calling her by her first name, not to her face. She shrugs, but seems a little pleased; taking it, I suspect, as respect. I continue: 'Born and bred in Whitebarrow. My mother dead these two years, my father unknown to me and no other family to claim me. I made my way as best I could, did whatever work would pay enough to keep body and soul together, then found employment at Mater Hardgrace's Academy, in exchange for classes. I learned everything I could and she was kind to me, the principal. Asked if I would stay and become an instructor – but I didn't fancy teaching grownups. I'm better with children to be honest.' Not much of that is true; it merely sounds genuine.

'You poor girl, all alone in the world,' she says sadly.

I smile. 'There are many of us; we make our way well enough. We have our dreams and our drives. We will get what we desire, never fear.'

She stares at me for a long moment, then nods. 'I believe you will.'

'Goodnight, Mrs Charlton.' I rise.

'Goodnight, Asher Todd.'

4

'This is the angel oak!' says Albertine and points excitedly. 'This is where the wicked wolves of the wood were defeated!'

I say, 'Indeed?' and try to keep the worst of the scepticism out of my tone. I should know better – I *do* know better – there are more things that roam than anyone suspects. The tree is enormous, its branches spreading up and out, the leaves on the turn, green to gold to fire. Soon they'll fall entirely, leaving only a skeleton.

The tarn isn't a large body of water, but Burdon said it's deep enough to drown in; when I touched my fingers to the surface I found it icy. 'You watch those children,' Mrs Charlton said as she handed me a picnic basket this morning, as if it's not my job. I may not know much about children – although *she* doesn't know that – but I'm aware of that much at least. *Don't let them drown.*

There's a park on the far side of the village by a pretty stream, but we have chosen instead to take our picnic near the church, which is far enough away from other buildings that it almost looks like a conscious attempt to put distance between them. The tiny grey stone cottage where the priest lives is a miserable-looking place. We are sitting beneath an oak just outside the churchyard; the children's coats have been discarded in the sun, but when the wind comes up it's cold. We're not so far from the tarn itself, and we can lean against the low stone wall that surrounds the graveyard, which looks rather cramped, tombstones at angles like badly grown teeth. If folk insist upon dying, the bone orchard will need expanding. My eyes keep straying expectantly, nervously, I must admit, to the church. I swallow hard, try not to stare.

Albertine senses my disbelief – this is our fourth day together, she's a perceptive child – and takes determined steps closer to the trunk. 'See? Those claw marks were made by the wolves as they fled.'

There are claw marks, yes, at such height as might be made by wolves, but they are fresh; so fresh that there is sap still seeping from the gouges in the bark.

'And that,' she says with triumph, pointing to a rock not so far off in the field, 'is the last wolf, turned into stone by the good priest.'

It's unlikely a priest would have wielded such magic, yet she's right: the large stone lump *does* look very much like a wolf slinking off. I nod to hide a smile, then pause: if the last of the wolves were destroyed in the mists of time and memory, then what made those scratches? I don't ask the question aloud; it's enough that I'm made nervous by it. I recall the whatever-it-was that followed me along the drive my first day here, then file it away for later consideration.

We wandered through the town this morning under the guise of a lesson about town planning, but really it was a chance to have the children tell me about the Tarn. To see what they might let slip that adults would not. But they are still a little formal, a little standoffish – I think because they are still trying to get the measure of me. Or because they were urged to be on their best behaviour by their mother as we left the manor. Or perhaps, just perhaps, there's still the memory of my temper on our first meeting.

The lesson content was somewhat beyond Sarai, but she's displayed rather a talent for identifying plants and fungi, drawing them and flowers and leaves into her exercise book (no writing yet, she's not quite got a hold of that). I have been telling her their official names and she in turn supplies the local names. When she pointed to a strange crimson flower growing over the oldest of the graves and said 'Blood-bells', I found myself at a loss; I've never seen their like before. I must investigate at some later date when no one's paying attention. I think she enjoyed the chance to teach someone else something. Now, with the blanket laid out – a safe distance from the edge of the tarn – and our basket unpacked, the lessons are over for the day. Sarai is curled against my side, the boy is climbing the tree – 'Stay in the low branches, Connell' – and Albertine is dancing beside it.

'Come and eat your lunch,' I instruct. Connell is faster to obey than his sister.

'Wolves of the woods, hey?' I say and it brings Albertine to kneel on the rug, snatch up a sandwich in a fashion I'm sure her mother would find unbecoming. 'Then tell that tale in full, my miss.'

She chews quickly, anxious to get the story out lest one of her siblings takes it into their head to do so – badly – and swallows. Albertine crosses her legs beneath her pink skirts, then draws herself up, hands clasped in her lap, head tilted just a little. Someone's taught her how to *tell* and I recognise the gesture. It makes my chest ache for it reminds me of my mother perched on the edge of our tiny bed when I was a child and she still had the breath and the desire to entertain me. She might tell me tales of girls who became queens, of witches who flew, of boys who became pups; when she really wanted to frighten me, she'd tell me of her home and what happened there.

'Once on a time and twice on a time, and all times together as ever I heard tell of, there was a family who owned this land. Their name was not ours, and it is lost, for they were wicked. So wicked that they chose to be wolves, once a year. They would hunt the people of the village for sport. The villagers knew no better, and thought it was their lot to sacrifice until the good priest arrived.'

I try not to scoff (a god-hound would not want sacrifice made to anything but the Church), but Sarai gives a puppy howl, which makes me laugh; to cover up, I nod encouragingly. Albertine smooths out her frown, continues.

'And the priest fought the wicked wolves of the woods; though he was badly wounded, the good God preserved him, and in the end he prevailed until there was but one beast left, a great she-wolf. The priest cursed this last creature and it turned to stone. Then the priest chose the strongest family in the area and gave them stewardship of the land and the people.' She smiles and finishes the formula. 'This is the story you asked to taste, whether it be sour or sweet, it is done.'

'And this once-upon-a-time? It was before us?' I ask, then wish I had sharp wolf teeth to bite off my own tongue.

But the child's too self-centred to think anything of my slip except to correct it. 'Us, the Morwoods. *Us*.' And why would she think any more of it?

'Who told you this tale?'

'Tib Postlethwaite when she used to look after us, before we had a governess.' I met Tib the other day, who grunted at me as

39

she delivered the milk and Burdon introduced us; gods help any child whose education is left up to her! All they'd have heard was story and superstition. Ah, perhaps she simply didn't like me. But I think also about how Albertine's eyes slid away from mine when she said the word "governess". Should I ask questions now about the one who came before me? No. Too soon.

'That was a wonderful recounting, Albertine.'

She blushes under the praise and looks around for the sandwich she discarded. Her brother's eaten it during the telling, so I hand her another. I'm about to ask more questions, when a voice comes from behind the angel oak.

'You shouldn't be telling such tales, Miss Albertine. You know your mother doesn't like them.' Eli appears, leans against the trunk. 'And they're ignorant besides.'

She colours deeper, from a pleased pink to a roaring red.

'Don't be ridiculous,' I say, wishing I wasn't sitting; he's so huge as he looms. 'It's just a tale. No harm in stories, no one takes them seriously. At least no one with half a brain.'

'Only half a brain, you say?' He stretches a long arm down and plucks a sandwich from the basket; I have to resist the urge to smack it from his hand. The mutton and cheese and bread are gone in three bites. 'Still and all, no point in telling stories that make priests out to be heroes.'

I can't fault him on that, and perhaps he sees it in my face for he smiles. Then Eli nods towards the church. 'Exhibit A.'

A tall, round-shouldered man appears on the steps. He wears purple robes, though the colour is faded with age so it's almost as lilac as my bedroom furnishings. It gives him an air of levity that's at odds with his expression, which is unfriendly to say the least. Yet I know enough that a mere village priest has no right to wear such a shade – he should sport nothing more than mole brown. My throat closes up to see him. I don't know what I expected. He might have been handsome once – surely he must have been? – but bitterness at the loss of things he thought he deserved has turned his face to stone. He raises a fist, shakes it, shouts, 'This is the Lord's place.'

Before I can reply, Eli yells, 'It's Morwood land and these are Morwood children. Take your complaints up to the big house, you old crow. You know what sort of a hearing you'll get there.'

The god-hound huffs and puffs, shakes his fist a little more, but Eli just crosses his arms over his chest, plants his feet solidly and stares until the priest shuffles back inside. There's a moment of stunned silence, then the children erupt into giggles; I force myself to join in. The laughter helps release the tightness in my chest but I can't help but see him as if he's painted on my eyes: the once-dark-now-granite hair, the stooping posture; the weight of disappointment. What did I expect my first glimpse to be?

I pull my attention away, look at my charges: the girls rolling about with mirth, Connell staring up at the groundskeeper with unabashed admiration. A proper governess would tell them this is inappropriate, bad manners; would tell them to respect their elders and those who hold themselves holy and can make your life difficult if you do not. But I'm not a proper governess; *Not a governess's bootstrap*, my mother would have said with equal relish and disapproval.

'As if he'd get a hearing up there,' says Eli. 'That being said, there's a good chance he's gone inside to collect holy water to throw on us. So, we'd best move along.'

41

* * *

Some five minutes later, I speak up, raising my voice so Eli Bligh can't pretend not to hear me up there in front.

'The god-hound? Would he not be welcome at the manor?'

Eli snorts. 'He's been out of favour for a long time, since I was a boy. Though the master and young mistress attend services when the spirit moves them, the old lady' – he coughs and corrects with a glance at the children – 'that is, Mrs Morwood the Elder and the Church apparently had a disagreement of some proportion.'

I'm itching to ask more, but it's best not to be gossiping in front of the old lady's grandchildren. He seems to realise that, and grins over his shoulder. 'The details of which I am not privy to.'

I almost pout.

'This doesn't appear to be the way home,' I observe. I'll not hurry along behind him like some wife harrying a long-legged husband.

'I thought you might like a little tour – a detour,' he calls over his shoulder, and Connell laughs with delight. Small boys are easily amused.

I don't say anything, just keep walking. We've headed away from the church and Tarn, but not towards the manor. The trees grow more thickly here, closer together; the path is hard to discern yet Eli's march forward is unerring no matter how dark it gets beneath the branches. I say nothing, reminding myself that every opportunity is a chance to learn something.

At last, light!

We break out into a large clearing ringed with trees and nothing in the middle. Or rather, a deep hole in the middle of it all. The

42

quarry. Where we stand, looking down, there is no path. Across the way, however, I see a switchback track that snakes to the bottom. One side is gravel and dirt and I assume stable, the other is mud-brown water. I wonder how deep.

'It's not used much,' says Connell. Albertine has no interest in it, I can tell, or she'd be instructing me.

'The same stone as the house?' I ask.

Eli replies. 'And the church and rectory, and some of the bigger houses further away.'

'Neighbours,' Connell says as if they might be unspeakably exotic.

'Where does your mother take you to visit?'

'The Penpraises and the Willows, the Madrigals and the Solomons,' Albertine chimes in – a subject of interest to her clearly – 'although Father says they're beneath us, and I think Grandmamma might have said that too.'

I'll dig into that more later. Instead I look at Eli, back at the quarry. 'It's dangerous.'

'Only if you're not careful.' He grins. I pull Connell back from the edge. Not such a problem with the girls, they're both staying close to the solidity of the trees. Eli continues, 'It's far from the Tarn and the house. No one comes out here much unless there's stone needs cutting for repairs. Long time since it's been worked properly.'

It's not big enough for a commercial concern, and the stone's not lovely enough to be sought-after. It's terribly plain. A movement catches my eye across the great gaping hole. Something white, flashing between the boles, moving very quickly as if not to be seen.

43

'What's that?' But I ask too late and it's gone before Eli and the children turn its way. Flustered, I stare. 'Nothing. Just my imagination.'

And perhaps it was. I try to recall if this place was ever mentioned but find nothing. Doesn't mean there isn't something buried deep, only that I can't access it. I shiver and Eli notices. The sun's getting low in the sky.

'Right,' says Eli. 'Home then before your Miss Todd gets a chill.'

'We're allowed to call her Miss Asher,' says Connell shyly, proudly.

'Indeed?' Eli raises a brow at me. 'Perhaps one day I'll earn that privilege.'

'Highly unlikely,' I say and raise my own eyebrow in return.

* * *

Back at the manor, Eli leaves us at the front door. We barely spoke on the walk; he paced ahead with Connell doing his best to keep up, firing questions at the big man; the girls and I came along behind, me quizzing Albertine on her spelling. Once inside, I've barely had time to remove the children's coats when Luned appears. She's become less snippy with me, possibly because I've resisted all her efforts to bicker.

'Get along. I'll take care of these. The old lady wants to see you. Second floor, the suite first to the left of the staircase.'

'Thank you, Luned.'

Leonora Morwood did not send for me when her son said she would, nor any day since. When I met briefly with Jessamine yesterday morning about the children's lessons – she did not criticise or suggest anything, I think she simply wanted to be

44

involved in a small way and I was happy for her to be so, though jealousy at her care for the children did prick at me – she explained her mother-in-law had been ill. There was something in her tone that told me it was half a lie, but I did not question.

My pace is measured, not wanting to present myself either out of breath or madly perspiring. When I finally arrive at the relevant door, I take a few moments to compose myself: smooth my yellow skirts, tidy my braid, wipe away the tiny beads of sweat at my hairline and upper lip. Leonora Morwood is the one who hired me via the Academy in Whitebarrow (and the one before me). I have read her letters to Mater Hardgrace, seen the strong, elegant handwriting, noted their tone of demand, expectation of obedience. I raise my hand and – balled into a fist and shaking – after only the briefest hesitation, knock.

The voice that answers is firmly uninterested as it bids me enter.

I step into brilliant white light. When my eyes adjust I make out a large room with three tall arched windows, curtains held back by silken cords and ten fully lit candelabras placed carefully around the space. To one side is a large bed, a wardrobe, duchess, a writing desk and a small closed door. To the other is a sitting room, the walls covered with bookshelves, armchairs tightly crammed beside delicate tables piled high with volumes that are either being read or simply cannot fit on the shelves. Even at this distance I can see many of the spines bear a gold embossed *M*.

'Oh!' I say before I can stop myself.

'What is it, girl?' It takes a moment before I locate the speaker, whose tone has lifted from indifference to annoyance. She's just a silhouette and at first I think she's small, but then realise she is hunched over a wooden lectern right in front of the middle window. Her hair is a faded red, turning to snow, and hangs loose across her shoulders, down to her waist; she doesn't turn to me.

'You have so many volumes of Murcianus! They are very rare.' And expensive, but I do not say that – a sure giveaway of one's poverty is the mention of something's value. I have been poor, but I have also been rich-adjacent and benefited from that. The few tomes owned by the university library at Whitebarrow are not merely kept behind lock and key but chained in place as well, viewed only under the strict supervision of the chief librarian (unless one has other, more surreptitious means). Yet here. So many! Unfettered and free!

The woman straightens; she's quite tall, almost my height. Her dress is a deep burgundy and she wears white cotton gloves such as the archivists at Whitebarrow do. She turns towards me, beckons. As I draw closer I think her eyes are silver. Her face was lovely once, I can see that, but a tracery of wrinkles and sagging have marred it. I quickly calculate: she must be sixty; not old, but old-seeming. It's not simply the furrows – that's never enough to ruin beauty – but there's some suffering beneath her skin. Yet the bones of it are familiar, the architecture is *known*. Though I recognise something in her, she'll not do the same with me; this face will raise no alarm bells. I keep a distance between us, a good several yards.

'You've heard of these works?'

Be brave, Asher. 'Some of them, yes. And I know that Murcianus was not a man, but rather Murciana of the Citadel at Cwen's Reach, first of the Blessed Wanderers.'

The woman raises a brow, nods. 'Very few know *that*. Some

46

of these copies came with those who fled the Fall of the Citadel. They passed to me from my mother, as they did from hers to her in a very long line. Others I have had found over the years.'

'Marvellous,' I say and I mean it. So much knowledge! 'Are you descended? From *her*, I mean?'

She gives a laugh. 'Easy to allege such a thing, yes? Who's to gainsay you so long after the dead are dust, so very long after Murciana passed away. But no. I'll not lay such a claim – one of the Little Sisters escaped, came here, married in. They say Murciana bore no offspring, besides.'

'They say she did not die,' I breathe, a little carried away to speak of such things with someone who understands them. 'They say she wrote herself into a book, with ink of her blood, and pages of her skin, a quill of her bones, all threaded together with her own hair.'

'I've not heard that before. Fanciful, but I must write it down.' She says it so quietly it's almost like a prayer. She raises a hand once more. 'Come closer.'

So I step into the brightness that pours in with the afternoon's direct sun, and I realise that her eyes are not silver. There's the cast of oncoming webs in both iris and pupil… a milky fall of cataracts that will entirely take Leonora Morwood's sight soon if I'm not badly mistaken. I don't restrain my intake of breath.

'Let me see you while I may, girl, you're little more than a series of smudges at a distance.' Her mouth thins.

'My name is Asher Todd,' I say to assert myself. 'And I might be able to help.'

5

The sun on my back is wonderful and I stretch like an old cat. I have the afternoon free for Jessamine has taken the children visiting some neighbour or other, Luther is off somewhere on the estate, so I'm stealing some time for myself. The western parlour is kept for formal occasions, no one will look in here and find me curled on a seat in a patch of warmth, book on my lap. Oh, I'll offer to make myself useful elsewhere soon enough. Not that I'm obliged, but it will be appreciated.

Yet even my best laid plans cannot compete with the ructions of a household, and I hear Mrs Charlton shouting at Burdon, demanding to know where Luned is. I sigh, and rise, make my way along to the kitchen door which is ajar; I peek in.

'You know,' says Burdon stiffly, 'very well where the girl is.'

'Not again! Aren't there enough Morwood bastards running around the Tarn? Bad enough having the Binions creep about here once a week, rubbing my poor girl's face in it! The indignity! The cruelty!' The housekeeper's mouth is drawn, lips thin and tight. Her hands are clenched into fists as she faces the butler across the table. I've not yet sighted the Binion twins, but now I'm eager to do so.

'The master will do what the master wishes. Do *you* want to go and fetch her?' he challenges, and begins to lean back as

48

if he might cross his arms over his chest, but thinks better of it. Undignified. 'If the girl's too stupid—'

'Don't you dare blame her!' Mrs Charlton's voice is a knife cutting the air.

I push the door open, step in, smile as if I've not just heard their argument. 'I'm at a loose end, Mrs Charlton, with the children gone for the afternoon. Is there anything I may help with?'

Those lips get thinner and tighter as if she might begin to swallow herself – then she relaxes. Gives a sharp nod. 'There's mending needs collecting from the Tarn. Heledd Jones should have everything ready by now. She's in the house across the way from the apothecary, the one with the green door. Ask Eli to saddle you a horse.'

'It's such a beautiful day, I think I'll walk.' It'll only take me the better part of twenty minutes; I learned to ride in various houses we lived in, but I'd rather gnaw off my arm than ask Eli Bligh for anything.

Mrs Charlton shrugs as she hands me the silver bits to pay Heledd Jones. 'Don't forget your coat, it's turning colder and colder.'

'Is there anything else you need from the Tarn?' I say. 'Or you, Burdon?'

They both shake their heads, but when I come down from my room a few minutes later, coat in hand, I find Burdon in the foyer as if waiting for me. I grin, slant my eyes up at him. 'How kind, Burdon, I'd never have been able to open the door on my own.'

'Saucy miss.' He holds out a hand and I offer a palm in return: he drops four silver bits into it. 'If you don't mind, at the inn they have a peach brandy I'm fond of. Just don't let Mrs Charlton see.'

'Your secret is safe with me.' He helps me on with my coat and soon I'm striding across the gardens, then the fields and into the woods to take the shortcut into Morwood Tarn.

* * *

I break through the trees and the church and tarn are on my left. No sign of the god-hound, probably for the best; I'm not ready for that confrontation quite yet. I walk briskly (just in case) past the graveyard and the angel oak; I look at the scratches in its trunk once again and note no new ones have joined the originals. Perhaps a very large fox or badger made them and nothing more? Without predators (no wolves) they might grow big enough in the woods to make marks so high.

The road leading into the village is smooth beneath my boots. When I had the children with me the other day, I did not linger because I was doing my best to keep my charges in check. To keep Connell especially from climbing anything that would bear his weight. Today, however, I take my leisure, moving slowly, staring at whatever gains my interest, noting where things are, how they look. The cottages on either side are neat and tidy, white-washed daub and dark wooden beams, the glass of the windows thick with a greenish tinge; flaws in their make-up are whorls and pits that look rather pretty. Gardens are well-tended, although most have succumbed to the autumn chill. Smoke billows from the smithy and the sound of hammers on anvils is loud, rhythmic; the two women working the forges don't lift their heads to watch me pass.

Mrs Charlton has been generous with local knowledge and gossip. Perhaps a thousand souls inhabit Morwood Tarn, living in all manner of houses from tiny black-and-white cottages to red-brick two-storey abodes for those with more money and stature (although no one the Morwoods consider their social equals). There is a lazy constable who attends to the small matters of crime that occur in places such as this, and reports to Luther. A lawyer who deals with the legalities of life and death. A blacksmith and his daughters who tend to the need for horseshoes, ploughshares, scythes and other instruments, while the son does leatherwork: shoes and boots, belts and bridles, bags and saddles, what-have-you. An inn is run by a widow and her three children, providing decent meals and passable accommodation for travellers through the village on their way to other, more important places. There's a bakery, a butcher, a grocer, a jeweller, a seamstress, a tiny coffeehouse for those wives who consider themselves above the common rooms of the inn. All with a hundred tiny details of gossip attached – so many, in fact, I can't keep track.

I drift by a dozen or so other places of business until I reach the inn. Its sign swings in the breeze; the name is The Good Wolf, freshly picked out in gold, with a rather handsome-looking beast – black-furred, green-eyed, sharp-toothed, razor-clawed – beneath it.

Inside, the atmosphere is warm, a little smoky, with a hint of meat pies and a fair whack of grain alcohol – the scent of it having been poured, imbibed, burped and sweated out again. Unavoidable for such an establishment, but it's not unpleasant and there's no accompanying odour of vomit, which cannot be said of many hostelries I've frequented in my day (often trying to extract my mother from one). No one notices me; my sparrow's appearance makes me almost invisible. It's a decent-sized public house – the Tarn is one of those locations that's on the way to a lot of other locations, but otherwise offering no compelling reason for a traveller to stay.

I make my way over to the bar, admiring the look of all those glasses suspended in front of the mirrored wall. Tapping the counter, I gain the attention of the girls. All three are blonde, blue-eyed, and give me a look of bored curiosity. They're all dressed in red skirts and white low-cut blouses. Pretty enough now, late teens, early twenties, but their edges are beginning to fray – crow's feet too soon, hard mouths – and this life will only continue to take. None look happy with their lot, but that might be boredom. It could simply be that I'm not male and some women won't light up for one of their own. They are familiar, however, and it takes a moment for me to realise they were my fellow travellers on my last coach journey to Morwood. If they recognise me, they give no sign.

'Help you?' drawls perhaps the oldest, but she doesn't push herself away from her position leaning on the benchtop. I'm sure they'd be different if it were busy. I'm half-tempted to stay around and find out what the evenings are like, but then I'd have to walk home in the dark, and somehow that makes me far more uneasy than it ever did in the city.

'May I have a bottle of your peach brandy, please?'

'Don't got none.'

'Never sold it.'

'Nothing fancy here.'

A little chorus of malice. The longer I look at them, the stronger the familiarity; even the tone of their voices is like hers.

'You'd be Luned Wynne's sisters.' I fold my hands in front of my waist, like a nun going about her day. They shift uncomfortably, caught so easily. I took a chance, didn't know she had any siblings, but it was too obvious.

'What's Madam Muck up to then?' one of them scoffs. The other two have expressions I don't like. I take another chance: that they know Burdon and that he'll have no patience for their games. 'Mr Burdon has asked me to purchase this brandy on his behalf. Perhaps you would prefer that I tell him he must come himself to conduct his business?'

The oldest one straightens, reaches beneath the counter and produces a brown bottle with a stopper. She plants it on the nicked benchtop in front of me. I pull the cork out amidst protests and sniff at the contents – I'd not put it past them to give me the wrong thing; but no, peach brandy, very strong. Nodding, I toss the coins so they bounce once, twice on the benchtop then fly off onto the floor at their feet so they scramble to collect. I'm out the door before they reappear.

That was unpleasant. Imagine, a whole family of Luneds. I continue on until I see the apothecary's shingle – a mortar and pestle – then look to the right. There it is, the house with the green door. There's a white picket fence and an arch over the wooden gateway twined with the last of the season's roses. I pass beneath, take the cracked stone path, to knock.

'Come in,' is called.

The small room that acts as a parlour is bright. There's a woman in a corner, nestled in a chair by a small fire, nursing a child with fine silver hair that matches her own. An idea begins to form, a solution to a problem I've been turning around for a while. She looks tired, as if the earth is pulling at her features, but she smiles at me coolly.

'Heledd?' She nods. 'I'm Asher Todd,' I say, 'the new governess at Morwood Grange.'

Her expression clears but the smile grows no warmer, nor more genuine. In fact, there's a little wariness in it. Still, I move my lips up in a friendly fashion. 'I've come to collect the mending.'

'On the table,' she says and gestures with an elbow, helpless beneath the weight of the babe.

And it is, folded neatly in a small basket; I pull one of the petticoats out and examine it. It's only on my third attempt that I find where she's darned the tears, and I nod. 'Excellent.'

She looks at me with pride and not a little amusement – seeming to warm towards me. Then again, we both know I'd be a fool to deliver work to Mrs Charlton without checking it first. I take the silver from my pocket and go over to her, put it directly in her hand. There's a low footstool she's not using, and I sit on it without asking permission. It makes me smaller, less threatening.

'I wonder…' I say delicately and pause until she snorts with laughter.

'Out with it. Subtlety will gain you nothing here, Asher Todd, so just ask me straight and I'll say yea or nay with no suspense.'

I grin, a little ruefully, all my cleverly selected words worthless. I like her, but I must now throw the dice at her feet. 'Forgive me for being so bold but… I would buy some of your breast milk.'

She looks taken aback. 'What on earth for?'

'For a poultice for the older Mrs Morwood.'

'We've not seen her here in perhaps three years. Some folk say she's dead.'

'Very much alive,' I say and laugh a little. 'Is she missed? Was she popular?'

'She was hard but still better than her son.' Instantly she seems to regret saying anything. 'I'm sorry, you're of the house. Please don't tell Master Luther I said that.'

'Never fear, I'd not tell him anything for either love or money.' And I say it with such conviction that she believes me. It is the truth, a rare thing from my lips. 'But I… want to help the old woman.'

'And you can do this? You can make magic?'

'Medicine,' I say hastily, although yes, magic will be part of it. We are remote here, superstition abounds, naturally she leaps to magic before medicine. 'But nothing a doctor would recognise; and something a priest might fear.'

'Met ours, have you?'

I nod.

'Old goat,' she sneers. 'Alright. But what's in it for me?'

I nod, then draw two gold crowns from my pocket: they are rare and unscored, not meant for the making of change. Very old and not needed by those who gave them to me. 'These. And your silence about it.'

She narrows her eyes, gaze flicking between me and the coins burning cold in my palm.

'The old woman,' I say hesitantly, unsure how much to trust, 'is losing her sight. I believe I can help. But I need an ingredient I cannot provide myself. When I saw you with the baby, I thought it was an opportune moment – unless you can direct me to another breastfeeding mother in the village?'

'You're a cunning woman,' she says and it doesn't sound like a curse. It's not quite true, but I take heart. She stares at me for a while, then says, 'I don't want your money. But I'll have your help instead.'

In turn I nod, though I know that *help* is often more expensive than silver or gold. I slip the crowns back into my pocket.

'My family,' says Heledd, 'don't live in the Tarn, but in the woods – my father's the coppicer – manages the forest on the estate. They're ill' – then hurriedly adds – 'not contagious, though, not a *plague*,' she emphasises. 'But they've been unwell for a few months now.' She lifts her chin. 'If you can cure the old lady, maybe you can help them too.'

I say, 'If I aid your family, I have your promise of silence? Such things might be regarded as hedgecraft and it's best if no one hears whisper of it.'

'Certainly not the priest,' she says slyly.

I snort. 'Then we have an agreement?' She nods. 'Tell me about their symptoms.'

'Fevers and rashes, which go away for a while, but return. It's confounding: not enough to kill, but sufficient to make life difficult, always being not quite well.' She smiles. 'I visit them, and I've not caught anything.' There's a pause. 'But don't tell my husband I've seen them; he's fearful of infection with the babe.'

'Perhaps it's something near their cottage, something they eat? Water supply?' I tilt my head, thinking.

'But you'll go? Go and see them?'

'Yes, of course. Point me in the right direction. I can go on Sunday, it's my day off.'

She pulls the baby away from her breast and holds the child up; it begins to cry immediately, deprived of its meal. 'Take this'un then, and I'll get you what you need.'

6

'How much longer, Asher?' asks Leonora Morwood.

'Two more days,' I say. 'The same length of time as when you asked this morning, really.'

'You are far too snippy for a governess.'

'The paste must ferment for five whole days, Mrs Morwood. Anything less and you will have no benefit of it. Then I will apply it to your eyes three nights in a row – and make no mistake, it will sting. Be patient. Now, do you want me to finish this chapter or not? There is but one entry left.'

I'm reading to her, for she cannot do so herself at night, but she does love a story before bed, much like her grandchildren. Most nights Jessamine tucks her offspring in and tells them a tale, so I come to Leonora's room. Tonight she's in a fine sulk and it makes her short and snappish; she's demanded something more academic than fantastical and I'm reading from *Murcianus' Book of Magical Creatures*. The section on wolves is interesting, but I've found nothing relating to the tale Albertine told me of Morwood's wicked ones.

'Yes,' grumbles Leonora from her seat across from me. We sit in the confined sitting room which need not be so cramped – it is a very large suite – but I've come to the conclusion she likes it thus. 'Go on, finish it.'

I clear my throat and begin:

The tale of the wolf's wife originates from an ancient idea that a woman – maiden, thornback or crone – in want of a faithful husband might seek one from amongst the four-footed, wolves being known for their devotion and mating for life.

Were such a woman so inclined, she might betake herself to a pond located in a wood on a night of the darkest lunar phase. It is a known fact that when the moon disappears, she hides in water to refresh herself. The needful woman should sit by the tarn and wait. The moon is the mistress of the wolf and they will roam, seeking her out when she is not in the sky.

A wolf that drinks from such a pool in the presence of such a woman will immediately be transformed from his lupine shape and take on the aspect of a man. He will go where he is led by the one who takes his hand.

Children born of these unions sometimes have tails, and it is wise to be aware of this.

A woman who acquires this sort of mate must, however, be wary. Should her husband, for whatever reason, eat a meal containing wolf's bane, he will revert to lupine shape, forgetting his family and taking once more to the wild woods. And he shall never again be drawn from his beast's life.

Leonora sneers, 'Poppycock!'

'You don't believe in wolf wives?' I ask.

'Oh, their existence is documented. But wolf's bane! Any

woman feeding her husband wolf's bane – aconite, monkshood, devil's helmet – is trying to get rid of him. So if he keels over or simply runs off into the forest the result is much as was required.'

We both snort with laughter. The old transcribers were simply that: recorders of the tales they were told, not critical thinkers, although in some margins I have found notes by the scribes expressing their own doubts as to tales' or histories' veracity. In the volumes I've read held in the Whitebarrow Library those notations had been blacked out by the hands of the librarians and archivists who preferred not to see any sort of dissent. The laughter has the advantage of dissipating her tension.

'Shall I help you into bed?' I ask.

'I'm not entirely useless,' she snaps, but it's without fire. She's been getting worse, her sight failing as each day passes; the bright light she needs to continue to read is precisely the thing that causes an ocular irritation. It might seem a cruel punishment.

'I know. Sleep well, Mrs Morwood.' I take up a candle to show my way.

'Goodnight, Asher.'

Outside her room, I pause, listen carefully. Nothing to hear, not even Leonora moving around to get herself ready for slumber. I step quietly along the corridor, away from the staircase, towards the door at the far end. There are two rooms between it and Leonora's suite. The children's chambers are down on the first floor close by mine; Luther and Jessamine's quarters share Leonora's level, but on the other side of the staircase. Far enough away for privacy. Burdon, Mrs Charlton and Luned have rooms up in the attic.

Portraits line the walls. There is Leonora in her youth, flanked by a husband who looks something like a potato with wispy blonde hair, but whose breeding, I'm sure, was impeccable. Donnell took her surname she told me, became a Morwood so the family name would continue on, with her the sole heir to the estate. Images, too, of each of my charges, somewhat younger than they are now. And Luther and Jessamine on their wedding day, I think, he in dignified greys, she in a dress of cobalt blue; her veil appears as fine as mist, not even obscuring her features in the slightest. She seems happy there, then; no lines had been carved into her face by worry or discontent. She looks much older now, but it can only have been little more than a decade ago.

Here: a blank space between paintings. A rectangle that's darker than the rest, where something once protected it from light. I run my finger around the shape of the absence, wonder what it looked like when it hung there. Then I move past.

The door handle is thick with dust: no one bothers to polish anything this far along the hallway. The brass feels gritty against my palm as I try to turn it; it shifts the tiniest amount, then grinds to a halt.

Locked. I lean my forehead against the wood. What did I expect, really?

'Miss Todd? What are you doing here? Snooping?' Luther Morwood's stern voice reaches me; he's much closer than he should be without me having heard him. I startle, stumble back from the door. Luther is quick to catch me before I fall. Still he mocks: 'Sneaking?'

I put a hand to my forehead, which is hot to the touch. 'Mr Morwood. I was seeing to your mother, I came out here… I must have become disoriented. I feel so terribly weak.' Only one of those things is entirely untrue. '*Not sneaking.*'

'I do hope you're not sickening for something. If my mother's demands are too much on top of your duties with the children, you must simply tell her no.' His arm is still around my shoulders; I can smell his cologne. I do not like him this close, I do not like it at all. I look up into his face; nothing sparks there, nothing more than vaguely irked curiosity. A dull little sparrow excites no interest. I'm merely an inconvenience foisted upon the household by Leonora.

'Oh, not at all, sir. It is a delight to read to your mother. It was simply a momentary unsteadiness – I do believe I'm still fatigued from my journey here. How silly.' I pat his hand and step carefully out of range; I do not pull away too strongly lest I make clear the lie of my fragility. 'Thank you for your concern, Mr Morwood. I shall be well.'

My heart is beating hard as I take the stairs down. I could not have stayed in his arms any longer lest he realise that I was afraid, adrenaline coursing through my veins for fear at being caught. I begin to breathe more evenly until I hear his steps behind me; not trying to catch up, but matching mine. Almost as if he's stalking.

But then I forget he's there because a shrill thread of noise comes from below; the particular pitch only small girls can achieve tells me it's Sarai. My shoes clatter, Luther's still keeping time. The children's rooms are on the opposite side of the stairwell from mine, close enough that I might hear cries in the night but still ensure some seclusion.

I throw open the door, expecting the worst, only to find Jessamine sitting in an armchair by the fire, Albertine beside her on a stool, Connell on the rug at her feet, and Sarai face down on the floor, arms and legs flailing and a fresh howl issuing forth.

'Whatever's the matter, Mrs Morwood?' It doesn't sound to my ears like an accusation but the expression on Jessamine's face tells me she hears it as such. She goes pale and her lips pinch – or perhaps it's the appearance of her husband hot on my heels. Trying to make up for it I ask, 'Are you well?'

'I read the story, that is all,' she says, defensively. 'I began to read the one she asked for and then…'

'She didn't read it right!' the prostrate child wails. For a moment I'm stumped then I remember: after lunch every day I've read her a favourite tale from the book in Jessamine's lap. It's the carrot I hold in front of her to get her to complete some small lesson each day. Sarai's not stupid, but she's very young, still flighty – might remain so her whole life, of course – and judiciously applied bribes work best with her. The story of the girl who turned into a butterfly is her favourite; its telling requires a lilting voice, almost singing, and fluttering motions of the hands and lashes.

I don't go to Sarai. I want to comfort her but to do so in front of Jessamine would be foolish; I've seen enough women in Whitebarrow take a dislike to nannies and governesses, even to their mothers and sisters and aunts, whom they perceive to have greater favour with their own offspring. Instead I say, 'Sarai, don't be silly. There's never only one way to tell a tale.'

'There is!' she insists and it becomes a scream at the end. Jessamine stands, stricken pale, but she doesn't go to the child either. She comes to me instead, snapping the book closed as she does, then thrusts it against my chest with enough force to hurt and push the breath from my lungs.

'Mrs Morwood,' I manage.

From behind me comes Luther's voice, 'Jessamine!'

And that breaks her. Tears start in her blue eyes, her bottom lip trembles. It did not take much, and I'd not realised quite how fragile she is. I eat down every aggressive instinct I have – every shard of jealousy that these children have a mother who loves them so! – and touch her hand, hold it when she would otherwise have pulled away. I make her look at me. 'Mrs Morwood, this is but a child's tantrum. It will pass like a storm, and tomorrow she will not remember it any more than the sky does the rain clouds. It hurts you, I know; your mother's heart is scarred and will be more so as time goes on from such whims. But I promise you this: a daughter always loves her mother no matter what. Even the worst mother still holds a part of her daughter's heart – and you are the kindest of mothers! She is so small, Mrs Morwood, forgive her this – and me.'

There are moments when I think the words have no effect, but then she smiles tremulously.

Then Luther strides past us. He grabs Sarai up by one wrist and draws his arm back; it descends before anyone can react. Everyone watching, a frozen tableau, only Luther is free. The flat of his palm connects with his youngest daughter's backside with a resounding thump – not quite a slap for she's protected by her skirts – but the noise is loud in the otherwise silent room.

'Luther!' Jessamine cries as if the blow struck her. Sarai's mouth opens wide, but before anything can come out, her father sets her on the floor, one finger held up to her face.

'Silence,' he says and the child's lips quiver but close obediently. He grabs his wife's arm and tugs her to the door. 'Attend to the children, Miss Todd,' he says, as if I must be told what to do.

Jessamine's head is bowed, shoulders slumped like broken wings, and I would give anything to drag her from him and protect her.

But now is not the time.

I simply nod and turn away from him. There's the thud of the door closing, then footsteps growing fainter. I bundle Sarai up, cuddle her close, but she doesn't cry. Their parents' room is above this one. Connell looks up at me and though he's trying to hide it, he's afraid. He says, 'Father hurts Mother.'

I cup my hand around the back of his neck. 'Come along, you three.'

Herding them out like ducklings, we go to my room. The space is much smaller, but it is cosier and whatever happens next between their parents the children will not hear it. I sit in my armchair, the storybook in my lap, and they sit in a semi-circle at my feet.

'Now, Sarai, first thing tomorrow you will apologise to your poor mama – and I'll not read about the butterfly girl tonight for your actions have consequences. You might not like how your mother reads stories, but you will be polite and kind to her. Do you understand?'

Her bottom lip wobbles, but in the end she nods. I lean forward and pat her hair; she pushes against my palm like a cat. Connell scootches closer so he can rest his head on my knee.

'One tale, then, and off to bed.' I open the book and begin, 'A great while ago, when the world was full of wonders…'

7

'And where might you be off to?'

The voice comes as a surprise. I left the manor behind some while ago, following Heledd's directions to her parents' cottage. I've not yet left the main thoroughfare between Grange and Tarn, but will do so just before the church. The last thing I need is company or anyone knowing where I'm going. It is Sunday, after lunch, though I chose not to take my meal with the family this day for it's too much like work (though I recognise it's a privilege not to be shunted off to eat in the kitchen with the servants). Everyone's been at their worship – or making excuses like Leonora and I – had a feed and are now lazing about. The priest will be sleeping off his repast, I hope. I cannot do everything I need to do at night for without sleep I shall fail. And some things require sunlight. If I were sensible I'd have begged Eli for a horse, but it's best if no one questions me, best if the household simply think I'm taking a walk for my health and quietude. How annoying to find Luned trailing along behind me. I wonder how long she's been following.

'To church,' I say. 'I felt unwell earlier, but now I shall make my own devotions.' I shall not. I do not wish to set foot in there. At least, not yet. Small places like this? Far away from the big cathedrals? It's easier to slip under the eye of the Church at least as far as regular worship is concerned – harvests and the like, work on the land that cannot be delayed, is a fine excuse not to attend. Mind you, these country priests may well be quicker to burn you than in a city if they think you're not-quite-right.

'I'm sure.' She comes alongside, gives me a look. 'I hear you met my sisters the other day.'

'They're very like you,' I reply, and she can make of that what she will.

'They said you were a bitch.'

'They struck me as uniquely qualified to recognise a kindred soul, then.'

She guffaws, surprised. 'You're not wrong there.'

'I take it you don't get along?'

'Well, there's a reason I'm working for the Morwoods and they're still at the inn.'

'What reason is that, Luned?'

She pauses. 'I want more. I want better than the Tarn and a shitty cottage and ten screaming brats before I'm thirty.'

'Ambition isn't a bad thing for a young woman if you know what you want.' My tone is neutral, but in my experience for women ambition needs to be paired with intelligence, talent or great beauty. Luned's like her sisters, pretty enough but how long that will last is anyone's guess. Even her housemaid skills are questionable, and she's sly but I detect no great genius behind any of her actions. If she was at all clever she'd have made friends with me from the first rather than beginning with outright aggression those couple of weeks ago.

'Oh, I know.' She laughs loudly and it's unpleasant. I think of her sneering about the former governess.

66

We come level with the church and Luned stops, as do I. She's going to wait, damn her. I smile, tilt my head and turn to the cracked stone path that leads through the low drystone wall. My boots clack and crunch on the worn paving, up to the heavy wooden door with its ugly bands of iron, splinters poking out, some tipped with old-blood brown where heedless fingers have been caught. Carefully I grab the rusty metal handle and push; my hands are shaking a little for fear of finding the place occupied. I don't hesitate – to do so would be to show my lie – and step into the darkness. I close the door mostly behind me, just leave the merest sliver so I can watch her even as I listen carefully for the sound of someone else in here. Little bitch waits a full five minutes before I see her wandering off down the road towards the Tarn and presumably a visit to her family – such acts do not require one to like one's relatives.

I sigh, wait for her to be out of sight, then heave the door open. I step into the sun, skip down the steps, throwing glances at the cheerless little cottage that serves as a rectory. I'll not lie: I scamper. I run. Then head off across the graveyard, over the wall, into the woods, in the direction Heledd advised. Only when I'm under the trees do I start to breathe more easily. *Don't be a fool*, I tell myself, *he does not know your face.* I put those thoughts from my mind, promising to deal with them later.

My sense of direction is good but I've always been a child of cities: so much easier to navigate by buildings and streets, by the chipped cobbles at the corner of one avenue or by the statue in the middle of a plaza. Trees and shrubs, stumps and rills are much harder to distinguish if you're not used to a place, if these things do not act as a map in your mind. Three times I fear I've gone entirely astray.

When I'm sure I'm lost in the cool shadows I stumble upon the stream Heledd said would be there, and the small rock bridge that stretches across it. The water is cold and fresh when I drink. I sit beside it for a while in a patch of sun, and take the ham and cheese sandwich Mrs Charlton made from my satchel. I feel the knots in my neck and shoulders untying themselves, and I lift my face like a flower. There's only the sound of the rill racing by, some few birds too stubborn to fly away for the cold months, and in the undergrowth the stealthy scratching and grunts of unseen creatures.

A fox barks close by and I can see a red snout poking from beneath a frond of foliage. I sit very still and the vixen eventually comes to sniff at the fingers in my lap (smelling of sandwich, no doubt), then pushes at me for a scratch. The fur is warm and soft; she makes squeaks as I pat her ears, run my nails along her spine, then the brush of her magnificent tail. Sharp little white teeth show in a grin as she stretches back and forth under my ministrations. I give her the last slice of ham from my sandwich and she seems happy to sit on my green skirts for the duration.

Then there is a thud in the thicket.

The vixen stiffens, and is so swiftly gone that all I see is a blur of fire.

In theory, I shouldn't be far from my destination: cross the brook, walk to the fallen yew with branches like wings, then I should see the garden gate. I listen carefully but there's no other sound. I do notice that the birds have gone quiet. I remember my arrival at Morwood, being stalked. Whatever's out there hasn't attacked me thus far, so perhaps that is not its goal. I feel a little less concerned but perhaps it is a false security. Nevertheless, I rise and smooth my skirts as if I've not a care in the world, then set off across the stream, stepping delicately over the narrow bridge so I don't overbalance.

I reach the fallen yew in no time at all, and yes, its branches do look like skeletal wings, sticking up in the air. And there is a small garden gate, covered in greying ivy, and beyond it a cottage that seems to grow from the ground itself, an A-framed thing of split larch planks turned silver by the elements, windows of glass blown thick and green and imperfect, a small porch with a wooden swing moving in the slight breeze; and trees, trees so close to the house and each other that they seem to form part of the structure. They *do* form the back wall as far as I can tell, part of the sides as well. In the forest and of it.

A crash behind me, a growl, and I fling myself forward like an arrow, hurdling tussocks and logs in my skirts, bashing through the garden gate so hard I fear its hinges break. I hammer on the door, throwing looks over my shoulder as I begin to shout, 'Open up!'

I look away again, back into the green of the woods, see nothing, then the door is gone, pulled open and I'm tumbling forward into someone's arms.

'What's the noise for?' A gruff voice, loud in my ear, and I wrench away from the man, then turn to push the door closed. So much like my first day all those days ago. Is it a joke? Am I imagining things? Am I going mad? Madness… I often think it's never far from my mind; after all, that's the way my mother went, in the end.

'Who's there?' Another voice, this one weaker, a woman's, comes from another room. I'm standing in a small space, half kitchen, half parlour; tidy but timeworn. Somewhere beyond

69

the poky doorway will be a bedroom or two, perhaps a lean-to bathroom; part of the walls *are* growing green wood. I do my best not to screw up my nose: the place smells stale, shut up for too long, and there's the taint of vomit too. An old shaggy dog, red-furred, lies by the hearth, eyeing me but not getting up.

'You're shaking, lass, have you got a fever?' I finally get a good look at the man before me: short, with the same silver hair as his daughter; grey skin hangs on him as if he once filled it better. 'What are you afraid of? You're pale as a cloud.'

'Heledd,' I gasp, then gather myself, take a breath, choosing not to answer the question. 'Heledd sent me, Mr Lewis.'

'Who is it?' the woman calls once again.

'Still don't know,' he says.

'Asher Todd is my name. I'm the governess at Morwood Grange. I met Heledd and she said you'd been ill. I might be able to help.'

He raises his bushy silver brows in disbelief. 'Master Luther's sent medicine, but we might as well be drinking our own piss for all the good it's done. Still and all, can't see what good a *governess* would do.'

I pause, consider, but don't express my surprise. Connell told me when I casually asked that the little building with the millwheel off the side of the big house is his father's private space, but when I've wandered past and casually peered in the high windows, all I can see is a layer of dust over every surface, cobwebs on windows and in corners. There's a covered well behind it that appears not to have been drawn from in a long time. I wonder what Luther has been giving them. I wonder why they've gone to him rather than a physician.

'I have some knowledge of healing, Mr Lewis. If I might speak with your wife? And there are other children here?' He stares at me, so I touch his hand. 'And you've been ill too? I can see it, sir, please confide in me.' I grin. 'I promise not to make it worse – and I'll not make you drink your own piss, I swear.'

He laughs unwilling, nods, says, 'Come through,' and leads me into the next room.

It's a cramped bedroom with a double bed containing a woman whose locks were once bright gold, but are now greyer than her face says they should be. Beside her lies a girl, perhaps sixteen, silver-tressed. In an armchair, covered in a blanket yet shivering, is a boy with mouse-brown hair. Heledd's family.

'This is Asher; our Heledd sent her. Thinks she can help.'

'Hello, Mrs Lewis.' She just blinks at me. At a glance I can see she's suffering the most, as mothers generally do. 'I'll start with you if I may. Mr Lewis, perhaps you and your son would give us some privacy?'

He looks as if he might say *no*, but then gives in. 'Come along, Ifan, help me with the tea.'

I doubt the boy will be much use as he heaves himself from the chair and stumbles behind his father. But I notice the battered tin buckets by the bed, two, a miasma of stink rising from them. 'I know you're exhausted but please take those, empty and wash them,' I say severely.

'Our Heledd's been doing that,' Mr Lewis says defensively.

'But she's not here now,' I point out. He nods, irritated, and grabs one, gestures for the boy to bring the other, then they're gone.

Right. First things first: I push the row of windows wide, feel cool air rush in. I approach the bed. 'Keep these open during the day; you'll feel better if you're able to breathe freely. Now, can you sit up, Mrs Lewis?'

She struggles and I slip an arm behind her to help. The neck of her nightgown is loose – like her husband, she appears to have lost weight – and I can see red dots of a rash across her shoulders, up her neck into her hair, down her back. But... they don't look like something that's springing from the inside, from an illness. There's no festering or eruption. I don't touch them, but I look closely. I've seen something like this when skin's been subjected to a powder designed to cause irritation. There's no sign of pus or infection, the skin is not broken, merely reddened. I look at the girl.

'Do you have this rash too?'

She nods, hooking a finger to tug at the neckline of her gown: red spots speckle her chest, up her neck.

'Mrs Lewis, your husband says Mr Morwood visits?'

'Once. When we first became ill, then he sent that maid to deliver a bottle of medicine. For all the good it does.'

Luther dropping in out of the goodness of his heart? 'Mrs Lewis—'

'—Eirlys—'

'Eirlys, did he also send powders for bathing?'

She shakes her head, turning with difficulty and digging beneath her pillows. 'But these were brought, to go under the pillows.'

In her hand a small calico sachet, unbleached linen, tied with a red ribbon. Some of the apothecaries in Whitebarrow trade in such things, some of the witches too; such items can be used for any number of purposes. I take it from her by the ribbon and sniff at it cautiously. There's lavender to cover everything else but I can

72

detect baby's breath, nettle, ragweed, and something else I can't quite identify.

'I see. And how do you feel? Are you experiencing vomiting or diarrhoea?'

'We're all puking like there's no tomorrow. Can barely keep down dry bread. Not enough goes through us to shit.' She looks exhausted by this speech. I glance at the girl again and she nods.

'Has he sent more potions?'

'No,' she grunts, then looks afraid. 'Not that we're thankless; don't tell Mr Morwood we are! We're grateful for everything. And I know he was at one of the universities, was studying to be a doctor…'

Indeed? Something to investigate further, although perhaps not here. 'I'll not say anything, never fear. Exhale for me, a long breath.'

It's foul when it comes and I recognise it from some of the cases I saw in the slums of Whitebarrow, filthy beds where the inconvenient were left to die after someone had slipped poison in the food or drink. 'You were ill before Mr Morwood sent the medicine?'

She nods. I help her lie back against the pillows then go around the other side of the bed and examine the girl more closely; her symptoms are identical. 'I think, Eirlys, that perhaps you are allergic to the treatment. No fault of Mr Morwood's,' I assure her. 'But don't take any more medicine and if you have any other of these sachets, burn them.' I slip the one she gave me into a small leather pouch from my satchel, then secrete it away. She stares. 'I have seen such illness before and sometimes perfectly good remedies don't help simply because of a patient's own bodily humours.' I smile. 'Will you trust me? Give me a week and if you are not on the mend by then we shall speak with Mr Morwood together. But I would like to try to help you first – better I beg forgiveness than ask permission.'

She nods slowly. I can't help but feel she doesn't entirely trust Luther Morwood.

Her husband and son are out in the front garden by a small well, finishing the business of cleaning the buckets. I scan the woods for any sign of what drove me in here so abruptly, see nothing, and so give them a cursory check, but there's nothing new from what I've seen inside. I tell Heledd's father what I told his wife and he looks disinclined to argue.

'I don't suppose you've any of the medicine from Mr Morwood left?' I ask.

He shakes his head, but rummages around in his pocket, draws forth a small blue bottle. 'Came in this though. Thought you might like to look at it.'

I take the vial, hold it up to the light, take the lid off and sniff at it, but there's nothing there. No trace.

'We washed it out, sorry.'

'No matter.' I put it into the leather pouch with the sachet. 'And this is where you draw your water from?'

He gives me the same look one gives an idiot.

'But you're close enough to the stream to get it from there, yes?'

'Why would we?'

'Because, Mr Lewis, I think your water supply might be tainted. A dead animal perhaps, or something seeping from the ground into the liquid. Don't use the well for a while.' I nod at the lad.

'Bring me some water from the stream – not in those buckets.' He goes inside, reappears with a large bowl, shambles out the gate. I drop the wooden pail attached to the well, hear it splash, then pull it up by the rope. I take one of the small clear bottles from my satchel and gingerly fill it. Holding it up to the light, I can see no obvious reason for their illness. I wrap it in a kerchief to pad it, then stuff it into the bag.

'Now,' I say, glancing around the little garden. 'Borage?' I spot it quickly and pick a good handful and take it inside. The boy soon returns with the bowl, liquid spilling as he walks slowly. 'In the kettle, lad, on the hob quick as you can.'

I make a tisane while they watch, and give them instructions as I crush the leaves, then cut them finely to steep them in the newly boiled water; I add a dash of vinegar. 'Each of you should take two glasses of this before bed. In the morning, make a fresh batch – you've seen how much I've used – and drink it throughout the day, and do so for the next seven days. I will return to see how you fare.'

Thomas Lewis sips at the mug I pour for him, makes a face.

'You'll get used to it, and I think you'll find you prefer it to vomiting. If you've stale bread, toast it well – burn it a little; the char will help calm your stomach and digestion.' I raise a finger. 'And remember, do not use the well water.'

He takes my hand and says, 'Thank you, Miss Todd.'

'Asher.'

'Thomas.'

'I will see you soon, Thomas. If things get dire, do send for me.' Although who of this lot would be well enough to drag themselves to the manor? Still, I don't imagine they'll get worse once they

75

stop drinking the well water, once they burn those little sachets. I pat the old dog as I walk past; he gives a sigh.

Back outside I take a deep breath. I tap the pocket of my skirt, feel the reassuring length of the long knife. Then I step out into the darkening afternoon.

8

I walk so quickly from the Lewis cottage that by the time I'm within sight of the Grange I'm puffing; but that's the manner of things: the road home from a new location always seems shorter than the journey there in the first place. Though I listened so hard my ears ached, there's been no sign of pursuit the whole way. With a sigh of relief I'm about to step from the small clearing onto the fields that lead up to the rear of the house.

Before I manage that, however, I'm broadsided.

I fall to my right, the breath knocked from me. I smell… smoke and dog. I sit up, look around. Nothing. Getting to my feet, I run towards the gap between the trees. I'm hit again, and I rise again, this time managing to get my hand in my pocket. Fingers curling around the leather hilt of my long knife, I slide it out, concealing it by my side. I take steps again as if to attain the gap, then feint back as the scent becomes stronger. I whip the blade up, feel it connect with something in a long slice.

There is a yelp and a silver-grey something flying past me. A body hits the grass and slides to the base of one of the larger trees with a whimper. Except by the time it fetches up against the roots, it's no longer lupine in shape, but human. A long-limbed male, naked as the day he was born. Eli Bligh gives a cough, raises his head, and coughs again.

'Bitch's bones,' he moans. 'That wasn't meant to happen.'

My fear and disbelief burn up as a flame of rage consumes them. The sort of rage I've kept under control all these years no matter what's happened because I learned early on the consequences when I did not do so – as did the lad in Whitebarrow who told me my mother was a whore. Then I'm sitting astride Eli before the crimson in front of my gaze fades and there's just the utter shock on his face. I'm holding the dagger so close to his left eye it must be all he can see.

Then he laughs; like an idiot, he laughs. As if this is the funniest jape ever.

I drop the dagger and tumble off him, crawl a few yards away. I want to be sick; fury always has that effect. Slowly he sits up, dabbing at the cut across his chest. It's bleeding well, but I don't think it's deep; his momentum, the angle of my blade, saved him that.

I feel hollowed out by truncated ire. 'Why? Why?'

'What?'

'What was the point of that?' I shout.

He looks abashed. 'A bit of fun. Tormenting you.' I stare at him, open-mouthed. 'The day you arrived, walking along the drive, you were so… full of yourself. So stiff and proper and uppity. Assured when you shouldn't have been. Queen of the bloody forest, as if you belonged here. Even when I shifted and let you hear me… gods, you were afraid, I could smell it on your sweat, but too proud to run.'

'Fun,' I say, wishing I'd stabbed him properly. 'I should have flayed you alive and hung your skin on a branch to see if you had fur on the inside as well.'

I don't look at him again – do not ask him about what he is, it's clear enough – just pick up the knife and wipe the blade on the grass until it's clean. Then I return it to my pocket; I check the contents of my bag and find the wrapped bundle of the water sample miraculously intact. I rise and stride towards the house without a backward glance; at least there'll be no more stalking of me around the estate. It's a little while before I realise my face is stinging. It only occurs to me later when my mind isn't so frazzled that Eli might be the one person who'll tell me the truth about the other governess – and that I should have asked him when I had him at a disadvantage.

* * *

'Miss Todd, you look as if you've been dragged backwards through a hedge.'

I come in through the kitchen garden, hoping to avoid anyone, but the housekeeper is there, preparing the evening meal. Mrs Charlton's customary brusqueness is overt, but when I'm close enough she softens. 'Oh, your face!'

Broad fingers touch the spot on my right cheek where the skin has peeled off from contact with the ground. My hair's fallen mostly out of its bun, the pins dislodged annoyingly easily, and locks curl down to my waist. There are grass stains on my white blouse, dirt marks on the green of my skirt and short jacket. The mourning ring is still on my finger and that's all that matters.

'What happened?'

'I got a little lost in the woods and panicked. I tripped and fell. Sometimes I'm terribly clumsy.' I lie easily; I'm good at it.

'Let me clean that up. Sit.' She pulls a chair out from the stripped pine table and there's no gainsaying her. Soon she has a bowl filled with warm water from the pot over the hearth, a clean white rag and a small jar containing purple ointment. She sees my gaze and says, 'Lavender,' as if I wouldn't know it from a lump of coal. I lift my face so she can get to the wound better.

'Mrs Morwood – the elder – has been asking for you,' she says.

I don't remind her this is my day off; we both know it. I keep my head still as she gently bathes the graze, making sure to remove any fragments of grass and dirt with a tiny pair of silver tweezers. When she's satisfied, she dabs the ointment onto the wound and the smell of lavender is so strong that I'm thrown back to a sickroom in Whitebarrow, a room where my mother lay dead and I'd brought armfuls of lavender to ensure her spirit remained quiet for as long as I needed it to. In my memory her eyes fly open, though I know they never did. I gasp.

'Did I hurt you? I'm sorry, hen, sausage fingers.'

'No, it's not your fault.' I grab at her hand, hold it for a moment, then release her as I stand. 'You're very kind and I appreciate it. Thank you, Mrs Charlton. I'd best go and see Mrs Morwood.'

She says lightly, 'You hardly seem a one to panic.'

'Anyone might do so, Mrs Charlton, in an unfamiliar place.'

'Fell, did you?' she asks.

I throw a smile over my shoulder and say, 'Like a stone.'

To my surprise she yells, 'You pair!'

I follow her gaze to the laundry room; two round faces peer from the doorway, expressions guiltily blank. Identical. They come into the kitchen only when she waves violently. They walk in step, which takes some doing given how tentative they are, yet they still manage to synchronise, even when stopping a few yards from us.

'This is Miss Todd, the governess. Asher, these are the Binion twins, Solenn and Tanet. If I'm not around, seek her out and listen to her. Understand?'

It's like watching a mirror image as their neatly braided red heads dip in a nod. Both slender in black sack dresses with white aprons showing the dirty fruits of their labours as they've cleaned the manor under the housekeeper's direction. They might be about sixteen.

'Hello, Solenn. Hello, Tanet.' I smile at them, but there's just that shared stare that goes on for so long I become uncomfortable. I wonder if they can see something they shouldn't.

'Shoo, off you go now, home time,' says Mrs Charlton. 'Don't forget to take the basket with the bread and your payment. Straight to your gran now.'

When they're gone, I ask, 'Are they…?'

'No more simple than anyone else. Just quiet, I think.' She answers a question I didn't ask. I'd meant *Are they Luther's?* but I think it's clear they are. I could tell they were a little afraid of her, but I don't think she's cruel to them; don't think she blames them for what they cannot help. 'You won't see them much, but just in case – they're good cleaners, follow directions well, don't need supervision.'

I nod. 'Good to know.'

'Now you'd best—'

'—get to Mrs Morwood.'

* * *

81

'Will it hurt?' Leonora asks, although there's no hint of fear in her tone. Her nerves, I suspect, were forged in fire. She ate dinner early, knowing this would be how she would spend the evening.

'It will sting, I am told,' I say as I stir the poultice; five days of ferment and it's a bright bloody pink and it stinks. 'But far less than an operation I have seen performed.'

'Can you do that? That operation?'

'I will not. The eye must be cut. You must remain awake for it. You'd be tied down, held down. It is dangerous and so is the risk of sepsis from such an invasive procedure.'

'Does it succeed?'

'For a time, but I never yet saw a patient who did not suffer an infection and die in terrible pain a few months later.' I whisk the mix around and around to make sure it's blended properly. 'A few months of perfect sight is, I think you will agree, far too high a price to pay for an agonising death.'

I took the time to tidy myself up before coming to Leonora's room, but there's no hiding the graze on my face. When I walked in she was snippy until she noticed, then she was all solicitous. Her hand on my cheek was cold but gentle and for a moment, I leaned into the palm, just as Sarai had to mine not many days since. For a second, it was like the touch of a grandmother, one of the kindest things in the world, or so I've been told by those who have them. Then I pulled away and to forestall queries I said, 'I fell in the woods,' and she did not ask any questions.

'Come along,' I say and hold up the small mortar, 'it's time.'

She wrinkles her nose at the smell coming from the contents but says nothing else. I follow her to the bed, and give the poultice one last stir.

'Remember, you must keep your eyes open while I apply this, Mrs Morwood. It will not be entirely pleasant, but you're a woman of will. I'm told it will hurt less than childbirth and you've done that once!'

She does not contradict my joke – does not sigh *Twice* – merely says, 'Yes.'

'Hold still, it must remain for an hour.' And I gently begin to layer the paste, careful to pull back the lids as far as I can to ensure coverage.

Leonora Morwood makes no sound beyond a single sharp intake of breath. I am quick and efficient, and soon she lies still as a statue on a tomb; the two pools of bloody-pink mix make it appear as if her eyes have been carved out.

I ring the rope beside the mantlepiece; down in the kitchen a bell will sound.

'What shall I read, Mrs Morwood?'

'Whatever you choose, Asher.' The sign of distress: she always has strong opinions about what's read, always makes the choice, and I am never troubled for my suggestions. A rare chance, then, for most of the books here are strangers to me and I learn something new every time. I select *Murcianus' Book of Curses*. Upon opening it, I discover it's not, in fact, a list of hexes, but rather stories involving such things. I should not be as disappointed as I am, and choose a page, begin at random:

Once upon a time, there was a queen. She was beautiful as they all must be, but she was sad as they aren't supposed to be. Her husband loved her and he wanted children. She did not. In the course of time, though, she fell pregnant and two daughters were born.

The pain of the first, the pale twin, she tolerated, but the second caused her such agony, such a rush of hate, that she cursed the child. The dark twin did not cry; she was and always would be a well of silences and depths no one could plumb. The other was shiny and shallow, a sprite of light and laughter. Two babes of the same womb, of the same birthing, should have been loved equally, but they were not. We were not. I was not.

Ultimately, love hangs on acts, however unimportant they may seem at the time. It attaches to what people do or say and our memory of those things. Gestures that travel to the heart and lodge there for a while at least. They build a foundation for kindness and love from which a child can learn.

I have no memory of such acts. I remember the chill of indifference. I remember living in the shadows of my mother's unhappiness. I remember being famished my whole life, yearning for a crumb of affection, just one that might somehow quell the hunger inside me.

But I starved. My sister ate her fill and her heart grew expansive and happy. She did not know want, she did not know how sharp your soul grows when it's deprived, how its ribs stick out like dead trees on a bare landscape. She did not know what it was to never be sated. She could no more escape her fate than I could, but even knowing this, I hated her. Hate her still, I think; perhaps more than I hate our mother. I don't know why; I just know that I do.

'Mothers shouldn't favour one child over the other, but somehow we always do,' muses Leonora, sleepily; the posset I gave her earlier is doing its work.

84

Before I can ask more, say, 'But you only had one, did you not?', there is a knock and I go to answer. Burdon awaits, his expression saying he is not pleased to have had to mount the stairs for anything other than going to bed at night or attending to Mr Morwood's gentlemanly requirements. His job is not on the upper floors; he is the butler, he *buttles* below, the entry level is his domain. But he smiles when he sees me.

'Miss Todd.'

'Burdon. Has the medicine I brought for you helped?'

'Undoubtedly, Miss Todd.' He eyes the mark on my cheek, but makes no comment. 'Thank you.'

'Would you be so kind as to bring up a bowl of warm water and perhaps six soft cloths? I'm sorry, I should have thought of it before I began.' I smile. 'Or send Luned, perhaps.'

'Luned is indisposed,' he says in lofty fashion.

'She's not returned from the Tarn?' I ask.

'Luned has other duties of a Sunday evening, Miss Todd.' And his lips clamp tightly together and I know better than to try to prise them open, but I can guess that Luned is pursuing her plan to have more than just the Tarn. Does she think Luther will set her up as his mistress? Buy a fine townhouse in Bellsholm or elsewhere to visit once a month? What *does* she think will happen?

'Then I shall see you again soon, Burdon. Thank you.'

When he returns and I have tidied up my mess, when Leonora's breathing is low and even I stop reading and put the book aside. I take one of the candles from the mantlepiece and pick my way across the floor, to where the doors of the dressing room lie. Inside: dresses of silk and satin, velvet and bombazine, cotton and wool. On the floor, three long rows of shelves where all manner of shoes wait; and a recess with drawers and hooks whereon hang necklaces and bracelets, tiaras and rings. So many gems and jewels, enough to fund a lifetime or more. When did she wear these? I pick through my memory for mentions of balls held here or in the larger cities; she'd have travelled when she was young, seeking a husband, and then again looking for a wife for Luther.

I think, for a moment, about setting all these dresses alight. I raise the taper higher and see what is at the back of the space. A rectangle. Gold-framed. A portrait.

I think of the spot on the wall out in the hallway, where the colour of the panelling shows something once hung. I move closer: the sharp pale features, the blue eyes, the line of the jaw, the red, red hair. A green gown, a necklace of pearl and emeralds. The breath punches out of me, my knees feel weak. The face I've not seen in two years, but so much younger, before I knew her. Black dots gather at the corners of my vision; there's not enough blood getting to my head and I'm so faint. I lurch forward, put out a hand, miss the wall, get the painting instead. The canvas shifts beneath the weight of my fingers; I feel a tear, and pull away. I examine the portrait closely. The rip is so small no one would notice it who isn't looking for it. I hope. I back away, not taking my eyes from the thing until I can close the doors behind me.

* * *

Back in my room, I lever up the floorboard and look at the items all huddled together in the bottom of the hidey-hole. Two tasks. I reach in, take up the one that means the least. I open the letter again, pull out the drawing of Mater Hardgrace and her niece,

86

Miss Hilarie Beckwith. I must start asking questions about her but be careful how I go.

I look down at the other things, my *duty*, and sigh. That will take some time yet. Cannot be rushed.

9

'Good morning, Miss Todd.'

'Good morning, Mrs Morwood. Are you well?'

Jessamine sits beside me. I'm in the small walled garden to the side of the house, where there's a goodly crop of medicinal plants. The children are sketching a selection of those – or rather Albertine and Connell are doing so, while Sarai picks flowers and turns them into chains and crowns – and I've settled myself on a stone bench with a notebook to plan the week's lessons.

'Thank you,' she says and I note she merely acknowledges the enquiry, does not say 'yes'. Out in the daylight her skin appears translucent as if, on the right angle, the sun might shine through her. There are streaks of white in her hair that can be seen up close, though she's tried to hide them with careful coiffing; I could tell her that wilder locks and curls would be a better concealer, but I don't. She's not coming to me for fashion advice. Her smile is brittle as she looks at the notebook in my lap.

'You are very clever,' she says.

'I believe most women are, Mrs Morwood, whether it's acknowledged or not.' We smile, but her own is brief and fades quickly.

'I am not. I am beautiful. I'm sufficiently clever to know *that*.

It got me a husband.' I say nothing. 'My father was a merchant with enough money to attract a bridegroom of pedigree, if little fortune.' She looks at the children, and her expression is complex. 'He thought that was important, the name, the lineage. He thought such a match was the greatest kindness he could do for his dim little daughter.'

'The Morwoods were rich, surely?' I say before I can stop myself.

She shakes her head, lowers her voice. 'I was told by Leonora, when first I came here, that Luther's father had been a spendthrift. He would travel to the city of Breakwater and gamble for days and weeks, as long as the coin held out. Sometimes he won, but as is the way of such things he eventually began to lose more than he gained...' She purses her lips, as if she regrets beginning the story. 'It was not how he always was, but there was a tragedy – I know not what – and Mr Morwood depleted the family fortunes and died soon after.' She leans closer, lowers her voice: 'Leonora's room? All her precious things? She hid them so he couldn't sell any of it.'

I touch her hand. 'It's an old story, Mrs Morwood. I take it your husband did not inherit this particular flaw?'

'Not that one, no.' She shakes her head, lips a thin line. 'He was gone before Luther brought his suit to my father's door.'

I nod slowly. 'Did you love Luther?'

'He was handsome,' she says and I take this to mean she thought she did. 'But men are often different inside than out. My own father was a singular man, open and honest; what came from his mouth echoed what was in his mind.' The corners of her lips quirk upwards, but it can hardly be called a smile. 'What was your father like, Miss Todd?'

'I never knew him, Mrs Morwood. My mother raised me alone.' I remind her. *Truth*. Mostly. My mother's periodic consorts could hardly be called "fathers".

'And you have never married?'

'Never.'

'Then perhaps you are as inexperienced as I was in the ways of men.' She looks at me with what seems to be grief. 'I was not prepared for Luther.'

'I'm sorry,' I say, for it's all there is to say.

There is that strange quirk of her lips once more.

'My children are my joy,' she says and her voice shakes.

'Of course, and they adore you, Mrs Morwood.'

'My mother-in-law decided the children were ignorant, I think, though she's not seen them for some time, not since she took to her rooms. She said she did not wish to see anyone. There was but one governess before you.' She stares at Sarai, who is staring back, watching us both; in her now-still hands, a chain of tiny crimson bell-shaped flowers that look like drops of blood on her white dress. Then goes on: 'The children liked her well enough but never loved her.' She shrugs. 'Perhaps she was simply not here long enough.'

Jessamine slips her hand from beneath mine, switches her grip to dig her nails into my flesh; her eyes jump back and forth between her children. 'Don't take my children's affections from me, Miss Todd. Take my husband if you will—'

Oh no. 'Mrs Morwood, I—'

She speaks as if I did not. '—He doesn't look at you the way he looks at others.' *You are so plain.* 'But perhaps there is something else about you. Luther has never been a faithful man… I could bear that… but my children's love… that is the one thing I cannot lose. Not their hearts.'

'Mrs Morwood. Mrs Morwood, you're hurting me.' For a moment she tightens her grip. Then I'm freed before I need to struggle.

Jessamine rises. 'Please, Miss Todd, I beg of you.' She moves off, stopping by each child in turn to touch their faces and give them a trembling smile, before walking out beneath the archway of the garden. I rub my hand, feel where the skin almost broke, now marred by halfmoons. It stings much as my cheek still does.

In Whitebarrow I saw many women whose husbands called them hysterics, and whose doctors' diagnoses supported the verdict. Indeed, some of them were mentally unwell, but sometimes as a result of ill treatment, constant bullying and abuse. Women with nowhere else to go; women from all strata of society; women who, subjected to relentless torment, finally snapped. I saw them in hospitals and examination rooms, paraded through lecture theatres for clever doctor-professors to opine over. I saw them in marketplaces, in modistes' shops, at operas and on cold slabs. Each and every one wore the same expression, the one on Jessamine Morwood's lovely face. I cannot know what's been done to her over the years, but I can imagine.

'Are you alright, Miss Asher?' Albertine calls. Did she notice her mother's behaviour? Or is it simply that I've been staring into nothingness for a few minutes?

'Yes, Albertine. Thank you. Just daydreaming.' I smile. 'I do believe it's time for your lunch. Go and wash up. Tell Mrs Charlton I shall be along presently.'

* * *

Sometimes stealth is called for, other times a more direct offensive is the best choice. I cross the gardens towards the small building with the millwheel. Should anyone see me, I'll not look like a sneak. The little structure is surrounded by high-set windows to let in light, so until now I've merely gotten the most passing of glances inside as I walk by on tiptoe. The door looks stout. I knock loudly. If it is answered, I will have a question, if not... I knock again; while my right hand *rap-rap-raps*, my left jiggles the handle.

It swings open. Unlocked. Unloved. I step inside, pulling the door closed behind me.

Big enough to hold four rooms, it's been turned into one large space. No other entrance, but a tapestry (a hunting scene) hanging where one might have been expected. There's dust on the shelves, but the flagged floor is remarkably clean – I wonder if the Binions come in here and do the bare minimum? It is like some of the teaching laboratories at Whitebarrow University: against one wall is a long bench holding a collection of glass jars, mortars and pestles, tubes of clear glass, bottles of powders; there are bookshelves on another wall, and yet another is covered by glass-fronted cupboards. Inside are rows of tiny bottles in blue, green and red – several of the blue vials are missing from a row; blue vials that were sent to the Lewis family, filled with "medicine". Those on one shelf are empty, those on another are full of liquid or powder, yellowing handwritten labels peeling away; they've been here a long while. There's an apothecary's set of drawers filled with needles, spatulas, scalpels, bandages... a perfect collection of a doctor's tools. A hearth, stacked with dust-covered logs, stands cold.

There is a desk, cabinets with drawers, a chair at the desk, and one beside it as if for a visitor or patient. In one corner an entire skeleton, human, hangs from a frame. Beside it is a glass-topped display case: inside is a skeleton I do not recognise. It appears human but for the skull, which is elongated, its jaw distended, lined with long sharp teeth. One of Eli's ancestors, perhaps, a wicked wolf boiled back to the bone and put on show? I know several men of Whitebarrow University who'd give their eyeteeth for the chance to examine such a thing. It almost distracts me from my task.

In the middle of it all is a table, metal and stone with a thin mattress, for examinations. To the right, part of the room drops away to show it's built over the river, and part of the waterwheel is actually inside the house. I smile; a mill once, then repurposed.

Yet the air of neglect cannot be ignored, and it's more than merely weeks or months, but years. This place waiting as if prepared to receive a medical man who never arrived… I think of Eirlys Lewis saying Luther had studied once…

Suddenly there is a noise, a rattling. The hanging at the back is flung aside to show Connell pale-faced, wide-eyed in another doorway. He hisses, 'Father is coming!'

I hurry towards the boy, slip out. Connell closes the door swiftly and quietly. He grabs my hand, dragging me towards a gap in a hedge behind the building. He pulls me on, down the sloping bank to the edge of the river, then tugs me with him beneath a very low overhang that I can barely fit under, then I'm slithering after him into a short trough-like depression and end up in a muddy hole, splashing as I hit. I look at the ruination of my white blouse and blue skirt. I feel the damp seep into my boots. Surely this was not necessary.

'Connell—' I begin but he puts a filthy finger to my lips; his face is so bloodless in the dimness that he almost shines. I struggle to right myself, lying against the cold muddy ground beneath the riverbank, and peer over the edge of our hidey-hole. The water's flowing swiftly by, the other bank looks terribly far away at this angle, and above it fields roll to the tree line where the woods proper begin. I'm about to speak again when I hear heavy footsteps. Then a voice, crooning, although there's nothing consoling about it.

'Connell?' Luther Morwood. 'Connell, where are you? Have you been sneaking again? You know what Father promised last time.'

I glance at the boy beside me and his eyes are dark pools of fear, enormous. When I touch his shoulder, he's shuddering. I know why *I'm* fleeing the man above – why is his son? I pull him into a hug; for my own comfort I spin the mourning ring around my finger, a nervous habit, recently developed.

'Connell? Cooonnneeellll?' The singsong of Luther's voice is eerie and I begin to tremble myself, wondering how often his wife and children – *all* his family – have heard that tone and felt their guts turn to water. I fight against memories of a similar tone in my own childhood when fire rose in my mother's temper. I wonder how Leonora feels about him; she never eats with the family for any meal and it occurs to me only now that I've never seen her interact with her son. That doesn't mean it never happens, but... It's another few minutes before Luther leaves; I hear his tread retreat. Five minutes more before I speak again, five long minutes of lying in mud and fluid, of crawling things skittering across my hands, over my back. Twice, otters peer into the hole with umbrage.

'Connell,' I say. 'Thank you.'

'Father's mean. He gets angry,' he says with a trembling pitch.

I touch his face with my grubby hand – it doesn't matter, his cheek is equally covered in muck – and he gives me a tremulous smile. 'I will protect you from him, Connell. I promise.'

'No one can.'

'I swear to you, I can. Trust me, Connell: ogres can be defeated.' I smile and he returns it. 'You come to me anytime you need to; hide in my room if need be.' Fine enough with my secrets hidden beneath the floor. 'Even if I'm not there.'

Slowly he nods.

I've never taught before, never had the care of children, but these – I can identify with them. Feel their needs and wants, what will appeal to them best. And I *do* want to protect them. How strange.

We scramble out of the hole. In the sunlight we look even worse. It will be difficult to go back into the house like this. 'Connell, is the water deep here?'

'Here yes, but not a little further down.'

We wander past a bend in the stream and he points. 'Here is shallow.'

'Right. In. No, don't remove your boots and make sure your head goes under too.'

Once we are both thoroughly soaked and much of the mud is washed away, we head back to the house, shivering. I grab a handful of plants on the way. He's a good lad, not complaining about the icy bath and the cold of the day, but both our teeth are chattering.

We tramp in through the kitchen door, much to Mrs Charlton's surprised displeasure.

'Gods, what happened? Look at that shirt, Master Connell, ruined! And Miss Todd! Your lovely skirt!'

'It's just water, Mrs Charlton,' I say mildly, dripping on her clean floor.

'Wait there,' she grumbles. There's a wicker basket of fresh laundry on one of the benches and she extracts two towels from it. She hands me mine, then begins to rub Connell down with a fervour that might start a fire were he not so wet. She asks again, 'What happened?'

'Yes, what *did* happen?' Luther's voice sounds from the door that leads to the rest of the house.

Connell's gone paler still. I step in front of him and Mrs Charlton, and smile, undoing my hair. It unwinds like a dark serpent to below my waist. Luther watches its journey.

'Connell was helping me search for this.' I hold up the stalks of water betony. 'It grows by the riverbank – very good for cleaning wounds.' I indicate the graze on my cheek. 'Connell was being a good lad and it got him soaked. He slipped and fell.'

'And naturally you jumped in to save him?'

I feel irrationally aggrieved that he's not making an effort to hide his disbelief. 'Of course. How would it look to let your son and heir drown when he's in my charge?' I shake my head. 'Bad enough he's wet through.'

'I commend your diligence, Miss Todd.' Luther nods slowly, but I can't help feeling he knows I'm lying. 'A warm bath for both, I think, Mrs Charlton, lest a chill set in.'

As if I too am a child beneath his hand. Then Luther is gone and Connell is staring at me like I'm the sun and moon all rolled into one.

10

Two days later, I'm bringing the bowl of red-tinged water and used bandages down from Leonora's room after her evening treatment; she complained there's been no change and I told her to be patient. I'm just outside the kitchen when I hear raised voices: Burdon and Mrs Charlton and Luned. Usually there is a veneer of harmony amongst the staff – or at least since my arrival, or at least in front of me. I remind myself that there's only so much I can know of what went on prior. I pause, wait by the closed door, listening.

'It's not her fault, Cadec Burdon, I'd swear on it.' That's Mrs Charlton.

'The girl's slack as a sow's tits and you know it. Getting worse by the day.' Burdon, with a nastiness I've never heard from him before. 'She left it out by the hearth, then panicked when she realised what she'd done. Luned, be honest: you put the ruined milk in the cool room after it spoiled, didn't you?'

'I put it away when I was meant to, Mr Burdon, I swear! As soon as Tib Postlethwaite delivered it.' She sounds like a wounded child; where's the piss and vinegar I've become accustomed to?

'Then why is it curdled, girl?'

'I don't know, sir.' Luned's voice trembles.

'She did put it away, Burdon, I watched her do it.' Mrs Charlton sounds as if she's about to lose her temper.

'Well, that's as may be but the milk's still spoiled. It's a bloody waste.' His voice is shaking, the anger burning down.

'There'll be more brought in the morning, you know that. In plenty of time for their breakfast.' There's a pause and I imagine her raising a finger to Burdon's narrow face. 'And you won't say another word about it, not to Mistress or Master.'

'No point saying anything to Master,' he snipes.

I push into the kitchen to see them huddled by the table, glaring at the three large blue jugs thereon and each other. Luned's been crying and she swipes at her cheeks in embarrassment as she sees me.

'Is all well?' I ask and go to the sink to wash the bowl and bandages. Luned flounces out without a word, and Burdon follows her a few moments later with nothing more than a nod to me. Mrs Charlton remains staring at the crocks. I hang the bandages by the fire to dry, then approach, touch her arm.

'Mrs Charlton? What's happened?' As if I'd not been eavesdropping.

She points at the table. 'That girl... she put the milk away. I *saw* her take it from Tib's hands, pour it into these containers, hand the pail back, and then take them straight to the cool room. Even if she'd left it out a few hours in this weather? Nothing would have happened like that.'

I lean closer to the table and the smell rising from the vessels makes me gag. It's ridiculously strong, terrible as decay. The milk is a dark grey, an oily slick covering the top instead of a layer of fresh cream. It might have curdled if left by the heat of the fire, but this colour? I've never smelled anything like it, but I've *heard* of it happening. A shiver creeps up my spine.

'What could do that?'

'Sometimes such things happen, Mrs Charlton. Perhaps the cows had eaten some plant that was not healthful. I have seen it happen.' *I have not.* 'There's nothing to worry about – beyond Burdon blaming Luned.'

'Miss Jessamine's complaining of a cold spot in the hallway outside her room.' Seemingly off on a tangent, she twists her hands.

'Mrs Charlton—'

'And last eve I found the front door wide open well after midnight. I don't know why I came down, but there it was, agape to the night and whatever's in it. How did that happen?'

'Perhaps Burdon forgot…'

'Does that man strike you as likely to forget his duties?'

Perhaps if he'd overindulged in his preferred brandy, I think. 'Mayhap Eli…'

'Boy's an arrant fool but he knows better than to leave the house unsecured. There *are* times when you leave the ways open – and you take precautions – but last night wasn't one of them. Last night was the ordinary sort when things slip in that you don't want in your home.'

I stare at her. She's not stupid, Mrs Charlton, but I don't know what else to tell her. Certainly I don't need her speaking of ghosts, bringing the priest up here to cleanse the place – then I remember Leonora won't have the god-hound in the house. 'I've not felt anything. Nor seen anything.'

'Nor me, but who knows when such things make themselves known?'

'I think it best to be calm, Mrs Charlton. Let's not panic until we need to. And if there's anything about, well, then there are ways to deal with it. I'm sure you've got some ideas.'

'And I'm sure you do, too, Asher Todd, for all your clever ways.'

You don't know the half of it.

'Let's wait, then? Make plans when and if we need to. But perhaps put those outside the door and deal with them in the morning? Too late to start with such a mess.' I smile. 'I was going to make a pot of tea. Will you join me? No milk, of course.'

She nods. When I'm done, I find a bottle of ordinary old whiskey in the pantry and throw a generous drop in each cup. We sit by the fire, as we've done before. When I sense she's calmed, her shoulders have lowered instead of hunching about her ears, when her hands loosen their grip on the mug, I clear my throat.

'That little building by the stream, with the millwheel?' I ask, and she raises a brow. 'What's it for? No one seems to go there.'

'*That*,' she says, 'was made over for Master Luther when he went off to Whitebarrow University to become a doctor. It was a mill from when this family were less important and there was no big house here – now the Aclands in the Tarn are the millers. Mr and Mrs Morwood had it converted into a little surgery for Master Luther.'

I blink. A tremor runs through my right arm, a strangely localised shock. *Whitebarrow*. 'Mr Morwood is a trained physician?'

She sniggers, leans close, shakes her head. 'Burdon told me. The young master was sent off to the university town; it was his finest wish to study, though his parents weren't too keen. But Luther insisted and they gave in, which I'm given to understand had been the way of things. They converted that little structure so Luther Morwood would have somewhere to play doctor and look after the health of those on the estate and in the Tarn.'

'What happened?' I almost say *No one's been in there in years.*

'Failed his studies. And behaved abominably by all accounts, such that he was sent down. All that wasted money. A matter of great shame. Burdon said that's what set the old man off on his own merry path to the grave via every gambling den and whorehouse he could find along the way.' She sits back and looks very satisfied; Mrs Charlton truly does not like Luther Morwood, but keeps it well concealed from him. Whenever I see her interacting with him she's nothing but polite, businesslike: *Yes, sir. No, sir. Three bags full, sir.*

'Yet there's no doctor in the village?'

'Was one but he died and Mr Morwood's never let him be replaced. If it's not too bad it clears up. If it's otherwise then nature takes its course and we all go down to the bone orchard. Women in childbed rely on the women around them; when Miss Jessamine's been pregnant, the doctor comes from Bellsholm to make sure she's safe.' I stare at her. 'Those in the Tarn make do with whatever the apothecary knows; some of the women have remedies, but no one wants to be too obvious about it lest that old priest screams, *Witch.*'

'But what about the family?'

'The old mistress called in a man from Youngling's Brook about her eyes, but he wasn't able to offer any help. Nor any specialists from the big places.'

'There's a convent not far from here,' I say, almost to myself. 'They've a sanatorium attached.' The tea in my hands is cold now and I've barely taken a sip. 'The nuns are clever healers or so I've heard.' It's also where the clever Whitebarrow doctor-professors send any cases they cannot cure or kill off, a convenient hiding place – except for the fact that the nuns there *do* often manage what the medical men do not.

I wonder at Luther not allowing a physician here – could he really not bear to have one around? To see someone succeed where he'd failed? To let the folk of the Tarn suffer because of his ego? It is not beyond imagining. Mrs Charlton sighs and rises. She reaches for her empty mug; I raise a hand. 'Leave it, Mrs Charlton. I'll tidy. Off you go, you look tired.'

I clean up after she's gone, but I do not go to bed.

* * *

I knock on the cottage door and listen; I seem to do that a lot. Truly, much of my life seems to have been spent waiting outside rooms, hoping to be let in. The memory annoys me and I turn the handle, pushing just as he calls, 'Come in.'

I've only seen him at a distance these past few days, and the desire to take the knife again, do a proper job, has only marginally lessened. I know it's nothing more than anger and humiliation. That he made me afraid and I don't like being afraid; so much of my early life was spent in that state.

I want myself back, I want my equilibrium returned and I will take it.

The cottage is an open space, small; a big bed in one corner, a tiny kitchen in another with a table and two chairs, a settee by the fire, its fabric worn but once pretty, a blue and gold brocade, something discarded from the big house as no longer good enough and that washed up here as too good to throw away. The only part of the room that's closed off is one corner; a bathroom, I imagine.

Eli's standing by the table, pouring water from a heavy iron kettle into a blue enamel mug. He's wearing dark trews and an undershirt that's got pink stains across the chest.

'You're bleeding.'

'I wonder why,' he says.

'Take your shirt off.'

'Now, now. A man likes a little romance first.'

I move to where he stands, put my hands on my hips. 'Perhaps you'd rather I tell Mr Morwood he's got one of the wicked wolves in his employ?'

'What makes you think he doesn't know?'

'Because I think if he did he'd have either hunted you over hill and dale, or pinned you on the table in his little surgery trying to figure out what makes you tick.'

Eli removes his undershirt and sits heavily on one of the rough-hewn kitchen chairs. I put my satchel on the table.

The laceration is longer than I recalled, from the mid-point of his chest to partway across the top of his arm before it becomes shoulder; it's scabbed over but there's some pallid liquid seeping. I take a bowl from a range of mismatched crockery on the sideboard; some white with blue patterns, others with pink and orange roses – old lady's crockery, inherited from a mother or aunt or grandmother, gathered together as pieces break. I pour in hot water from the kettle, add a little cold from the tap over the stone carved sink, then fish a pouch from my satchel. I roughly tear the water betony stalks and leaves to sprinkle them into the container, then leave it to steep. I pull the other seat up and sit in front of Eli,

103

our knees almost touching. I take a soft cloth from my bag, dip it into the fluid, dab tenderly at the wound.

'Why are you doing this?' he asks in a low voice.

'Because if it gets infected, I'm given to understand there's no doctor closer than a week's journey. And if you die, who will answer my questions?'

'What makes you think I'll answer your questions?'

I press none-too-kindly at the cut and he sucks in breath through clenched teeth. I grin.

'Tell me,' I say, 'about the wicked wolves.'

He hesitates and I press again.

'Ah, gently for the love of fuck!'

'As gently as you knocked me over?'

'I don't... don't know my own strength when I'm in that shape.'

'Indeed.'

He looks away, shakes his head. We both know it's no excuse.

'I'll start: Once upon a time, the wicked wolves of the woods had the run of this land, before the Morwoods came. The wicked wolves hunted the people of the Tarn until one day a good god-hound took it upon himself to destroy this terrible scourge. Just one god-hound against a legion of wicked wolves.' I grin. 'This is the story Albertine tells me, and I've not been able to find anything – thus far – in my reading to either support or disprove this.'

He glares.

'Yet here you are, clearly wolfish, or worse than a wolf and clearly neither dead nor vanquished. A wolf of the woods and, my experience would suggest, wicked.'

He raises a hand in surrender.

'I know nothing more than my grandmother told me when I

104

was a littlie,' he says and I'm much gentler as I pat the wound dry. Reward good behaviour. 'We were never the predators they said we were, and never hunted children. Bad husbands, dangerous men, cruel mothers; folk no one would miss if they thought about it.' He smiles without mirth. 'Those who weakened the village, who made it worse. And we kept the rest from harm, from outsiders, raiders and robbers and the like. It's a very long time ago, Asher Todd, but the Tarn was always safe because the wolves maintained the borders.'

'What happened?'

He shrugs. 'A Morwood happened. That's all my gran would say. We were slain.'

'Not all of you.'

He shakes his head. 'Some slipped through and away, hid in plain sight. Some neighbours remained kind. The line weakened. Here I am, the last of the blood.'

'Why are you still here?'

'Where else would I go? My people bled into this land. I stay here… I'm part of it.' He hoods his eyes, turns away. I wonder if at night he dreams of once again running freely, of being lord of this place like his ancestors once were.

'I've never seen anything like you, but I've read about them.' I sit back. 'All that power to shift and you use it to frighten governesses.'

He blushes. 'Only one governess.'

'Not the one before me?' I risk asking – Jessamine mentioned her openly the other day, so perhaps I will get away with it. There is a jar of ointment, calendula and goldenrod in a suspension of lanolin, and I tenderly apply it to the cut.

'A soft silly little girl? Where's the fun in that? No challenge.'

'Where did she go? The one before me?'

He shrugs. 'Here one day, gone the next. Master Luther said she'd had a family emergency.'

'Leave your shirt off a while, let that soak in, let the wound dry.' I hold up a herb sachet and the jar of salve. 'Bathe it with the water betony and apply the ointment morning and night until it runs out.'

He grabs my hand; his palms are prickly, his grip strong. 'You're not going to come and attend to me yourself morning and night?'

'I've better things to do.' I rise, pulling away. He doesn't fight me, but raises a brow, leans back in the chair, crossing his arms over his chest and winces as a result. 'And if you try to scare me again, be in no doubt that I'll finish what I started.'

He gives something that's a little grunt, a little snort of a laugh. I repack my bag ready to step into the night. 'Eli?'

'Yes?'

'Did you leave the front door open at the big house last night?'

'What kind of fool do you take me for? And have Mrs Charlton after my hide?'

I shrug and turn away, put my hand to the doorknob.

'Asher Todd?' His tone is tentative. *Surprising.*

I look over my shoulder. His expression is one of shame, a boy caught out.

'I'm sorry. I'm sorry for trying to scare you. I'm sorry for knocking you over. It was stupid and cruel. I *am* sorry.' He nods.

'Yes,' I say. 'It was. But thank you for apologising.'

I can count on one hand the number of apologies I've had in

my life from men. Then I'm out the door, striding back through the darkness towards the last light of the manor. I only just set foot in the kitchen when there's a bloodcurdling scream from the floors above, loud enough to reach me and communicate pure terror. I set off at a run.

11

The shrieking does not stop as I hurry to the second floor and the suite Luther and Jessamine share. Mrs Charlton is there just before me, in a dark pink dressing gown, a white sleep cap askew on her hair. I'm fearful of what we might find – what might Luther be doing that caused his wife to make such a noise, for her fear to overcome her natural desire to pretend everything is well enough?

We thrust open the door and barge in.

In the middle of the room, in the sitting area, is a white-nightgowned Jessamine Morwood, dark hair loose, giving a series of high-pitched howls, flailing like a mad thing. She's hitting at the air in front of her and her own face and chest. Turning in a circle like a top, the motion moves her around and around, miraculously avoiding furniture. There is no sign of her husband.

Mrs Charlton goes to her charge, tries to calm her, but Jessamine slaps at the older woman now. I grab at her arms, hold them to her sides. She keeps pressing out screeches, however, and I exchange a look with Mrs Charlton. She slips a hand over Jessamine's mouth, and begins to make shushing noises, soft and low.

'Hush, my dove. We are here and you are not alone. Quiet, my girl,' she croons.

'Mrs Morwood,' I say. Jessamine's eyes above Mrs Charlton's hand are terrified, darting from me to her old nanny and around us. 'Mrs Morwood. What happened?'

Tiny peeps come from behind the housekeeper's fingers. I can see the flesh of Jessamine's face is being pressed white. I gently pull Mrs Charlton's hand away; Jessamine's panicked breath becomes a series of sobs.

'Jessamine, what happened? Was it... Mr Morwood?' Her eyes go wide, the fear seems to increase, so I put a finger over my own lips.

'She... she walked through the wall.' Ragged, her voice, and harsh.

'Who?' I ask and Mrs Charlton echoes me.

'A woman. Red h-h-h-h-hair.'

My heart stutters. I touch the mourning ring.

'Who was she?'

'Red hair. Red hair.'

Given the racket, I'm astonished there's still no sign of Luther. Nor Burdon, nor Luned. But I notice three heads are peeking around the doorframe, eyes enormous, faces pale and fearful. Jessamine's shaking like a leaf in a storm and looks set to begin her shrieks anew. I change my grip, catch her fingers gently in mine.

'Jessamine. You're frightening the children,' I say and her gaze follows the direction of my nod. She sees her babies and slumps; we have to hold her up. I jerk my chin at Albertine. 'Back to your rooms. I'll be there shortly.' I don't check to see if she obeys. 'Let us get you lying down. I think you'll feel better.'

Between us Mrs Charlton and I help Jessamine beneath the covers of the black oak bed with its red velvet canopy; the other side is untouched, the linens still intact. The housekeeper has the look of a mother in despair.

'A damp cloth, Mrs Charlton?' I say, and she bustles through a narrow door leading into the bathroom. I sit on the edge of the mattress and take Jessamine's hand; her wrist, I notice, is bruised. The other matches it – dark contusions, going yellow with age, precursors to the new. 'What woke you, Mrs Morwood?'

She turns her head on the pillow, her eyes like pits, her lips bloodless. 'I… don't know. I thought I heard… someone crying… the children… but there was that woman. I got up. She was moving around the room, touching things, then she looked at me – and she was so angry. She flew at me…'

Her eyes fill with tears. I look more closely at her throat: there are old bruises there too, usually covered by the high necks of her dresses. Luther.

'Did you know her? Did you know her face?'

'I've never seen her before. I don't know what she wants.'

I could tell her it was a dream, that she imagined it. I could do that but perhaps it would make her worse, to be disbelieved. 'Jessamine, I don't believe she's here for you. Old houses sometimes… throw up things such as this. But you mustn't speak about her again. It wouldn't do for anyone to think you were… unwell.'

Her eyes go wide. She takes my meaning. Mrs Charlton returns, a cool damp cloth in one hand. I let her replace me. Jessamine might ignore me, might repeat what I said, then I would deny it; it would make things worse for her. Perhaps she senses that.

'I will make a tisane to help her sleep. Will Mr Morwood—'

'He won't be back tonight,' Mrs Charlton says with certainty. I doubt she'll leave the girl's side this night, even if Luther tried to physically remove her. I close the door softly, find my hands are cold and shaking. But there's no time to indulge myself, the children will be waiting.

They are in the girls' room huddled on one of the beds like terrified chicks. When you realise a parent cannot look after themselves... well, it's a terrible moment. I fix a smile, sit beside them. They lean into the circle of my arms, and I hold them for a while.

'Your mother had a terrible nightmare, but she'll be fine now. What a shock to wake up to!' Their faces clear; if I'm not worried, then it must be alright. 'Come along, back to bed.'

I tuck the girls in first, then escort Connell to his chamber. 'Will Mother be well?' he asks in a trembling voice. I hold his hand, find it colder than mine, and rub the fingers, breathe warm air onto the icy skin until he laughs that it tickles.

'Yes, Connell, your mother will be well.' I say it though I cannot know if I lie or not. 'I will do my best to help her any way I can. Now, sleep.'

When I finally return from the kitchen, a cup of sleeping draught in hand, I notice something shining at the bottom of the stairs that lead up to the attic rooms where the servants sleep. On closer examination I realise it's the heavy-chained chatelaine Mrs Charlton usually wears at her waist. Perhaps she grabbed it in her confusion or out of habit when the ruckus began. I pick it up. Not so many keys, so one must be used for all the internal doors. I slip it into my pocket.

Back in the room, Jessamine takes the cup from me and drinks like an obedient child. 'You'll stay with her tonight, Mrs Charlton?'

'Of course.'

'Then I will see you in the morning.' As I close the door the housekeeper begins to sing, one of those songs I half-remember from childhood. It takes me back to a tiny house in Whitebarrow, to my own mother's voice sweet and low, one of those times there was no need of a protector and it was just us. I shake myself, feel the past cascade from my shoulders.

I quickly check on Leonora. She's breathing deeply, sleeping under the influence of the possets I've been giving her for some relief from the pain of the eye treatment. She'd not have heard Jessamine's ruckus at all.

Then I'm out in the dim corridor, gazing to the far end, where the locked room lies. I touch the chatelaine in my pocket. This might be my only chance. I tiptoe along, try all the keys until there is just the last one left; it slides into the lock almost unwillingly. It doesn't turn at first, but then finally grinds over grit and gilings. But click it does at last, and I push the door open.

The air is cold, cold, colder. Colder than it should be.

I breathe dust and cough. All is dark but for the moonlight coming in the tall windows; there are no curtains and the bed is free of hangings and coverlets as if everything was stripped away after she was gone in an attempt to wipe her out. Everything except the painting hidden in Leonora's dressing room, taken from the wall in the days after her child was sent away. There is a chair, though, beneath the window, the only other piece of furniture, and a slim spectral figure perches upon it. The moonbeams pass through her, yet I can make out the crimson of her hair, the strange blue fire of her eyes, the pale spill of her skin. The dress isn't the green one of the portrait, but the plain grey rough wool shift she died and was buried in because we couldn't afford anything else.

112

I approach but not too close. I sit on the edge of the four-poster bed. Particles rise around me.

I stare at her and she acts as if I'm not there; perhaps she doesn't recognise me. It's five minutes or more before I find my voice, and I know that the moment I speak things must change. I will have no choice but to do what I'd hoped not to.

Ghosts can be left behind, but they can find you too. I had hoped I'd travelled far enough. Hoped she might never follow me, though I had made promises to her. I thought she might forget, but in life she was never one to let go of anything so why would she change in death?

At last, I say, 'Hello, Mother.'

* * *

My earliest memories are of my mother's hair, so bright it seemed stardust had been sprinkled through it. Some days I forget the shape of her face, the slant of her eyes, the tilt of her nose and the set of her lips but I can always recall the fall of her copper-crimson locks as she leant over me in my crib when I was a baby. No one else I ever saw had quite that hue; she would let me brush it when she was in a good mood and I was old enough to hold the implement. It picked her out in a crowd, made people stare at her, and for the longest time I was proud of that: that everyone looked at my beautiful mother.

I didn't understand, then, not entirely, their gazes. I saw the envy and awe, certainly, but didn't comprehend the rest, the darker shades of what was in their expressions. Not until later when I grew older and began to listen, *really* listen to what people said as we passed. Only when I understood what she was and did to keep us – how others regarded her – did I become less proud.

She was well known in Whitebarrow was Heloise, by men and their wives – sought by the former and loathed by the latter, although it must be admitted that some of those women might have had very mixed feelings about her. Some approached Heloise too, and were rebuffed unkindly, which was unwise; if only she'd been gentler towards them perhaps her later life would have been different. But I suspect her past had been so fraught with gazes and touches she did not invite that she had no grace left for what she did not feel and therefore did not understand. When her looks began to fade and her hold on those husbands who were not her own loosened, when the madness tightened its grip on her, in those days she might have done better had she been kinder to those wistful wives.

Yet in those early days in Whitebarrow when her beauty brought us prosperity, when I was dressed like a little princess and taught to behave as one, when she was wanted and envied by all, in that cold golden time my mother mostly loved me.

Now, here in the place she'd fled, in the place I promised to return her to, I tell her all I've done since I left the university town. I don't mention that I ran away, or that I hoped she'd not follow or ever find me even if she did – it makes little sense, I know, for *I* fled to her childhood home, but hope is not a rational thing. It was always a vain wish when I carry the item which is intrinsically hers – but even if I did not, how could I escape when I am so intrinsically *hers* too? My blood and bone, the very fabric of me came from her. How could I hope to dig those bits of she who birthed me out of my skin?

I tell her all these things knowing she cannot reply; the illness that ate away at her in great ragged bites took her tongue a year before it rotted everything else. She made her wishes known, then, when she still had the wherewithal to write, by use of a small chalkboard. When she did not, it was with furious blinks and grunts and groans that still make me shudder when I hear them in my dreams. In her last days, if she even knew what she wanted all she had was rage to offer.

But I tell her that all I promised, all I learned at such great cost to myself and others, can be done and will be done, but it will take a little time yet. That she needs to be patient a while more.

Long after I've finished speaking she turns towards me at last. Surely she recognises me though I look different. Surely she knows her own kin no matter their skin. I stare into her eyes and see that the agonies of her last days have not deserted her. Staring into her pain, I wonder how I could have ever run from my promises to her. And I wonder, not for the first time, if all that's gone before hasn't made me a little mad, that I should ever have thought those promises reasonable. And so the thing I thought perhaps I had escaped, the vows I thought I might avoid, must now be honoured, all because of this spectral thing sitting voiceless by the window.

'Stay in this room, Mother, I beg of you. Leave the inhabitants of this house alone; you'll have your due soon enough. Do not wander lest you make my task more difficult. Lest it take longer. Remain here. I will come again.'

When I leave, I lock the door as if that will stop her. Back in my room, I press the key into the small wax tablet I carry for just such purposes; I must return the chatelaine to Mrs Charlton in the morning, but I need to be able to come and go as I please. I must find a means of making a duplicate.

At last, I lie on my bed; I don't bathe or remove my dress. I'm too exhausted for these rituals tonight, even though I know they are such small things and would make me feel better. I don't want to feel better. I don't deserve to do so. Every time I close my eyes all I see is the burning blue of my mother's eyes, and the guilt threatens to overwhelm me.

* * *

I sleep only a little before dawn begins to splash itself across the sky. In the end I give up, make myself a tonic, and dress warmly. I'm still hooking the satchel over my shoulder by the time I step outside. My breath mists the air as I walk briskly across the fields, then into the woods.

I took careful note when Eli brought us back this way.

The sounds are strangely clear in the freshness of the morning, yet also strangely dulled by the trees and bushes. I see no small animals but I hear them; and nothing like Eli Bligh's creeping in the undergrowth, so there's that.

When I reach the quarry, there's still a thick fog on the water, and it hasn't quite dispersed by the time I walk around the rim of the crater to find the path down. The gradient is comfortable and generally the track is free of scree that would cause a fall. Still, I'm careful. If I trip and fall, who's to find me? No one knows where I've gone or even that I've left the house. Just another girl to disappear from Morwood.

When I set foot on the ground, it's fairly firm but damp and the fog seems to have lightened. I go to the edge of the water and, taking a jar from my bag, kneel. Then I plunge my hand into the water – it's breathtakingly cold – and dig around. A handful of white goop comes up and I examine it minutely. Kaolinite clay. I suspected as much from the colour of the liquid that first day Eli led us here. I've a use or two for it, and it never hurts to have such a substance on hand. I fill the jar to the brim, screw the lid on tight.

I rise, looking up at the walls of the dig, admire the neat cutouts where stone's been taken to build things. Then I realise I'd best hurry to get back in time to clean up, and present myself at breakfast. But when I turn around, the fog has thickened again.

I take a few steps forward in the direction I came from. A few steps, just a few steps, then look behind – and the pool is gone, the wall of cut stone similarly disappeared. The fog begins to move around me, swirling slowly then with increasing speed until it's like the hard flurries of a snowstorm and I can barely keep my eyes open to see.

Something tugs at the back of my coat, like a child seeking attention, and I swing about to face – nothing. The tugging again, behind me once more, this time at my skirt. Again and again and I swing about like a fool until I'm dizzy. Then a sort of tunnel forms in the whiteness, head-height only, and then there's a face looming at the end of it, not enough detail for me to think I know who it is, but it dives.

Dives towards me at speed and I collapse to my knees, a cry on my lips that I hate letting out. My mother would be ashamed of me. As I'm on my hands and knees, forcing back tears – why am I so rattled? *Why?* – I notice something in the damp earth: my footprints from when I went to the water's edge. Whispering *Thank you* to I don't know who, I crawl back along the trail I unwittingly left myself. I keep crawling until I'm halfway up the switchback path, well above the fog – yet when I turn and look back where I've been there's no sign of the whiteness. All is clear: the water, the wall; I can even make out the spot where I dug up the clay, the pool murkier, the shallows disturbed.

My breath catches in my throat and my feet make a decision for me: I run.

12

Last night, I removed the final poultice from Leonora Morwood's eyes, laved them clean, then dripped in a solution of eyebright. She complained once again, and bitterly too, that she still couldn't see properly. And I, short on slumber and patience, told her to shut up her whining and sleep, for pity's sake.

This morning, she appears at the breakfast table for the first time since I arrived at Morwood and, if everyone's reaction was anything to go by, for the first time in some years. It occurs to me only then that I've seen neither her son nor grandchildren visit her rooms at any point since I've been here, nor Jessamine either. That's not to say it hasn't happened but I have spent a goodly while in her second-floor suite, and though occasionally I've run into Luned as she collects trays from outside the door, as for the members of her family? Not a one. Before I came, to whom did she speak? Did she simply stay in that space, reading, reading, reading until her sight grew dim, edging her lectern and books ever closer to the light of the windows? When did she take to her room for good? How long was she holed up there? Jessamine mentioned it in the garden that day but it did not seem so significant until now. Three years! Heledd said three years.

As Luned serves porridge, the door of the small dining room

opens and there's Leonora in a gown of purple shot silk. The sleeves reach halfway down her forearms, and there's silver lace inside, silver bows around the elbows. The bodice is tight and cut low, again with silver lace around the neckline, more silver bows in rows down the bodice. The style's antiquated, but fit for a ball. Her hair, which I've never seen any way but loose down her back, has been swept up into an elegant chignon and the necklace around her wrinkled throat is a blaze of emeralds and amethysts. Her fingers are weighted down with rings.

All to break her fast.

We're underdressed by comparison, no one's ready for an impromptu gala.

'Mother,' Luther says, dropping his spoon with a loud clatter against the bowl. The children stare, as does Jessamine, shaken by surprise from her funk. She has enough wit to order Luned to set another place, which the girl does with alacrity.

In grander homes, ones in the larger cities, I would not eat with the family that employs me. I'd dine in my bedroom or the kitchen if the other servants would tolerate me; but here I've been favoured. I suspect it's because Luther wants to keep an eye on me, and also because I keep the children in check. He sits at the head, Jessamine at his right hand, Connell at the left, Sarai beside her mother, Albertine by her brother, and I beside Albertine. In any other household, I'd not be privy to this performance; but I'd also not be in any other household. The table is a small one; she chooses the free spot at the other end, opposite Luther, and that's where Luned fumbles with cutlery.

I rise and approach the old woman. She turns her head left and right as directed by my fingers under her chin, using the light of the long window that looks out onto the gardens to examine her. The eyes are now clear, their blue restored, the pale webs gone. We smile at each other.

'How do they feel?' I ask.

'Well enough,' she says and I raise an eyebrow; she relents. 'Much better. They do not sting and I can see everything.' She blinks rapidly, her lashes a butterfly's wings that might change the world. 'So. That's what you look like; not as pretty as I expected. Funny, when you were little more than a shadow, I thought you reminded me of someone, but now I see you properly…'

'You might simply say thank you,' I point out.

She grins. 'Thank you, Asher Todd.'

Luther has gathered himself, risen and approached. 'Mother. How is this possible? Your sight—'

Leonora nods at me and I feel much happier than I should. 'My dear Asher has unsuspected talents. It's refreshing to have a competent physician on hand. You could learn something from her.'

That lands like a blow on both of us. Luther, his face red, plants a cold kiss on his mother's cheek, then steers her to the vacant chair, which he pulls out for her. Leonora sits to my left with all the intent and grandeur of a ruler setting up a rival court; although it's the foot of the table, she makes it seem otherwise by her very presence. Luther returns to his place, clearing his throat as if something's stuck there. Luned deftly slides a bowl of porridge in place, then the jug of cream, the plate with a pat of butter, a bottle of mixed berry preserve and the sugar bowl.

'Mother, what an unexpected pleasure,' says Jessamine wonderingly. 'It's been so long.'

'Yes, Jessamine dear, far too long.' She holds up her cup, waves it for Luned to fill even though the pot is on the table in front of her. She takes a sip, makes a face. 'It's too cold, girl, bring me a fresh pot.'

I can see steam rising from the coffee in her hand. Luned exits swiftly – the fastest I've ever seen her move in response to orders from anyone in this house. Luther stares at his mother until she meets his gaze in her own sweet time. He pauses, says, 'But how?'

She clicks her tongue in annoyance. 'I told you. Asher has learned some clever things in that university town.' She doesn't say *Unlike you*, but the implication hangs in the air.

He looks at me.

'A simple poultice, Mr Morwood. I had seen it used with some effect on older people by doctors at Whitebarrow.' *A lie.* I'd only ever seen it used by certain women, done quietly for those who knew better than to boast of it. Women clever enough to let any successes be attributed to miracles wrought by the Church, by worn and wearied wooden saints in alcoves and alleys around the city or looming above fountains, hands hovering in a constant state of blessing. 'I'm pleased to have been of assistance.'

'Luther, we have matters to discuss now that I am functional once again.' She adds everything she can to the porridge, mixes it like a witch with a cauldron and takes small, well-bred bites.

'Indeed? I was unaware you had any complaints about how I've been managing the estate.'

'Easy to remain so if you never come to my rooms, never speak to me, stay away for the better part of three years. Let your children run wild.'

Ah.

'Mother, I—'

'After breakfast we will discuss the tenancy agreements which I believe are up for renewal. Then the investments in Bellsholm, the properties there which came as part of Jessamine's dowry.' She nods towards her daughter-in-law. 'And the practicalities of taking on more staff to replace those you dismissed – a properly qualified lady's maid for myself at the very least. I can hardly be expected to do my own hair every day.'

'Mother, I—'

'And we shall begin entertaining again. I have so missed the company of gentlefolk.' She nods to herself. 'A ball, I think, to celebrate spring when it next arrives.'

'Mother, I—'

'*And*, Luther, we shall make some small changes to mealtimes. I can see standards have been allowed to drop.' She eyes every member of her family and clearly finds them wanting. 'From now on, we shall dress for dinner. Formal gowns and suits.'

'Mother, I—'

'We are not so isolated that we need to look like commoners.' Leonora glares at her son and he looks far less secure at the head of the table. 'And I shall be discussing menus with Mrs Charlton from now on. I know you won't mind, dear Jessamine; it will relieve you of an onerous duty, give you time for more of whatever it is you do during the day when Asher looks after your children.'

Jessamine drops her head, not before giving me a searing glance. All my good work, gone so quickly.

'Connell, sit up straight. Albertine, you're using the wrong spoon. Sarai, don't pick at your bread like an urchin.' Leonora looks

123

at me and smiles. 'Your posture and table manners are perfect, Asher.' I think of my mother poking and slapping me until I sat up straight. 'I hope you will be able to turn these feral creatures into something more presentable. Now, where is that girl with my coffee?'

Leonora requires no reply. My stomach is twisting and turning. I helped the old woman because... because I could... because I wanted to show off... because I wanted to give her something, like a child seeking approval, yes, that. I did something I shouldn't have bothered to. Yet I did not think how she might react to having her sight restored. I did not know what she was like before, beyond the tales I was told – I thought perhaps the pain of her infirmity had changed her for the better, that suffering had wrought a miracle in her heart. I did not think she would revert to who she had been – or at least not so quickly. I did not think that she'd have learnt nothing from these past years since her daughter was driven forth.

And now Luther is looking at me with undisguised hatred – so different from his usual vague annoyance at my presence.

I'm not sure what I've done.

Leonora is a horror.

She's the horror my mother told me about and I chose not to listen.

I look down at my toast, rapidly cooling and hardening, blink, then glance up at the children's pale tense faces. I smile reassuringly but feel less than reassured myself. Yet I have spent too many years coming to this point. I will not fail, not now. I will adapt as I must, for it's the only way to survive and keep my promise.

* * *

Jessamine, pricked by Leonora's comments, cancels classes and takes the children into town. They suddenly require new clothes and shoes; this will take all day. I am not required. In the kitchen, the news spread by Luned no doubt, there's nothing else that can be talked about.

'Wonderful what you've done for the mistress, the *old* mistress.' Mrs Charlton is washing dishes and Luned is nowhere in evidence. I pick up a tea towel and begin drying. She repeats, 'Wonderful.'

I say nothing.

'Wonderful. No doctor's been able to do anything to help, all those visits away in the beginning, when she started to lose her sight. All those who came later when she refused to travel.' She sniggers. 'And that priest, used to come up here, trying to get in to see her, convince her he could perform a miracle if only she'd have faith. She had Eli throw him off the front stoop.'

No wonder the god-hound looked at us with such dislike that day.

'Nothing miraculous about it, Mrs Charlton, just a treatment. Nothing more than medicine I picked up in my travels.' *Knowledge I stole.* 'Sometimes it helps, sometimes it does not.'

'Well, you've put a cat amongst the pigeons, no doubt about it,' says Burdon as he dumps a tray of dishes on the table. He leans over to me and says, 'Had it been me, I'd have left well enough alone.'

And I think he might be right, but I'll interfere with more than this before I'm done. Perhaps it will not last long, perhaps it's just the newness of her restored freedom. But whatever else I have done, I've given her the power to take on Luther.

125

* * *

Later still, when I check on Leonora before bed that night, to apply more eyebright, I find her sitting in front of her dressing-table mirror, a barrage of lit candles around her. She's not reading, or attending to her hair, but staring at her reflection so she might see every detail of the face before her. Sight restored and this is what she wants to do. I don't sigh. She was beautiful once and, like my mother, when a woman thinks it's her only currency, it's hard to lose. Her expression is a mix of sadness and rage; I recognise it easily for Heloise wore it long enough.

'Perhaps it was better that I couldn't see this...' She touches delicately the crow's feet by her eyes, the deep lines around the mouth, the furrows across the forehead as if she might cut her fingers on them.

'My, your gratitude is a short-lived thing,' I say, and take up the silver-backed brush and begin brushing her long hair. 'We will see what can be done about everything else next.'

There's only so much I can do, only so far the rigours of time can be reversed. I can make her unguents to smooth out wrinkles, plump the skin, but she will never have the bloom of youth again and that is what she's grieving. And I should resist, I know I should, this urge to help her... but the urge to please, to seek approval as if it's love is too strongly ingrained.

She gives me a smile. 'Sharpish child, you remind me of – someone else. But you are right. I am thankful, and now I can read once again. That is something, isn't it?'

'That is a very big thing.' I pause in my task, think how a lady's maid will take my place here soon, feel strangely bereft. 'Forgive me if I am bold—'

126

She gives a sharp laugh. 'When are you not?'

'—I did not realise you are at odds with your son?'

'Is that how it seemed?' she asks, sounding both surprised and amused. 'Let me tell you a tale, Asher, I know how you like them.

'Once upon a time, there was a she-wolf, who birthed two cubs. She loved them more than anything in the world; she was fierce, protected them against every threat. But one day there came a change upon the world. The forests were ravaged by fires, droughts dried up rivers and lakes until there were only puddles. Food became scarce and though the she-wolf hunted herself to exhaustion she could not find enough to keep both her babies – and herself – fed. The day when she realised only one of them might survive, a crow sat in the bare branches of a tree, and observed the she-wolf watch her cubs play and complain how hungry they were.

'"You'll have to choose between them," said the crow. "Better times are coming – I can see them, when I fly above – but not soon enough for them."

'"I will not choose," said the wolf.

'"*You* might survive if you ate them both," suggested the crow.

'"Would you do that? Would you choose such a thing?"

'"I do not know," said the crow. "But your options are limited. One or the other, you or them."

'The she-wolf was silent for a long moment, until at last she spoke: "No. I have one final choice." And she bit down on her own paw and chewed it until the blood flowed. Then she called her cubs to her and urged them to eat and drink of her body and her blood. And this scene was repeated day after day until nothing remained of the she-wolf, no voice to call or sing as her offspring devoured her, no body to eat nor blood to drink. She was gone. And her children survived. And they ran off into the world and spared their mother not one more thought after she was gone.'

'I—'

'When I first began to lose my sight… I did not realise he would seize the opportunity to try to take everything I'd built from me. After a time he refused to bring any more doctors to see me. Told me to accept my fate, what God had decided for me. To conduct myself with *grace*.' She says the word as if it's the greatest insult ever given. I think about what Heloise told me, how her mother and brother colluded to send her forth from her home in shame; how it benefited Luther to remove the heiress. I think about the portrait Leonora keeps in the dressing room. Has she been staring at it today, now that she can? 'I stopped going down to meals, he stopped coming up here to visit. He dismissed my lady's maid, left me without allies. I've not seen him in literal years, though we live in the same house, on the same floor, separated by a hundred yards and too many resentments. How could I have known, Asher, that he would prove so worthless?'

I think about what Luther did to his own sister, my mother. I think *How could you not have known?* But what I say is, 'I'm sorry.'

'Don't be. I earned it,' she says very quietly, almost under her breath so I barely hear it. But then she adds, 'Yet I'll be no self-sacrificing wolf.'

13

Sunday morning comes around, I sleep late and feel like I've lived a year in seven days. The only reason I wake is because the Binions tap at the door and look expectantly at me. They leave when I tell them they may return in half an hour. They say nothing, just slip away.

Sleep was hard won last night, and I spent hours tossing and turning before at last dropping off in exhaustion. Even then my dreams were fraught with imaginings – of my mother as she was when I knew her, and as she might have been when I did not. The bedtime tales Heloise told me, of what happened when she went to her mother, told her about the child – me – growing inside her. How Leonora raged at her ruin, at all the plans she'd had to make a good marriage for her daughter; how she'd locked Heloise in her room for days until the morning Burdon came for her, with a stout coat, a single carpet bag containing a few changes of clothes, and a purse of coins to pay her way wherever she went. No one else in the house spoke to her or even saw her off – her father so recently deceased, there were only the servants and her mother and brother who might have said goodbye – and the butler walked her up the driveway, through the woods, to the front gate where the coach soon stopped on its way away from

Morwood, the Grange and the Tarn, and everything she'd ever known. When she'd asked Burdon where she should go, he'd replied, 'Wherever you might hide what you've become.'

So, when I look upon the old man's face, I remember that. Heloise said he was kind until then, I *do* remember that. I wonder if I'll ever be able to ask him about it.

I remember his words from my mother's mouth, and I remember her expression, her tone as she told me. I remember her every resentment because that's what she fed me, and even if I went hungry for food, I was ever sated with my mother's bitterness and her desire for revenge. And I grew with one aim in my life, to bring her back where she belonged.

I roll out of bed and pace up and down the small, pretty room, the room that girl had before me, my predecessor, and I recall that I've neglected the other task I came here to do for someone else. I will do it, soon, I will.

Filled with energy and rage, I'm almost running from one wall to the other, a rat in a cage, a cat in a box, a madwoman who may as well be in an attic. All those thoughts, all those emotions – years of thoughts, years of feelings, not all mine – mine, all pressed down under Heloise's, under everything she fed me, told me, all my life – all of them feel like they're burning in my head and I must do something, destroy something, push the rage and sadness outside before I tear someone limb from limb.

A walk, I think; a walk, fast and warming; a walk across the fields and into the woods, away from this house. Time to visit the Lewis family again, as I promised. Or a ride. Perhaps take one of the horses from the stables; faster, wilder than I. Eli owes me a favour. I'll not feel so uncomfortable asking for something.

I see Burdon as I'm making my way downstairs. I've dressed neatly in a dove-grey dress, my hair is a tight braid curled into a bun, my satchel over my shoulder, stout boots on. He's at the top of the staircase as I reach the bottom and though he calls for me I ignore him and am out the front door at speed. I cannot look at him, not at the moment, not when my mother's memories are so close to the surface.

Out the door, down those stone steps, quietly around the side of the manor, and along the path to the stables where Eli spends a goodly part of his day. I pass the structure where the carriages are kept – two full ones, a caleche and a brougham – and nod to Owen Reiver, the some-time coachman, as he polishes the large black conveyance with the Morwood crest on the doors. The structure is the same stone as the house, and I step inside to note that it's pristine. There's the smell of hay and horses, of well-cared-for beasts. Eight stalls, six of them occupied. Two enormous draughthorses to plough the fields, black as night, feather-footed, their coats brushed to shine. The others two roan geldings, and two ebony. All looking at me over the doors to their stalls, curious, hoping for a treat I suspect.

'Eli?' I call and receive no response. I walk further in, past the stalls to the very back where the tack room and feedstore wait. 'Eli?'

I call all the way along and am met with silence. When I finally reach the feedstore, there he is, resting against a bale of lucerne, staring at me.

'Why didn't you answer?' I snap.

'I figured you'd turn up eventually and find me.' He shrugs and it enrages me – I was ready for a fight, wasn't I? I don't want a horse, I know that now; I didn't come down here looking for that.

'This means nothing,' I say before he kisses me. 'Nothing.'

* * *

'And no more vomiting?' I ask. 'Nor shitting through the eye of a needle?'

Eirlys Lewis smiles. 'All well. We can't thank you enough.'

I think back to the sample of water I'd taken from their well, think about the dead mice I found around the plate of bread I'd left in the kitchen, soaked in that very water. So I was right the well had been poisoned – just not very efficiently. The dose was deadly to the mice, smaller creatures by far than a human, which suggested however much went into the well wasn't large enough or the poison strong enough to kill anyone. Enough to make them ill, however. I wonder if death was the aim, but the poisoner was simply incompetent? Or if the illness was a warning? What might this family, or one of its members, know that someone wanted kept quiet? They were unable or unwilling to tell me – perhaps they didn't even realise it was a warning?

'Eirlys, is there anyone who wishes your family ill?' I ask and she looks at me strangely.

'What an odd thing to say. No, we live out here, we live apart, my husband works hard for Mr Morwood, and he's never had any reason to complain.'

I nod. 'Forgive me, a stray and silly thought. But continue to get your water from the stream for another few weeks. I have given your husband some items to help cleanse the well. Be careful of what you drink and eat.'

She nods. They've all got their colour back, the rashes have

132

disappeared from their skin and the children are running around outside, their energy returned. Hardly recognisable from the barely living creatures I saw a week ago.

'Thank you, Asher. We can never repay you.'

'Just stay healthy. And keep drinking the tea, it's good for you any time.' I repack my satchel and rise. The little kitchen is clean and bright, the air in the entire cottage is fresh with all the windows open, and bunches of lavender hanging by the fire, ready to be thrown in.

I bid her farewell and go outside. Thomas Lewis is by the well; in his hands and at his feet are the ten balls of kaolin clay and assorted herbs I brought. Easy enough to use the clay from the quarry (less easy to forget the fog and being lost in it), all the herbs in the gardens, easy enough to make these balls and let them dry by the fire in my room in the evenings, then hide them in the hidey-hole until this visit.

'Just toss 'em in, you say?' he calls as he sees me.

I go over to him, nodding. 'They'll dissolve and the herbs will neutralise anything in there that's unhealthful.'

'Neutralise? Now there's a big word.'

I shrug. He throws them in, four, five, then finally the last two. We listen as they drop into the liquid. I repeat what I said to his wife, in hopes they will both remember – or if one does not then the other will. 'Water from the stream for another few weeks; by then this should be drinkable again.'

'Thank you, Asher.'

'You're welcome, Thomas. You're back to your tasks?'

He nods. 'I've been able to finish planting a new copse to the north corner.' A cloud passes over his face. 'Had to leave it unattended for too long. Tried my best but I couldn't even walk that far.'

I pat his arm. 'All back to normal.'

I did not ride, finding myself a little too tender for that after my encounter with Eli. Yet when I begin my walk back, I find myself unwilling to return to the manor just yet. Still too much energy, still too much lightwood in my soul ready for the touch of a spark. So I make a detour, though I don't quite know why. Perhaps it's the appearance of Heloise when I'd thought myself free so briefly. Perhaps it's simply that I *want* to pick a fight and this one has been put off for long enough. I return to the church yet again.

The door's unlocked, no one around with services done for the day. Inside the air is colder than out, all that stone keeping the breath of autumn trapped. It's dark, too, but for some few candles lit up by the altar. I can see white cloth upon it, embroidered with gold. Last time I was here I did not look around, was not prepared to remain. A monstrance studded with precious gems, and two silver vases filled with those blood-bell flowers that even at this distance I can see are wilting despite the cool that should keep them fresh. I wonder how old they are and which good-wife tends to this church on behalf of the god-hound. Someone not especially devout it would seem; the not-quite-a-cathedral in Whitebarrow was ever spick and span, its bouquets fresh and the finest, its good-wives attentive and prideful. Having seen the priest here I'm in no way surprised he inspires no devotion to either himself, his church or his god. It's a very long time since he was handsome enough to seduce my mother. To father me. To leave her to the fate she ultimately met.

I walk quietly towards the altar. The old man's not in evidence; perhaps he's holed up in his little house behind the church, perhaps in the village haranguing someone for sins real or imagined. Hypocrite. How long I've got is anyone's guess so I pick up my pace and circle around the altar to find the gap in the stones. A finer place of worship would have some kind of covering, a trapdoor or a balustrade of sorts to warn the unwary about this void: if I did not know what I was looking for in the dim space I might have fallen. I take one of the candles; its flame flickers with the movement, then steadies. Down the steps, my paces echo only a little.

The crypt is, strangely, warmer than above. That might concern someone more superstitious than I, but I've got other things to take my attention. There are niches around the walls filled with death-beds in dust-covered wood, gold locks and hinges catching at the gleams of the flickering candle. Money enough for the Morwoods to pay for expensive coffins to keep their dead beneath, but not enough thought for them afterwards to pay someone to rub the gilings away, to polish the little brass nameplates on the side beside the main latch. I walk around the space, candle held high, and examine each and every nameplate. There are twenty coffins here, twenty filled niches. I wonder where earlier Morwoods lie, surely there must be some, then I notice the flags at my feet are engraved with names and years long ago. There. They rest there. But the recent dead are here and five empty niches await, reserved no doubt for the current occupants of the Grange.

I navigate the room twice, three times, and do not find what I seek.

So.

Did they say she had died? Did they tell anyone who asked that Heloise had passed away? Cover the shame that way? Or did they simply not mention her again? No announcement, merely perhaps an offhanded 'Oh, she's gone, some months ago, private funeral, don't you know?' if anyone ever asked. Not even a pretend interment, no men of the house to carry an empty coffin – so light, so light! – down here for her. Just sent her forth and acted as if she had never existed. And who might I ask about that without giving myself away? No one. Not yet.

I do find the box containing Donnell Morwood's remains. Leonora's husband. Heloise's father. My grandfather. Dead before she was shamed, I think my mother said. When did he die? The brass plaque tells me it was the same year Heloise was sent forth. So: after Luther returned and before Heloise was exiled. And my mother seldom spoke of him; never mentioned him as a tormentor or protector. Perhaps he was simply nothing. Did she even much remember him, after he was gone? Being dead he'd failed to save her from anything and I suspect simply wiped him from her mind. When news of Luther's disgrace came home to roost, carried in the folds of a letter, he set about dying of shame and impoverishing his family. Now that I know of Luther's abortive stint in Whitebarrow, did his father die before he had to see his son again?

Without her husband around, without her daughter, how did Leonora change? Only one child left, the other banished, no one else to temper her tendency to control everything. Morwood, hers after all, her blood in the soil, her family's lot.

From above comes the distant sound of the church door opening, the warning creak travelling down to the depths. My heart stutters; I think to blow out the candle, to carefully make my way back up the stairs, and sneak into the shadows, try to make my escape. But something inside me says *No*. Ever so quietly but ever so firmly. *No*.

Whatever fills me makes me slip the mourning ring from my finger, stow it in my skirt pocket. I feel no change. Perhaps there is none. Perhaps I've had this face too long now. I pull the pins from my hair, shake out the tresses that I can now see have changed hue. I take to the stairs, hold the candle high and make no secret of my presence.

'Who's there?' The trembling, rasping voice. What did Heloise say? He had the finest voice. He was thunderous in the pulpit, persuasive elsewhere; sometimes he would sing to her.

Before I take the top step, round the altar, I call, 'Hello, Father.'

'Who's that?'

The candle in my hand is held high just enough to illuminate my face, my hair. My mother's face, my mother's hair; only my eyes aren't hers, not that particular, peculiar blue. Mine are green, like she always said my father's were. Are. But he's probably not in a state to realise that at this very moment.

'Hello, Father,' I repeat. 'Don't you recognise me?'

And from the way his eyes widen, I know he does. Or rather, he recognises her, the lover he cast away. I'm older than she was then, but in this light it will hardly matter. I move around in front of the altar, to face him as he stands in the narrow aisle.

'Heloise.' He says her name like a breath, like a curse, like a prayer all in the one exhalation. 'It can't be.'

'It isn't. I'm her daughter. *Your* daughter.' It won't matter, telling him this; he's not seen my other face, won't associate this illusion with the quiet brown-haired girl and not a single fine feature to distinguish her. And there's a good chance he won't even speak of it – would he dare approach Leonora? After what he did to – with – her daughter? Whatever he says he'll sound deranged. And I cannot help but enjoy the mean sense of delight this gives me. All the things he helped take from Heloise. I'm not fool enough to think there'd ever have been a happy family for any of us. But somehow there should have been something better than there was, but for this man's weakness.

'You... she didn't die?'

'She did, but not when you thought. Did you imagine her dying by the roadside? Giving birth there as her last breath left her? Or perhaps being buried by some well-meaning stranger, kinder than you or her kin? Burying her and perhaps a child brought forth in the coffin? What did you imagine happened to her, Father?'

'I...' He stares at me as if he can make neither head nor tail of my words; as if he cannot separate me from my mother. 'She ruined me.'

I shouldn't be surprised. Why am I? What did I expect? An apology? Why does this feel like a blow?

'She ruined me!' Even louder this time. He prowls, raging, back and forth along the aisle; flecks of spittle fly from his mouth. 'Don't you know who I was? What I was going to achieve?'

'No.' Although Heloise told me. She said he'd been sent to Morwood for a year – a year's service in a small and unimportant place before he returned to the cathedral-city of Lodellan to begin his journey upwards. I do not know how she thought it would be – did she dream of joining him there? Living perhaps in a fine house he'd set her up in? Though princes of the Church

138

do not marry, they're happy enough to father children hither and yon. But I never asked her because by the time she began to tell me more about my father (those secrets trickling like sand through an hourglass), she had nothing but anger left for him. I don't know if she kept any memories of her hopes, and I was not fool enough to ask her about those. Whatever hers were, he did not share them.

But the incident with Heloise was enough to keep him here in Morwood. Somehow those in power found out. Somehow the flow of his life was diverted from the mainstream of ecclesiastical authority in this tiny backwater. And he's been sitting here all of my life, stewing on it. I wonder if Leonora had influence? If ensuring he suffered close by was her revenge?

'She told what I'd done! What we'd done! She… she seduced me away from my god…'

'And you've clearly spent all the time since trying to get back into his good graces with kindness, charity and service to the poor,' I say, and he stares. Perhaps the sarcasm is lost on him. He stops pacing, comes closer to me.

'And now you're here. To ruin me…'

'Hardly seems like there's anything left to ruin, Father.'

He leaps at me and I'm not prepared. Hands to my throat, thin strong fingers like iron bands. I drop the candle and it is extinguished. Now I'm on the cold stone floor, the back of my head striking the flags, bouncing a little, but cushioned by my fall of hair. There's just me and the man who fathered me, frothing at the mouth, spittle striking my face as he tries to throttle me. I try to peel his fingers away but he's too strong. I can hear him shrieking. It's a most awful noise. Telling me what I did to him, what I cost him, conflating me with Heloise so it doesn't matter at all which one he strangles. Black spots at the corners of my eyes, then a great silver flash that takes the priest with it, and I can suddenly breathe.

And the sound of feeding, the shrieks silenced, and I roll my head to the left, see the great wolf worrying at my father's throat, and I've got just enough sense to slide the mourning ring back on my finger. My long hair is brown once more.

I close my eyes for what seems a very long time.

Eli's hands on my shoulders shake me awake, gently. In the dim light of the last candles I can see he's tried to wipe away all traces of the priest but there are bloodstains on his shirt, his chest where he's not closed it again. I look past him at the small ridiculous pile that's all that remains of he who fathered me, and I feel nothing. This was not what I'd intended. I had not planned any of this – ridiculous when you consider how much else I have planned – but how else would this have ended? A quiet death for him? One not at my hands? Or Eli's paws and claws?

'Are you all right, Asher?' Eli says and it sounds like he's calling from far away. 'Did he hurt you?'

He sits me up and I put a hand to the back of my head. No blood, just a slight ache. My throat's another matter, and it will only get worse. I'll need to rub calendula into the skin for it will bruise and bruises will require some explanation. High-necked blouses for me for a few days.

'Did he hurt you, Asher?' Eli asks again and I can hear that he cares and I wish he wouldn't.

I nod, croak: 'But not as much as he would have. Thank you. Why are you here?'

'I was coming back from the Tarn – had to get a new bridle.' He looks at the body. No regret on his face. 'I heard him screaming. Didn't sound sane.'

'No. I came to light a candle, offer a prayer. He attacked me.' I shake my head. 'I didn't know he was so…'

Eli looks at me, peers into my face.

'What?'

He shakes his head. 'Nothing. I just thought I saw… red hair.'

I laugh. He joins me.

'What'll we do with…' he asks at last.

'In the crypt below. There are death-beds. He'll fit neatly in one.'

14

'You look awful, Asher.'

'I believe "tired" is the polite term, Mrs Morwood,' I say evenly. But Leonora's right. I *do* look awful, dark circles under my eyes, dry lips, wisps of hair escaping my usually immaculate braid, and I spotted a stain on the cuff of my white blouse well after we'd left the house, too late to change. All I can do is tug down the sleeve of my short jacket and hope no one notices; it's bad enough I know it's there. I've been pulled from my teaching duties to accompany her this fine morning. We could have taken the caleche, but she felt like walking and I cannot blame her after all those years confined to her rooms. 'I did not sleep well.'

Again. My mind leapt between the memory of my father trying to kill me and my lover killing him. Of gathering his final remains in an altar cloth and stuffing him into my grandfather's coffin. I wonder how they'll slumber like that?

'Burdon tells me there was a commotion the other night.' She lifts her face to the sun. In the full light her wrinkles are clear, the tiny crevices that furrow the lips she's daubed with a bright tint. I'm glad she can't see herself like this. There's nothing bad about how she looks, but I have realised how very vain she is.

So. Burdon heard it all and chose not to appear. Too drunk? Or perhaps Mrs Charlton told him?

'The younger Mrs Morwood had a nightmare.' I feel protective towards Jessamine; mind you, it would do me no good to tell the truth.

She arches a brow at me, tastes the lie. 'A nightmare? I was given to believe it was more than that. An episode. A fit. Hysteria.'

'She was afraid. Mrs Charlton and I managed.' And I regret saying that because it sounds as if we needed or wanted help, as if we did the next best thing to failing.

'Jessamine has ever been delicate. She had episodes after the birth of every child, and we were all obliged to be patient.'

I suspect Leonora was *not*.

'I've seen enough women suffer such things after childbirth, and worse still if they lose a little one in the birthing bed.'

'I think you have seen many things, Asher Todd,' she muses and gives me a sideways look to tell me she'd like to pull the secrets from me.

'At Whitebarrow, it was hard to avoid such knowledge, Mrs Morwood. The clever doctor-professors regarded women from the lower orders as little more than experimental subjects, unworthy of compassion. Fit only to be rendered down to note form in their diaries and journals, their books and gazettes. Discussed and laughed about over port and cigars.' My voice sounds too high-pitched so I stop speaking, rein the anger in.

'One day, you will tell me about your education there.'

'How are your eyes, Mrs Morwood?' I ask as we pass the church. I imagine the priest standing in the graveyard pulling up blood-bell flowers. I wonder what he'd have said if he could see

143

Leonora Morwood walking beside me, resplendent in a crimson silk gown, and a jaunty black hat of tulle scrunched into the vague shape of a rose and dotted with rubies. It offers no shade from the sun, merely sits on an elaborate pile of curls. Well, we'll never find out now.

Casually Leonora turns her head and spits over the low stone wall. It's a neat trick, a skilled shot, decidedly unladylike; I can't help but admire it. I wonder how long before the god-hound is missed?

'My eyes are exceedingly fine, thank you, Asher.' She smiles, smug, as if it's her just reward. 'So fine in fact I can see someone trying to change the subject a mile off. Jessamine was ranting about ghosts, wasn't she?'

'She… said she thought she saw someone.' I pause. 'A woman with red hair,' *take a chance*, 'and blue eyes.'

Leonora seems to stiffen, there's a hitch in her stride, but that's the only sign of a reaction.

I carry on, 'She was overly tired. And perhaps, such old houses, they keep echoes.'

'There are no ghosts at Morwood Grange, all have been exiled long ago.' Leonora speaks in an even tone. But I wonder what she's thinking. If she's pondering the chance that her only daughter is dead and has come home to haunt her. Will she look in that room? What will she see? Not everyone can discern ghosts, even if the spectre wants to be seen – whereas some folk see them whether they wish to or not, others only when the phantasm desires. Would Heloise want her mother to know she's there? To know how she looked when she died?

I note she doesn't say "exorcised", as if spirits can be banished

144

so easily with neither bell, nor book, nor candle to send them on their way. No ritual, merely a demand to vacate. I don't tell her that I've brought a ghost with me – or rather that it followed me and the things I carried. I don't tell her that my ghost is hers as well. I simply say, 'Mrs Morwood is delicate, yes.'

'Luther is not kind.' She says this with a sigh, as though he won't share his pudding. As though it's something trivial. 'And Jessamine is tender.'

'Was Master Luther always that way?' I ask casually.

She shakes her head. 'He is always like his father in that he's displeased to not get his own way. He's spiteful if denied.'

I think of Donnell Morwood throwing good money after bad when his son disappointed him, gambling away what little was left. I hesitate, then say, 'He was your only child?'

'Yes.' There's not even a pause before that single word, no hesitation before the lie. That's three times she's denied my mother.

'His father spoiled him and he was never disciplined until it was too late. But perhaps it wouldn't have mattered; perhaps the rot was always there.'

As my mother told it, Leonora was as indulgent of her son as their father. Yet he turned on his own mother the moment she showed weakness. And Leonora will not forget that.

'Did he ever travel from home? Apart from Bellsholm to woo Jessamine?'

'To your hometown, Asher. He was meant to study at Whitebarrow. His father indulged his whims. Luther thought himself medically minded. How wrong he was.' She sounds as if a short temper is on its way. She does not mention how he shamed the Morwood family name.

145

'Ah.' I clear my throat, decide I cannot get away with further questioning, not without raising suspicions. 'How long is it since you've been into town, Mrs Morwood?'

'Three years? I stopped going in, then I stopped leaving my room.' We pause at the boundary of the village and she surveys it like a potential buyer. 'But I recall it well enough. Walk with me to the solicitor's office, then you may amuse yourself for two hours I shouldn't imagine. Don't indulge in idle gossip with anyone, Asher.' She gives me a glance.

'You can trust my discretion, Mrs Morwood. I think you know that by now.' I do not keep the reproof from my tone and she gives a broad grin. I don't ask her why she's going to see a solicitor, but I cannot imagine it will please Luther. What will happen if she cuts him from the will? I must admit that every red-headed child I see has me wondering if it's a little Morwood bastard – and could anything I say be worse than what's already been done by Luther? Well, of course it could, but she doesn't know that. I simply walk her down the main street to the tall thin building that houses the lawyer. As we go, people stare. It's not entirely bustling, the main street, but there are enough folk to notice us. Notice *her*.

The people of the Tarn curtsey and bow, offer greetings and delight – and not a little shock – to see Leonora Morwood. They ask after her health; she tells them it is all down to me and my skills. People begin looking at me with a curiosity I'd managed to avoid before now, in my sparrow's skin. But this is a place without a doctor, with only some hedge-witches to quietly do what they can. At last we break free and make our way to the solicitor's office.

At the door, Leonora waves me away before she enters. I smile, thinking she likes her secrets.

'I too have errands to run, Mrs Morwood.'

'I think, Asher Todd, we shall meet in the coffeehouse for lunch at midday.'

When she's disappeared inside, I make for the apothecary across from Heledd's house. A bell rings over the door, and I spend almost an hour in there, an amount of time that might seem excessive but for the range of products he keeps in stock and tightly packed on shelves. I'm in need of some dry ingredients but also more calendula ointment for the bruises my father left on my throat. To look at anything requires the little man with his half-moon glasses to take things down for my close inspection. At first he was irked, but eventually realised that my purchases were going to be considerable — and that I was knowledgeable about my subject, sending him away when he offered me coltsfoot root in place of dandelion root — and by the end I part with two of the Witches' coins (which made his eyes widen) before he carefully places everything in the wicker basket I brought with me. He throws in a small jar of lavender salve and points at the almost-healed graze on my cheek and whispers, *It has a little rosemary as well to prevent scars*, as if it's our secret. His farewell and exhortation to return soon are genuine.

On my way out the door, I pause. 'Oh. Mr Morwood asked if you might compound that same mixture he purchased a few months ago?'

The old man's expression is puzzled. 'Why would he say such a thing? He's not been in this shop in years, girl!'

'Ah. My mistake. I must have misheard him.' I smile like a

silly chit and leave. Wherever Luther got his medicine for the Lewises, it wasn't here.

I did not fail to notice the faces that passed by the shop window, and did their best to see inside, to stare at me. I'd brought Leonora Morwood's sight back, what else might I do? I resisted the urge to poke my tongue out at every curious expression. Next, I knock on Heledd Jones's door.

Heledd, dressed in a sky-blue frock covered in golden roses, breaks into a smile as soon as she sees me. She folds me into a hug.

'Thank you!' she says. 'Thank you so much. My parents cannot sing your praises enough.' She pulls me across the threshold and into the small sitting room. I'm pushed into a springy armchair and she whirls about, into the kitchen then returning with two small crystal glasses filled with dark crimson liquid. 'Damson brandy.' She hands me a shot and we clink the pretty glasses carefully. They look like heirlooms, something from great-great-grandmothers, handed down and down and down. 'You're a miracle worker.'

'I thought it was meant to be our secret.' I sigh, almost to myself. 'Although it hardly matters with Leonora Morwood prancing up and down the high street.'

She giggles and it's clear she's already party to that bit of gossip. 'I can never thank you enough.'

'Well, you might try,' I say and grin. 'A favour.'

'Anything,' she says and I wonder at her willingness to say so. She's brave or foolish, perhaps a dash of each.

I produce the little tin filled with wax and the impression of the key. 'Can you have a copy of this made?'

She takes the item, looks at it and me speculatively. The wax tablet is a burglar's tool and she's too smart not to know it. I don't try to lie to her, not about this. I don't do anything but let the request hang between us. She says, 'It will be ready in two days.'

She can take it to the locksmith here and no one will question her, or ask what the key is for – if they do, it's easy enough for her to lie. If I were to do so, however, it would be the talk of the town and who knows where the information would end up? I hand her three gold coins – overly generous but it will buy silence as much as a key – and say, 'I'll come and collect then.'

* * *

I meet Leonora in the street outside the coffeehouse, and we enter together. The hum of noise ceases almost immediately.

Leonora's lips quirk up, but she doesn't give them the satisfaction of a full smile. She simply nods at the woman in a pink faille dress with a white apron over the top who is clearly the proprietress, and we are led to a table in the window, all the better for us to see and be seen. There are two girls, not much more than twelve years, dark curls beneath mobcaps and like enough to be twins, different enough to be distinguishable one from the other. They continue ferrying plates and platters to the packed tables, but they stare at us – mostly at Leonora.

Leonora orders lunch without reference to me or the parchment menus: finger sandwiches and cake and a silver pot of coffee. Leonora Morwood shall have what she wants. Food appears as if by magic. We eat under the weight of gazes sly and shy. The noise level grows as they become used to us.

'Did you have a satisfactory meeting with the solicitor?' I ask.

Leonora nods. 'But I would be pleased if you did not mention this visit to anyone.'

149

'I'll say naught; your business is your own, Mrs Morwood. But as you know, more than one person saw you enter those offices. I cannot vouch for their tongues.' I start with a slice of cake, eating my dessert first like a child.

She raises an eyebrow, whether at my choices or my comment is unclear, until she says, 'You'll find that the people of the Tarn know how to keep their mouths closed. Their loyalty is to me.'

'Your son… is not popular?'

'As I've said, Luther has his father's tendencies; he does not have the right touch with those for whom he is responsible. He sulks, loses his temper easily. I am a proper Morwood, born on this land. Luther is too much of Donnell. You've seen how they look at me?' I nod, although I think perhaps we've interpreted these looks differently. 'They are happy I've returned. To see me well. To see me in charge once again.'

'That is comfort, surely.' *And how will Luther feel about that? Will he surrender power willingly?*

'And you've given me that, Asher Todd. Don't think I'll ever forget that. Just remember whose side you're on.'

'Of course, Mrs Morwood.' And in truth I do not. But I wonder often if that side is ever to be my own, or am I always to be labouring for another's desires? What might such freedom be like?

'Leonora!' Almost a shout, it distracts us from our conversation.

A large woman approaches. She has hair so black it can only be a dye. Her face is overly powdered a dead white, and rouge has made two circles of high colour on the apples of her cheeks. Untinted lips, however, and her eyebrows and lashes are an ashy grey. The turquoise dress is richly made, embroidered with silver tulips; almost as excessive as Leonora's crimson gown.

Her reticule is a black velvet thing embroidered with colourful blossoms, and clutched tight in beringed fingers. She fair lunges at our table, at Leonora, mostly ignoring me but for a single double-take of a glance.

'Margery, what a pleasure.' Leonora's tone says it's anything but, yet the woman blushes with delight. Acknowledgement of any sort makes some folk happy no matter what its source.

'How wonderful to see you out and about, my dear. Your eyes?'

'The work of Miss Todd, here. Miraculous, as I'm sure you will agree.'

'I look forward to a visit very soon! A dinner party!' The woman turns to me. 'You must bring Luther and Jessamine and… why, I don't know who this young woman is but she looks charming.' She smiles brightly, brittlely.

'Miss Todd is governess to the children, Margery, but has some medical skill, as I am fortunate to have discovered. If you will be so kind, we are in something of a hurry and would finish our lunch quickly and in privacy. I shall arrange for an invitation to be sent to your home at a time convenient to myself.'

The woman seems caught between disappointment at the dismissal and glee at the promise of an offer. She drops a curtsey, and her expression says she did not intend it, that it's made her lesser in this interaction. But it's too late now. Margery straightens and moves away. She leaves the coffeehouse entirely; I suppose it is the only action open to her.

'Margery Marston was ever a gossiping shrew.' Leonora spits the words. I wonder at the intensity of her judgement; is it likely those flaws of which she accuses someone else are her own in some measure?

151

'You can hardly blame her curiosity when you've been absent so long, Mrs Morwood. You've observed yourself how happy people are to see you.'

'Better if I didn't wear my years so heavily,' she complains. 'Better if I looked no older than when I last set foot here. Better still younger than that.'

I point to the basket beside our table. 'I cannot reverse time, merely soften it. I hope to help with that as well, but you must have reasonable expectations.'

'Whatever you can do, Asher Todd, will please me.' She smiles and there's truth in that, although how much is difficult to discern. I wonder what will happen when I am, inevitably, unable to fulfil her wishes.

'I shall do my best.'

'Excellent. Now, finish up. I tire of eating under such scrutiny.'

Ah. So even Leonora Morwood's taste for attention might wane given time.

15

'Thank God, you're home.'

Burdon greets us at the door but he addresses me, rather than Leonora. It's in no way disrespectful, but it is notable. We step inside, place our purchases on the hallstand, and begin to untie the ribbons of our hats.

'What is it, Burdon, that cannot wait two minutes?' Leonora asks sharply.

'It's young Mrs Morwood, Mrs Morwood. She's had a fall.'

'A fall?'

'Down the stairs.' The man's lips are pale, his hands clasped tightly in front of him – I wonder if they might shake otherwise – and he nods upwards.

'How long ago and where is she now?' I ask before Leonora takes over. I collect my basket and wait, poised for an answer.

'Not half an hour. She's in bed; Mrs Charlton is attending to her.'

'Did she say anything? I mean, as to why she fell?'

He shakes his head but his lips press tightly again. I shall have to corner him later.

I hurry up the stairs, ignoring Leonora's grumbling about Jessamine's seeking attention. I wish I did not hear her telling

Burdon to bring afternoon tea to the library downstairs even though we've just had lunch, but perhaps it is best that I see her daughter-in-law without prying eyes and ears.

Jessamine is terribly pale against the white covers, eyes closed and there's a bruise already darkening on her forehead. Mrs Charlton has the younger woman's skirts pulled up to expose her bare feet. The right ankle is swollen and turning blue. Is it broken as well?

I put my basket down and gently shuffle the housekeeper aside. 'Would you mind getting a wet cloth, Mrs Charlton? And a wet towel too.'

She could have already done this but I fear she's panicking; her mothering heart makes her unable to think straight. Two incidents involving her girl so close together are worrying. But she obeys me quickly, happy to have direction, I think. When the housekeeper returns from the bathroom, I firmly wrap the cool wet towel around the swollen ankle, then I examine Jessamine's brow. There's no blood; the skin did not break. From the basket I take a small jar of calendula ointment; I dab a liberal amount on the egg on her forehead. I will do the same later to the ankle when it is cooled.

'What happened, Mrs Charlton?' I ask. There is a pitcher of water on the bedside table and a glass. I take a paper packet of ground dried butterbur and feverfew, recently and fortuitously purchased from the apothecary, pinch in a measure then mix it. I sit Jessamine up, prop myself behind her and open her lips. I pour a little into her mouth, and gently massage her throat to make her swallow. I do this twice more; not all the liquid is gone, but most. I continue to hold her upright a while longer as I wait for the housekeeper's answer.

'She fell down the stairs.' But her eyes slide away.

'Mrs Charlton, you may tell me anything. In fact, you *should* tell me everything. Did you witness the fall?'

Slowly, the older woman nods.

'I was barely three feet from her. She wasn't even near the top of the staircase. She hadn't slept well these past two nights. All she wanted was some fresh air, a little walk, so we left the room. Then…'

'Go on.'

'It was like a mist, thin and white as poorhouse gruel, but somehow… somehow it fair picked her up and carried her. I could see her feet, they weren't even moving, there was just her hair and nightgown trailing along as she was whisked to the staircase and tossed down.' She shakes her head. 'You'll think I'm mad.'

'No, Mrs Charlton. I don't.'

'And why's that?' she asks and it's a challenge, quite rich from someone who's just confessed to me what she did.

'Because, Mrs Charlton, I have seen stranger things than you might imagine. Now, please go and make a warm broth for Mrs Morwood – beef will be best, not too thick.'

She stares at me for a moment, then nods, says, 'Any vegetables, Miss Todd?'

'Only green ones and just a little salt; do not bring bread.'

'Yes, miss.' She almost bobs a curtsey before she remembers who I am. 'You'll stay with her?'

'I'll stay with her.'

* * *

That night I sit by Jessamine's bedside. Luther was determined to share his wife's bed no matter how she felt, and argued with me until Leonora appeared and settled the matter. He finally moved some of his things to one of the guest rooms on the lower floor. It was difficult to send Mrs Charlton away but at last exhaustion if not common sense prevailed; she'd sat up the previous night with Jessamine after all. She was easily persuaded to leave her chatelaine with me in case I should need to open a door or cupboard in a hurry. If she'd been more alert she might have questioned that more closely but she did not.

I sit by the big bed with its blood-red hangings. The colour of passion, they say, my mother said. Whenever we'd change house, change patrons, she'd redecorate her bedroom in the new one. An array of crimsons, carefully calibrated to inflame the senses, oil burners for heady scents, silky sheets – honestly, I don't know how she didn't slide off them, but perhaps that was the point.

Now I sit beside Jessamine, who lies in this bed, my uncle's bed, and think there's been no passion here, at least not for a long time. Power, yes; domination, yes; pain, yes. Passion, no.

Jessamine whimpers in her sleep, tosses her head from side to side. I touch her shoulder, stroke her hair, whisper *Hush*, and she settles.

'I'll tell you a story, shall I?' There'll be no answer, but this will help me pass the time, for my interest in *Murcianus' Book of Strange Places* has waned.

'Before the world became as it is today, there was a witch who fell in love. She was the daughter of a woman who knew the secrets of gallowberries and how to walk between worlds, but that's a tale for another time.' I clear my throat. 'The young girl – her name is lost for all our names are lost in the end – watched her mother leave this world, hounded. Then the girl took her revenge on the men who'd caused it and left her alone. She did not think that they'd had families themselves.

'She found refuge with another woman, another witch, who was kind, kinder than her own mother had been (even if our mothers are unkind, Jessamine, we love them, we cannot help it, and we will avenge them). And she fell in love, though she'd not sought it, with the son of one of the men who'd killed her mother and whom she in turn had killed.

'For a time, life was sweet, but all refuges are brief things. Her friend died. And the man she loved discovered her true nature, that of a witch, and every bit of love he'd felt for her was magically, alchemically transformed to hatred – so fast, so fast! And thus she did the only thing she could…

'She whispered a word only witches know and he became a hound, a wolf of sorts, and he remembered only his devotion to her for wolves have no hatred of witches. He was loyal beyond all creatures and followed her through flood and fire – he followed her into the maw of a most terrible winter, and who knows? Perhaps he follows her still.' I realise I've crept forward as I've told, my fingers clutching the bedsheets. I release them and sit back, clear my throat. 'This is the story you asked to taste, whether it be sour or sweet, it is done.'

She doesn't stir.

'The point is, Jessamine Morwood, that most men will turn on you. And the only way to guarantee their loyalty is to make them into something else. Someone should have told you that before you married.'

Who told me that story? My mother? Or one of the old women in a variety of kitchens in a variety of houses? Those behind whose skirts I sought refuge from my mother's temper, or from the master of the house who wanted me to disappear for my presence reminded him that my beautiful mother was *encumbered* with more than simply some challenging personality traits.

Who told me this tale? I cannot remember. Too many recountings collected over the years, too many heard and read and used as salve for wounds I did not invite. I wonder that I chose to tell poor Jessamine this one; I wonder if it will give her ill-dreams. I feel bad – surely she's got enough.

* * *

Eventually, I doze in my chair, until I feel a shift in the air, a drop in temperature, hear the strange whispering I've heard before, in the houses I shared with my mother after her death. I open my eyes as Heloise moves in front of the last of the embers glowing orange in the hearth (I can see them through her, slightly obscured as things are by a thick rain); tiny flames flare, lick up in the wake of her passing as if to follow.

'Mother,' I say, soft and low.

She comes to stand in front of me. I put my hand out and touch Jessamine's arm so gently that she does not wake. The light in Heloise's eyes blazes. Dead though she might be, she still looks ill, still looks like she did in her last days of life, lying on that sweat-soaked mattress, unable to speak, sleeping more than anything, glaring when she was awake, grasping at my hands and digging her nails through the skin and into the flesh. I still have scars there that can be seen; little knots I can always feel under my fingers.

'Mother, do not harm her. She's done you no ill.'

Again, the fire in her gaze seethes; she gnashes her teeth, jerks

158

her head forward on her neck like a snake. Not a noise in any of it, but her meaning's unmistakable; I've only ever heard the whispers in my sleep, or rather in that place between sleeping and waking where nothing is quite real.

'Mother, you do not even know her.' But I think I know the problem: she thinks this woman took her place in this house she was meant to inherit. She thinks if she hurts Jessamine, she'll hurt Luther. 'Mother, she has stolen nothing from you. And she has suffered in her time here, trust me.'

Still there's no softening of her expression; her hands wring as if around Jessamine's throat. 'If you haunt her, I will not help you, no matter my promise.'

That seems to get through and Heloise leans down, her face to mine, her breath like stinking rime even though there's no air to come from her lungs. I feel flecks of ice hitting my skin. I don't breathe, I don't wish to take her death in, yet I do not sit back or try to avoid her. That was never the way to manage my mother in life and death hasn't changed her. I learned early on that cringing away made everything worse; being brave didn't stop her tantrums but somehow lessened their impact. In Whitebarrow, as a ghost, she did not leave the rented room, remained there as she'd done in the last part of her life; at least until I moved and she found me after a few days. I wondered then if she was too afraid to wander or felt she could not. I'd set no traps for her, when there seemed no need. How long after I'd left the house that was not mine did she go looking for me? How long before she ventured forth to find me? She travelled swiftly, but then they say the dead often do.

'Leave her be, Mother. Leave her safe. You will have what you want, just as I swore, but her safety is the price.' I do not tell her about the priest, my father; not yet. Who knows what she might do?

Heloise straightens slowly, gives Jessamine one last baleful look. I'm not certain I can trust her. Other measures will need to be taken. I watch as my mother leaves, ignoring the door, passing through the wall, off in the direction of her own room.

I do not sleep the rest of the night.

* * *

In the brief breath before proper dawn breaks and the servants rise, I leave Jessamine alone. I slip down to the kitchen and find a sack of salt, then creep back up the stairs and along to the locked room that used to belong to Heloise. That belongs once more to her. The key turns easily this time; soon I shall have my own.

I've lived so much of my life in darkness, taking secrets without permission. I fall so easily back into the habit of a lifetime. Quickly, I open the door and step into the cold, cold room.

My mother sits by the window again. She doesn't bother to look at me, which makes my task easier. I open the neck of the sack and begin to pour salt along the lines where the walls meet the floor. Around the edges of the room I go. Heloise only takes notice as I trickle a thin trail by her; thin but it's all I need. She stares at me but doesn't seem to comprehend. Why would she? No one's ever done this to her before, she's never been contained. She does not know the lore of ghosts and spectres, whereas I stole it from all those clever books I read when I should have been cleaning shelves, emptying bins and pails.

Finally, I close the boundary, across the threshold. I open the door, carefully hopping over the line of salt, making sure the hem of my gown doesn't disturb the integrity of the new border. I turn. Heloise is looking out the window.

'Mother,' I say. 'You must stay put for the moment. I cannot trust you to do that, can I?'

She doesn't even glance over her shoulder.

'I will release you when I can. Be patient.'

Heloise will know what I've done only when she tries to leave here again, when she tries to pass through the walls easily as breath through muslin. She will be enraged. But she needs me; I have made my promises and I have never yet let her down. Except once – when I let her die. But I will make amends.

I do not believe she will leave Jessamine alone. I bear the woman no ill will – she had no real choice where she married – and I would not have her children lose her so soon. But whatever happens, Jessamine cannot remain in this house. She cannot remain in easy reach of Heloise. I would not see Jessamine harmed further. I need to consider my options. I will need Leonora as an ally.

16

'What of Caulder, Miss Asher?' Connell asks.

We are in the small room designated as a classroom: there is a chalkboard on wheels at the front, and I must confess we spend less time here than we might. I prefer – and so do the children – working around the house and gardens. There is a long bench and an equally long desk in front of it, with faint-ruled notebooks and sharpened pencils on top – I'll not allow them ink and quills for some while yet, especially not the littlest, although Sarai's page is already filled with clever doodles and drawings of the things she would like, kittens and puppies foremost amongst them; she has considerable talent for one so young. Albertine and Connell dutifully take notes as I speak, and they ask questions only after raising a hand and receiving a nod from me; discipline is the first lesson of any worthwhile class or so I've been told. A painted map of the known world hangs on one wall – I cannot say how old it is, but some of the newer towns are missing, and smaller villages too, but that might simply be because the cartographer thought them beneath his notice. Today is geography although admittedly I know more of history and tales than geographical details. But I know enough. It's fortunate that my stolen education has been so very broad.

'We were not discussing Caulder, Connell,' I say.

'No, but Bellsholm is boring.'

'Bellsholm is a useful city, a port-city, a critical part of the trade routes that keep food and goods moving back and forth. People are fed, they are paid a wage, lives are made easier by the supply of necessities, and pleasant by the supply of luxuries. And it is where your mother is from, so it is relevant to *you.*'

The boy pouts and I cannot help but smile.

'A little diversion, then. Caulder is one of the cities of the Darklands. It is located in the mountains and its major export is silver of very high quality. Although the best silver, it is said, was always in the coffers of the O'Malleys of Breakwater; they are now extinct.' But that's not what he wants to hear. 'It is ruled by the Leech Lords who live on human blood.'

Albertine and Sarai gasp like delicate misses.

'But how do people survive there?' Albertine asks breathlessly.

'The Leech Lords are few, and they know, for the most part, that their own existence depends on a populace that gains benefit from their rule. Towns and cities with a lord or lady must make tribute. In return, they are fed and protected. For the most part.'

'And for the other part?' asks Connell.

'Not all leeches value their folk or believe in… responsible farming. And not all live in castles and manors. Some roam and feast and murder.'

'What's to stop them coming here?'

'The borders, Albertine. The borders are protected forever. Such as they cannot cross over.' I smile. 'We are safe.'

I could tell her that the borders are held by the will of witches, that even the princes of the Church recognise that there are some who cannot be got rid of entirely. But there's nothing to be gained by that sharing or by making too many aware of my knowledge of witches or those who told me; a secret has little chance when too many begin to breathe it.

'Now, may we return to Bellsholm?'

'What of Whitebarrow, Miss Asher?' asks Connell.

'You are trying to distract me from my course, young man.' I smile. 'It is a city of learning, a place of study, of doctor-professors and clever men.' *It is a place where women pretend to be less than they are, but that does not differentiate it from anywhere else.* 'Why do you ask? Would you study there?'

He shakes his head. 'Father thinks I should, but...'

'It's not your dream then. So, somewhere else, some other subject?'

'Literature.'

I smile. 'Then tomorrow we shall begin a study of the works of Murcianus. I'm sure your grandmother will be happy to let us examine her collection.'

He looks dubious.

'Leave it to me, Connell.'

'Will Mother be well soon, Miss Asher?' Sarai asks. She has been even less attentive than usual, concentrating on her drawings. I crouch down to look into her eyes. I touch her hand, pudgy fingers between mine.

'Yes, Sarai. She will be well. You must just be patient with her.' I feel a little jealous that she has a mother who returns her adoration; I'm tired from the hours spent talking to mine, who barely acknowledged me. It makes me a little thin-skinned.

'Is she ill because of you? She does not like you, Miss Asher.'

Albertine hisses and Connell says, 'Sarai!'

That hurts as much as anything I've ever suffered – such a tiny thing, yet its effect is like a lightning bolt. And it's true, I know it, but for her to speak it aloud? A cut so sharp. I know it's based on maternal jealousy, but I have cared for the woman, am doing my best to keep her safe. It's all I can do not to withdraw my hand like a petulant child who wants to offer hurt for hurt. Yet I know my smile's lopsided when I answer, 'No, Sarai. Your mother is simply over-tired and a little sad.'

'Mother is unwell because Father is cruel,' says Connell and his tone is so bitter for one so young.

'Connell,' says Albertine with reproach but she does not contradict him. These two oldest have eyes to see, where Sarai understands both too little and too much and has not enough wisdom to distinguish where the truth lies.

'Your mother will be well, children, it might simply take some time.' It's all I can say. It will not do to speak ill of Luther, not when he has already done such a sterling job of turning his son against himself, of making his elder daughter doubt him. 'Now, let us return to Bellsholm.'

* * *

Luned is sitting with Jessamine while Mrs Charlton, who has sleepless bruises under her eyes despite my taking last night's shift, makes lunch. She moves slowly around the kitchen placing dishes too carefully on surfaces to ensure she doesn't drop them. I suppose I hadn't really thought of her age before, but she's easily sixty, the same as Leonora, but where the mistress of the house has energy to burn, the housekeeper is all but spent. I mix her a tonic with lemon juice and mineral salts to make it fizz, then

165

a little sugar to sweeten it. Then I make another for myself; the hours of watchfulness weigh heavily on me. Somehow I still fear Heloise will get out of the prison I've made for her, find some way to subvert every bit of lore and magic I've learned.

'Were there any... interruptions in the night?' she asks. The first words she's uttered to me since I wandered into the kitchen. The first words since she entered Jessamine's room this morning and I left it; not unfriendliness, just exhaustion.

'She slept well, woke twice.' *The truth.*

'And... did you see anything?'

'I saw nothing in the dark hours.' *A lie.* 'But I don't believe there's nothing there.'

The door opens and a cold breeze blows in, bringing Eli with it. I've not seen him since Sunday, since... He's wrapped up in a greatcoat, a scarf around his neck. His cheeks are red from the wind. I feel my own face redden as I recall our time in the stables. Then I remember it was *not* the last time I saw him. *Sharp of tooth and red of claw.*

'Mrs Charlton. Miss Todd.' Eli has two sacks over his shoulder and he thumps them onto the tabletop. One has blood stains. 'Potatoes and coneys.'

'It's cold?' I ask. Yesterday it was no cooler than autumn should be, and in the sun it might have been spring. Now winter's here for sure.

'It turns fast hereabouts. You'll be wanting your coat from now on, Miss Todd; places like the stables can be chilly without enough clothes.'

'I'm surprised you need a coat, Mr Bligh.' I slant my eyes at him as I turn away. There's broth on the stove; I ladle a bowl for

Jessamine. 'I'll give Luned a spell, Mrs Charlton, but I must attend the children this afternoon.'

'I'll be up after lunch.'

I leave the kitchen, but I'm not alone. Eli follows me. We're through the door into the corridor that leads to the foyer and he grabs at my arm. The soup splashes but does not clear the rim.

'If you make me spill this, you'll get worse than a scratch, Eli Bligh.'

'Talk to me, Asher Todd.'

I frown. 'What about?'

'About the light I see at night from my cottage. The strange blue light from the second floor, from a room that's been locked for years. The light that wasn't there until you came?'

I swallow, pause to gather my thoughts. 'I don't know what you imagine in the night, Eli Bligh, where your wolfish mind wanders.' I look at him at last, hope the lies are hidden by the veils in my eyes. 'Why would I care for your nightly imaginings?'

'Because I saw *you* at that window,' he says and breathes into my face.

'You fantasise, Eli Bligh.' I smile. 'I have no key but the one to my own chamber – how could I enter a locked room? Do you suggest I am some sort of burglar, given to lock picking? What would such an activity get me when I am gainfully employed in this house?'

He says nothing but lets go of my arm. He reaches into his coat, to an inside pocket, and pulls out a small parcel wrapped in off-white paper. 'Heledd Jones asked me to give this to you when I saw her in the Tarn this morning. Said you'd be waiting for it.'

So much sooner than expected, so much more inconvenient

than expected! He shakes it, something inside rattles, metal against metal. I reach for it; he pulls it away.

'Eli, be so kind as to give that to me. It is a gift from Heledd.' I feel the breath press from my nostrils, hot and annoyed. 'Or do I need go tell her you cannot see your way to passing on my property? Do I need tell anyone that you go sometimes on two feet and sometimes on four? That if they want to find the priest they need look no further than your gullet?' There I go, using threats to get what I want; too much like Heloise, too much like Leonora. Too much like a Morwood.

'You might then need to tell why you were so helpful scooping his remains up.' He's got me there. There's a long pause until at last he grins reluctantly. Eli hands me the small box. 'You'd have told them by now if you'd wanted me hunted.'

'I can always change my mind.'

'But you won't.'

'I probably won't.' And I grin in spite of everything, think about kissing him; but I don't.

* * *

Luned is leaning over Jessamine; the well-oiled door does not creak and my steps are naturally silent from a lifetime of sneaking. The maid is whispering to her mistress. It takes a few moments for me to get close enough to hear her, but the tone is clear: hatred. All well and good for me to come to this house with my plots and plans, but what about those who are already here? Those with their own designs?

'Luned,' I say for I've heard enough. She spins around but I keep my expression carefully blank so she won't know. 'Has Mrs Morwood woken at all?'

A sheen of sweat begins to pearl on her forehead. 'No.'

'Really? You've been here the entire time?'

Her expression is sour and she doesn't meet my eye.

'Luned.'

'I went to my room for a little. To rest.'

'Go and help Mrs Charlton in the kitchen.' I think, if there is a need, it will be best for Tib Postlethwaite to sit with Jessamine in future.

She gives me a look and I wonder at what she thought of the governess who came before me. I wonder how she treated her. 'Thank you, Luned, for attending to your mistress.'

When she leaves, I examine Jessamine closely. The lump on her forehead has gone down and her ankle is far less swollen. There are no broken bones, and I hope she will be able to walk on it soon.

'Mrs Morwood? Mrs Morwood, wake up. I have something for you to eat.'

She doesn't stir and I'm quite glad for it means she did not hear Luned's malicious whispers: *I will have everything you have. You will be gone. He's promised me.*

'Mrs Morwood, you must wake.' From my pocket I take a small bottle of smelling salts; I waft it under her nostrils. I can smell the ammonia from here; it makes my eyes water. Jessamine's head twitches from side to side, her eyes flicker open. She startles, pulls away from me.

'N-n-n-n-n-no.'

'Mrs Morwood. Jessamine. I mean you no harm. Please believe me. Tell me: have you seen the ghost again?'

'You… you believe me?'

169

'I do. I have seen stranger things, Mrs Morwood.'

'No, I have not seen her since yesterday… the stairs…'
She closes her eyes, tears squeeze. I touch her hand, hold it. She
squeezes back.

'Jessamine, you will not see her again, I promise. But I need
your help. And I have a proposal.'

She pauses but not for very long, then nods.

* * *

In my room, as I pull the curtains to shut out the cold night, I idly
wonder if Eli Bligh is watching from his cottage. If he watches
this window – or the other one. If he sees the blue glow of Heloise,
if he continues to wonder what it is, but decides he has enough
ghosts of his own – or the house has ones that are not his concern.

17

Two days later, Leonora does not come down to breakfast. The morning table, which has been a field of battle since her sight was restored, is strangely quiet. Not as if the war is over, but perhaps there's an uneasy truce no one quite expected.

I'm interested to watch him: without his mother here, Luther begins to reassert himself. He snaps at Jessamine, whose nerves are not ready for it and she shakes whenever he speaks to her; he picks on Connell, though Albertine tries to distract her father. Sarai sings to herself. It's fascinating to note that Luther, the moment his mother made her triumphant return, put up only a token defence against her grabs for territory. He showed her all the books, all the accounting of how he's invested the family fortune – Jessamine's dowry – these past years, and Leonora told him that most of them would be changed. That she would also be renegotiating the tenancy agreements. That Mrs Charlton and Burdon would report to her now, and that she would begin the search for extra staff in the next week, that her passing mention of a spring ball had become a grand event such as had not been seen in these parts for a very long time. Some of that I knew from her directly, some from standing just long enough outside the ajar door of the office when they spoke that first morning.

And Luther? Luther lay down and took it without a peep. He absented himself from the Grange, took himself off to the inn and other less salubrious drinking establishments, and found himself other beds to sleep in. I wonder how Luned feels about that?

I'm unsurprised to realise he's a coward, lording it over those who are weaker than he is. His mother? She's always been stronger, until her eyesight went, then he took advantage of her vulnerability. She won't forget it, neither will he. I see how he looks at her when he thinks she doesn't notice, thinks no one's paying attention; a whipped dog, resentful, scheming. I hope she knows what she's doing.

So Leonora's absence this morning is notable. *Deor's Art of War* advises that one does not normally abandon a position of strength so quickly after having won it back from the enemy. She's made a point of instructing Albertine and Connell in etiquette and the duties of a landowner. Sarai says 'mmmm' when addressed but she doesn't really pay attention; she's too young and, I am beginning to think, a little fey. *I've* made a point of causing a distraction, asking Leonora a question about something, anything, anything to get her attention away from the dreamy child, to keep her from deciding the little thing needs disciplining. She tends to give me a sideways glance each time but answers, following my distraction, and leaving the child be. I think she knows what I'm doing and allows it for now. I am unsure how long this will last, this willingness to tolerate my interferences. As long as she owes me her eyes, I suppose.

After breakfast, I send the children to the ground-floor classroom with instructions to practise their letters and to write me a poem; Sarai will draw and dance and sing.

I knock on Leonora's door.

'Mrs Morwood? Mrs Morwood, are you well? We missed you at breakfast.' I step inside.

'Here, Asher Todd.' She's over by the window, in an armchair; the lectern is pushed aside. She's in the bright morning sunlight and as I approach I can see that she's not brushed her hair at all, it's a washed-out red storm around her head, and she's still in her nightgown, a purple embroidered housecoat over the top. Her thin feet with their pearly nails are bare and look cold.

'Mrs Morwood, are you ill?' I'm close enough to touch her shoulder, and I feel the chill coming from her even through the thickness of her housecoat. On her lap is the portrait of Heloise and I have to swallow my breath; she doesn't seem to care that I see it. But why would she? She cannot know who her daughter is to me; who she herself is to me. I look around, find the discarded slippers, then kneel to rub some warmth into her feet.

'Mrs Morwood?' Given how carefully coiffed and attired she has been this disorder is distressing. Even when I first knew her, even before the return of her sight, she dressed tidily: the bright exotic bird colours since have been her celebration, the jewel-coloured gowns shown the light while she can enjoy them. I cannot take my eyes from my mother's image. 'What's wrong, Mrs Morwood?'

'I'm in mourning, Asher.' Her fingers dance over the canvas – I can see the small tear I made all those days ago. 'In mourning for my youth. My beauty. All my plans to hold this grand ball? To what end if it's only so they can all see how decrepit I've become?'

There was a moment I thought her mourning was for my mother. More fool me.

173

'Can you not do something for me, Asher? Clever Asher, my cleverest girl?' And for a moment she sounds like the grandmother she should have been to me. And my heart hurts for what's never been, and that makes me weak and needy. I know I'll curse myself afterwards. Because she's asking for *more*.

There are tales of a woman who had the secret of restoring beauty; it was said she could even remake limbs, faces, from some sacred compound known only to her. They say she lived long, far beyond a natural span, but no whispers have been heard of her for many, many years. The Witches of Whitebarrow told me about her, their own voices hushed with a reverence that might have been fear, or fear that might have been reverence. But those powers are beyond me – whatever magic's in my veins I've directed to great and darker things. I have a will and a way with ritual; anyone might commit craft with those things, but the power differs depending on where you sit on the witches' scale.

I *can* do something for her, for this grandmother who has never been, yet it will require a price higher than some begged breast milk. Why do I continue to offer this woman aid when I've seen what she becomes when there are no fetters on her? But I know. The same reason I obeyed my mother all my life: hope of love. Approval.

Besides, if I leave her defenceless against Luther? Luther unchallenged will have no distractions. No distractions and he may well watch me more closely, and with Heloise here I cannot afford to be under such tight scrutiny. I cannot leave her locked in her room forever – though I cannot deny I dream of it – but it's too cruel after all she suffered in life. I must keep my promise and I must begin to move forward with my plan. Leonora must remain a piece on my board and she must be more than a pawn. The Queen must be free to move as and where she may, for she will keep Luther off-balance.

'Asher?' she pleads.

'I might be able to do something, Mrs Morwood, but it will not reverse time. You will not look as you did in your youth, but you will look more youthful.' I point to the portrait in her lap. In the daylight I can see the cracks in the paint. How old is the thing? I'm almost twenty-nine; Heloise was sixteen when she was sent forth. In the painting she's perhaps that age? Or a little younger. Painted not long before everything came apart in her life. I ask, 'Who is she?' and hold my breath.

'My daughter. My girl.' She does not say my mother's name.

'Is she…'

'Dead? I do not know. She left here long ago; I don't know where she went. She might be no more than dust and bones. Perhaps she lives still. Perhaps I have other grandchildren.'

She *left* here.

She had no choice, I want to scream that. I want to shout that they exiled her without money or resources, only me in her belly to burden her. Only me to drag her down. How much of her life would have been different if not for me? I remember Heloise and I remember these words from her mouth at her worst times. Not just when the sickness got hold of her. Before the infection she would scream them at me so I could know from my first days that I had ruined her life. I would know even on the days that she loved me.

I swallow, clear my throat until I think my voice will be steady. 'You could look for her.'

175

Leonora shakes her head. 'Too many years, too much said and unsaid. What good would it do?'

'As you said, there might be grandchildren.'

'Haven't I disappointments enough?' She laughs, only a little bitterly.

'It might bring you peace, perhaps.' My voice trembles. 'I wish frequently that I had parted differently from my own mother before her death.' *True. I wish I'd not made the promises I had. That love had not made a slave of me.*

Leonora smiles and it's an unpleasant thing. 'Peace is for the fearful.'

What might life be like now if I could say, *You are my grandmother. I will tell you of my mother's life, of her last days. Might you love better? Might you live better? Might you try again with me to undo the past?*

Instead I say, 'I will have something for you soon.'

'Thank you, Asher Todd. What a wonder you are.'

'It will hurt.'

'Beauty always has a cost.'

In spite of everything I glow at her praise. I should not, knowing what I do, yet I feel the warmth that comes with a compliment, rare though it might be; there is, of course, the cold limning that it will never occur again. That this will be the last kind word I ever hear. Oh, how much damage my mother did. 'Mrs Morwood, one last thing?'

'What is it, Asher?'

Now is the time to begin my negotiations, now that she wants something of me. 'I would speak with you about Jessamine.'

* * *

Out in the corridor not five minutes later, I'm on my way to the classroom when Luther Morwood catches up with me. Thus far he's not said anything about the aid I gave his mother, but he has looked at me more than he was wont to do before that. My sparrow's disguise had worked until then. Now, he pushes me against the wall so hard the paintings rattle.

The breath is knocked out of me, my back hurts and he grips my chin with one hand, grips my wrist with the other. He is not gentle. At least he doesn't grab at my throat; the bruises are beginning to fade. He leans in, breath reeking of whiskey, and hisses hot words into my face, 'Do not help my mother any further. Remember who hired you.'

I'm no stranger to fear and I'm no stranger to hiding it. Between grinding teeth, I say: 'That was your mother, Mr Morwood.'

And because I show no fear, because I remind him of the truth, because he cannot find any leverage with me, he lets me go. Pushes away from me, glaring, snorting like a frustrated bull, then turns and walks off. Wherever he touched me, I hurt; my bones ache from the strength of his grip. I watch him go and he does not look back, which is for the best or I think he might see too much in my gaze. I think about the other governess, the one who did not return from Morwood Grange.

* * *

'Eli?' I knock, then call from the threshold as I push the cottage door open.

I have everything I need for the new cataplasm but this one thing; the getting of it is not beyond me, but it can be better done by someone more expert than I. It is a favour I would prefer not

177

to ask, but my choices are limited. I enter the dim but tidy space. 'Eli Bligh, are you here?'

No answer, but I notice that the fire in the hearth is burning low; it won't be long before the temperature plummets if it goes out. I kneel, add more kindling and blow the embers back to life. Then bigger branches to build it up, then a stout log. 'Where are you, then?' I softly say when I'm done. 'Where is that stubborn beast?'

'I can only assume you mean me, Miss Todd.' Eli's voice is behind me and I jump-turn, still nervous from the aftereffects of Luther's attack. Thankfully my backside is padded by thick skirts as I hit the floor.

'Yes.' *Beast.*

'And what can I possibly do for you?' He's rugged in his coat and scarf, as I am – even the short walk from the house to the cottage in winter daylight is a chill affair. He closes the door, comes over to help me up. His hand is cold and large and hard; I can still feel the imprint of Luther's palm on my face. All I can think of is how Eli looks when covered in fur, white snarling teeth, all sinewy muscle.

'I need something.'

He cocks a brow but says nothing.

'I need a live animal.'

Still nothing, though the other brow lifts to meet its partner.

'I need a fox. Alive and uninjured.'

No reply, just a spreading grin.

'Can you help me? Will you?'

'Will you tell me why you want it?'

'I *need* it.'

'Need?'

This time it's me who says nothing.

178

'You can either tell me this or what was in the package from Heledd.' He leans towards me. 'Or you'll be finding your own live, uninjured fox, Miss Todd.'

I bite the inside of my cheek, thinking. 'I need the animal to help Mrs Morwood.'

'Older or younger?'

'Does it matter?'

He shakes his head slowly.

'Leonora,' I say. 'Will you help me, Eli Bligh? Now I've told you why.'

'Ah, you're no fun, Asher Todd.' He pulls me towards a chair, sits himself, then settles me on his lap. He nestles his face into my neck. It's strangely tender; he's careful, knowing the bruises are there. 'Does it still hurt? Your throat?'

No. Yes. I clench my hands into fists to stop me winding them into his hair. 'Yes or no, Eli Bligh. Will you help me?'

He leans back, stares at me for a long while then finally nods. 'Where and when? Your room? Tonight?'

'In your dreams, *beast*,' I say, though it might not be wise to bait him after he's finally agreed to help. And gods know I do want to kiss him, but if I do I'll never get out of here. 'I will collect it from you here this evening, after eleven.'

'It won't end well for the fox, will it?'

'It seldom does.' For a moment, I do bury my face in his hair, breathe the woodsmoke scent of him. He holds me tight but doesn't try anything else, and when I squirm, he lets me go. I leave him without saying goodbye, my heart going too fast and breath feeling stale in my lungs, whether from his proximity, owing him a favour, or at the thought of what I must do I cannot say.

18

'Mrs Charlton?'

'Yes, Asher?'

I'm helping her fold the freshly dry sheets in the laundry room, while we can hear Luned next door in the kitchen, cursing as she thuds the heavy iron from the stovetop to the curtains. A punishment, I think. Mrs Charlton had been protective of Luned in front of Burdon, but I'd told her what I'd heard the maid saying to Jessamine, because while I can keep Heloise at bay for a while, someone else needs to watch Luned; I cannot lock her in a room on her own at my leisure. I sense the girl's tasks are likely to become more onerous and unpleasant for some time.

'There was another governess.' She says nothing because it's not a question, but her lips compress thin, and her gaze is dark. 'What happened to her?'

I take up the corners of a fresh sheet. She does the same at the other end, and we begin the dance: folding it lengthwise, once, twice, then a third time; we step towards each other and she takes the corners from my fingers so I might bend and grab the edge and bring it up, an action to be repeated twice, each time bending a little less, until there is a neat rectangle of thick white linen in her arms. She places it carefully on top of the tower of those that have gone before. 'Who told you?'

'Luned mentioned her, but she was another from Mater Hardgrace's Academy – I could hardly avoid knowing.'

Her lips tighten and twist more, like she might disappear into her own mouth. 'She was unsuitable.'

'Mrs Charlton, that covers a myriad of sins,' I say and she looks away.

All my time scheming how to enter this place, then one day Mater Hardgrace appeared at the doorstep of the house that was not mine. She with her academy for governesses and her good reputation. We had met before when that reputation was in danger of being in tatters because some girl she'd sent off to a fine position had returned with a problem in her belly. Came to me – with said girl tagging along behind her, shame-faced, exhausted, weeping – because I'd developed my own reputation amongst the women of Whitebarrow, the ones who lived in the shadows and could not afford the fees for those clever doctor-professors of the city. Then she came again one day all on her own and told me how her niece had disappeared from a posting; imagine how my ears pricked up at the word *Morwood*. That placename so often hissed and screamed and sighed by my mother. There it was, suddenly within my reach.

'Mrs Charlton, I beg of you. Better you tell me now. I will care for your girl as best I can. But if I do not know the currents in this house…'

The housekeeper sighs and leans against the bench top. It's a small room, windowless, mostly given over to the copper for boiling laundry, and the mangle for squeezing it dry. There are

181

baskets and small buckets with wooden pegs, there are washboards and metal tubs for the more delicate items. The room smells of lye and lavender, and a little heady in the confined space. When it rains, we string rope across the kitchen and let things dry there, but the recent sunny cold days have done what was needed.

'She was here and then she was not.'

I clear my throat, speak low and steady: 'Mr Morwood?'

She nods, a jerky movement as if the admission comes out jagged, hurts her. 'She took his eye, though she seemed to have no liking for him. He'd follow her.'

'What manner of young woman was she, Mrs Charlton?'

'Not like you.'

'You mean she was pretty.' I smile, not in the least bit rueful.

'Very pretty.' She rubs her face with her work-reddened hands until it too is quite ruddy. 'And then she was gone. Left without so much as a by-your-leave. Mr Morwood said she'd had a family matter to attend to.'

'And no one would question him,' I say. 'What harm if Luther took his fun and got rid of the governess his mother had insisted upon hiring?' But I knew from Mater Hardgrace that her niece was not inclined towards men. Mrs Charlton gives me a look that's a little shock, a little warning, a little shame. 'How long has Luned shared Mr Morwood's bed?' I ask and her expression shifts entirely to affront, not because she did not know but because I have spoken it aloud.

'Some months on and off.' Mrs Charlton licks her lips as if they're very dry, glances away. In a low voice, she says, 'She's smart enough not to fall pregnant. Visits the apothecary regularly.'

'Clever girl. Fennel and pennyroyal will do the trick mixed

182

with the juice of a lemon. Anything that survives *that* can be voided by a concoction of black and white hellebore.' The housekeeper blinks. 'Don't play the fool, Mrs Charlton; many's the woman whose life would be easier with fewer children. I may not think much of the girl, but she's not a fool in that at least.'

She shrugs. 'Mr Luther whispers promises to her and gods help me, she believes him.' She makes an exasperated sound. 'I asked her, after you told me what you'd heard. He said she'd be the new lady of the house, that he'd put aside my Jessamine.' Her chin sets. 'But whatever else he might do, he'd never do that because if she's gone, the money goes too.'

'Whatever do you mean?' I ask, picking up a pillowcase and folding it even though Luned will need to iron it flat.

'Jessamine's father was a suspicious man. He wanted his daughter married well but he knew there'd be fortune-hunters even amongst men of impeccable breeding. So he made sure that her fortune was paid from a trust by a solicitor in Bellsholm. If anything happens to Jessamine, the money – both compound and interest – goes straight to the children and will be administered by the solicitor. Mr Luther will get not a penny.'

Clever. So very clever. Luther knows this and he cannot get rid of his wife, but he can make her miserable. He can torment her every day. He can take however many maids and governesses to his bed and ruin their lives. He can sow his bastards around the estate and village. But he knows the line he must not cross. Leonora must know it too. I wonder at her finances – what did her wastrel husband leave her? What did she manage to hide away? Does she even now skim funds off the top of Jessamine's fortune each month it is paid? I think of all those jewels in Leonora's dressing room: how many are heirlooms, how many have been purchased with Jessamine's dowry? What happens, however, if Jessamine is declared mad and unfit? How long before Luther thinks of *that*? How long might he leave her in the limbo of an asylum?

'Mrs Charlton, I think it best Luned not sit with Mrs Morwood again.'

'Do I look like an idiot to you?'

I smile. 'No, Mrs Charlton, you do not.'

The children are with their mother now, visiting. She was delighted to see them and she looked considerably better for a night of uninterrupted sleep, no incursions by my mother.

And I have wondered over and again why my mother targeted Jessamine.

Of all the people in this house – her own mother and brother foremost amongst them – why Jessamine? Even the children would have made more sense, though I am terribly grateful Heloise did not think to touch or terrorise them. Nor Burdon, nor Mrs Charlton, nor Luned. Eli – Eli doesn't sleep in the house; besides, would she even go near him? Would she sense his own strangeness and realise he would feel no fear at the sight of her?

But Jessamine, who has been sweet and gentle, even when she thought I would steal her children's affections; wrong-headed, but sweet. Jessamine who lived – to Heloise's mad mind – in this place, with her children, when the true daughter of the house and the heir had been sent forth. Heloise must surely sense that she's been erased from her family's history – I cannot imagine Luther or Leonora would have chosen to tell Jessamine tales of a banished daughter.

Heloise went after Jessamine because she's the weakest in the household and because she has what was denied to my mother. It matters not at all that she lives under the worst of Luther's cruelty. That she's already worn down, whatever resources she might have had stretched so thin. And Heloise, with her unerring instinct, sensed that and made her choice. Jessamine will not be safe in this household as long as my mother roams in her current form.

* * *

The fox is a male, large, and sleeping in front of the fire in Eli's cottage.

'It won't wake for a few hours,' he says, tone carefully neutral; he's fed it something. 'But I suspect it won't need to wake, will it?'

I don't answer but cross the room and kneel by the slumbering animal. Its fur beneath my fingers is like thick silk, its scent musky. The ears are velvet, the tail a thick brush. The firelight makes the red of its pelt glow. I close my lids, squeeze them tightly so tears won't come. If I let them loose now, I won't do what I need to. I clear my throat, gather the beast in my arms, and rise. I pass Eli at the door and mutter, 'Thank you.'

'I dug a hole, behind the old… millhouse,' he says just before I'm out the door. It makes my shoulders drop as if the weight of the fox has increased. Eli knew I could not do what I'm about to do in my room.

The air is cold and I wrap my cloak around the fox; no reason for it to be uncomfortable. It's heavy and warm against me as I make my way towards the little building, sticking to the shadows so no one looking out their window might see me on the lawn and wonder what I'm about. The moonlight shows my path clearly. The door remains unlocked from when I brought the things I need down earlier, laid them out on the examination table, from which I've removed the padded mattress; I pull the thick curtains across so no one will notice the candles I've lit. A scalpel, mortar and pestle, dry ingredients and a lidded jar.

It's almost midnight and the hour will help my cause, the time of witchcraft and dark deeds. I gently put the slumbering fox onto the tabletop and I pat it one last time. I whisper, 'I'm sorry.'

The scalpel is sharp and bright and the fox's chest opens with relative ease. The heart is still beating as I prise the ribs apart; I snip the meaty thing away from its moorings and pluck it out. From the animal's slack mouth: a pale mist of breath and soul puffs pink from between the sharp little teeth. I grab up the empty jar and gently blow the delicate fog until it's captive inside the container. I screw the lid on tightly; it won't be there for long.

I grind the tiny, trembling heart in the mortar, turning it to a red jelly. It takes time and effort, but eventually it's the right consistency; I add some blood. The heart, the breath, the soul – the essence of life, repurposed for an old woman's vanity.

But I keep going.

I fold in the dry ingredients, turn the jelly into a paste, mix it thoroughly. The fog of breath and soul lies at the bottom of the jar; it's stopped circling its prison as if becoming dormant. I unscrew the lid and pour in the paste, swiftly before the fog can escape, then the lid is back on and I shake the contents. The viscosity immediately changes, bubbles, becomes more fluid, a living thing.

I take the poor fox to the back door, find the hole Eli dug, just through the hedge. I lay it in the depression and ask its forgiveness for what I've done, then with my hands – for Eli did not see fit to leave a shovel and I suspect that's on purpose, to make me work for my blood – push dirt over the poor thing whose fur is now

186

dulled by death, weeping silent tears. Back in the surgery, I wash the scalpel and mortar and pestle, brush away the remains of the dried ingredients, then blow out the candles. I leave the building and take a deep breath, standing in the darkness, feeling it seep into me, through my skin, into my flesh, my bones, the very core of me. The fox's death feels like a step that cannot be untaken. Somehow, it feels like the worst thing I have done, although it is not. Not really.

19

'Children, go to your rooms.'

It seems irrelevant to Leonora that her grandchildren haven't finished their breakfast. Wrapping several small pastries into one of the damask napkins, I shoot her a look.

'I will be along later. Albertine, read to your brother and sister from the book of fables.' She touches my shoulder lightly as she passes by, and I pass her the parcel; they'll not starve and I'll bring some other treats to the classroom. Connell looks at me and I nod. Sarai wanders out, holding Albertine's skirt in one hand and a piece of jammy toast in the other. Leonora doesn't seem to notice their reluctance to go without my confirmation.

'Luned, you are no longer required,' Leonora says and doesn't even look at the girl, who seems confused, dishes in her hands. The older woman, with little patience for being questioned, shouts, 'Go!'

As the door closes behind the maid, Luther rises from his place at the head of the table. He's halfway up before his mother's voice stops him.

'Luther, you're not going anywhere.'

He raises a brow at me, not in collegial query but to wonder why I remain. 'I thought I'd visit Jessamine.'

He's not shared their suite for some days now.

'Your wife is unwell.'

'My wife is hysterical,' he says dismissively. 'It will pass.'

'She needs better attention than she can receive in this house. Asher believes—'

'Oh, Asher's diagnosis? What a qualified governess you have hired, Mother.' It's quite the rebellious speech for Luther. But I suppose the loss of his preferred victim is making him feisty. 'We will send to Bellsholm for a *real* doctor—'

'Your wife needs time away from *here*. The atmosphere is not conducive to her… peace of mind. Asher tells me there is a convent four days from here. The nuns at St Dane's run a sanatorium. Jessamine will go and stay for a month.'

'Mother, you're overreacting. Jessamine has always been dramatic. She will—'

'Luther, Jessamine will leave as soon as possible. Mrs Charlton will accompany her.'

'And who will run the household? Who will cook?' Luther's lips are white with anger.

'Tib Postlethwaite will prepare meals, and your idiot twins will spend a little more time here if required. Burdon knows his job and Asher will keep Luned in line. The house will not fall apart for some few weeks, I would imagine.'

Luther begins to turn his gaze towards me; rage and astonishment that I had ignored his warning. Leonora's voice stops him. 'And you will escort your wife, Luther.'

'Mother…'

She raises her voice and it's like a storm about to break, all rage, no rain. 'And when you return here there will be other matters to discuss.'

Luther blinks rapidly; his hands clench and unclench until he can manage to say, 'Is there anything else, Mother?'

'That will be enough for now.' Leonora sits back in her chair. 'You should go and prepare for your journey, Luther.'

He rises, gives me a searing look that says *I warned you*. It will be best to have him away for a while. When he returns I will have to deal with the situation I've created, but for now there's breathing room. When he is gone, Leonora releases a long breath then turns her bright blue eyes to me.

'Are you happy, Miss Todd?' I note she does not call me *Asher* when she is displeased with me.

I nod. 'It will be best for Jessamine, Mrs Morwood.' I take a sip of coffee. 'And I believe her continued good health is in everyone's interests.'

She narrows her eyes, trying to divine if there's a double meaning to my words.

I examine her face over the rim of my cup. The skin is plumping nicely, the wrinkles have reduced considerably. Her lips are pouting-smooth, the bags under her eyes are no longer puffy, indeed the very flesh seems to have drawn back up onto her cheekbones, her jaw firmed. It isn't entirely noticeable – she looks refreshed. The effect will increase over the next month or so, not enough that anyone would remark on it in an uncomfortable fashion. Last night after I'd dealt with the poor fox, I woke Leonora and gave her two spoonfuls of the admixture to drink. She made a face and, in my weariness and guilt, I hissed at her to grow up, almost saw red with the temper threatening, that a creature had lost its life for her so the least she could do was show some stoicism. I then plastered the rest on her face, neck and décolletage; I know it stung, but she kept her mouth shut, did not even whimper – perhaps so no more would get in her mouth. I sat by her for two hours, trying not to smell the odour that rose from her as the mask did its work, trying not to hear the hissing as it ate at her in tender nips. She never said a word the whole time, not even to ask if I was sure *this* was what it was supposed to do. For the best really, or I might have had to truthfully answer that I'd never done it before, never seen it done, only read about it, and kept the recipe in my notebook. But this was the cost of getting her to do what I wanted: sending Jessamine and Luther away. Jessamine will be safer: he won't touch her in Mrs Charlton's presence, won't do anything in public. And she's terrified enough of my mother's ghost to go, to trust me with her children.

'Are *you* happy, Mrs Morwood?'

'I am content for now.' She turns to the mirror over the fireplace and touches her face, smiling. 'How long will it last?'

Your contentment? Who knows? I shrug. 'A year or more.' I don't know, but I will be gone by then.

'Can it be repeated when required?'

'Yes.' But I would sooner take off one of my own limbs than do it again. I feel exhausted after last night (and the night before); the darker the magic, the more it demands from you. And I need to gather my reserves for what's coming.

She says, 'So. In return, I've done what you asked. I trust you are content?'

I nod.

'Good, then you can go into the Tarn this morning.'

'The children—'

'The children will survive without you I am sure. I have

191

something else for you to attend to while you're there.' She shakes her head, *tsks*. 'I'm sure I'm capable of supervising my own grandchildren, Asher.' Then adds as if in surprise, 'And I suppose it's time I got to know them better.'

* * *

I find the solicitor's office and push open the door beneath the green and gold shingle that says *Taverell & Daughter*.

There is a parlour of sorts, green velvet chaises, a table with cups and a silver engraved urn perched atop the flame of a small candle to keep the contents warm. The air smells of coffee and vanilla. The walls are dark-panelled and instead of paintings there are small tapestries, scenes picked out in silk thread: shepherdesses and their flocks, wolves and pups, *rusalky* and rivers and lakes. There are three doors, all closed, and a set of stairs leading upwards, presumably to the living quarters. The wall-lamps are frosted glass encased in silver frames shaped like mermaids. Only a sliver of daylight comes in through the gap in the thick velvet curtains – perhaps a nod to privacy for clients, although how it would help when the office is on the main street and anyone might see you entering is beyond me.

'Hello? Do you have an appointment?' A female voice, soft but firm. I turn and find one of the doors has opened. The woman is thin and wan-looking, white streaking the temples of her otherwise dark hair. She has a sweet face and large, intelligent dark eyes. Her dress is yellow, red roses embroidered around the hem and cuffs.

'I'm Asher Todd. Mrs Leonora Morwood sent me to collect a parcel from either Taverell or Daughter.'

She smiles. 'My mother no longer practises, and I am "or

daughter". Mrs Morwood mentioned you would come.'

Did she? Of course, Leonora would plan ahead to have someone else do the boring parts of a task for her. Plotting and scheming. Perhaps it is something that travels in the blood.

'I'm Zaria Taverell. Everything is ready, if you will follow me.'

She leads me into a tidy office, the walls covered with bookshelves filled with leather-bound books. A quick glance at the titles says they are all some kind of legal tome – no reading for delight here, or at least not for me, but perhaps for Zaria. There is a small neat desk with a small neat chair on either side, precisely the same in egalitarian fashion. Directly behind the desk a set of pigeonholes waits, each with a rolled parchment inside. Zaria unerringly plucks a scroll from one of the slots, not even having to search for it. Her eyes scan the document for last-minute mistakes, but I suspect there are none, that this precise woman does not commit errors.

She sits and gestures for me to do the same. She smooths the sheet, then folds it until it is like an envelope. On one corner of the desk, a silver tray holds a red candle and a metal stamp. Carefully Zaria lights the candle and lets the wax drip onto the parchment, then presses the seal into the scarlet mess. She holds it there for a few moments, then removes it to leave the shape of a wolf in the warm wax. That will take some skill to open without leaving a trace. Perhaps something of that curiosity shows in my face, and she smiles as she hands it over.

'Thank you, Mistress Taverell,' I say and carefully push the thing into the side pocket of my satchel.

'Please tell Mrs Morwood that we are delighted to be of service as always. When she has checked the contents and made any amendments, we will be happy to witness it for her. We can either come to the Grange or she can visit again. We shall retain the final document for safekeeping if she so desires.' Ah, so this is merely a draft.

I nod, hesitate. 'She did ask me to enquire about another matter…' I pause delicately. Zaria leans forward a little. 'You have dealt, I believe, with arrangements for… a previous governess?'

She seems to freeze, disapproving. 'I made no such arrangements.' I sense I'm on thin ice, that beginning this conversation was, perhaps, more of a risk than it seemed when I first thought to take it. I keep my tone level, the pace of my words steady. I do not rush on like a liar or someone trying to gain information I neither have nor have a right to. 'Oh.' I frown, confused. 'I was told you had dealt with such things before?'

'Not for a governess.' Still stiff and distrusting. But there's a gap in what she's said, a lacuna: not a governess but other women, perhaps. 'I'm unsure I ever saw your predecessor here.'

'You will realise that Mrs Morwood has put her faith in me – sending me here on her behalf. Me. Not another member of the household.' I'm at pains to point this out but trying not to sound too importuning.

She nods yet again, a little more freely.

'I am not,' I say proudly, 'of the same cloth as others in her employ. I am a little older and wiser, my head is not so easily turned, my guard not so lightly surmounted.' I pause again, lower my voice. 'We – the household – might once again find ourselves in need of your services in this regard. Another local girl. Would the arrangements made for the others suit her… problem?'

Zaria Taverell takes a deep breath and glances away, to the

corner where there's nothing but a bookshelf and some cobwebs up towards the ceiling, out of reach. The lawyer looks irritated.

'I understand this is… inconvenient,' I say, and her eyes slice towards me; it's not annoyance, it's anger.

'That man thinks he can do as he wishes and others will clean up his mess! That these poor girls – foolish though they might be – are disposable!' Her voice breaks like glass, and the last note is one of despair. *Oh*, I think, *you don't know the half of it.*

'I'm sorry. I cannot say I disagree with you. But Mrs Morwood asked me…'

She shakes her head, releases a ragged breath. I wonder what happened to make her feel like this – is it personal or merely a dislike of men who push their way through lives not their own as if they are scythes? Cutting down and taking what they want, then discarding it blithely. How old is she? Old enough to have known my mother? She looks mid-forties, a little older than Heloise when she died, but that might simply be the passage of time; gods know Heloise looked older than her years. But I can't risk asking, not so soon after this stirring her suspicions.

'Do they all stay here?' I ask instead.

She sighs. 'Most. If they're stupid enough to sleep with Luther Morwood, they're hardly likely to survive out in the world. Perhaps this latest might like to travel, get away from here so no one knows her shame?'

I weigh things up and decide not to push my luck. 'Things are not certain with this one as yet. There is still time for nature to take its course and solve the problem. I will return when we know better how the land lies.' I hesitate. 'I imagine things would have been very different if Mrs Morwood's daughter had survived.'

'I imagine so,' she says but gives nothing away. Neither disapproval or otherwise. I resist the urge to probe, to dig out more information. This one is a lawyer, not given to gossip. I'll need to find another source. I feel less concerned now, asking about Heloise, now that I've seen Leonora with the portrait, heard her speak of her daughter. No one will ask now *How did you hear about her?*

I rise, as does she. 'Thank you for your assistance.'

She holds her hand out, grasps mine, grips it tightly so I cannot break away. 'I hear you have some talent for healing.'

I smile, the coldest way I can. 'Who told you that?'

'Heledd Jones mentioned it. She's a friend – forgive her, I know you asked her to keep it a secret. But with Mrs Morwood so much better it's hard to keep your ability hidden.' She points at her own eyes to illustrate.

I relax. But no point in admitting too much. 'Sometimes I can help. I have some knowledge of medicine.'

'My wife is unwell. An issue with her breathing.'

'Are the aspirations wet or dry?'

'Wet.'

'Does she cough or wheeze?'

'Both.'

'Is there blood in the mucus?'

She shakes her head.

'Is she here? May I examine her?'

'She's travelling – a fabric merchant – and I do not believe she'll see a doctor while she's away. Alize is an especially stubborn woman, much though I love her.'

'I will send a tincture tomorrow' – thinking the Binions might be bribed into running errands for me – 'if you or your cook can slip it into meals? One tablespoon – it shouldn't change the flavour of what she eats and alert her. How long will she be gone?'

'Another two days, I believe.'

'Then when she returns give her the mix for three days in a row and send a note to me at the Grange if she is better or worse. If the latter, I will examine her whether she likes it or not.'

She laughs loudly and it makes her beautiful. 'Thank you, Miss Todd.'

I nod. 'You are welcome, Mistress Taverell.'

* * *

As I walk back towards Morwood, the carriage passes me, the one with the Morwood crest on the side. One of the big matching black pairs draws the shining ebony conveyance along. Inside, I see briefly Jessamine and Mrs Charlton on one bench seat, and Luther on the other. Owen Reiver, the coachman, notices me, tips his head. The thin boy beside him stares straight ahead; that will be his son Tew.

Jessamine's face is pale, her expression distraught; Mrs Charlton and Luther both have taut lips, tight cheeks, narrowed nostrils. Better if I could have sent Jessamine in the company of Mrs Charlton alone – better for her to be away from Luther as long as possible – but getting her out of Heloise's reach is paramount. And some days without Luther Morwood around the place won't hurt me. When he does return, I will be ready. None of them see me.

I'm a little surprised they are gone so soon – I thought it would be at least another day to allow for preparations. But Leonora. It was Leonora, getting rid of them quickly. She agreed with my plan to remove Jessamine, but she cannot help herself: she must

197

put her mark on it. It has left the children alone without their mother, unknowing that this might happen, unprepared. I should have been there.

I did not think, when I set this in motion, that I would grow so fond of them. In all truth, they were simply a means to an end, the job a key to this place, this family. I hardly thought of them at all, if I am honest. Yet here I am, with three little ones at heel, caring for their bodies, minds and hearts and hoping to not hurt them more than I must. Had they been happy, perhaps I'd have cared less, but they are afraid of their father, afeared for their mother, and wary of their grandmother. And we are related, after all, though it's a tie they'll never know. How could I not sympathise with such children, given the shadows I grew in?

I pick up my pace until I am running towards the manor.

20

'Oh, shut them up, Asher Todd!'

In the library Leonora is sitting in Luther's preferred chair by the fire, a book open on her lap. On the red velvet chaise longue is Albertine, who is holding Sarai, with Connell beside them, but not touching. All are crying, but Sarai is by far the worst. She weeps and hiccups, gives little howls, a small sad wolf, and clings to her sister like a limpet. I kneel in front of them, put my hands out to take Sarai and she screams.

It's a terrible high-pitched shriek, and she kicks at me with angry little feet. I'm off-balance and I tumble backwards, hit my back on the coffee table, fall to one side and hit my left temple against the stones of the hearth. Black flickers at the edges of my vision, blood seeps from the tear in my skin.

The room is silent-still for long seconds while everyone stares. Slowly, I sit up, feel the throbbing ache begin as I blink and blink and blink. I look at Sarai, who is staring at me in horror now. Connell is first to move, pulling a white cambric handkerchief from his pocket and holding it to the welling crimson.

'Sarai,' I say and my voice is raw. 'Sarai, what have I done?'

She peeks from under Albertine's arm and says in a tiny voice, 'You sent Mama away.'

Guilt; I can hear it, see it. She had begun to prefer me to her mother, she knew it hurt Jessamine, and here is the consequence, or so the little one thinks. Her mother is gone and it's her fault, my fault.

'Shush, Sarai, Miss Asher is not to blame! Mama is ill,' Albertine says.

'Sarai. Your mother is very unwell. She has gone to a place to heal – it is called St Dane's. Your father is escorting her there, and Mrs Charlton will stay with her – so you know she will be well looked after. This is not my doing.' *A lie that only Leonora knows.* 'She will be absent but a little while. Sarai, I swear your mother will return to you. In the meantime, she has commended you to my care. I know you are sad, Sarai, but please trust me.'

She says nothing but buries her face in her sister's side and continues to cry. Connell helps me up, steadies me when I sway. 'Thank you, Connell.'

Leonora has not moved or spoken in this time; her mouth is still agape. I think of my mother's temper and wonder where it came from. Heloise would have been out of the chair, hand raised before I'd even hit the ground; Leonora is frozen in place.

'Mrs Morwood, I will take the children to their rooms. I think this day has been distressing enough for them, and there is no point holding classes. I will have Luned take them up some lunch soon.'

She nods. 'When they are settled, come and see me.'

'Of course.'

I hold out my hands. Connell takes one, Albertine the other; Sarai holds her sister's hand, thumb stuck in her mouth, giving sideways glances to her grandmother and I. 'Come along.'

* * *

Once the children are calmed – and Sarai has muttered an apology – I leave them in their rooms with nothing more than the instruction to remain there, to read, to sleep, to do whatever they will. I promise to check on them later.

In the small bathroom along from my bedroom I carefully wash the cut, a wet white cloth turning red from the blood that's already begun to coagulate. It's darkening, setting like jelly. The wound isn't too deep, though it will scar, giving me a match for the one on my right temple, a souvenir of Heloise in the early days of her illness, when she still had strength to throw things, before I learned to remove items from the rickety upturned box beside the bed. I wipe lavender water over the red line for disinfectant, then dab an ointment of calendula. It stops bleeding. I carefully rearrange my hair as well as I can, loosening the thick bun at the base of my neck so shorter tendrils fall free and go a little way to hiding the injury. I drink a cordial of feverfew to prevent a headache. Later I'll take the mortar and pestle from the chest of drawers and crush a mix of herbs for something stronger, something to take away the pain entirely and make me sleep like the dead.

I look in the mirror for long moments. I should be used to this reflection after all these weeks, it should not surprise me every time I catch sight of myself. Yet it does, this rounded face, these brown eyes, this dark hair, the ordinariness of this visage.

Unbidden, Zaria Taverell comes to mind again, so calm when she insisted nothing had been done for the other governess. No contact, no arrangements; I wonder if the girl even made it into the Tarn or was she too busy with the children and assorted tasks?

Mater Hardgrace said she'd not requested a rest day and I'm sure Leonora took advantage of that. Zaria… Zaria struck me as truthful – her anger at Luther a sign of that – which makes me wonder how short a time my predecessor lasted? She was in the house, certainly – her few small treasures I found in the hiding space prove it – but perhaps she never made it to the Tarn at all. No one saw her, not simply Zaria. How long before she disappeared and Leonora wrote to Mater Hardgrace, complaining of the girl's flightiness and demanding a replacement?

When my nerves are calm once again, I smooth the front of my skirt. I think of the thick parchment in the satchel now in my room; will I give it to Leonora? Will I tell her it wasn't ready, that her solicitor was less reliable than expected, that I will go back for it in a few days? Too great a risk: she might send someone else; she might go herself. Best to hand it over and find some other way to discover its contents.

I take the document out, slide it into the deep pocket of my dress. At this very moment I feel as if I have pushed too many things to the brink, that at any moment something might overbalance and shatter. I take the staircase down and find Burdon waiting for me in the entry hall. 'Miss Todd, there is a gentleman to see you. I have taken the liberty of putting him in the western parlour.'

'Thank you, Burdon.'

I'm so distracted I do not even think *Who might be here?* My fingers shake on the doorknob, however, and I make a concerted effort to steady it, then open the door. The room is decorated in primrose and even on the most overcast days it seems light and airy. There is a fire in the grate, two golden velvet chaises facing each other over a marble coffee table. There are paintings on the

202

walls of bucolic scenes, but there are no books here; that is not the purpose of the space. This is a room for polite discussion; should Margery Marston ever darken the doorstep and manage to breach the house's defences, I imagine Leonora will speak with her in here.

A man of medium height stands by the tall window, looking out. He's a silhouette against the daylight. There's something…

'Sir, may I help you?' It is only then that I recall on this day of disturbances that I neglected to ask Burdon who the visitor is. The gentleman turns at the sound of my voice, hesitant, then comes towards me. As he gets closer, his face begins to make sense and my heartbeat slows as if ice is running through my veins. Dressed in his usual finery, the embroidered red silk waistcoat is one I know well, the crisp linen shirt beneath it, the beige trews, polished brown boots and black frock coat with all the pretty touches and pleats and gold buttons of which he is so fond.

Closer now, he squints, uncertain. 'I am sorry, I asked for Asher Todd.'

I cannot get any words to pass from my lips.

He steps even closer, is almost on top of me now. He reaches out and grasps the wrist of my right hand. 'Wait… Is it you?'

I still do not speak. If I say nothing perhaps he will go away. Perhaps he will assume he's made an error, taken a wrong turn.

'Is it *you*?' He pushes his face into mine, his grip tightens. 'It *is* you. But not you. Almost…'

I consider, for the breath of a moment, lying. Saying, *You are mistaken, sir, be gone!* But that would solve nothing. There is no running from this house, it is where I need to be. He touches my cheek, then. 'How? How are you her and you? How are you—'

His brown eyes drop to my hands, his gaze widens; he has seen the ring. He grabs at it, he pulls hard, not caring if he hurts me. For a moment or two it will not come loose; a cry escapes me though I don't struggle, then the ring slips away into the palm of his hand. I feel no change but I can see from his expression that I am different. In the mirror over the hearth there is the face of another woman, my true face: the red hair, the milky skin, the green eyes. A face very like the portrait of Heloise that my grandmother keeps in her dressing room, and the one this man can identify, for he knows me, knew my mother too although not in her better days.

'Hello, Archie,' I say.

'You took her ring.' He holds it up like an accusation, his voice shaking; *her* ring because it contains her hair. 'Why would you steal her ring?'

I gesture to my face. 'You can see why. I cannot be recognised in *this* place.'

'But how?' His disbelief is laughable.

'Archie, you know how. All the things you've hired me to do, how can you be shocked at this smallest of feats?' I pluck the piece of jewellery from him and examine it. 'I borrowed it is all, Dr O'Sullivan.'

The mouse-brown hair braided beneath the glass dome belonged to his wife Meliora. I spoke a spell over it, made a small sacrifice for all magic requires the red price, turned it into a charm to transform. I slip it back on my finger: in the mirror, the changed features reappear, not entirely mine, not entirely Meliora's but enough of both to make a different woman, a woman who would not be recognised by her own grandmother because she is an imprint of Leonora's daughter. A face as dull as a sparrow so as not to excite interest in anyone but Archie, for he adored his drab little wife. 'And I need it a while longer, Archie, but I will return it, I swear.'

'You ran away.'

'I had matters to attend to and I knew you would not want to let me go.' I touch his arm. 'I was always going to come back, Archie. I promise you.' *A lie. But I did not cover my trail well enough despite all my efforts, all those detours and feints, all those coaches and carriages to places I did not need to go, all to throw him off the scent. All to no avail.*

'You said you would—'

'I know what I said, Archie, but there are things I need here, things I need to do here before I can help you.' I frown. 'How did you find me?'

'Mater Hardgrace—'

Can I trust no one in this world?

'—I'd seen you had been speaking with her – and the neighbours mentioned she'd been a visitor – so I asked if she knew where you'd gone.' He stands tall, shoulders pushed back. 'I told her it was imperative I find you.'

And I, like a fool, had not thought to tell her to keep it a secret because I had not thought anyone in Whitebarrow knew of my connection to Mater Hardgrace, and she knew nothing of my true reason for coming here. She thought only that I did her a good turn. We had always met at night. But Archie, damn him, and the neighbours, damn them, had paid more attention than expected; I'd underestimated him.

'You said—' His bottom lip trembles, all rage gone, and Archie O'Sullivan of Whitebarrow University is reduced to a child. I sit on one of the golden chaises, draw him down beside me. His smooth-shaven chin wobbles; mourning often takes the appetite, but not for Archie. His clothing, while well-made, is tight with the feeding of his grief; he's paunchier. My disappearance probably made matters worse. I wrap his right hand in both of mine, caressing the delicate skin that does nothing much at all except point to notes on chalkboards already written for him by underlings, indicate ingredients for another underling to mix, to open his books, to light his pipe, to pour his orange-blossom whiskey with dinner and raspberry gin nightcap into cut crystal tumblers. He's soft, is Archie; in truth I'm amazed he made it this far in finding me. I'd have put money on him giving up easily. But perhaps I underestimated his love for his wife, his need to have her back, his belief in what I could do. And how much he watched me.

'Archie.' I wipe away the tears that have spilled over. 'Archie, I will return, and I will undertake all that I have faithfully promised.'

I kiss him on the cheek, feel his hand slip from mine and go to my waist so he can hold me firm. He turns his head, seeks my lips, and is soon making those noises I've come to recognise. Archie misses his wife terribly, this I know, but it's never stopped him from spending himself in me the eighteen months when other needs overwhelm the sadness. I've never complained for the contact is kind and warm, and I have had so little of that; yet I've been careful to make sure nothing more comes of it, drinking down black brews to ensure no child takes in my womb. Today, though, I rebuff him. It would be easy enough to straddle him here, exhaust him, make him malleable, but I'll not have anyone hear us. I'll not attach myself to him any further; I'll not make it harder to do what

I must do, to inflict the hurt I must on him and myself. I might have been able to love him had it not been for his shade and mine, Meliora and Heloise – perhaps I do, in my own way.

But perhaps not. He's a weak man and that makes the scorn rise in me. It makes it easier to deceive him when I need to. I push him away very gently. 'Not now, Archie. Not here.'

He breathes heavily, but says, 'Of course. Of course not.'

I take his hand again, move myself a little further along on the chaise. 'Archie, you must return to Whitebarrow. I will follow in a month at the most. My business here will be concluded and I will return to you. I will return and you will have your Meliora back.'

I will run and hide myself far better now I know you have this determination. I will do what I must do here and then my oath will be fulfilled, and I will flee once again, I will find a deeper darker place to hide and never see any of my sorrows again.

'But—'

'Archie, I beg of you. Leave. Do not return to this house. Sleep tonight at the inn – I assume you've already taken a room there from your tidiness, which is not such as a traveller bears – and then go directly to Whitebarrow. I'd prefer you tell no one you came looking for me, but I fear that is a vain hope.'

'Only the servant at your door.'

'No one at the inn?'

He shakes his head. 'Mater Hardgrace—'

'Had already told you where I was.' I nod stiffly. 'Then keep our secrets, Archie. It will do no good to share them. Now, please leave. I will see you soon enough. Trust me.'

After he rides off I stand at the door for a long time, wringing my hands.

21

I was born in Whitebarrow almost upon my mother's arrival there. She'd wandered after being expelled from Morwood Grange. She told me that she'd had no idea, truly, where to go and what the world held, that she'd stumbled upon the university town. Yet I think, knowing now that Luther had failed in that place, she gravitated there from some perverse sense of satisfaction. She'd never been beyond the boundaries of the Grange and the Tarn, only ever had tutors in the small room where I now teach her brother's children, and her mother trying to instruct her about the running of an estate. When they sent her forth she had only the clothes on her back, a few pieces of jewellery, a purse of gold and silver bits, and me growing in the pit of her.

When she finally arrived in Whitebarrow, or so she would tell me (and this is the story most oft on her lips, so I think it the most true), a man found her and took her to his home. A doctor, one of the new medical men, a professor at the university. Moved by pity, or my mother's beauty – I imagine she was glorious even swollen as an overripe fruit – he took her in. Installed her in the guest room of his fine home, had his servants and wife care for his "stray waif", his burden from God, his means of doing a good work. He delivered me, too, when the time came. My mother having found a safe harbour, it was a further ten days before I was born. He'd ensured Heloise did not bleed to death or take childbed fever; that I was healthy and clean and fed. She took his last name, Todd, for me and herself so no one ever knew us as Morwoods. I do not know where Asher came from, only that it means "happy" or "blessed". The irony is not lost on me. When Heloise was able to rise and undertake small tasks that did not overtax her, she began to earn our keep as well as she could, helping the mistress of the house with mending, sewing rough smocks that charitable institutions might give out to the poor, and in the evening reading to her new protectors from whatever improving tracts they deemed fit. And thus it might have continued for a longer while than it did, had the mistress not found her husband in my mother's bed one night, labouring as if both God and his demons urged him on.

At least we were not returned to the street, but passed on to one of the doctor-professor's colleagues. A man older, and unmarried and likely to remain so, less by his own choice than that of others. We remained in his home until I was five or six, so I have memories of him – unlike Mother's first "protector" – and so I can rely on my own recollections. He was plain, not quite ugly, and smelled fusty. He did not like me – did not like evidence of Mother's other lives – but he did not hurt me. I had my own room and, on the days when he was not at the university until late, I spent my hours within those four walls. I read from an early age and found my solace there. When the house was free of its owner, I was at liberty to wander its halls, enjoy Heloise's company when her mood was good, and sit in the library and read everything I could find from fairy tales to medical tracts, voraciously learning whatever I could.

Though Heloise's temper was unpredictable, I knew she loved me. She would never agree to any notion that I be sent to an orphanage, and soon he made the suggestion less and less often. But the time came at last when he decided he needed a wife, an actual one, not merely someone who tolerated him in her bed as an exchange of goods and services. And, much to the surprise of everyone, a bride was duly found for him by the spouse of another doctor-professor. A suitable girl, plain and undemanding in every matter but one, and that matter was us. We were sent forth once again, this time with no new home arranged, but all our lovely things (and any books I managed to steal) packed in cases, and a purse heavy with coin. Heloise found us a place to live, a tall pretty house with high windows that flooded the rooms with light.

The money in the purse, however, ran away rather faster than Heloise would have preferred (her mother's lessons about managing funds had never seemed to stick) and she once again traded her beauty for our sustenance. I do not truly know how much she minded. Though she screamed at me more than once over the years that it was my fault, that if there'd been only her she'd live much more cheaply, more easily, she made no effort to learn another skill, made no move to find an "honest" profession (yet I've often wondered what is more honest than whoring).

And this way, she chose who shared her bed, she set her own prices and made sure to collect. When we walked in the streets, bought our daily bread, those who glared at her discovered they had no power over her; she'd withstood the worst of her family so she would not be brought low by mere whispers. Heloise held her head high, tossed her bright red curls, arched her brows, and smiled coldly at them. She knew what their husbands wanted, knew what they'd pay for it. She held all their secrets in her hands, and she would be afraid of no one.

The first time I asked her about my father. A priest who'd seduced her, she told me, in between slaps – I was light, my mother was strong. She held my wrist tight, dangled me by an arm so my feet didn't reach the floor, and spanked my arse as I swayed. He'd promised her everything and given her nothing except me. His kind, she told me, god-hounds, were not to be trusted under any circumstances. He was so handsome, she told me, hair as black as night, his eyes so green you'd lose yourself in them – *You have your eyes from him, Asher* – but he was as deceitful as those who fell from the heavens. Sometimes she whispered other things about him to me over the years, but I seldom sought new details. She whispered, too, of her mother's rage when she learned how Heloise had ruined herself, set all Leonora's plans awry.

As I grew, I had tutors, for Heloise was very determined that I should learn better and more than she ever had. I had tutors for as long as she could afford them. But there were still days, weeks, months, years when she resented me. Resented not only that I had been the cause of her exile from Morwood, but also that I learned. I learned and I loved it. There were days when she threw books – hard-earned, expensive books – into the fireplace and held me back to watch them burn. All the while she would whisper how I must realise nothing was permanent, and that she was the source of everything I had – that I should not get above myself because each and every item might be taken away. Those were not all of my days, but more than enough to remember. To have their imprint, their fractures, on every part of my mind, heart and soul.

Eventually, however, my mother's clients fell away and our funds dried up. She grew older, less fresh and lovely. She became ill more and more often, unable to work. She became less willing to allow men to do as they wished with her. And she did not like the way they began to look at me – I think sometimes for fear of what might become of me, and sometimes because they no longer looked at her. Once I woke in the night with her whispering, wondering aloud what would happen if she took my face from me, if I no longer looked like her.

When I was fifteen, we left our pretty little house for the first in a series of smaller, less-pretty houses, further and further from the nice neighbourhoods. Eventually we had a single room in a boarding house, cheek by jowl with brothels, our living paid for at first as I sold the last pieces of the fine jewellery rich men had given to her, and finally by my own wages. Heloise – her looks gradually eroded by illness and alcohol – had taken to her bed and a kindly neighbour sat by her when I had to go out.

By then she was truly ailing; life and death were catching up with her.

I found employment at the university, cleaning the classrooms and halls where I could only dream of studying, for women were not accepted there. I dressed in drab colours, kept my eyes downcast, tying my bright red hair up and away under a scarf, so it would draw no attention. So none of the clever doctor-professors might recognise Heloise's bastard daughter, or think me available for such services as she had rendered. I made myself beneath their notice, I learned to move oh-so-quietly along the corridors, to slip in and out of places I was not meant to be. To enchant the soles of my shoes so I could pass unremarked.

As a cleaner, I was given keys to certain doors. Here's the thing about having a single key: it begets another. Open one door and you will find, invariably, other keys left carelessly about. Keys to doors and windows and desks and safes, to locked cabinets, to laboratories. I worked at night after most of the lecturers had gone home. I was not the only cleaner, but I was the only one in the building that contained the library and the doctor-professors' offices.

I made the university and all its secrets my own.

All those clever men wrote such clever notes, all their lectures and all the results of their treatments and experiments. I read each and every one until I knew more than any spotty student who roamed the corridors, who'd bought his way into the institution – certainly more than my uncle ever did. I began, also, to help the women around us with the medical knowledge I'd gleaned, and the other knowledge I'd learnt from the more esoteric books in their collections, and from some of the old women who knew more than they should.

Everything I studied was aimed at one goal: making my mother well. I would spend as much of my earnings as could be borne buying ingredients and potions from apothecaries, then eventually I simply stole the ingredients from the laboratories I cleaned. I made tisanes and elixirs. I could brew anything from a love philtre to a sleeping draught, I could compound a cure for headaches or rashes or nausea, relieve a cold or arthritis, set a broken limb and have it heal faster than should have been possible, prevent a pregnancy or abort one that had already taken. But I could not find a cure for my mother's ailment. Sometimes she might rally, be bright for days, but in the end she would fade and she'd be dragged back down once more. Yet she lingered for years.

Still I fought.

Still Heloise died and I was left alone.

Heloise died, but I did not stop looking for a means to save her, to fulfil the promises she'd wrung from me because she never forgot that night when I'd first committed sorcery, when the fire danced at my very whim.

22

'Asher?'

I don't know how many times I've been called, but it's clear from the impatient tone it's been more than once. I shake my head then my whole body as if to settle back into shape, into the place I've made in this house, this world. I still my fluttering hands, clench them into fists so they're not betraying my discombobulation before Leonora, and turn.

'Are you quite well, Miss Todd?' She's frowning, standing a few feet away, come out of the library to look for me, no doubt, when I failed to reappear as expected. Her face seems to have gotten younger even in the short while I've been away from her.

I smile, clasp my fingers together. 'Quite well, Mrs Morwood.'

'Who was that man?' She nods towards the open door even though Archie O'Sullivan has long disappeared from view. I should have known Leonora would not miss a thing.

'An old friend of my mother's. Kindly come to check on my wellbeing.'

'He did not stay long to do so,' she observes, then heads back to the library, expecting no answer for it was not a question. I follow.

'I asked him to leave, Mrs Morwood. I'm here to work for you, not to socialise.'

'What a good girl you are,' she throws over her shoulder.

'My mother raised me to be so,' I reply. *But Heloise didn't really, merely to be obedient, and those are two different things.*

'Do you have my paperwork from Mistress Taverell?' Leonora returns to her seat.

'Oh. Yes.' I draw it from my pocket, the wax seal intact. She takes it without haste, her movements confident as if she's got no doubts about what she will do, about what is contained therein. She rests it on her lap, fingers laced over the top.

'Excellent. Now: I wish to spend part of each day training Albertine.'

I blink, search for something appropriate to say, settle on, 'Afternoons would be best. I teach in the mornings and their afternoons will be free of the time they would spend with their mother, at least for the next month.'

She nods. 'That will be satisfactory. We will begin the day after tomorrow – I will have ordered my thoughts by then.' And because I did not ask anything, she seems to decide to reward me. 'The girl must learn how to manage an estate. This estate.'

'Not your son? Not Connell?' *And because you did not get the chance to pass all your knowledge on to Heloise? Is this your next chance? What if you knew I existed? Would it be me, next in line?*

'Connell's a nice enough child but Albertine is the oldest.' She does not mention Luther, does not acknowledge that part of my question.

I nod. Does she mean Albertine will inherit? Does Leonora think the girl will stay here, and any husband she might have will take her last name (as Leonora's did) and be content to sit by the

216

lady of the manor as she makes decisions? That worked so well for Leonora and Donnell, after all. 'I will tell her, Mrs Morwood.'

* * *

It's only when I finally retire to my room in the evening after overseeing a cold supper left by Mrs Charlton, supervising the children's bath and bedtime, then collapsing into the chair by the fire, that I allow Archie O'Sullivan to creep back into my thoughts.

He was one of the doctors I sought out in the early days of Heloise's illness; he was not the last but he was always the gentlest. It was only later that I heard his own wife was ill and suffering an ailment neither he nor any of the clever doctor-professors could cure – any more than anyone (myself included) could cure my mother. Later still that I learned Meliora had died not long after Heloise.

He was kind, too, which struck me when I'd had so little kindness in my life. He remained kind even when he discovered me in the Whitebarrow university after dark, resurrecting a dead wolf cub that had been brought in for the classes. I got to it before it was given to the students for dissection practice – it would have been no good to me after they'd done their worst with it – and he watched from the shadows as I, all unaware of his presence, worked a spell I'd found in a book. There were notes in the margins in a blocky hand, an untidy script seemingly written in haste to get things down as they were done, observations with the unalloyed enthusiasm of a mind curious about cause and effect, about making things happen that perhaps should not. A mind untroubled by any sort of moral compass or fear of consequence – someone who would do something simply because they could exert their power thus, and never question whether they *should*. The name on the front was faded but I could make out *A Manual for the Students of the Tintern Dollmakers' Academy*.

I wondered what other feats the author of those notations had managed, where they'd gone, when they'd died. A long time ago, I assumed, from the book's publication date. Copious notes about how to bring an animal back to life but nothing about a human. No matter. Somewhere in that library, in the depths of the proscribed section – to which I had, of course, acquired a key – I was sure there was the means to do so. Instructions in another's hand – or perhaps the same hand, older, wiser, even more filled with a thirst for knowledge – and I would find it. It was only a matter of time.

I never did – find it, I mean – but I found something… greater. Worse. Better. Stranger.

That night, Archie made no sound as I worked, no sound until he saw what I'd done: brought the tiny wolf back by a mix of words and herbs, blood and breath. Its eyes opened, red, and it rolled to its feet, snarling and snapping. I stared at it, fascinated by what I'd wrought – horrified, terrified without a doubt, but not enough to stop. I'd probably have stayed that way until the creature attacked me, but for the gasp from the shadows. I clutched at a scalpel; the undead wolf turned too, growling, towards the source of the noise.

'Who's there?' I asked and I cannot recall ever feeling more afraid either before or after that moment. Discovery meant my own death. I imagined the dungeons, the torture the god-hounds would inflict on me even if I confessed immediately to witchcraft. I imagined the flames, searing, burning, dead before I could do what I had promised Heloise. I whispered *Mekham* and the little pup fell, back into its death.

But it was Archie O'Sullivan who stepped from the gloom, his face lit by fear and strange hope.

'Can you do that to a person?' he asked, breathless.

I shook my head. 'Not yet.'

Heloise was three months dead, but I had what I needed of her. Had everything except the key, the formula, the way. I had nothing of his wife, doubted he did either. And certainly not the *right* things.

'Meliora,' he said, and the name caught in his throat. I recalled too late that his wife had died. Remembered I had heard the other doctor-professors gossiping about her death, about how hard he'd taken it, and how he should buck up and find a replacement. 'Will you be able to…'

And I should have said *No* then and there. Should have told the truth and simply said *No, not now, not ever; it is beyond me* or *Not for you or anyone else* but I did not. I'd learned from my mother that honesty often led to the closing of doors, the loss of opportunities, and I thought of all the resources Archie might supply if I told a lie. So I said, 'I will.'

'I want my Meliora once more. I will give you whatever you want, need, I will keep you safe. I will tell no one what I have seen here tonight' – and in that moment I imagined I could smell the cooking of my own flesh, the smoking of me like a side of bacon, but he did not notice my fear – 'but return my wife to me and everything I have is yours.'

I thought how much easier it would be to not sneak around and steal things, materials and knowledge, how nice it would be not to have to scrape for a pittance of a salary to survive, to not have to make myself invisible every waking moment. How nice not to live in that room in the boarding house, not to sleep across from the bed where my mother had died. If and when I found out how to resurrect a person, I would only do it once then disappear from his life, for I had no desire to become a mistress of souls. It was easy to lie to him – and so I did.

And I stayed under his roof for not quite two years; I wanted for nothing. I had an allowance for my personal use, and an account for whatever research items I needed; he gave me keys (more keys!) to the university and he called me his assistant – I went where I wanted and no one questioned me. I was able to do as I wished in the daylight hours, although admittedly some activities were best reserved for night. Perhaps I'd have stayed there forever in his house, gradually losing faith in what I was trying to do, and instead growing content to settle into a life beside him. Perhaps I'd have kept trying despite all signs that I would never succeed, and go a little mad in the process; perhaps he'd have let me. Perhaps he'd have forgotten his Meliora after a while and decided I would do in her place.

But there came the day when I found what I needed and remaining with Archie O'Sullivan was no longer an option.

* * *

Standing outside my mother's room, I notice some few salt crystals have crept beneath the door. I wonder if she's been trying to remove them so she might escape, wonder if she's been down on her ghostly knees blowing with all her might with breath she doesn't have, and this is what she managed to dislodge. Or perhaps it's simply from the breeze that creeps in under the sash of that cold, cold room.

Should I go in there? Speak with her? Recount how things are

220

progressing? That's why I left my own chamber, isn't it? To see her? But she'll simply look at me with that burning blue gaze, and wordless though she is I'll know she's demanding why I've not yet fulfilled my promise. Letting me know in no uncertain terms that I have failed her in the past and will doubtless continue to do so forever.

I push away and turn, back to my room, take up my winter coat, and leave the house entirely. My feet move, but I do not think and it seems no time at all before I'm standing in front of his cottage, entering without knocking, then he's staring at me, one eyebrow cocked and quizzical.

'It means nothing,' I say for the second time, and reach for him, and he for me, and for a while I do not have to think of anything else that might be required of me.

23

I wake so late that dawn is breaking a cold bright white. I hear the sound of hoofbeats and know I must hare back to the manor so as not to be caught. He tried to hold me there, keep me warm, but I shrugged him away, refused to kiss him goodbye lest he capture me again and this all start to feel like something that could become a habit.

I sneak in through the kitchen door but Tib Postlethwaite is already there, standing by the table, cheeks red from the cold. She's tying one of Mrs Charlton's white aprons over the top of a faded forest-green dress, but she's still got her black bonnet on. She spots me and one greying eyebrow goes up. I throw my shoulders back, refuse to look guilty, and say, 'What a lovely hat, Mrs Postlethwaite.'

Her hands fly upwards; she'd forgotten to take it off. Too busy looking around no doubt. I swallow a smile. 'Did Mrs Charlton speak with you before she left?'

She nods. 'She did.'

'The pantry is well stocked. If there is anything you require, please ask Luned. If she is unhelpful then please tell me. Don't let her put one over you.'

'It'll be a cold day below before the likes of her sends me

astray.' Her voice is deep, a little thick as if she's speaking through treacle. I need to listen carefully if I'm to pick out all the words. I've not spoken to her at length before. She delivers the milk early each morning, is generally gone before I make my way downstairs.

'If you need more hands in the kitchen, the Binion girls can be called upon. They will continue their weekly cleaning duties.'

'Yes, Miss Todd.' She doesn't curtsey – nor does she need to – but I feel there's at least a modicum of disrespect. Not simply that she thinks me a slip of a girl to be giving her orders, but that there's something she doesn't like.

'Come along then, I'll show you where everything is.'

'If I can't find my way around a kitchen by now…' she grumbles. She's probably right; she's probably been in and out of this kitchen since before I was born – but if I let her get away with this tiny rebellion now, I'll never gain control.

'Then you should hang your head in shame. But Mrs Charlton is somewhat eccentric in her organisational habits, so hush and listen to me. There's little time before I must go and make myself respectable.'

Her look says *That will take hours*.

'Do you want my help or not? Because if Mrs Morwood doesn't get her porridge at its perfect consistency and warmth, or her toast browned to just the right shade, there will be hell to pay… and I'll not stand between you and her for anything in the world.'

She throws up her hands in surrender. Good. I take her on a tour of the kitchen, pantry, the storage rooms in the cellar below. As I give instructions I consider asking if she remembers Heloise. Yet there's something about this woman that's formidable in a way that Mrs Charlton isn't. Or perhaps it's that I sense she cannot be charmed – that I won't be able to get away with anything in her sight. It seems I've rid myself of Luther's oversight and replaced it with hers. I'll need to watch her as she watches me.

* * *

While I'm bathing, my mind turns again to the poisoning of Heledd's family. And I'm convinced it was indeed poisoning, not some animal dying in the well or something leached in from the stones and soil. Intentional and malicious. Yet the apothecary denied having sold any poisons to Luther and my gut tells me he was genuine. Someone contaminated that water supply. Luther sent Luned with "medicine" to the Lewises soon after they first began to sicken. Unable to examine it, I can only assume it was another dose, designed to make them worse or finish them off. Is it possible that Luther only wanted to warn them? Or frighten them? Surely, as lord of the manor, he could simply turn them off the estate? But then they might wander away with whatever knowledge he fears they possess.

So. Poisoning. Or here's a thought: was he so incompetent with his doses that he didn't put enough into the well to do the job? And repeated this with the "medicine"? It's not beyond the realms of possibility. Ah, I wish I could ask around Whitebarrow University, talk to the oldest instructors who might recall Luther Morwood; dig out all his secrets and humiliations.

I cannot ask Luned what she carried for Luther either. She probably would not know, but there's a good chance she'd report back to him that I'd asked. Would she have obeyed him without question purely in the interests of maintaining a life here? Does she truly dream of becoming the Mistress of Morwood? Possibly. She strikes me as sly but I can't quite tell how clever…

Luther and Jessamine's suite is empty. No great thing to search it tonight, see if anything can be found to either prove or disprove my thoughts. And Luther's other room, unless Luned is in there, sleeping more comfortably than her small attic space allows. I'll need to be wary; perhaps I'll look tomorrow morning when she's preparing the children for their day.

The bathwater has gone cold and I am now likely to be late down to breakfast. I heave myself out and begin speedy preparations so Leonora has no excuses to comment on my tardiness.

* * *

The children are listless in the morning, missing their mother, but none of them mentions Luther. Sarai warms to me a little; she keeps looking at the wound on my forehead, her brow creasing with guilt. We trudge through lessons – reading and mathematics – and after lunch I think it's a relief to all of us when I hand them over to Eli for riding lessons. He touches my hand as I leave, but I avoid his gaze.

Back in the house I go upstairs, seeking Leonora to see if she has any tasks for me. Her suite is empty. I go in though, out of curiosity, and the first thing I notice is that the portrait of Heloise is gone, back into the dressing room, on the wall there, hidden from sight. I suspect she'll not discuss her daughter again, not willingly, for it would remind her of a moment of weakness and that'll displease Leonora Morwood. We're both aware that I've gathered some of her secrets – though she doesn't know how many others were gifted to me by my mother – but it would be unwise to remind her. Most people will share a confidence then regret it, and treat

225

you as if you've already betrayed them. Those with the means to hurt you will do so to punish you for what they let slip.

One last look at the record of my mother's living face, then I turn around to leave. On the desk I see the familiar colour of the parchment from Zaria Taverell, unsealed, unfolded. I pick up the two sheets, small writing on one, a legal opinion: Leonora's original investment of Jessamine's dowry has borne considerable fruit – because the amount settled on Jessamine was enormous. Even if she were to leave Luther, taking the original endowment with her, more than sufficient wealth has been created that the Morwoods would remain monied – yet I cannot imagine Leonora wanting to hand back any of that original capital in the event of a divorce; I think of Jessamine whispering how her mother-in-law had hidden all her "precious things" when the family was in penury. Should Jessamine, however, die, the inheritance would bypass Luther entirely and go into a trust fund for the children, to be administered by lawyers in Bellsholm – and Leonora Morwood would not get her hands on that.

Zaria also advises that Leonora would be entirely within her rights to make Albertine the heir, replacing son with granddaughter. She would be wise to set up a small stipend for Luther's support to keep him contented (or as contented as he is ever likely to be), and then to ensure there is a separate trustee appointed to take care of the children's financial needs until Albertine attains her majority. If she wishes to go ahead with this change to her will, then on the second page are the recommended terms and clauses. Leonora should make any amendments and notations thereon and return it to the office for a final document to be created.

I put the parchment back where I found it and return to the corridor.

I understand why Leonora would want to make this change.

I'm certain Zaria would be delighted to ruin Luther's comfortable life.

Such a change would make Luther powerless.

Such a change would ruin my plan.

Such a change would put Albertine in a perilous position.

What can I do?

What can I do?

I stand at the top of the stairs, clench my shaking hands, slow my breathing. There's nothing I can do just yet. I must be patient. I must do something. There's nothing I can do. Not yet. I blink hard to stop the tears of frustration. All my plans, all my promises, will they be all for naught because of an old woman's whim?

A voice calls up from the foyer. Burdon, yelling my name in a less than butlerish fashion.

I take the stairs at a sedate pace until I reach the ground floor. His expression is one of utter displeasure. 'Some people here to see you, Miss Todd.'

My heart flips – the last time someone arrived for me it was not welcome. He flings open the front door. A group of perhaps ten folk, mostly women; I think I recognise some faces from my trips to the Tarn.

'They apparently have health issues, Miss Todd, and seem to think you are the person to talk to.' Burdon's tone is neutral but he can't control the set of his lips.

'Thank you, Burdon.' I remain calm, look at the group. 'If you'd

227

all be good enough to go around to the kitchen entrance? I'll chat with you there.'

* * *

No good deed goes unpunished. I'd seen to twelve individuals by the end of the afternoon, under Tib's curious and vaguely disapproving gaze. I saw everything from haemorrhoids to infected scratches, bruises inflicted by husbands, painful monthly courses, indigestion, bad breath, headaches, colds and several things in between. I sent each and every one away either with a mix if I had it to hand and instructions on how to take it, or a note for the apothecary so the right thing might be dispensed. At one point Leonora wandered in, stared, eyebrows lifted, as the Tarn folk bowed and murmured greetings and well wishes. She said not a word, but nodded, sharpish, then departed. Heledd Jones arrived just as I was seeing off the last patient.

'And here she is, the source of my current misfortune,' I said.

'Now, don't be like that.' She grinned and hoisted the plump baby into my lap. 'Many's the woman who'd kill to be so popular without having to open her legs.'

We both burst into gales of raucous laughter, and I heard Tib Postlethwaite snorting in the laundry room.

'What's with this one?' I ask, dangling the infant as if she might have forgotten it's hers.

'A rash.'

'Arrowroot powder,' I say. 'It's not as if you wouldn't have known what to do yourself – it's common enough knowledge, don't need a doctor for that. So, why are you really here?'

'Zaria—'

'Oh!' I'd forgotten my promise. I lay the child on the table, careful to keep him on the shawl he's wrapped in – no bare baby bum on Tib Postlethwaite's cutting surface! – and gently peel away the swaddling. Bright red skin and I can feel the heat coming off it. The lad grizzles. 'Hush.' For all the lawyer has been in my thoughts, it's because of my obsessing over the contents of her letter to Leonora. 'The tincture for her wife. Hold him here.'

Once she's got a hand on his fat little leg to stop him from rolling off the table, I go to the pantry, to the shelves where I've started storing more and more herbs so I'm not constantly up and down the stairs for such things. I collect what I need and return. I take a little hot water from the kettle over the hob and mix in some feverfew, then add cold water and honey for sweetness. I coax it into the little one's mouth to prevent any illness from the fiery rash. Then I lave the area with lavender wash and pat it dry before sprinkling arrowroot powder onto his skin. Delighted at the relief he begins to gurgle and kick his feet in the air.

'How are your family?' I finally think to ask.

'Entirely well and they can't stop singing your praises.'

'Runs in the family apparently,' I grumble as I begin mixing a tincture of pellitory of the wall. 'Your father works a lot with Luther Morwood?'

'Of course. Da manages the woodland. He's answered directly to him these past few years since the old lady's been poorly.'

Poorly.

'Ah. Kind of him to send them medicine when they were ill.'

She just makes a *Hmmmm* sound and I wonder if the coincidence of her family's worsening illness with Luther's kindness has been a matter of discussion. I say no more about it. I decant the liquid into the last of my small bottles, and seal it with a cork.

Handing it over, I say, 'For Zaria. I've no doubt she'll remember my instructions.'

'Thank you. What's she owe you?' Heledd dips a hand into her pocket, but I shake my head.

'Nothing today. But let her know I might beg a favour in return.'

Heledd nods. 'Come for afternoon tea tomorrow if you can get away?'

The idea seems delightfully shocking: social interaction just for the sake of it. I hesitate then accept. 'Thank you.'

* * *

When I finally dragged myself to the table – having remembered to dress for dinner and ensure my charges were also suitably attired – the children were filled with their riding adventures and seemed to have forgotten for a while at least that Jessamine was away. I'd wondered if Leonora might decide to banish me from the dining room as part of her quest to "raise standards", but then she would have to manage her grandchildren on her own. She did, however, listen to them with greater patience than I'd ever witnessed, and asked more questions of Albertine than she was wont to do, about her studies, her reading. The girl noticed her grandmother's attention and, after an initial period of nervousness, began to glow. When the meal was done, Leonora instructed Luned to take them for their baths and bedtime as she wished to speak with me for a moment. I promised I would look in on them before they slept and read a story.

As the door closes, Leonora Morwood fixes me with a look. 'You're popular, turning my kitchen into a regular market square.'

Too tired to dissemble, I reply, 'Shouldn't have told everyone it was me who restored your sight. You could have said it was a miracle, then they'd all be beating a path to the priest's door

230

instead of ours.' *Ours*. Of course, there's no point anyone going to the priest – Father – anymore, is there?

'That priest,' she fair spits. 'His only miracle is turning perfectly good wine into piss.'

I laugh.

There's a great flame of temper in her eyes and so much hatred – and I suddenly understand why she didn't send him packing back to Lodellan, tail between his legs after my mother was sent forth. She kept him here to know how he suffered, deprived of any chance of advancement. Kept him here to watch his suffering – and then her sight left her. But then the fire goes out, she's back in control.

'You really are the most facetious creature, Asher Todd.' She sighs, sits back in her seat – she's taken over Luther's head of the table position and I think he'll be hard-pressed to wrest it back when he returns – points a long finger at me. 'And here I was going to say that you should use the surgery for your physician's duties. Don't want the great unwashed traipsing through my lovely home. And if you think Mrs Charlton will put up with it when she returns, you should think again. Now close your mouth, you look like a simpleton.'

'But the surgery is—'

'Luther hasn't set foot in there since the day after he returned from Whitebarrow trailing his shame behind him.' She shakes her head.

'What did he do there, Mrs Morwood?' I ask quietly, not really hoping for an answer.

She makes a strangled noise. 'There was a girl... always a girl where Luther's concerned, but this one wasn't the sort who

231

could be paid off. The Chancellor's daughter… I was given to believe she'd have married Luther, but her father did not consider my son a good enough mate.' Leonora wipes a hand over her face, then says so low I almost don't hear it, 'I heard later that he'd subjected the girl to the medical attentions of a colleague to remove the object of her shame.'

'It did not go well,' I say, for I had heard rumours of a former chancellor who'd lost his only child and his reason. He was found wandering in the labyrinth of the library many nights in a row, until it was too late and he'd discovered a place to hang himself from the rafters. It was the smell that led the librarians to his body at last. *Oh, your messes are far-reaching, Uncle Luther!*

'I believe if Luther had not already left the university he'd have been arrested.' She smiles grimly. 'That will teach the Chancellor to act precipitously.'

I open my mouth, about to pursue the thread, but she clears her throat and gives me a hard stare.

'Asher Todd, the Tarn needs a doctor or at least someone who knows what they're doing. There's been an ancient hedge-witch or two, but I think you're more able than they. This is something I can do for the good of the people who rely on me. Something that's been denied them by Luther, and I can do this because I can unseat Luther. And I can unseat Luther all because of *you*. So, I suppose it's a reward of sorts, although there's plenty of work to be had. Eventually the children will be grown, but you can stay here, continuing to help.'

I don't know what else to say except, 'Thank you, Mrs Morwood.'

Something sits in my throat and I don't know if it's rage or grief or gratitude, or perhaps all three. An offer of a place. An offer of a continuing home. No doubt it's powered by some self-interest – why would she want to let me and my skills go? – but a kindness of sorts. And a blow to Luther.

Morwood is changing. Morwood is changing because I came. Morwood will change further still.

'Mrs Morwood,' I say, knowing I should stop myself from speaking. 'Teaching Albertine to run the estate… the document from Zaria Taverell… are you thinking of changing your will?'

She quirks one eyebrow at me, amused, not irritated. As if to say *Can't put anything over you, Asher Todd.* Then my grandmother grins, wickedly, and says, 'Shall I tell you a story, Asher?'

24

Once upon a time, there was a little girl called Matilda. Her hair was dark, her skin olive, and her eyes as yellow as corn. She lived in a small village with her parents and brothers. Some days she was industrious, working hard to help her mother around the house. Other days she would sit at the window and watch those who passed with the same stare men and dogs use to eye meat and women. No one quite knew what to make of her, but she harmed no one and was loyal and loving to her family, so the villagers tolerated her eccentricity.

Matilda's maternal grandmother lived in a small cottage in the woods. She had a reputation as a wise woman, a healer, and – if crossed – as an efficient caster of curses. Matilda loved to spend time with her grandmother, who taught her herblore and told tales of women who chose to be something other than what society thought they should. Matilda's mother did not like her daughter to spend too much time with the old woman, for her mother scared her and Beth feared that in time her daughter would grow to be like the old witch. Then God only knew what would happen.

A good few years after her bloods started, Matilda was still unmarried in a village that married off its females at a young age. It kept them busy – rearing children and tending a house left little time for questioning. Matilda, though, was different. What had been tolerated as amusing eccentricity in the child was seen as a streak of danger in a young woman.

At seventeen, Matilda walked with a swaying gait that mesmerised and unsettled those who watched. For a girl as yet unbedded she seemed to know how best to affect the men around her, and even some of the women. Her attraction was effortless, like a scent that floated from her skin and tickled the nostrils of her admirers.

Village boys her own age would have liked to know what waited under her skirts. They had tried to find out; some had worked up the courage to ask her to walk out with them, but when she rested her yellow eyes on them, their cool depths turned the would-be suitor's knees to jelly and his heart to lead. Matilda smiled and walked on.

Her mother noticed the gazes that followed her daughter. Best, she thought, to take advantage of them, of the girl's beauty, of the desire she roused. Beth approached several families with the offer of Matilda as a wife. While no one was so rude as to laugh out loud, no one accepted. As the tone of her offer became desperate, Matilda's mother sensed pity in the eyes of those she entreated, shaking their heads and saying no.

Something about Matilda suggested she would not be easily quelled, would not go quietly to a bed not of her own choosing and, perhaps, children gotten on her and left in her care would turn out as different as their mother; a yellow hue of strangeness running in their veins.

* * *

Each time a boy faded from her daughter's side Beth's hopes shrank. They mingled with her fear and tasted of bitter almonds at the back of her throat.

One afternoon, she called her daughter to her. Beth's voice was harsh, with disappointment, with the fear that put a hard edge on her concern for her child. And failure – she could smell the scent of failure on her own skin – in spite of her best efforts the child had turned out too much like her grandmother. When she closed her eyes, Matilda's mother saw her daughter living alone and strange in a cottage deep in the woods.

On this particular afternoon, she handed Matilda a basket of food and told her to take it to her grandmother. The old woman was ill, unable to care for herself, and Matilda was to stay with her as long as she was needed. If the old woman died, then Matilda was to come home and the men would go back and bury the old witch.

'Don't you care, Mother?'

Taken aback, Beth slapped Matilda so hard that blood spurted from the girl's nose. When the yellow eyes turned on her mother's furiously pale face, they didn't even blink.

Matilda wrapped herself in a red cloak that her grandmother had knitted. The wool was the same shade as the blood trickling from her nose; as she wiped the fluid away it settled into the warp and weft of the fabric as if it belonged there. She plucked the basket from her mother's hand and turned. Beth's voice stopped her momentarily.

'She's not how she should be. She never was, not a normal mother, not a normal woman. Nor are you.' The yellow eyes flicked to her once more, amused, fluid, fearless.

'No. Not like you,' Matilda said, and with that the last apron

236

string snapped as if severed by sharp, angry teeth. Matilda left, her hips and hair swaying. She did not see the outstretched hand reaching to pull back the words, nor the tears that ran down her mother's face.

* * *

The way to Granny's wended through the woods. Stick to the path, *was the village wisdom. Don't leave it or you might be lost – worse still, you might be changed. Change was worse than loss; change meant you no longer fitted into your place, you couldn't be recognised by your kin, and that was the greatest danger of all.*

A boy followed her. A little younger than her, but almost a man, and desperate to win the admiration of the older boys. The task he had chosen to prove himself was Matilda; his goal was amorphous. "Matilda" encompassed a myriad of things: walking out, kissing, sliding a hand up her skirt, or perhaps something more brutal, something he did not dare name.

He watched as the red cloak disappeared into the woods, flashing in and out of the trees and undergrowth. He hung back until they were far enough from the village that any protests she made would not be heard.

She cast a furtive look behind her and left the path, stepped into the undergrowth and tugged on the tie of her red cloak. The warm wool slipped from her shoulders as she disappeared between two enormous tree trunks.

Swiftly he moved forward then saw, coming from the other direction, an enormous grey wolf. A male, in its prime, almost five feet tall at the shoulder, with grey eyes to match its fur. It stopped, sniffed (the boy was grateful he was downwind), then followed Matilda's scent.

The boy had only a small knife. He didn't like Matilda enough to risk his life for her; then again, her gratitude might be worth something. Hearing nothing more, he moved forward.

The first noise to come to his ears was growling, low and hard. Next came a whimpering, a moan: deep, but female. He crept through the trees, his boot catching on something soft. Her cloak lay like a spill of blood, still warm from the touch of her skin, intimate against his hand. His eyes alighted on the rest of Matilda's discarded clothes and then on Matilda herself.

She knelt on all fours, naked and brown, her face against that of the great grey wolf as they licked and sniffed at each other. Then she turned and offered herself to the beast, shaking with excitement, whimpering. The wolf covered her and she howled as he entered her.

As the boy watched, hard and panicked, he saw fur sprout over her limbs, saw her teeth lengthen and her jaw distend, saw her yellow eyes slit in lupine desire as the great wolf moved over her. Unable to stop himself, the boy rose. His movement caught Matilda's attention. She howled in fury and, with an effort, pulled herself from her mate.

The boy's eyes widened. He saw sharp teeth in a wet mouth, a white circle set within a red one. Saw the muscles in her forelegs tighten and bunch in the moment before she leapt. There was only sky above for the briefest of moments, then pain and a wet sound, and, finally, nothing more.

When the boy was still and bloody, she gave him one last shake. At this sign, the male, who had waited patiently, joined her and they ate their fill, as though at a bridal feast.

* * *

Matilda shrugged back into her human skin. She picked up her basket and her cloak and continued on her way. The great grey wolf loped beside her, sometimes pushing his head against her hand.

Behind them, a woodsman stumbled onto the remains of the boy. His distress was multiplied by the fact that he was the boy's father. He tracked the wolf's prints, noticing how they intersected with a human set of prints.

Matilda and her mate arrived at Granny's house. The wolf waited patiently, lying across the doorstep like a large dog while Matilda entered.

'Still alive?' she asked the lump in the bed.

Laughter answered her as she put the kettle on the fire. Settling herself on the edge of the bed, Matilda held the old woman's hand and peered into her face. Surrounded by hair that had once been black but was now almost white, the face was strange: thin, the angles more lupine than human, the pale eyes tilted towards the sides of the head, yet beautiful in the same way as a wild thing. She looked weary but well and Matilda thought she would recover.

'Still alive, little sweet. What did you bring me? Some of your mother's broth?' Her eyes greedily picked at the basket lying on the table. 'Did she send good wishes, too, my daughter?'

'She fears.' Matilda dropped her gaze, sadness that she had hidden from her mother showed there.

'She always has,' said Granny. 'Beth fears for you more than she can love you. Because you're different.'

'Because I'm like you.'

'Yes. Like me.' She opened her mouth to continue but growling and shouting outside the cottage interrupted them.

Matilda put her nose to the windowpane in time to see a woodsman raise his axe and cleave her mate in two. She howled in despair. Her grandmother struggled out of bed.

The woodsman hacked at the body of the wolf, his sobs punctuating the slap of the axe in the wet flesh. The trees rang until the mingled sounds were absorbed into their bark, marking them as surely as age would.

The man stopped only when he heard the grandmother calling to him.

'Thank you for saving us,' she croaked. She touched his shoulder and urged him inside. He blinked his eyes to accustom them to the gloom of the cottage. 'But we didn't need saving.'

'You killed my husband,' said Matilda. She dropped her red cloak to the floor as her real covering made its way from inside to settle on her flesh.

* * *

In the autumn darkness, Matilda's mother lay straight and stiff in her bed.

Her husband's snoring stirred the air with a strange violence and she felt the urge to poke him awake, make him roll over, have him share her sleeplessness. But she had done it before and knew that it would earn her a slap across the ear, a casually bruising blow that would ache in the morning.

She turned on her side, facing the window, seeing the full face of the moon stare down at her. Beth could feel the pull of it in the tides of her blood and tried to studiously ignore it just as she had her whole life. Denying her mother, denying her self, denying her difference. Denying her only daughter.

Matilda had not come home. It was three days since anyone

240

had seen her. The boy's body had been found soon enough. When the party of hunters descended on the old woman's cottage they found the remains of the woodsman, of Granny's white nightdress and of Matilda's red cloak, smouldering in the last coals of the fire.

A wolf had gotten in.

No, more than one: a pack.

Had to be a pack to slaughter three adults.

Matilda and her grandmother had been dragged away. Their bodies were being kept in some lupine larder.

Beth knew better. Her blood knew better. Somewhere they trod worn forest trails, the soft pads of their paws soundless and strong, eyes bright and all-seeing, coats soft as velvet and warm as wool, tongues long, wet and obscenely red.

A scratching at the door brought her back to the sleepless bed on which she lay. She slid from the sheets, slipped through the few rooms of the cottage silent as a shadow. In the front garden sat a young wolf. Behind it, outside the gate, sat another, older, its fur almost white. Two gazes, both intent, both cold, held her. Briefly she regretted opening the door, but it was a dried leaf of a thought, picked up and blown away as soon as it entered her head.

The young wolf rose and made its way down the garden path towards her mother. Beth, knees weak, sank to sit on the stoop. The yellow eyes mesmerised her and the beast stopped in front of her. Beth lifted her hand, rough and red with years of toil, reached out and fastened onto the fur, burying deep into the warmth and texture. She closed her eyes.

Surely now, *she thought,* surely now I am dead.

Then the fur, the warm body, were gone and when she opened her eyes the two beasts were fading into the night, down silent streets until they found the woods. In her lap, Matilda's mother found a long red skein of wool, damp with saliva and strong with the scent of wolf. She wrapped it around her wrist as tears slid down her face, stinging like nettles.

* * *

Leonora sits back, looking satisfied.

The whole time she was telling the tale her smile did not waver, and I felt pinned beneath her gaze. Listening, I couldn't help but wonder how much she knew. About me. About Eli. So, I held my breath, said nothing though my heart seemed to thud more loudly than it should. I said nothing, gave nothing away, not even to ask what she meant. Eventually, she tapped the table with one long finger.

'The moral of the tale, Asher, is that when your child disappoints you, you may find a grandchild to fill the breach. Sometimes drive skips a generation. Sometimes you make mistakes with your own children, but time gives you the opportunity to make it right with their offspring.'

And part of me wants to howl. Part of me wants to shout, *But I'm your granddaughter too! Your blood is in me, look at all I've done – don't you see yourself in* me?

Yet I don't. Even in this moment – when I want to scream, when I want to strike out at poor Albertine, whose fault none of this is – I know that I can never disclose what I've done. What I still do. What I will do.

I nod, say, 'I see. How fortune has favoured you with a second chance, Mrs Morwood.' Then I rise. 'I should see to the children. I must keep my promise.'

242

* * *

The morning is a blur. There is too much to do in the surgery but I do what I can: dusting, sweeping up mouse droppings, laying traps for those who remain, polishing as many pieces of glass as possible, washing and sterilising each instrument. Things are pristine and unused, untouched by Luther. I send the Binions to the apothecary with a list of herbs that do not grow in the manor gardens, and they not only bring back every single one, but find clippings of most for me to transplant. I give them a few more of the coins Leonora's allocated as a budget for my little practice and thank them. They don't reply, but I realise they're not the fey idiots others believe. I fill jars, slip small neatly written labels inside each one, line them up in place. There is still more to do, but I am as close to ready as I can be. I had thought, when I was young – far too young to realise what the world held for me – and reading those books in our second saviour's library that I would have professional chambers. That, as an adult, I would help people, dispense things to make them better. But as I grew, I eventually realised that no matter how much I read, how much I learned, whether it was freely given or knowledge I stole in the depths of the night – that no matter how clever I was – I would never have such a place to call my own.

Every night, cleaning laboratories and classrooms, offices and the narrow aisles of the enormous library, the days too after Archie gave me a means to be present in those spaces without hiding so much. Every second of every minute of every hour of every day… seeing those idiot boys with their privilege and power and no care for anything beyond themselves… seeing them getting the education I'd have slit more than one throat for. Seeing them

243

fail, appear in classes drunk and loud and ignorant – yet remain. Remain and make their way through their studies, achieve their degree (whether with honours or otherwise, it did not matter), grasp their title, go out into the world to assemble surgeries such as I would never have. Knowing how badly some behaved and still retained their place at Whitebarrow made Luther's failure all the more impressive.

The university provided learning, but only for a chosen few. A gathering of scholars to pursue their new theories – specifically to pursue a science untainted by the old ideas of magic, superstition – independent of the Church but still aligned with it and its goals of digging out anything they could not understand or control. That meant all the women who practised such cures as involved ritual as much as medicine. Some of the histories I read told how folk deserted the cunning women and witches, turned their backs and chose *modernity*. But the truth was that the Church hunted them, made them hated, made them dead. Drowned them, burned them, hanged them. The highest of the god-hounds encouraged and funded the neoteric medicine and destroyed anyone who failed to change. The women who could offer help soon began to disappear, living hidden deep in forests where they could remain unmarked and unburnt. Some continued to visit them, trading food and goods for healing. But for the most part, without an alternative, people had little choice but to turn to the doctors and their ilk.

Now. Here I am with everything I dreamt of – or a large part of it. The thing, at least, that I wanted for myself. I think I could be happy here, but for the other things that I did not wish for but are too difficult to be rid of. I could be happy here but for what

I know about this family, my family. But for the things I have promised and cannot escape.

As I scrubbed and washed the sanctum I could forget, for hours at a time, all the matters that I did not wish to think upon. The acts I cannot escape. Leonora's plans for Albertine, to make Luther nothing in his own home. But a tension runs beneath my skin, waiting for Mrs Morwood to hand me a sealed document, to say *Take this to Zaria Taverell*; for her will to be done. I've no fear now she'll ask anyone else to do it for she doesn't trust anyone in that house. I know I need to be ready when Luther returns; I will need to act quickly. But for some brief periods, I can forget.

In the afternoon I walk into the Tarn and take tea with Heledd, listen with a surprise that's not entirely manufactured about the disappearance of the priest. Genuinely I have tried to put him out of mind, but my father's insisted on appearing in the corner of my eye every so often – not in ghostly form, but an echo of some sort. A very weak one, mind you, but I do not think it's guilt; I'm quite well acquainted with that.

When I ask how long he's been missing, Heledd looks somewhat embarrassed. No one knows, she says. No one noticed until the congregation turned up this morning to find the little church empty, the little house too. The man so unpleasant – and with a history of wandering off drunk for days on end – no one had bothered to seek him out. *Will the constable look?* I enquired, and she shrugged. The priest would return in his own time or he would not. I wonder how long it will be before Leonora writes to the cathedral-city to ask for a new one.

We talk about the surgery and I can at last show someone how excited I am. I feel like a child with a new toy – even though it won't last, this sanctuary. And I know that as soon as I leave she'll be telling her neighbours, that gossip will speed the news around the Tarn, that there'll be a string of villagers waiting for me tomorrow.

And when I return? Hurrying in the cold, barely beating the darkness? I go once more to the surgery. I make a fire for warmth, which I will bank before I leave so it will be easy to breathe life into tomorrow. I sit for a while because it is quiet and it is *mine*. I determinedly keep my mind clear of troubling thoughts and for a while, such a little while, I am calm, I am *home*.

And when I am suddenly hungry and in desperate need of dinner, I rise and turn around to see a figure in the doorway. A sharp intake of breath – I didn't hear anyone – then they move, step from shadow into light.

It's Luned.

I laugh, clutch at my chest. 'You startled me.'

She doesn't say sorry or even shrug, she just paces to the desk, to where there's the spare chair for the patient, and takes a seat. Luned lifts her face, watches, waiting for me to join her. There's no less dislike in her expression, but it's twinned with desperation. I sit.

'What is it, Luned?'

Her mouth opens and a howl issues forth. She cries like a child and I suppose that's really what she is, not much more than eighteen. I wait. I don't hold her hand or offer platitudes – we've not liked each other enough (or at all) to do that. But I'm patient, hand her a handkerchief, then pour her a glass of the lemon-blossom brandy I've brought over for patients. She takes a sip, hiccups, sips again, wipes her eyes and nose.

I repeat, 'What is it, Luned?'

246

Her voice is flat. 'I'm pregnant.'

'Ah.'

'He'll get rid of me if he finds out.'

'Who?' I ask as if I didn't know.

'Mr Morwood, you idiot!' she yells.

'And did you simply come here to insult me?' If I hadn't thought before that she was hard to like, I certainly do now.

'I need your help, you bitch.'

'Then be a little more polite, you cunt,' I hiss at her, and the language shuts her up. She stares in shock. 'Now. How far along are you?'

'A month?' She shakes her head, looks away.

'I thought,' I say thinly, 'you were taking precautions.'

'So did I, but it turns out sometimes things don't work.'

'Indeed.' I scratch my head, rub my eyes with tiredness and irritation that I have to help this awful girl; that my sense of peace has been burned up like a moth too close to a flame. There's a moment when I feel everything – myself, my mind, the world – wobble. Tilt as if I might slide off its surface and fall into blackness. I clench my hands into fists, feel the nails cutting into my palms. The pain pulls me back, steadies me. 'What have you been using?'

'Silphium.' I raise a brow and she says, 'My old nan knew a thing or two. She was the cunning woman in the Tarn until she died last winter.'

'Ah.' *Pity she didn't teach you a few more things while she still breathed.* 'Well, sometimes it doesn't work if you've been drinking a lot of alcohol.' She looks away and I think of those empty bottles of wine that have appeared in the kitchen some mornings when there's been none consumed at the dinner table.

247

'I'll examine you.'

'No!' she fair screams and you'd think I'd made an indecent proposal. 'Just give me something to get rid of it. I can't have it. He can't know. Just help me! If I have it, I'll never get away from here.'

And because I don't like her, and because I like Luther even less, I don't insist. I don't send her away empty-handed. I grind bay leaves and chamaepitys in the mortar, add some stinking gladwin for good measure, then put the powder into a small blue bottle. I tell her how to take it, the measure of it, how much hot water to steep it in and for how long before she drinks it on going to bed. I warn her it will cause cramps, but as she is not so far along they should not be too awful. She does not thank me when she leaves. I find my hands are shaking long after she's an absence.

* * *

I put the children to bed after dinner and read them a story about a mother who turns into a swan and must fly away, but in the end she is reunited with her offspring. When I've tucked the girls in, I escort Connell back to his room, tuck him in even though he asks if he's too old for that.

I smile. 'Do you think you are?'

He shakes his head. 'Not too old tonight.'

I kiss his forehead and agree, 'Not too old tonight. But perhaps tomorrow night.'

'Perhaps.' He grips my hand as I'm about to turn away. 'When will Father come back, do you think?'

'A while yet,' I say. 'Four days' travel to St Dane's, then perhaps he will rest for a few days more, then another four to return.'

'So, not too soon then?'

248

'Not too soon,' I say softly and squeeze his hand. 'Sleep well, Connell. You're safe.'

I searched Jessamine and Luther's rooms last night and found no sign of any poison or herbs that might be used to make it. I only know that Luther made another attempt; he knows the Lewises have survived for he speaks with Mr Lewis on an almost daily basis (or did until Leonora unseated him). Surely he'd have said something to me if he thought I'd saved them and thwarted him? His reaction to his mother's recovery was a sign enough of how he felt about such interference. Perhaps it was only a warning? Or perhaps it was nothing more than an amusement and experiment? Or perhaps he simply cannot be bothered to try again.

When I go to bed – my own, not Eli's – I sleep deeply and dream of the night I found the Witches of Whitebarrow.

25

In the first days after Archie found me and moved me into his home, I became more diurnal than I had been, less inclined to stalking the corridors of the university at night. I revelled, I think, in at last being able to be seen doing what I could do – or at least the research part and some of the smaller experiments (all science, those ones, no magic).

But eventually I missed the darkness and the quiet of those cold hours. I'd never been afraid there with only a lantern for company. Never felt the blackness as a threat, and my favourite place was the Great Library with its labyrinthine shelving system, a maze that you could get lost in if you didn't know the signs carved into the sides of the bookcases, little nubs and dips to show whether you went left or right. Students had been known to become disoriented in there, shouting out for someone to come and collect them and lead them to safety so they didn't starve, only to be found as bones years later or as unhappy wandering spirits. The head librarian had taught me the codes as soon as I'd begun cleaning there – I don't think he liked sharing those elevated secrets with so lowly a creature, but equally he'd misplaced cleaners before and didn't want to repeat the experience, not least because it's hellishing hard to get decomposition stains out of book leather. And eventually I realised there was another pattern to them, not simply a means to navigate the stacks, but a way to find a path through to the centre of the library, the dead centre of all those books.

It took me a long time to figure that out – I'm embarrassed by how long – but I wasn't looking for a cipher in the building itself, just in the books it housed. And while they were all valuable and furnished me with much of the knowledge I have today, it was in fact the structure that contained the greatest secret.

In the middle of it all, a painting on a pillar, I thought at first, of a door, with an inscription:

WHAT WE COME FROM,
WHERE WE GO TO,
WHAT WOMEN WILL COLLECT ALL THEIR DAYS.

I laughed, thought of my menial job here, and snorted, 'Dust.'

The door was a real thing, wasn't it?

It popped open, didn't it?

Hesitating only slightly, I passed through and found a set of stone stairs circling down and down and down. My footsteps echoed so that when I finally arrived (and make no mistake I became concerned after a while that I would descend for eternity), they were waiting expectantly.

Three old women, beldams, pale as pale could be, paler than the moon because they saw no sun at all, nor had they for too many years to count. One said a century; another scoffed and claimed two; the third said both were idiots, as if it could have been less than three.

'So long since there's been a guest!' said one, breaking the spiral.

'Oh, at least a century or two,' another croaked.

'No one since that one with the red hair,' whispered the third and they exchanged a glance that could only be called fearful, then back again to examine my own brilliant red locks. '*That* one. She who might dare anything.'

'I wonder if she still walks above?'

'I think we'd know of her passing, sisters. When one such as her goes beneath? The world whispers of it. The air would tell us, the earth and water.'

'What was her name?' I asked, thinking of the book I'd found, *A Manual for the Students of the Tintern Dollmakers' Academy*. Of the notes therein and my sense that whoever had written them would dare almost anything simply because they could.

Yet they'd not answered, but rather taken another tack. 'How did you find us? Find your way in?'

'Your riddle. I doubt any man would know the answer, and there are no women up there.'

'None but you.'

'Curious creature you are.'

'Well, you've found us. What do you want of us?' They spoke in the same sequence every time, a chorus, a round, a set order. Perhaps a habit or perhaps a sort of binding.

'Who are you?' I'd asked.

'We are the mothers, the sisters, the daughters, the aunts, the cousins, the nieces, the grandmothers of all the burned and drowned and hanged.'

'We are the first.'

'We shall probably be the last.'

All together: 'We are the Witches of Whitebarrow.'

I tilted my head. I'd seen no reference to anything like them in any book I'd read. Heard nothing of them from any other woman to whom I'd spoken. Might they be something so old they'd been forgotten? That so few sought them because their entire existence was unknown? How did that other, that one they wouldn't name, find out about them? So many questions I'd never have the answer to! My hesitation left a gap they did not like.

'Whatever flows in your veins that makes you different and dangerous? It comes from us. The things we did, what we became, whatever we released into the sky and the dirt and the seas? It chooses at its own wild will. It's found a home in you.' With this speech the first seemed she might apologise for that, but before I could dig further – *What had they done?* – the second chimed in:

'If you are here, you have a request, you wish to learn something – so, what do you want?'

'And your time with us is finite, child, so ask.'

'But…'

'Come, come! Time has wings and surely you realise this place is not one where you can stay? Not as you are? Alive?'

'The living may only dance with the dead for a little while, girl.'

'The world leads you where you need to go. It brought you to us, and we are bound to answer by the laws that hold us here. But you must hurry.'

'Who bound you?' I asked, and only then worried that perhaps I might only have a limited number of questions and I was wasting them like a fool.

'Her name was—'

'Can you recall, sister?'

'Surely we've written it down somewhere?'

They all gestured with identical vagueness to the room around them – and I finally took note of it. A high-ceilinged cavern more like, with three beds, many bookshelves overflowing with tomes, threadbare carpets on the floor and light, I realised, coming from orange globes that floated around the room giving off warmth and illumination. Desks covered with papers and more books, open notebooks blank and filled, inkwells and quills, pencils and brushes. I wondered why the dead might require such things, but restrained myself from asking – besides, wouldn't I choose these exact items for my afterlife?

The witches wore ebony dresses of indeterminate design, their hair white and eyebrows feathery (as if with great age they'd not thinned and fallen out but grown like developing wings). Their eyes were uniformly black, nails trimmed neatly and clean, each one's face a roadmap of lines as if each wrinkle represented a year. I'd have given anything to know where they'd come from, who they were before they landed here, but I did not know how long they might tolerate me and my queries – and if I might be trapped here if I tarried too long – so I asked the one thing I'd been trying so desperately to discover.

And when I did they gave a little wail, said I was as bad as *that* one, another one with red hair, the one who *dared*. Who'd asked for the very same spell. But they were bound to answer me, weren't they? Had told me so themselves. They protested, yet still spilled forth more tales of that woman in a tone of gleeful gossip; they named her reluctantly – *Selke* – spoke of all the great and terrible things she could and did do.

They found the right book and gave me pen and paper so I could copy the spell, the ingredients, the ritual – only that one, they said. One was all anyone got. Then I folded the paper and put it carefully in my pocket and prayed this wasn't simply some dream and I wasn't still in Archie's bed in his house, sleeping beneath his weight, the sounds of his snoring a constant saw that I'd learned to ignore.

When I was done the Witches gave me gifts: a mortar and pestle, and a bag of coins, strange ancient things, unmarked for making change, and I was sure I'd never be able to exchange them for their true value, for the gold was so bright and soft and pure-looking. The old women warned me to be wary of what I might do, what I could do, what I would do – but they said it without much hope. After all, hadn't they themselves ignored any warnings and changed the nature of the world in doing so?

And then at last, they urged me on my way, up and out, back to the spiral staircase, my lantern held high, up and up and up to a darkness that seemed wrong when I was rising, rising, rising until finally I stumbled into the library, into that secluded spot in the centre of the great building. I found my escape from the labyrinth, wandered home as if starlight lit my path. As if all my obstacles were behind me.

I still think of them sometimes, how they were not strange in their appearance, only hazy in their recall and conversation. There was no sign of food or drink – perhaps they had grown beyond the need for anything but knowledge and spells. Perhaps the dead – if they were truly so – do not eat. They didn't strike me as malign or threatening, only to say that the cold black hours were best for the making of dark and terrible things.

And in the morning when I awoke fully clothed on top of the covers, I thought I must have dreamed it all until I reached into my pocket and found the piece of paper there, a little crumpled but real enough; that and the heft of the coin purse, the mortar and pestle. I went back that very day, to the Great Library, retraced my steps but could not find where I had been. But from then on I began to plan my departure from Whitebarrow and Archie.

* * *

I awoke heavy-eyed, exhausted. Though the dream of the Witches was never frightening, it bore a weight each and every time. I grumped at the children in the morning and snarled at Albertine before lunch with such venom that we were both shocked and burst into tears. She apologised that she didn't know what she'd done, and I apologised because I knew full well what I *had* done. The child had never caused me harm, but I knew Leonora's plans for her had dug into my skin, my heart, my mind. The jealousy of one grandchild to see another favoured so – neither of her siblings seemed bothered by the time she was spending with their grandmother (indeed Connell had whispered he was glad it wasn't him), but they had not lived the life I had.

They'd never been deprived of a grandmother – she might not have been the best of them, but she was something. I'd had nothing. I'd had my mother and all her tales and her tempers. I had the version she'd given me of Leonora Morwood, and then I came here. Came to a place I might have belonged but could never claim. Came here and found that I did not entirely hate the woman – that she was like Heloise in some ways, she was as Heloise had said after a fashion, but entirely different in others. And I wanted, idiot child that I was, to be loved by her. To have her approval and her pride. And I thought – more with heart and less with head – that if I helped her gain her desires, I would be given love in return. I would be special. I would be seen. I'd be something other than Asher Todd who hid her hair, made her face plain, kept to the shadows too scared to even let her shoes make a sound in the world.

After all I had done for her, and then to see everything handed so easily to Albertine, through no fault or will or wish of her own… it hurt. It was neither rational nor fair on my part, to strike out at a child who loved me – and I loved in return. But it hurt nonetheless.

When we were friends again and all tears had dried, I was still glad to pass Albertine off to Leonora and the younger ones to a sullen Luned. I encountered Eli as I marched from the house to the surgery; he drew me behind a tree and kissed me, then I sniped and snarled. I was equally short with my first *real* patients, but no one seemed surprised or complained. Perhaps they simply expected this of both doctors and cunning women.

I'm tidying up when I hear a noise at the door; thinking it might be Luned giving me warning, today I turn. I wonder what she'll say after yesterday's performance, but it's not Luned. It's Archie O'Sullivan and he does not look at all pleased.

'You're a liar,' he spits with more fire than I've ever seen from him. He comes towards me and his gaze is locked not on my face but my finger – on Meliora's ring. I step back, keep the stone table between us, hold up the opposite hand signalling him to stop.

'Archie. What are you doing here? I told you I would meet you in Whitebarrow.'

'You're a liar,' he repeats. 'Thinking you can get me out of the way like I'm some simpleton. Well, I didn't go home when you told me to. I stayed and I watched. I watched you.'

I've had no sense of being observed. But then, I never thought Archie would find me, did I? But he did. He's clearly got skills unsuspected, has Dr O'Sullivan. 'Archie, what is wrong? What has brought this on? Why did you stay?'

He pouts, an unloved boy. Mama hasn't paid enough attention. 'I felt ill. Something I ate. So I stayed another night.'

Which means he gorged when he returned to the inn that day, ate himself sick when deprived of what he'd come for. Oh Archie. You child. Silly little brat. Then I notice flecks of foam are forming at the corners of his mouth, his eyes are wild and wide like a horse under duress. His voice goes up a notch. 'I listened to them all talking last night about their marvellous fortune, how wonderful to have a doctor for good. *For good!*'

'Archie, you're being—'

He gestures at the surgery, the little kingdom I've made. Even he can see the care I've lavished on it. 'Your promises have no value. I trusted you!'

'Archie, that's just—'

'And I saw you with him!' He leaps at me, but can't surmount the high table, sort of crashes into it with a thigh, a knee. The pain registers on his face but he keeps talking. 'You whore.'

'Who? Who did you see me with? Archie…' I speak as if aggrieved. But every fibre of my liar's heart knows I'm caught out. Yet that word, that single word thrown so often at my mother – that's a dart. I try to ignore it.

'That man outside this afternoon, some… common

258

groundsman.' He says it with such contempt I almost want to laugh. As if I've sullied myself. I say, 'Peeking, Dr O'Sullivan? Surely that's beneath you?' And that's quite bad enough. Should have kept my mouth closed, but it flies out, roars out, sick of being hidden inside me, behind this façade of a sparrow. Sick and tired of pandering to spoilt little boys. And that word. Again.

'Liar and thief. Whore!' He begins to sob and I don't think he knows how much is jealousy, how much is fear of losing Meliora – or me. 'You promised you'd give her back to me. Then you ran away. And now you're here with another man.'

'Archie.'

'I *know* what you can do. I *know*. I've seen you resurrect the dead – that little wolf!'

I don't tell him that was different, that what went into that cub wasn't its own soul. And it doesn't seem to occur to him the irony of mourning my faithlessness when he's begging his lover to bring his wife back to life. I could never have done it anyway – for she died before I even knew it and I was not in a position to do what was needed, what I had done to Heloise as she breathed her last. To take what was necessary. But if I'd told Archie that all those months ago, he'd not have given me everything I required to keep conducting research on how to fulfil my promise to my mother.

I'm abruptly exhausted. By everything. By everything I have done and said, by everyone who's demanded something of me these past years. By every lie I've told and promise I've made. So, I tell him the truth, or part of it at least.

'Archie. I'm sorry. I can't do it because I don't have a body to put her into.' He gives a cry and moves much faster than I'd have thought possible, dashes around the table and I'm too slow, not expecting him to put on such a burst of speed. He has me. His hands are in my hair, then around my throat and he's squeezing and squeezing and squeezing. Staring into my face while I try to pry his fingers apart. A sliver of me thinks *Stop fighting* because if I die then I no longer have to carry on with this awful, awful plan. The lack of oxygen burns my lungs; I can feel my eyes bulging, my tongue thickening.

But then I think *Whore*.

The word rolling off his tongue so easily. All that he wanted of me, all he gave to get it, all the time spent in his bed listening to him weep for another woman. And that word was the first thing he reached for.

I bring up a knee, between his legs, hear the breath puff out of him, then push him away as hard as I can. He stumbles backwards, is brought up short by something. Then long thin fingers reach over his shoulder, something sparks silver, and is drawn across his throat.

Bright red and arterial is the spray, slowing to a cascade, then a dribble, and he finally drops to his knees, eyes glazing over.

Leonora Morwood stands behind him, one of my scalpels clutched in her hand.

26

I stare at her, at my grandmother, for what seems like a very long time. Her expression is… satisfied, and I file that away to ponder later. If I start to think on it now, I don't know if I'll be able to do much else. At this very moment, Dr Archie O'Sullivan is bleeding in front of me and I should do something about *that*. I step forward, looking at him.

Archie gurgles as the flow slows – she did a good job – and I don't try to stop the bleeding. Even from here I can see the cut's too deep, he's too far gone already, so quickly. I don't help him and so I'm as guilty as Leonora for his death. Then I realise I'm crying. Tears are streaming down my face and it's hard to see; sobs are forcing their way up, heaving through my chest and I'm weeping like a child who's suffered her worst loss, worst grief. For everything I've ever done, I've not been responsible for anyone's death. I remember the priest – *Father* – or not the death of someone I knew and cared for – and I did care for Archie, though I used him. He was not cruel, he was simply… soft and sad. He wanted his wife back but was happy enough to replace her for a while with someone who filled the absence in his bed.

'Pull yourself together.' Leonora's voice is harsh. I blink away the tears so I can see her properly, her hand and the scalpel both dripping red. I shake my head. 'Come along, Asher Todd. There's a mess to clean up, girl.'

Archie is now "a mess", something to be discarded.

I'm dizzy – the strangling didn't help. Steadying myself against the table, I blink more, wipe my eyes, then watch as Archie gives one last gasp, a red mist coming from his mouth in time with a weak spurt from the hole in his throat, then he stops moving, eyes glazing, gaze aimed at the ceiling. They say the last thing you see is engraved on your ocular nerve – will Archie forever see the two women who killed him? One who looks a little like his wife.

I check the mourning ring on my finger, ensure it's still safely there. It wouldn't do for Leonora to see my true face. But she's not looking at me, she's peering around the room, seeking something; she slaps my shoulder. 'Asher! Focus.'

Nodding, I straighten. In a cupboard are sheets and towels, and I retrieve one of each. We wrap his head and neck in a towel first, then roll the rest of him into the sheet until it looks like a shroud. A headache's creeping up on me, but my mind is clearing. I grab his shoulders, and she his feet, after dropping the scalpel onto the tabletop.

'The well out the back,' says Leonora. 'It hasn't been used for years, not since they sunk a new one in the kitchen garden.'

It's covered over, but three of the planks are easy enough to remove, splintered with age. It's already winter dark out, the light having died since Archie's arrival and demise. No one will see us from the house; this is a house that eats secrets, besides. We heave Archie up, angle him into the gap, then have to push to get his gut in through the slim opening. In death he's both resisting and not, and the combination makes him difficult to manoeuvre. Finally, with one last shove, he's gone. A small splash comes to us, and a thud – not enough water there to drown in, just enough to rot in. *I'm sorry, Archie. You should have returned to Whitebarrow as I asked.*

I run back inside while Leonora curses, looks at me curiously as I return with fistfuls of dried lavender. 'To lay the ghost,' I say, sprinkling it into the black mouth. Then I put the planks back into place with shaking hands. They fit together like a puzzle, dovetailing so no nails are required, and I'm thankful to whatever long-ago workman made this. Leonora grabs my upper arm with harsh fingers and leads me inside the surgery once more.

She sags into one of the chairs, suddenly older, and watches as I find another towel, wet it then begin wiping up the pool of crimson on the floor. It comes up easily, cleanly, soaks into the towel. I sit back on my heels when I'm done, staring around me.

'Put it away. When it's dry, burn it,' says Leonora, and again I'm struck by her pragmatic train of thought, by the echoes I find in myself. Ruthlessness, I think, also travels in the blood.

I bundle the thing up, stuff it in the back of the cupboard. Tomorrow it will turn to ash. I wash the scalpel and put it on my desk; somehow I can't bear to put it in its place, with its siblings who've never done anything so terrible. I turn to Leonora, waiting. She rises and comes to touch my face. She *tsks*, says, 'Filthy child,' and dampens a cloth from the sink, and washes my cheeks and neck; it comes away red. The front of my dress is soaked with slowly coagulating gore, but it can't be seen on the black fabric. 'Burn the dress, too. We can replace it.'

As we depart, I blow out the lanterns and close the surgery door. We walk back towards the lights of the house, and she links her arm in mine, perhaps to keep me upright. She seems to sense that my knees are weak, that I'm almost done in now the rush of adrenaline and fear have ebbed. She escorts me to the bathroom and runs a bath, helps me strip off the ruined gown, washes my hair as I sit shivering in water from which steam rises, turning my skin pink. She makes me stand, dries me off, wraps my head, then leads me to my room, puts me to bed tenderly as any grandmother.

I think I whisper *Thank you* as she leaves, but sleep claims me so quickly I cannot be certain. I do not dream.

* * *

It's late when I wake; the sun is already well in the sky, heading towards midday. I ache all over and feel the fresh bruises on my throat. Gingerly I rub calendula cream on the skin; if one more person sees fit to strangle me I think I shall scream. I find a high-necked white blouse to go with my grey skirt, tidy my hair into a long plait, and go downstairs in search of food because I missed dinner and breakfast and in spite of everything – or because of – I'm ravenous.

In the kitchen, the children are sitting at the table eating bread and jam. Tib is leaning over a pot on the fire; the smell of meat and red wine is strong. A stew for dinner; my stomach revolts. Bread it is.

'Miss Todd! Grandmother said you were ill.' Albertine rises and comes over to grasp my hand. 'How are you?'

'I still feel a little unwell, Albertine. Thank you for your concern. I'm sorry to have missed your classes.'

'Connell and I read three new chapters in *Murcianus' Mythical Creatures* and Sarai drew the creatures.'

'Perfect,' I say, not having the energy to demand anything else of them (or myself) this day. 'Shall we sit?'

Tib Postlethwaite gives me a look that's unlikely to be described as sympathetic, but she does say, 'I'll make you some porridge.'

When she serves it, there's a knob of butter on top to melt in; it's plain, a little salty and tastes wonderful. I thank her and she grunts, goes back to what she was doing. She's no Mrs Charlton, but her food is tasty, she's unbothered by Luned's moods and Burdon's periodic bullying, and the Binions obey her without question. I miss our housekeeper, but Tib Postlethwaite, though she doesn't like me, is a good and stable woman to have around.

The time passes so normally, eating and chatting. When Burdon appears and tells Albertine it's time for her afternoon lesson with her grandmother, she goes eagerly enough. The girl's being taught things she never thought to learn – things her father would have denied her, given to Connell. Let her enjoy it while she may – it will teach her to be more than is expected of her. I suspect she's a far better student than Heloise ever was.

I ask Tib to tell anyone who comes that I will not be seeing patients today; she grunts again. I'd almost laugh if it didn't hurt my throat. I make sure that Connell and Sarai are wrapped up warmly, and take them for a walk around the estate, through the woods, to the Lewises' cottage. Best to be out of the house if I want to avoid people; besides I have some questions to ask.

I find only Eirlys at home – Thomas is out with their boy, working, making charcoal, and the daughter is in town collecting some groceries. The children play with the large shaggy red dog who seems to have more energy now the family is well again. I ask Mrs Lewis if they've had any relapses and she says no. I tell her about the surgery but of course she already knows – word travels fast when borne on Heledd's tongue.

'May I ask if you've seen Mr Morwood recently?' I know her husband must have in the day-to-day running of the estate, at least until Leonora's coup.

She shakes her head. 'Mr Morwood never comes here. He and Thomas meet at the big house in the morning to discuss what needs doing. Sometimes at the quarry, other times wherever the estate needs attention. Sometimes Eli Bligh brings a message. Only the girl that once.'

I nod, but I don't really know what I've learned, if anything. I had so many questions but they seem to have dried up. One more, in a low voice so the children can't hear: 'Did you ever meet my predecessor? The governess before me?'

She looks at me strangely and shakes her head. I must seem bizarre to her, all these unconnected queries. I smile, cut my losses and thank her. We head home soon after.

Being outside, answering the chatter from Connell and Sarai helps me to not think about Archie for a while, but when we are back in the house, I hand them over to a pale-looking Luned. I don't ask how she's feeling – the stinking gladwin in particular will make anyone ill. I go to the parlour and sit by the fire, stare into the flames. I can no longer ignore the memories of what happened last night.

I didn't kill him but I didn't save him either.

The more I think about it, the more I realise that Leonora didn't need to end him. She could have hit him on the head, knocked him out. But then, she didn't know who he was or why he was attacking me. Perhaps she panicked. The scalpel was the first thing she saw.

Her care was for me – or, at least for the person whose skills have given her back her sight and her looks, or part of them any road.

Poor Archie.

Would he have killed me? Having surmised – quite correctly – that I'd lied to him, thinking that I was settling in here, all his hope turned to rage. All his trust in me seemed misplaced. Not because he didn't believe I couldn't do what I'd promised, but because he realised I wouldn't.

Had he been more rational, had the world been other than it is, I might have explained that while I could, in a greater sense, do what I'd promised, I could not actually do it for him because his wife had died without me beside her. I'd not been able to bottle her last breath, the essence of her, a final spark that might be reignited later. And I'd not been able to take a piece of her flesh, an organ of import, for the soul to cling to. It wouldn't have mattered if she'd left a ghost behind – and she did not: I'd spent more than long enough in their home to know if she had, though Archie would not have seen her even if she stood in front of him – because ghost and soul are different things. Linked certainly, but not the same. A ghost might wander, follow as Heloise did me – drawn perhaps by the song of its own soul, or another such call, for most souls do not remain *here*. But I could never have done what he expected without those elements – and without another body to put it all into.

I lied and told him I could. I lied because doing so meant I did not have to live in a tiny room with my mother's spectre, stealing everything I needed, working in the darkness fearful only of discovery but not of what I did. I lied because it made my life and my search so much easier.

Poor Archie.

I didn't kill him, no, but he'd never have been here, at the end of a scalpel, if not for me and my lies. So grief-filled, so greedy, hoggish, at the inn's dining table.

The inn. His things. His horse.

Where's his horse? Surely he rode to the manor? I cannot imagine him suddenly deciding exercise was required in order to spy on me. The poor creature will be wandering. I must look for it. There will be a room at the inn, with Archie's fine things in it (not too many, not more than would fit in his saddlebags). How long before someone realises he's not paid his bill? Goes to his room, and decides to sell whatever they find? At a market stall, or to a seamstress to remake and pass on. He'd have had a key on him, but we'd tossed him in the well, hadn't we? No going back for that.

What to do?

My hand shakes as I count off my points:

One. No one knew why he came here and I do not imagine he would have told. Two. No one would have known where he was going, that he was coming out here. Three. No one knew he'd returned here last night – he'd been sneaking around, so the whole point was not to be seen. Four. Burdon welcomed him to the house those days ago. Five. Leonora knew he was here, but she has more to lose than I.

So: the safest course is to hold on for dear life and do nothing. Deny all knowledge of him but what can be proven. Express surprise if the horse is found – I had believed Dr O'Sullivan had already returned to Whitebarrow. Soon, Luther will return. I will be free and I will disappear and no one will ever find me. I'll make sure of it this time.

The door opens without a knock. Burdon again.

'You've missed dinner, Miss Todd,' he says, mildly reproving, a little concerned.

I smile. 'I'll have something later, Burdon. I'm not very hungry at the moment.'

'Luned's not well either – normally I'd think she's malingering, but she's almost green around the gills.' He shakes his head. 'Hope no ailment's going around.'

'I'm sure it's nothing. I'll go up and check on her later.' *As if I didn't know.*

'Very good, miss. Tib's seen to the children.' She'll not have read them a story; I'll have to check on them too. 'And Mrs Morwood would like to speak to you in the library.'

'Thank you, Burdon.' I rise and follow him out.

Leonora is standing, back to the room, staring at the black glass of the window. She's looking at her reflection, I think, then mine as I enter. We wait for Burdon to go, having been assured that he's no longer required this evening.

'Asher,' she says as the door closes, then gestures to the long seat by the fire. We sit at opposite ends. She stares at me, and I wonder what might happen if I were to take off the ring, show her my face, her daughter's face, her own face. If I were to tell her all I've done and all I've planned to do. Tell her about my mother and what happened to her in Whitebarrow. Tell her that Heloise is quite literally above us, even now, locked in her childhood room until I come and let her out. But I don't and she says again, 'Asher.'

'Thank you, Mrs Morwood, for what you did last night.'

'Who was he?'

269

'A man from Whitebarrow. A doctor. He had been… a friend. He lost his wife, maddened by grief as you saw.' I hate my deceiving tongue. Although it's not entirely a lie, is it?

'Where was he staying?' she asks, strategic as ever, and I run through my earlier train of thought, or at least the bits of it I don't mind her knowing. She nods approval.

'And he believed you could bring his wife back? Into another's body?'

Gods. How much did she hear? I doubt there're many lies I can get away with now. I nod, slowly. 'But I didn't want to. That's one of the reasons I left Whitebarrow. He was growing insistent, and I did not want to choose someone to… be a vessel.'

She shifts against the cushions behind her, considering. 'But you *can* do it?'

And here's my mistake: I should have denied it. Said Archie was mad. But I've already admitted it, haven't I? Trapped like a rat in a maze of my own making. I nod, a small jerky movement.

Leonora looks at her hands, at their wrinkled skin and age spots, the knuckles enlarged by arthritis. She rises, goes to the mirror above the fireplace and examines her face. Since the treatment she looks a good deal younger, but still not young. Her expression is greedy, so avid, avaricious. Like she might eat someone else's youth. 'So. You could put my soul into, say, Albertine's body?'

'Albertine?'

'My granddaughter will be my heir. It's only logical.'

'She's your granddaughter.' I clasp my hands in my lap to stop them from shaking.

'But you could do it?'

'You would both need to die first,' I say in the hope it will be a deterrence. I swallow hard, the bruising hurting more than it should. 'Mrs Morwood—'

'Asher Todd, you owe me your life. What would the constable say if I were to tell him what transpired last night? How you threw a man down a well and covered him up?'

'I wasn't the one to kill him.' My voice trembles and I hate it.

'But who will that stupid man believe? The person to whom he owes his living? Or you?' She grins and it's an ugly thing. 'What of the Church? What if I were to mention all you have done? If I were to go to the priest?' She seems to remember he's gone a'wandering – and she hates him – and corrects herself: 'Or send word to Lodellan that we'd caught a witch who was dealing in souls and death?'

I look away, find the flames in the hearth, think of what they would feel like around my feet, climbing my body.

'What if, Asher Todd?'

I look at her, the woman who banished her own daughter for getting pregnant, punished her for little more than causing disappointment and the upsetting of Leonora's grand plans. I look at this woman so in love with beauty that she'd steal someone else's life to keep it – her own grandchild's, as if Albertine were nothing more than fodder. I look at my grandmother and say, 'It will take time to prepare, Mrs Morwood.'

I rise. 'If you will excuse me, I'm rather weary.'

At the door, her voice catches me like a hook. 'Asher? I rely on you. You are my ally in all things.'

It's not a question, but a statement. This is what I'd aimed for, what I'd wanted, to make my other plans easier. Yet here everything is, so much harder than I could have foreseen. Or so I'd like to believe. Nodding, I do not reply, and step into the corridor.

The front door beckons and I step into the icy black.

I walk across the lawn, ignoring how the wind plucks at me, bites through my thin indoor clothes. The cold is sobering; it seems to slow my thoughts, make them sharper, easier to grasp. *Calm, Asher, calm.* I need only put Leonora's demands off until I have done what I came to do. Then, I will vanish, disappear into the night or the day or the mid-morning, whenever I can step from view. *Hold fast, Asher, only a little longer*.

In front of me something rises, it seems, from the very earth. Dark and solid and blocking my view. Then it snorts, steam pours from nostrils. A weak whicker.

Archie's poor horse.

Speaking quietly to the beast, my own trembling matching his, thud for thud, I lead him to the stables. There's a free stall at the far end, closest to the tack room; I remove the animal's saddle and bridle, rub him down, throw a blanket across his back and make sure there's feed within reach. I will speak to Eli in the morning, tell him I found it wandering. Going to him now is unappealing; I feel as if I couldn't keep my lies from dancing on my face. But there's one thing I must do before I sleep, no matter that I don't want to.

27

My steps are heavy as I go up to the attic; I've not been here before, there's been no need. Checking on Luned means I don't have to think about Leonora and Albertine, at least not yet. The girl doesn't answer when I knock. I put my ear to the wood, hear the sounds of harsh breathing, grunts and groans. If I didn't know Luther was away I might simply turn and leave. So, I open the door and peer inside.

'Luned? Luned, are you well?'

The small room is close and the air stinks of blood and excrement. Dormer windows with drawn curtains, a fire barely breathing in the hearth, a chest of drawers, a tiny desk, and a narrow bed in the far back corner. I can make out a tangle of white sheets; there are blankets on the floor. I lift the lantern high, then approach the bed.

Luned lies in a mess of linen and bodily fluids; a slim young woman, her stomach is distended. Not hugely, but she's much further along than she admitted. Three months, maybe four. A corset's amongst a pile of clothes on a chair by the bed – it's been wrapped tight about her day in, day out, to hide any swelling that might be noticed by a sharp-eyed Mrs Charlton or Tib Postlethwaite – or even Leonora if she took a moment to notice a servant. Luther… Luther wouldn't notice for a while longer; might tell her she's getting fat without twigging. But one thing's for sure: she's too far along for the mix I gave her to be at all gentle. At this point it'll be death for her as well if she's not tended.

'You stupid girl,' I whisper. I pull her up onto the pillows, tidy the bed as well as I can, all the while she hisses profanities at me because I've found her like this.

'I'd rather die than to have to thank you,' she grunts.

'I can leave you here, Luned, if that's what you want. If you want to die in your own blood and shit and piss. Die here and let Burdon find you in the morning when he realises you've not done your duties. Find you like this and you'll be six feet beneath the earth by the time Luther Morwood comes home and starts to look for his next silly little whore.' My voice breaks a little on that last word. I'm meaner than I might be because I'm scared and tired and stretched to my final nerve. 'You,' I tell her, 'are the last thing I feel like taking care of, so what's it to be?'

She sobs. 'Help me.'

I pour a glass of water for her from the carafe that's located on the desk – not within easy reach – and hold it to her lips. When she's done, I say, 'Wait here.'

'Where the fuck else am I going to go?' she spits then begins another series of moans and grunts that she swallows – Burdon's room is on this level, at the far end of the attic. Hopefully he's already in the embrace of his favourite brandy.

In the kitchen I fill a ewer of hot water, take an armful of sheets and rags from the laundry room, then to my own room to gather my satchel and its potions and powders. Back up the stairs as fast as I can.

Luned's gritting her teeth – I hand her a flat piece of wood. 'Bite down on it. You're too far along – you're already in labour. Stop fighting because it's coming out one way or another.'

I'll give it her: she didn't scream once, not even as she tore. Not even as the little scrap (with those few strands of bright red hair) slid out into the world. Not even when she asked me in a ragged voice if the child breathed and I said *No*. I wrapped it gently and held it out to her. She wouldn't look. It was so warm in my hands, this small thing who shared my blood, her blood.

'You'll regret it,' I said. 'Not now, perhaps not for weeks or months, even a year. But you will at some point. You'll regret not holding it. You'll always remember that you didn't do that. I've seen it time and again. You might not want the child, but you *will* regret this.'

Reluctantly she accepted, let it rest against her chest. I watched a while and could barely breathe for the lump in my throat for someone I didn't like and a child I'd helped to get rid of. But she hadn't been wrong. Luther would have set her aside the way he had every other woman in the Tarn who'd been fool enough to lie with him. She'd have gone back to her mother's inn in shame, tied there forever.

While she's holding the child, I stitch her up, make sure she won't bleed to death in the night. I think about what I could take – birth blood, the sac, the first-last breath if it had been alive – things to use in dark magics, things hard to find, things I do not want. Luned's breath hitches as I apply a poultice, then I make her drink a mixture to fight off a fever from childbed, yet another to make her sleep. I help her into the chair while I remake the bed with clean sheets, wash her down as best I can with a cloth, put her into

275

a fresh nightgown and settle her back under the covers. I pour her another glass of water, leave it and the carafe on the small bedside table. I open a window so fresh cold air flows in, then I build up the fire, and when it's blazing I put the ruined sheets on top. They begin to smoulder, still damp, and so I do something Luned can't see, something I couldn't in the surgery when Leonora Morwood watched: I whisper a word and a wish, twitch my fingers, and the flames blaze up, eat the sheets in a trice.

When she's ready, I take the baby from her. 'I'll tell you where it lies.'

'Don't.' She shakes her head. 'I don't want to know.'

In the time it takes for me to nod, Luned's eyes are closed, either already asleep or pretending so she doesn't have to watch me leave with her child.

* * *

I find a shovel in the stables then, out behind the surgery, I bury the remains. The earth is winter-hard but I persevere, digging the grave not far from where I buried the fox all those nights ago – why does it feel like a lifetime? In spring, I think, I'll plant lavender over the grave – then I remember I won't be here. I'll not throw it away like Archie. I'd say a prayer if I had any to give, but I don't so I just say *I'm sorry*.

I return the shovel to the stables, then go to Eli's cottage. He's already asleep when I arrive, but he wakes as I slip naked into bed beside him. 'Shit, you're cold.'

'Warm me.'

* * *

In the morning, I don't rush. I roll over, touch his face. Listen to the noise his stubble makes beneath my fingers, scratch him like he's a dog until he wakes. He growls, 'I'll bite you,' but smiles as he says it. I slither on top of him and wake him properly.

When we're done, I nestle in his arms, run my finger along the healing scar I gave him.

He grins. 'My aunt says you're dangerous.'

'I thought you were alone in the world. You said you were the last of the line.' I prop myself on one elbow, look into his face.

'*The last of the blood*, I believe, was the phrase.'

'Semantics.' I poke his ribs. He grunts. 'Who is your aunt, then?'

'Aunt Tib.' The grin fades. He gently touches the fading bruise on my temple.

That explains some of her hostility. She thinks I'll hurt her boy; she's not stupid. 'Ah.'

'Don't worry, she didn't like the previous governess, either.' He puts his hands behind his head and I swing out of bed, begin looking for my clothes. When my expression is neutral, I turn back.

'Why didn't Aunt Tib like my predecessor? Does she simply suspect every young woman of setting her cap at you?' My fingers fumble at the buttons of my skirt.

'She said the girl was uppity.'

That's more than possible. I think of Mater Hardgrace and her manners – all learned, all better than her beginnings, all to impress her clients. She'd have passed them onto her niece. And Miss Hilarie Beckwith might have made the mistake of thinking she could get away with being rude to anyone she considered beneath her. A shiver of guilt goes through me: I was meant to be looking for her, discovering her fate so I could write Mater Hardgrace before I disappeared and set her mind at rest; whether good news or bad, at least she would know. But I've been too busy pursuing my own course.

'How long did she last, Eli?'

He answers without hesitation. 'Not long. Two weeks, perhaps? Then she turned around and left. Family emergency Mrs Charlton said.' He shrugs. 'Asked for her bags to be sent on, she was in that much of a hurry. I dropped them at the inn to be put on the next carriage to Whitebarrow.'

'Oh.'

He watches me dress. 'Did you know her?'

'No,' I say quite truthfully. And I know that no baggage was ever returned to Mater Hardgrace's Academy because the principal herself told me. All she'd ever had was a letter from Leonora saying that the girl had proved flighty and left. No one's told Eli to keep this knowledge to himself. I'll ask no more questions, it would draw attention. But I wonder if Archie's things will disappear the same way the governess's did?

* * *

After dinner, Leonora hands me an envelope and tells me it's to go to Zaria Taverell first thing in the morning. I do not point out that she is becoming very cavalier with the children's education – I might be a pretend governess, but I've always taken the job seriously. If nothing else comes of this adventure, at least the Morwood children would have learned something – hopefully not simply to distrust governesses.

I nod and say *Of course*. When I've herded the children to their beds and read a story, I go up to the attic. Luned's not eaten the soup I brought earlier, so I sit and spoon-feed her. She doesn't mention the child, doesn't ask where it sleeps, and I don't bring it up. I give her more medicine, change her nightgown again, empty the chamber pot.

As I'm leaving, she says almost in a whisper, 'Why are you doing this?'

And I say, as truthfully as I can, 'I don't know.'

* * *

Later still, when the house is entirely quiet, I go to my mother's room and open the door. I'm careful not to disturb the salt crystals. She's sitting by the window still. I wonder if she's been there ever since I locked her in.

'Hello, Mother.' I sit on the edge of the dusty bed again and look at her. I could never watch her enough when I was a child, she was so beautiful. Sometimes she'd get annoyed, then angry, but I couldn't help myself. Who wouldn't want to gaze upon such perfection, something that rewarded the eye so?

I don't want to stare at her now; she's not the lovely girl in the portrait Leonora keeps hidden in her room. She's the woman who died screaming and gasping for air, in a sack of a nightgown, her hair wild. And she's not solid – I can see through her to the chair she's sitting on, to the wall she's in front of. The spectral bones of her face still show a hint of what was there, the architecture of her loveliness, but it's been eroded by the pain of her last years and, of course, death.

But after her passing, she was not gone from me. Her ghost – this thing before me – shared the boarding room with me, my own special little haunt, voiceless, aimless, waiting for me to do as I'd promised. Staring her reproach at me. And when I moved into Archie's fancy house, she followed me soon enough, took up residence in the attic there; sometimes I'd wake to find her watching me as I slept. Archie never saw her, sometimes would simply walk through her, disrupting the substance of her as though she was nothing more than a fog he might encounter on the street. I always found it interesting that he had no sense for anything eldritch – a ghost lived in his house! – yet he believed utterly in me and my ability to make something magical happen.

'Do you remember, Mother? The day you died? Do you remember the days before it? The promises you wrung from me?' Heloise looks at me. I wonder, *Does she even understand?* She's just a ghost, a thin skin left behind; sometimes they are powerful things, sometimes there's a something left clinging to them – it depends on the circumstances of their life and death, the strength of the person, the determination – and with a skerrick of soul still in place such a spectre is more... themself. But she's just an echo left behind with enough spite to target the weakest person in the house, poor Jessamine. I whisper, 'Do you remember, Heloise?'

She turns away, attention back out the window.

I stare at her for a while longer – so I recollect, recall, everything – because soon enough she'll be gone.

28

'Sarai, don't stray too far ahead.'

Leonora has taken Albertine riding around the boundaries of the estate. I've brought the younger two with me as I walk to the Tarn – Tib Postlethwaite's expression was forbidding and I wasn't game to ask her to mind them again. I'm sure she's added "shirker" to her list of my sins. Oh, Tib, if only you knew.

Sarai still havers between standoffish and sulky. Today she seems to have settled somewhere between the two. Along our way she's been picking blossoms and leaves that have already turned brown. Every so often she swings around, holds up her trophy and tells me the common name, then waits for me to give the botanical term. I can't quite tell if it's a sort of truce or if she's waiting for me to fail; to find a gap in my knowledge. It won't be long now before the snow comes and everything's white – will she have forgiven me then? Then I remember I'll be long gone.

'Is Luned feeling better?' asks Connell. 'Sarai has been wondering—'

'But she still won't ask me.' I smile.

'Well…'

'Luned's getting better, Connell, but she will need a few more days. Sarai may go up and visit her if she likes. I think it would cheer Luned no end.'

'You're very kind, Miss Asher.'

'Why thank you, Connell. Anyone would want Sarai to be happier.' I smile. 'It's nothing any governess wouldn't do for her charges.'

'I think you're wrong, Miss Asher,' he says. 'The other governess said our happiness was irrelevant.'

'How so, Connell?' I raise my brows. I've avoided asking the children about my predecessor for fear it'll be reported back to Luther somehow – because even the most casual of queries might alert a guilty conscience. But he's away and I did not ask.

'You're friendlier. And you're not afraid of Grandmother or Father.'

I smile. 'Was she afraid?'

He nods, biting his lip.

'What's wrong, Connell?'

'Father said we weren't supposed to talk about her.'

'Who would I tell?' I ask and smile. His expression clears.

'Miss Beckwith was nice enough, but she wasn't here long. Then she was gone.'

'Did you see her leave, Connell? Watch her walk to the Tarn or up the drive to where the carriage sometimes stops?'

He shakes his head. 'She was there one evening, then gone in the morning. Father said we mustn't ask about her or talk about her. He said she wasn't "fit".'

'Thank you, Connell, for trusting me.' I take his hand, give it a squeeze. He doesn't let me go. 'Now where's your sister?'

We're passing the church and I shudder. I look around for the little girl and her red, red hair – a quick nervous glance at the tarn itself, but there's no sign, no ripples on the surface to say I've been so lax in my job that the child is gone.

Connell tugs my arm and points: Sarai has scampered over the low stone wall and into the churchyard. She's skipping amongst the gravestones heading towards the crimson blood-bells that grow over the oldest graves.

'Sarai, come back here,' I call. She ignores me. Connell's grip tightens and I realise he must be concerned about the priest. 'Don't worry, Connell. There's nothing to fear here. The old god-hound can't hurt you.' But he hangs back, so I gently untangle my fingers from his. 'Wait here, I shan't be long.'

I pick my way to where Sarai sits, turning crimson flowers into a chain. She doesn't look at me, not even when I crouch in front of her. Things seemed to be getting better but now she's moody, sullen; I don't react to it. She's a child controlling the world the only way she knows how – withholding affection. It hurts a little, I must admit. 'Sarai, time to go. Come along.'

'Since you came, everything's changed. Mama's gone away, so has Papa, Grandmother is mean, Albertine never plays with me anymore, Luned is unwell, and it's getting cold.'

I suppress a smile. I'm responsible for many things, but not the weather. 'None of those things are my fault. I understand you're upset. Change is very unsettling. But shall I tell you a secret, Sarai?'

She looks at me reluctantly, but who can resist a secret?

'You mustn't tell anyone, but I will be gone soon too.'

That seems to cheer her up; she smiles and a weaker woman might take offence. But I just put a finger to my lips, then offer my hand, which she takes. 'Would you like to give those flowers to Luned? I think they might cheer her.'

She shakes her head. 'Luned said I mustn't touch them. Bloodbells are poison.'

'Indeed? Yet here you are. Let's leave them here. We'll find something else for her. Perhaps a treat from the bakery? Or the coffeehouse? Perhaps a treat for you and Connell too?' I take the pretty weeds from her and pocket them while she's looking at her palms.

'And for Albertine? So she plays with me again?'

'And something for Albertine, of course.' If Leonora has her way Albertine's childhood is over, but Sarai doesn't know it yet.

I wash her hands in the tarn, careful to scrub them free of the sticky sap; she complains about how cold it is and I sense her adding this to her list of resentments. She pats her little fingers dry on my skirts and I think ever so briefly of dropping her into the pond. Instead I hold them to my mouth and blow on the skin as I rub warmth back into them. It won't be long before the surface will ice over and no one will be able to drown in it for months.

* * *

In the Tarn, we gradually make our way towards Zaria's offices. I know she's away because a note came yesterday afternoon, thanking me for my help: Alize is doing better and they are taking a week's respite with friends. I could have told Leonora that but walking into the village was a preferable task. When we get home I shall make my excuse and tell her I will return in two days (when the lawyer will once again not be home). So I have no qualms in marching up to the door and knocking very loudly. There's no answer, of course. I was prepared for a maid or a housekeeper, but clearly whoever keeps their house has taken the opportunity to absent themselves. Wise. The paper in my pocket remains safe and I can safely fail to deliver it for a while.

The coffeehouse is packed, so we do not go in, but the bakery which supplies it with its delicacies isn't so busy. Connell and Sarai select treats for themselves, Luned and Albertine. I choose something for myself, the Binions who have been picking up the slack whilst Luned is abed, Eli and Aunt Tib, though I'm sure she won't thank me for it. Leonora doesn't have a sweet tooth, and Burdon will be happier with another bottle of brandy.

We sit in the market square in the sun and eat our morning tea. One of the stall vendors makes a hot chocolate that the children ooh and aah over. People approach and ask me if the surgery will be open this afternoon – offering gentle reproof for the day it wasn't. I hide a grin, thinking how quickly they've become used to the convenience of having me around. I tell them that yes, they may drop in any time after two and before six.

Groups of children run around the playground of the small school and my two watch them with envy. Poor mites, growing up in that house with only themselves and adults. Even Heloise made sure I played with other children as I grew. Never the offspring of the doctor-professors for their mothers would allow no such thing, but those of other kept women in Whitebarrow, of servants. At least I knew what it was to talk to others my own age. I think about sending Connell and Sarai over to make friends, but it would get back to Leonora and I've no doubt she would be displeased. Associating with guttersnipes! I could mount a convincing argument, I'm sure, but I don't believe I have the energy to do anything more than I absolutely must.

When we've eaten I tug them along to the inn; Connell carries the box of pastries despite Sarai's protests that she can do so. The children have never been there before and are wide-eyed as I herd them inside. Only one of Luned's sisters is around, the oldest I think. I smile, she does not.

'More brandy?' she asks with a sneer in her tone.

'Why, yes. Thank you for being so perceptive. Sarai, this is one of Luned's sisters.' Sarai smiles shyly and the girl's face softens, but not much. And not because of the mention of her sibling. I point the children towards the hearth. 'Go, warm yourselves.'

'Luned is well,' I lie. The girl shrugs, her sister's fate apparently of little concern. Luned's desire not to live her life here is entirely understandable – but she needs to set her sights beyond Morwood. The girl behind the bar thumps a new bottle of brandy on the counter; this time I politely hand her the coin.

'That it?' she asks.

'One last thing.' I make sure my charges are far enough away to not hear. 'Mrs Morwood has received a letter from Miss Beckwith's aunt.'

'And who's Miss Beckwith when she's at home?'

'The former governess at the manor. Her aunt asks whether the trunk was sent on as requested? It seems it has not arrived in Whitebarrow.'

Her face goes astonishingly still, her lips move as if she's underwater and trying for air. Finally, she shakes her head. 'That's because they weren't sent to Whitebarrow. Her note said Bellsholm. They should go to Bellsholm. The Shark and Lantern, I think it was.'

'Ah. Well that explains it. Thank you—' I wait until she supplies her name, *Mira* '—thank you, Mira.' I smile at her a little longer, wait until the tension made her white around the lips. 'Come along, children. Say goodbye to Mira.'

They do so obediently. 'Thank you, Mira, I will let Luned know you sent kind wishes.' I lead the children outside before she has a chance to respond.

We head back along the road to the manor. I have a clear sense of having committed mischief this day and it makes me smile. No one I like was hurt. I'll have to watch my back, however, and I'm wary as we walk home, listening for the sounds of anyone trying to follow stealthily. I'm certain of one thing, though, and that's Miss Hilarie Beckwith's trunk is somewhere in that inn. Or it was for a while, and now all her things have been divided up between Luned's sisters.

29

Late in the afternoon I see off the last of the villagers: mostly
a collection of children with incipient colds, two men with gout,
two more with indigestion and three women with arthritis. Another
woman, swollen with child, is short of breath, her skin is a pale
yellow, her hands and feet are cold and she complains of dizziness.
I tell her she's anaemic – common in pregnant women – and to eat
more red meat.

'At least tell me you're charging them.'

The voice makes a sweat break out immediately; I'd not
expected to hear it for some days yet. I wipe my forehead with a
sleeve before turning away from the shelves I've been reorganising,
making notes of what needs restocking. 'Good evening, Mr
Morwood. No, I do not charge them.'

'What?' He's standing in the doorway, hanging there as if
waiting for an invitation to enter.

'These people have had no access to a doctor for many years.
I believe it's the duty of a household such as this to ensure they
remain in good health – the village is part of the Grange; they are
your people, sir, they support this estate. Such a small cost to you
to help them, one that will pay you back many times – they will
remember the kindness and be loyal.'

He snorts.

'You've returned early,' I say, stating the obvious, hoping to distract him.

'Indeed. The idea of another four days in a carriage was less than appealing, so I bought a new stallion – he's magnificent – and made haste on my own. The Reivers and our grand conveyance will make their way at a more leisurely speed.' His words are neutral, the content quite ordinary, it's the tone that is all anger. Suppressed but not hidden.

'One might have thought you'd take some days to enjoy a rest before coming home,' I say, glancing down at the blue bottles in my hands.

'I'm sure you and my mother hoped so. While the cat's away…' He crosses the threshold and walks around the room that suddenly seems too small. 'And I'm sure my mother has been planning and plotting.' He gives a tight grin, gestures to the surgery. 'Stirring her cauldron.'

'Mr Morwood, any issues you have with your mother would be best discussed with her.'

'Ah but here's the thing: she does seem to deliberate everything with you, little Miss Asher Todd, before she puts anything into effect.' He pauses to stare out the window that looks over the stream; he's tall enough to see from the high-set things. 'So I thought perhaps I would ask you first, and perhaps you might do me the singular courtesy of telling me what I'm walking into.'

'Mrs Morwood doesn't consult me about her decisions, sir.'

'No, but she bloody well gets you to help with putting them in motion!' He shouts so loudly I can almost hear an echo. I can see Heloise's temper in him, better controlled at the moment at least.

'Now, a little bird' – at first, I assume *Sarai*, then I replace that with *Burdon* – 'tells me you went into the Tarn today. Knocked on Zaria Taverell's door. Now, what would my mother need with a solicitor?'

'Mr Morwood.' I look him straight in the eye. I shouldn't want to provoke him as much as I do, but all I can think of is my mother and what was done to her, how her own brother did not defend her, but thought only to take her place as the heir to Morwood. I think of everything that followed on from there and bled into my life even before I was born. 'I am *not* privy to your mother's affairs. You will need to ask her yourself.'

'Ah, but she likes *you*, Asher! Her dearest Asher who returned her sight – and blithely fucked my life. She's pleased with you, so very pleased she's set you up here, in the space that was meant for *me*. Shall I call you "doctor"?' He glares around at everything he cast aside. That he did not earn. That has sat neglected all these years.

'You know a woman cannot earn such a title, Mr Morwood, I do not claim it.' Briefly turning my back on him, I close the glass doors on the cabinet behind me, then go to my desk, two small bottles still in my grip: something for Luned to heal her faster, something to help me sleep.

As if my thought of her transmits to him he says, 'Burdon tells me Luned has been ill.' He stares at the stone table as if it might give up secrets.

'A passing unwellness,' I say. 'A stomach upset.'

He crosses the room in long strides, slaps the bottles out of my hand; they smash on the floor and I burn where he hit me. He yells, 'Do not lie to me!' and goes to grab me by my chin as he has before, but I'm ready for him, snatching up the scalpel from the desk where I've left it since Leonora used it on Archie. Still unable to put it away. Or unwilling. Unwilling to be surprised here ever again, unwilling to be vulnerable. To be strangled yet again. I have it up and at the tender flesh of his neck, the blade resting cool against the warm soft skin, the blue pulse beneath.

'If you raise a hand to me once more, Mr Morwood, I will slit your throat, or perhaps from gullet to groin,' I say coldly. 'And I do not imagine your mother would object overly much.'

He's frozen. I do not tremble, and imagine drawing the blade across, down. I could drag him out to the well and he and Archie could rest together. There's been no sign of Archie's ghost – either the lavender keeps him beneath, or I suspect he's found his Meliora. I could kill Luther now, but that would be such a waste after so much trouble. I thought I had a few more days to prepare, but no matter: everything I require is here. I just need a little longer to set up. Luther will keep.

'As I was saying, Mr Morwood, Luned has had an upset stomach. Something that has been going around the Tarn and which she doubtless picked up on a visit to her family there. She is mending but I would advise you keep your distance from her lest she remain contagious.'

Circumspectly, Luther Morwood steps away. He says not a word, merely turns and exits. I do not sag or fall, my knees are not weak, my hand does not shake. And I know for certain that I cannot delay. I lay out the tools and candles, the herbs and towels.

The only things lacking are what lies hidden beneath the floorboards of my room and Luther Morwood.

'Luned,' I call as I try to turn the doorknob, balancing a bowl of soup in the other hand. 'Are you awake?'

From inside there's a grumble, the sound of footsteps, something heavy being pushed across the floor, then a key turning. The door opens slowly, and there she is, swaying.

I hold up her dinner.

'No bread?'

I fish a spoon and two slices of bread from a pocket and wave them about; she steps aside and lets me in, closing and locking the door after me. 'How are you feeling?'

'Would have been better without the master of the house standing in the corridor, banging around and swearing at me.' She half-staggers back to bed. When she's settled, I put the bowl in her hands, and the spoon, stack the bread on the bedside table. I tidy the room, straightening the bedclothes, pulling out a clean nightgown from those Tib's washed.

'Well, I'd keep the door barricaded for a while. Burdon's told him you were ill.'

'Nosy old shit.'

'I don't know that he told him anything else – he doesn't *know* anything else – but your master's of a suspicious frame of mind.' I flop into the chair as she eats. Her colour is much better, her movements slow and careful but not overly painful. She is mending and she should consider herself lucky as it's no small miracle. 'I saw your sister Mira today.'

She grunts.

'She expressed great concern for your illness.'

She snorts. 'Can't have been one of my sisters. You must have been talking to someone else.'

'Not a happy family?'

'Happy enough until I grew old enough to have my own opinions. Until I wouldn't marry Sy Claffin with his fat gut and two dead wives gone before me. Until I wouldn't work in the inn.'

'So you got a position here and thought you'd fuck your way to the top.'

She chokes on a chunk of bread.

'Luned, you don't think you love him, do you?'

'Don't be an idiot.'

'But I heard you talking to Jessamine.'

'That's not it.' She shakes her head.

'Then why stay here when you can go anywhere in the world?'

'That costs money and I don't want to go through *the world* begging and scraping and *fucking* for my next meal.'

'So, what? You somehow marry Luther? When he's already got a wife? And there are children.'

'Don't be stupid. He said when the old lady's gone, Jessamine won't last long. Then he'd give me money. There'd be money to spare and I'd get my share.'

'So you don't want to marry him?'

She sounds a little desperate when she says, 'Gods, no. Don't want to marry anyone, but it's the only way to get money, isn't it? You've got to protect what little chance you've got in the world.'

Heloise certainly seemed to think so.

* * *

It's well after midnight when I'm finally ready.

I stand in front of the mirror in my room, take a deep breath, then pull the mourning ring from my finger. The approximation of Meliora's face is gone, and there is my own, near enough to Heloise's that we might have been twins. Near enough that I think it's one of the reasons she loved me – because it was like looking at herself – and later one of the reasons she hated me – because she no longer looked that way.

So strange to see this face after all these months.

So strange, this face.

I could leave tonight. Leave them all to their plots and plans. But Heloise's ghost will follow me. If I don't fulfil my promise to her soon, before Leonora changes her will, who knows what will be demanded of me next? And Luther hates me; he'll move against me soon, the moment he thinks I'm not paying attention.

The dress I pull from my trunk is green silk, like the one in Heloise's portrait. I let my red hair loose. I shiver but don't put on any shoes, easier to move quietly. My feet are cold on the stairs as I go up to the second floor, to my mother's room: she's still by the window, doesn't turn around when I whisper *Goodbye*. Along the hallway next, to the suite Jessamine and Luther shared until recently. The shape in the bed snores. I light one of the lanterns so he can see me.

I call his name and he stirs. I call again and again, until he sits up, confused and fuddled with sleep. I call one last time. *Luther.* He sees me finally.

My uncle's face goes pale, eyes become pits, his lips tremble. Before he can gather himself, I'm out the door, seemingly unhurried, but when beyond his sight I sprint along the corridor, and down the stairs, down, down, down until I reach the bottom. I hear his stumbling footsteps, see his tousled head peek over the banisters, to see me looking up, a bright spot beneath a lantern. When he pulls back to begin his descent, I'm off again, to the front door, which I leave open, and run down to the frost-covered lawn. It's sharp beneath my bare feet and I think I feel small cuts. I wait for him to stumble out, make sure he sees me before I glide around the corner, then bolt towards the surgery, where a single lantern is lit. I stand on the steps until he sees me, then drift inside.

I hide behind the door, listening for his heavy tread, the breaking of frost as he comes; tall though I am, strong though I am, I really don't want to have to physically fight him. He almost falls over the threshold and while he's off-balance, I hit him on the back of the head with the blackjack I've kept in my trunk for just such a moment. One word escapes his mouth as he goes down: *Heloise*.

30

Once Luther's secured to the table, I waste time. Not that there's a surfeit of it, but because this moment which has taken so long to arrive feels like it's here too soon. All the planning and preparing could not give a sense of what it would be like, here. For this *now* to actually occur. To see the jar on the benchtop, that fragment – call it what it is, Asher, *gobbet* – of my mother floating therein with a white mist bubbling and roiling in the free inch between the liquid preservative and the lid. To see all those herbs lined up and ready. To see the star in the circle I've drawn on the floor with chalk, overlaid with a line of salt just to be extra safe because you never know how strong what you summon might be, what else might come through with it. The Witches warned about that.

I have the piece of paper on which I wrote the spell, the instructions from the Witches' dark book. It all seemed so simple, so unreal then, when they sent me forth with admonitions and blessings and coin. I was like a child who prepares for something in hope, but deep down has no true belief it will come – then, suddenly, the shock of fruition.

I am waiting for Luther to wake.

There are things that must be said after all these years; not to say them would be a waste.

But I get tired of waiting, so I wave smelling salts beneath his nostrils, and he coughs to alertness. As he focuses on me, he tries to move but finds himself tied down. He stares and says once more, 'Heloise.'

I shake my head. 'No. Asher.'

'But—'

'Asher Todd, daughter of Heloise Morwood and a shitty god-hound. Sent forth by her family with nothing but a few coins and a babe in her belly,' I say. I drag a chair over to sit; he twists his neck to watch. I say, 'Asher Morwood.'

'Asher Morwood.'

'Do you know how many times I have tried on that name? I had a notebook when I was small and I wrote it over and over in the back pages so Mother would not notice and get angry. I'd change my script to see which one looked right. I thought, if I got it right on paper, it would feel right on *me*. It never did, Uncle. Why do you think that was? When Heloise found that book, she burned it and beat me.'

'Asher.'

'My mother would tell me tales of her life here, of what was done to her, how she was cast out. How in her desperation she confided in her brother, and he went straight to their mother and told like a little tattletale.' I examine my hands, such strong square things, they'd have no trouble wielding a scalpel. 'I should cut it out, that tattling tongue.'

'Don't hurt me!'

'Oh, don't worry. You're no good to me voiceless.' I run a hand through my hair. 'She didn't tell me you'd gone to Whitebarrow, though! How strange, don't you think, that she'd keep something like that from me when she told me so much else?'

'Please.'

'I've been thinking about it, a lot. Perhaps she didn't tell me *that* because she thought it strange she'd gravitate towards the scene of your greatest failure. I don't think it strange at all, Uncle. For the awful life we had, I think being where she knew you'd ruined yourself made her happy.'

It finally occurs to him to shout. He does so until he's hoarse, and then he seems to realise how untroubled I am by his noise. Luther Morwood looks at me.

'No point yelling. No one will wake.'

'Have you killed them all?' And this man, this brute, is horrified. Terrified.

'What do you think I am? Some sort of monster?' I can't hide my amusement. I know precisely what I am. 'They'll sleep until I wake them. Hands of glory are terribly useful things.'

He blanches – perhaps he knows how they're made, the left hands hacked from men swinging on the gallows, turned into candles. I lit two in the kitchen, six fingers, the name of each sleeper whispered above the flame – only Luther left unspelled. Another outside Eli's cottage door. Perhaps my uncle thinks I created them myself, but they were purchased from women in Whitebarrow who specialise in such things and carried around in the carpet bag along with the jar containing my mother's heart. Finally put to use. By the time the night's over they'll have served their purpose, and I'll destroy the things rather than risk being found with them.

'I have wondered why you did it, told on her – Heloise said you were not bad friends growing up. But perhaps when you returned from university in such shame she laughed?'

He nods slowly, reluctantly.

'It's the sort of thing she would do. And I don't imagine Leonora was very understanding. I imagine she told you exactly what she thought of you when so many sacrifices had been made to send you to your dream. The cost to convert this little surgery for you, to stock it with the finest instruments.' I gesture to the walls around us, the roof, the everything. 'So many sacrifices. Your father gambling money away hand-over-fist. Then he died and you were blamed for that too. You should have been able to make a living here, not a grand one, but a decent one. Yet all your potential spilled. Wasted.' I clasp my hands, as if praying. 'And my mother would have laughed, and you kept that anger and embarrassment warm. When the chance came to make her hurt…'

'Where is she?'

'She's dead. Of course. You don't need the details of her life or death, you don't merit them.' Because if he knew how she'd survived, what she'd done, he'd merely think she deserved what she did; that she was already inclined to be a whore anyway. 'But she left me in the world and made me promise to bring her home.'

'You can't kill me. They will look for me.'

'No,' I say, 'they won't.'

And in the end it's such a simple thing.

Light the candles at each point of the star, whisper the words to make what is needed, watch as a lattice of smoke rises and creates a dome above us.

Take the other jar, the one that's filled only with lavender because lavender keeps ghosts at rest. Speak more words, the spell, and watch as his soul seeps from his mouth, a grey-white mist, and goes into the open jar, settles amongst the purple blooms. Tighten the lid. Watch the body judder and jerk for it lives without an animating, directing spirit. Open the next jar: this one contains my mother's soul and the heart I plucked fresh from her dead chest so the soul had something to attach to – something to coax it to remain. Speak the next litany and watch as the mist shoots from that vessel, away from the heart, and goes to the nostrils and mouth of Luther's form, seeps in as quick as a mouse through a gap in the wall.

After all these years as simple as that.

And this is what Archie did not understand: to do this, the empty shell must come from a relative. Something to do with like calling to like. I read the notes in that dark book: there are other means, but the result will not be human, will not look human. Archie would not have wanted to cuddle with his wife's animated bones – or I cannot imagine so anyway.

I'd promised my mother I would bring her back to Morwood. Home. That I would find the means to give her life again. I knew I would need a cadaver for her, but Leonora – how many years might she have left? And the children had done nothing to deserve this fate. But Luther. Luther would give her the power she'd been deprived of in life. Luther was sure to inherit. Luther, the brother my mother cursed with her dying breath, the one she said *Give me his life* and I promised.

Or he was until I gave Leonora back her sight, her ability to fight against him.

The body on the table stops shuddering, takes in a breath as if it's the first in a very long time – and it is, really. The eyes flutter open; there's no change in them, they are the same colour, the same shape, but somehow I can see Heloise staring out.

'Mother?'

'Asher? My Asher?' Luther's voice, but softer, with a lilt, that musical tone her clients so liked, that helped her get her way when she felt like being charming. Drops of liquid appear on her face – his face – and I realise I'm crying.

'Mother. Mother, I did it.'

'Oh, my cleverest girl.' She – he – laughs. 'My strange, clever girl!'

She wriggles, and I undo the bindings, help her – him – sit on the edge of the table.

'Oh, my.' She looks down at her new body, at the large hands, the striped nightshirt, the long hairy feet. She puts one hand to her – his – crotch and squeezes, looks surprised. 'This will take some getting used to. Although, far more convenient to piss.'

I help her stand. She – he – wraps her arms around me, not knowing her new strength. I squeak and she apologises.

'How do you feel, Mother?'

'Alive. Exhausted. Displaced. Elated. All of the things, my Asher. I feel everything.' She laughs, and it seems lighter than Luther's booming laugh.

'You should sleep. You'll be exhausted and need time to – settle in.'

'I've been floating in a jar for longer than I care to think, I should have energy to burn, but you're right, I am tired. Bed will be welcome.' She kisses me on the forehead.

'Come, Mother, we can talk in the morning.'

'Yes! We have years to catch up!' she says and I smile in spite of everything. I smile because deep inside is the sense that this will be the relationship I always wanted, needed from my mother. That at last Heloise will love me enough. I have done this thing for her – this greatest and most terrible of things! – how can she not love me now?

I take the mourning ring from my pocket, slide it on my finger, slip back under cover of my false face. My mother-uncle smiles in wonderment. 'That I birthed such a clever daughter!'

After she's settled in Luther and Jessamine's bed, asleep almost before I close the door, I check the bedroom that my mother once, twice, inhabited, just to make sure. It's empty, the border of salt undisturbed. The ghost of her is gone. It's gone because Heloise is no longer dead.

I return to the surgery and tidy away every sign of what has been done. In the garden, I dig two deep holes and bury the jar with Luther's soul in one. I spit on it before I heap dirt over what remains of my uncle. Then, when there is nothing else left to do, I extinguish the hands of glory. I bury them, with more dried lavender sprinkled over the top. Buried separately from the soul jar because there's no point risking such things in proximity.

And when everything is done, I go to my bed and sleep the utterly dreamless slumber of the damned.

31

My mother – uncle? – is waiting in the breakfast room the next day, wearing what must be one of Luther's finest dove-grey suits and a blue waistcoat so icy it's almost silver, an azure cravat tied expertly; it was an art she learned for clients. But she's not alone; when I open the door it's to see Luned – out of her bed sooner than I'd thought – backed against the sideboard, serving utensils half-forgotten in her hands, a look of disbelief on her face. Heloise-Luther is smiling and the expression is one I recognise: amused cruelty. I think about Luther banging on the door of Luned's room yesterday, demanding to be let in. How much does Heloise know of Luther's memories? What still lives inside that body she's so recently inhabited? What can she access?

I clear my throat, and Heloise-Luther says, 'We shall continue this discussion later,' while Luned looks as if it's the last thing she wants to do in her life.

'Good morning, M – Mr Morwood.' I almost say *Mother*. 'I trust you had a fine journey, Mr Morwood, and Mrs Morwood is safely settled.'

Heloise-Luther's head tilts, and I can only imagine my mother is digging around any memories left in her brother's brain. There's a brilliant smile, an *Aha!* in her mind, and a tone of triumph as she says, 'Yes indeed. Both she and Mrs Charlton were well when I left. The nuns of St Dane's welcomed them and assured me that Jessamine will receive the best care.'

'What good news,' I say evenly. 'Luned. Are you feeling better?'

She flashes me a glance that's hard to interpret at first, then I realise it's fearful. 'I thought I was alright, but—'

'Don't worry about things here. Go back to your room and lie down. I'll take care of it.'

She thrusts the ladle and a stack of bowls at me then hurries out. Before the others arrive, I serve porridge into one of the bowls and put it in front of my mother. In a low voice I ask, 'How much can you see, Mother? In there? Of his remembrances? His thoughts?'

'Bits and pieces,' she replies with a frown as if sorting through a basket of odds and ends. 'If I concentrate, things are clearer, but hard to tell when events happened – whether sooner or later. With time I'm sure it will be easier.'

'With time,' I say as if I will still be here. As if I don't want her to find answers for me at speed. 'What did you say to Luned?'

And he gives me a look that is pure Heloise, all innocence and wonder. Before he can answer, the door opens and the children rush in. I don't believe they saw him yesterday afternoon, and at the sight of their father they freeze, stricken. Luther's mouth splits into a genuine smile. He rises, arms held wide. 'My babies!'

In all my time here, I've never seen him greet his offspring with such delight. Heloise, however, always did have a fondness for children not her own. If she does not remember how he acts – if she does not wish to act as he is – she must at least remember

304

to be careful. To change Luther too much, too soon, would be unwise.

'Welcome your father home, children,' I say quietly and smile to encourage them. Sarai goes first (she has the least to fear, or rather has had fewer lessons), Albertine next, and finally Connell, though the boy gives me a reproachful look. Heloise-Luther enfolds each of them in a hug, kissing the top of their heads, patting their cheeks, all the things she would do when she was in a mood to love me. There's a tiny stab inside; I recognise it as jealousy. *Idiot*, I think, but in my heart I'm still a child, still broken. I clear my throat.

When Leonora walks in, there's almost a stumble in her step as she sees the tableau before her. She gives me a sideways look and all I can do is shrug *How could I possibly understand?*

'Luther. Returned rather earlier than expected, I see,' she observes, her tone leaving no doubt that this turn of events displeases her. He did not come down to dine with us last night, not after our confrontation in the surgery, not after my threat. I suspect Leonora had more things to put in place before this moment – she did not expect a petty rebellion from Luther. She stares: Luther's affection appears genuine; the older children seem uncomfortable, nonplussed, although Sarai looks as though she could become used to it. She might yet be young enough to forget some things.

Heloise-Luther stares at her – his – mother for long moments. So many years since they last laid eyes upon each other, and every time Heloise recounted for me that terrible scene, she added some new detail, some fresh hurt. That her mother threw something, said something, turned away when begged not to, herded her only daughter out of the house and into the dusk, then the night, then the rain, then the breath of winter. Worse with every retelling.

Embellished each time until it was impossible to tell lie from truth – except the hurt. The hurt was always the truth.

But now… she – he – smiles. My mother-uncle smiles and it's as bright as the sun, a child seeing its mother, recognising her after a separation. All that joy, the expansion of the heart – just as I'd experienced last night when I saw Heloise staring at me from her brother's eyes – the moment when one is all hope of a relationship being what one wants so desperately for it to be. The brief, flashing, flaring shiny possibility. Before the hurt is remembered, the ache rushes back in and the moment is dead.

'Mother. I have missed you so.'

He's across the room in a few long strides – there's an ungainliness to the movement for Heloise isn't used to being in this body, to controlling it – and his arms are thrown around a startled Leonora. Heloise-Luther holds tight. Leonora's hands flutter in the air behind him, but do not land. She'll not be so easily won over. At last her daughter-son pulls away, seemingly without resentment. 'Mother. I know we've been at odds. And I have been unkind. But during the journey I considered many things – part of my reason for returning so early – and I wish us to be reconciled. For the hurts of the past to be salved. I know they cannot be forgotten, but I will do my very best to make up for all of my shortcomings. I understand it will take a while for you to believe in my sincerity, for me to demonstrate it adequately, but with time, dear Mother, I hope we will reach a much better place. That Morwood with both of us at the helm will become a great inheritance for the children.'

Leonora looks taken aback. There's nothing to fault my mother-uncle's earnestness. I doubt Luther could ever have managed to be so convincing. The elder Mrs Morwood gives a sort of a nod – it's mixed with a shake of the head – and moves towards her seat at the breakfast table (the far one, ousted however briefly from the head). Without Luned here, I serve everyone, a decided shift downward in my status.

I wonder how Jessamine will like her new husband. There are things I must explain to my mother about this place, this family – it's not the family she was born into, grew in, and from which she was then expelled. I must tell her these things before I make my departure. I've kept my promise to Heloise, she has her brother's life, and soon I will slip away to try and find my own existence now that this is done. She won't miss me; she must make her own way in this world I've handed to her.

* * *

Mid-morning, having left the children practising their letters, I go looking for Heloise-Luther. I find him at the stables, mounted on Luther's newest horse, face alight with joy. *I gave you that*, I think, *I gave you this chance to start anew.* And I'm so proud of myself that I can barely stop smiling. Mother sees me, thinks the smile is for her, and returns it hundredfold. Light might be spilling from the both of us.

'Where are you going?' I ask, somewhat breathless. Without thinking I put my hand on hers – his – clutched about the reins. Heloise-Luther places her fingers over the top, squeezes just as she used to when I was small and we would walk through the markets together, her head held high no matter what they whispered about us.

'Everywhere!' he says and gives a girlish laugh. 'It's been so long, Asher, since I've been home. I will ride from one boundary to the next, greet every tree and hillock, stream and fence.'

I press down my misgivings. 'Ride safely. Be home before dark. We must talk. There are things I must tell you, questions I must ask.'

'Of course, my Asher. Of course. But we have all the time in the world!' Then he releases me and I step back as the stallion surges forward, out of the yard, takes the house fence at a gallop and is up and over with a shout. My heart's in my throat until they land, the hard impact of the hooves like punches in my gut.

We really must talk. I clasp my hands in front of me, turn back and discover Eli Bligh is watching me with suspicion. I don't hesitate, walk straight up to him and kiss him on the lips. 'It's not what it seems,' I say and then leave before he can reply. All I know is that it's important he believe that, though he'll never get the truth.

As I'm heading along the corridor to return to the classroom, I hear Leonora's voice coming from the library, calling me to heel. Presenting myself at the door, I raise a brow. 'Yes, Mrs Morwood?'

'My son certainly seems in a good mood.' She's sitting with what looks like an account book open on her lap.

'Yes, Mrs Morwood. Perhaps some self-reflection has been beneficial.'

'You don't believe that any more than I do, Asher Todd. He's just trying a new ruse.'

I shrug. 'Only time will tell.'

'Indeed,' she says. 'The tenancy agreements are coming up for renewal. Make appointments for them all to see me by the end of the next month.'

'That's not my job, Mrs Morwood. Eli would be the person to do that.'

'I don't want Eli to do it. He answers to my son.'

'Eli Bligh will answer to whoever is running the estate to its best,' I say, unsure why I'm so determined to defend Eli. Or the boundaries of my position. Perhaps, having served porridge, I will never again have a chance to refuse a task. 'He is a good and honest man, Mrs Morwood.'

'Don't think I haven't seen you sneaking to his cottage.'

I can feel my face warming. 'That makes no difference to his character. Indeed the fact that *I* trust him should be reason enough for you to do so.'

'Indeed?'

'Mrs Morwood,' I draw myself up, 'you have trusted me with your grandchildren, your health and your secrets. Is this such a great leap? I keep to myself, I am discreet, I do not place my confidence lightly.'

'Asher, my darling girl, one day you'll be old enough to realise that fucking doesn't require faith.' She sighs. 'Be so good as to go into the Tarn and deliver that letter to the solicitor. I'm sure Zaria must be back by now.'

'Mrs Morwood,' I say, exasperated. 'You hired me to educate your grandchildren. A critical part of education is regularity and routine, yet you are wilfully interrupting my schedule. If you wish those children to grow up with more respect for others than your son has thus displayed, I suggest you cease and desist.'

She gives me a look like a snake almost trod upon and I think perhaps I've gone too far. Yet I stand my ground, hands folded in front of me, chin lifted, meeting her eyes calmly. Anyone would think me an actual governess.

'Oh, Asher Todd, some days I dislike you!' she exclaims at last.

'No, you don't,' I reply, and after a moment we both laugh.

'Get you gone,' she says, waving her hands towards the door. But when I reach it, her voice stops me. 'Asher?'

'Yes, Mrs Morwood?'

'That other matter. The matter of *moving*,' she says quietly and I know what she means. I wish she'd forgotten it. I wish I had too. I nod at her to go on. 'I would like to discuss a… *schedule* for that. You're so fond of such things, that should please you.'

'Yes, Mrs Morwood. But there are certain items I will need that are not easily available.'

'Such as?'

'Things that I shall acquire.' I lie to buy myself time.

She puts a hand to her cheek, feels the plumping which cannot entirely disguise the wrinkles carved there. Isn't this enough? Surely for another person it would be. But not my grandmother. She will take everything from her granddaughter – and then what? Shall I put Albertine's soul into Leonora's decrepit body? And when she tries to tell the truth, everyone will simply think she's the old woman become deranged. Will they lock her in the rooms above? Truly does Leonora think me capable of this? Then I recall what I have done to my own uncle. Perhaps Leonora Morwood knows me better than she realises; somehow blood recognises blood.

I clear my throat. 'When the time comes, we will make arrangements. I will take the letter to Zaria this afternoon when you are instructing Albertine. Will you tell Luned to look after Connell and Sarai? I believe she may be well enough.'

She nods, waves again in dismissal.

* * *

A few hours later I walk into the Tarn. The air is brisk yet my pace slow; I enjoy the last of the fugitive warmth of the winter sun. Soon enough the snow will begin and there'll be no leaving this place, not without leaving a trail. When I flee, I'll be wearing my true face; I'll leave the Grange, discard Meliora's ring – perhaps into the well with her husband – take the coach from the village to the next town, then the next, and the next—

No. A horse. I'll take a horse, make my own way so no one can see me, track me, ask anyone else if they've seen me. I'll ride until I find somewhere that feels safe. Like it might make a home. I've fulfilled my promise to Heloise. When I'm gone, Leonora Morwood will have no one to make her dark dreams come true. She'll never find another like me. The Witches said only one other had ever asked for the same spell, Selke of the red hair and terrible abilities – and she was surely dead by now. Without me, there will be no new life for Leonora Morwood.

And I have but one thing left to do, one promise left to keep, one I've neglected far too long while pursuing my own interests – or rather, my mother's.

In the village, I go to the store that sells pens and papers and art supplies, and browse the shelves. I leave with only a blank-paged journal. Perhaps I will write recipes inside, the little things that don't look like spells, that can't be held against you in a trial. I go to the bakery and buy a pastry filled with cream and fresh fruit. I go to the apothecary and stock up on the things I've used the most of at the surgery; things that are light and easy to travel with when I depart, things that will easily fit in a satchel when I leave everything else behind.

I do not go to *Taverell & Daughter*.

I turn around and walk home once more.

When I return to the Grange, I go straight to my room and lay a fire. For a few seconds I waver, then I grin, concentrate, whisper and *blow*. The kindling bursts into bright flame, hot and burning fast. I pull out Leonora's letter to Zaria Taverell and snap the wax seal in two – I'm almost proud of my neatness – and I sit on the floor to read the contents. Everything is to be bestowed upon Albertine in the event of Leonora's death; Luther is to be given an allowance, the right to continue living in the house or to purchase another in town should he wish. A small inheritance for Connell; a dowry for Sarai. Jessamine to act as Albertine's trustee until the girl reaches her majority – because Jessamine will be easy for Leonora to boss around once she's inside the child's body. Tidy bequests for the servants. A generous one for me and the doctor's living and the surgery until my death.

I watch the old woman's wishes and wants turn into cinders and ash, watch all those desires and plots become smoke and disappear up the chimney.

I'll tell her it was delivered, that Zaria said she would have it returned in a sennight. By the time Leonora asks after it, by the time she goes to the solicitor's office in high dudgeon to demand where her new will is, I will be long gone and all her plots in disarray. It is the best I can do for Heloise – the last thing I will do – from hereon in she will be the one to manage her mother's schemes. They deserve each other.

After dinner, my mother begs off chatting, claiming weariness, and I find I do not have the strength to insist. When the house is quiet and dark, I go to Eli Bligh's bed, and I do not sneak.

32

'You didn't ask me anything about him,' I say.

Eli, sitting on the edge of the bed, is buttoning me into yesterday's dress. 'No.'

'Why?' I shouldn't pick at it. He did what I wanted, didn't he? If I turn around, what will I see on his face? Instead I stare out the window at the bare tree branches, the frost that's silvered the ground. The mansion seems so far away, even though I can see it from here; so far away from the comfort of this warm small cottage.

'Because you told me it wasn't what it looked like. And I know you well enough by now that you wouldn't tell me what it was if you didn't want to. So, no point asking.'

I grin ruefully while he can't see me. Less trust than I'd thought. Dressed, I spin around, stoop to kiss him. When I straighten, his arms wrap around my waist and I hold his head against my heart for a while longer. He'll be able to hear how it beats, this broken thing in my chest, that keeps going no matter what I do. For a second, in the space between breaths, I believe I'm free: that what I've done is the finish of everything. That I can stay here with him in the cocoon of this place. We'll never go out again, no one can come in. We'll be safe, might even be contented. Eli and I will marry, have children (tiny pups, little wolves).

But outside I hear the wind begin to rise and howl, those bare branches scrape against the glass and I know I won't be able to remain inside with those sounds like a summons.

I pull away, cross the room, and am out the door.

Only to run smack bang into Burdon, who couldn't have looked more surprised if I'd appeared out of thin air. I don't colour up; this is the least of my secrets.

'Morning, Burdon.'

'Miss Todd, you're up early,' he manages politely. But he looks disapproving. He appears to be the only person who hadn't realised where I've been spending many of my nights. I know what he thinks of Luned and her habits – this old dusty bachelor with his brandy and his solitary room. I don't wish to think unkind things about him, he's never shown me unkindness. He begins to cough.

'Are you quite well?' I ask. He gives me a look that says if he were he'd not be barking. 'Come along.'

I grab his arm and help him into the kitchen. He tries to shake me off, but I manoeuvre him into a seat, hold a finger up to his face. 'Behave yourself, old man.'

The coughing means he can't quite show the affront I suspect he'd like to. There's a jar of honey in the pantry and I bring it out, twist up a spoonful. Burdon tries to tighten his lips like a wilful child, but when there's a pause in his hacking I stuff it into his mouth. His displeasure is clear, but he stops choking. I make him a hot lemon drink, loaded with more honey and a dash of whiskey. When he's halfway through, I ask, 'Better?'

He nods, gathers his dignity. 'Yes. Thank you. May I go now, Miss Todd?'

'Yes, but make sure you have another one of those before bed tonight. It will help you sleep, sweat the fever out, and it's better for you than a bottle of brandy.'

Burdon gives a harrumph and rises, leaving the kitchen with his fingers still wrapped around the warm mug.

I turn back to tidy up the small mess I've made and see Tib Postlethwaite watching me with a considered gaze. She's leaning against the doorframe of the laundry room, and I can only assume she's been there all along. I dip my head at her.

'Good morning, Tib.'

'You're kind, I'll give you that.' It seems a strange thing to say.

'Thank you?' I put the honey back in the pantry along with the bottle of lemon juice and the whiskey, and wipe down the table with a cloth. I turn and find she's standing very close, her face not far from mine, grey eyes like an ice floe.

'But if you hurt my nephew, Asher Todd – or whatever your name is – I will tear you apart.' It's hard to believe, for a moment, that she doesn't have anything of the wolf in her, the way her lips pull back from her teeth, the way the snarl lifts up the corners of her mouth. But she's nowhere near the most terrifying person I've ever encountered, so there's not even the slightest increase in my heartbeat, no trace of adrenaline. I think how near the knives are, how I cut the heart from my own mother, took the soul from my uncle. I think how her precious Eli killed the god-hound, my father; what if she knew that? There's laughter in my mind, high-pitched and a little unhinged as if everything I've done is beginning to unpick me from the inside. I pull myself back, tell whatever's in there to *hush*.

'My name's the only thing I have a claim to in the world, Mrs Postlethwaite.' *True.* I step back from her, unhurried, reclaiming my space without any fear. 'Eli is an adult. I've made him no promises, so I'll break none. He will make his own choices.'

Her bluff called, her shoulders slump. Then the little thought: *Would Eli come with me if I asked? When I go? With my true face?* I shoo the idea away, then turn to leave; I have only a little time to prepare for the day.

* * *

That night after dinner I put the children to bed. I send Burdon off with another hot lemon drink; he grudgingly admits to feeling better. I check on Luned, who says she does not need to be spoon-fed anymore, thank you very much. I tell her she can be in the kitchen first thing in the morning then, Tib will be expecting her. She makes a face. Back downstairs, in the library I assure Leonora that I've matters in hand for granting her greatest wish. Later still, I'm in my own room uncertain whether to go to Eli again tonight or not. A knock sounds on the door, which opens before I answer. Luther stands there. My earlier efforts to talk with my mother-uncle were stymied by other duties.

I hurry over, pull him in, shutting the door behind him. 'Mother! You could speak to me during the day, and best you do.'

'But I wanted to see you, my Asher. It's so hard when others are around, to find the moments when you are alone!' He leans down and hugs me. I wish my mother didn't feel so strange, didn't smell wrong – once it was the scent of roses, now it's brandy and the cigars Luther's partial to. The stubble of her beard scratches my cheek.

'You've done a poor job of shaving, Mother.'

'Hardly my forte. Not really something I've been used to doing, but I shall improve.' She smiles and sits in the chair by the fire, while I take the end of my bed. 'It is strange, Asher, how much of the memory of life lives in the muscle of this body. The things my brother did out of habit, I find myself doing them too, without so much as a thought. I do not do them so well, admittedly, but I *do* them.'

'Mother, do you have his memories? The ones of his past?' I sit forward eagerly, and watch her eyes become hooded. It's Heloise to a tee when she's not going to share everything, when she's picking through what she might give you. What worthless pebbles from her mountain of gold. My tone has an edge when next I speak: 'Mother.'

'Oh, quiet. I'm thinking.' She tilts her head. 'Some thoughts are so clear, easy to find, they rise to the surface like the lightest of things. Others… resist. No matter how much I dig. He hated you! So much, I can almost taste it. And me – he hated me even more.' She laughs at that, her brother's shout of amusement. 'But, he hates Mother most of all. Hates her even more than I do and that surprises me.'

'I think he still hated you for being favoured. For being the heir.' *Even though you had no aptitude for managing an estate*, I do not say.

She nods. 'I can feel what he felt the night he betrayed me. It makes me quite nauseous, in fact. Luther, Luther,' she says almost to herself, 'so many hatreds, brother!'

Which I must say seems a little rich given how long hatred was the engine of her own life. I wonder how long before this novelty fades? Before her anger and hatred return in full measure?

'Mother, I must ask and I beg you to be truthful: is there a memory in Luther's mind of a girl—'

317

'—so many girls!—'

'—the governess before me. A Miss Hilarie Beckwith. Did he kill her?'

'What concern is it of yours, my Asher?' Heloise-Luther's eyes narrow.

'The means of me getting here, becoming part of the life of Morwood – so I could do this for you – was bought at the cost of another promise. I must find out what happened to Miss Beckwith and set her aunt's mind at ease.'

'Ah.' Again, that tilt as if it makes the trip through her brother's recollections easier. She shakes her head. 'No. He didn't kill her, lucky girl.'

My shoulders slump much as Tib's did earlier today. *I was so sure!*

'I fear I've disappointed you, Asher. But as I said, the remembrances are different, some stronger than others. Perhaps I will uncover more with time, as I get used to this *persona*.'

'Mother. Your brother's wife will return at some point – you need her, she is the source of the money' – it seems important to tell her this, something she must know before I am gone – 'and, Mother, Leonora is making moves to change her will. To remove Luther from the equation. So I suggest you continue to be charming and conciliatory.'

Her gaze goes flat, then shifts swift as a serpent. Another smile, a nod. *I understand.* 'My good girl, you do look after me.'

'And, Mother, in this vein, I would advise not bothering Luned. Whatever your brother had with her, do not continue it. Send her away – I believe Luther had promised her money so she might leave, travel beyond Morwood.' I say delicately, 'Her feelings for

318

your brother have shifted to something akin to fear, Mother, so let us help her—'

But she's shaking her head before I even finish.

'I think not, my Asher. Or at least, not quite yet. It's so hard to resist those memories of her! And this body – this body is different. The flesh remembers…'

The shock must show on my face because a shadow passes over hers.

'Asher. My Asher. I've disappointed you.' His voice is so soft, only a little mocking. 'My darling girl, after all I've been through, would you deny me this little thing?' He rises, grasps my hands in his, squeezes gently. 'Asher, say you'll indulge me in this one little thing.'

And I want to scream that I have indulged her all her life, that my existence has been one long process of attempting to keep her happy. That I am exhausted, worn thin with efforts that never satisfied her, alive or dead. Then the voice in my head says, *Let them all take care of themselves. You have done enough.*

Whatever mess my mother makes for herself I will not be here to clear it up.

Soon, I will be gone. I will be free.

Another voice whispers, *But the children…*

I sit back, close my eyes, feel a fall of… something cascade over me. Invisible but actual, a physical weight, a pain, a pang. *But soon I will be gone.*

'Mother, be cautious, I beg of you. Whatever you do here affects us both.'

Until I am gone.

319

33

I'm distracted all the next day as I run through my duties by rote, my mind picking at angles of the problem that are, ultimately, all the same. Even when I sit watching Albertine tell a bedtime tale this evening, I'm barely in the room. If my mother is to be believed, Luther did not kill Hilarie Beckwith.

And why would Heloise lie at this point. At least about this? To tell me her brother had done this thing would simply be to confirm that my uncle got no more than he deserved at my hand. That not only was he an abuser of women and a bully, he was also a murderer. Mother has no reason to make me feel more kindly towards him – to make me think I was wrong about him in this one thing. But he did not do *this* one thing.

Therefore, someone else did.

I wonder for the first time whether she simply chose to disappear. Did she opt to leave her life behind and vanish so no one would find her? Yet she had no reason. She was fond of her aunt as far as I can tell, and her aunt returned that fondness – Mater Hardgrace's distress when she came to me was genuine. She begged me to help. The letters I found beneath the bedroom floor were gentle and fond, honest and open. No undercurrents of resentment that I could detect. A perfectly normal family relationship – I've witnessed if never experienced one. I'm thinking this way purely because I'm so strongly yearning to flee.

Sitting at my feet on the rug by the fire, Albertine's animated as she talks about the girl whose seven brothers were transformed into swans. The witch who'd done the deed told the girl she must remain silent for seven years, making shirts out of nettles for her siblings. But the boys hadn't been kind, not once. So she left them in feathered form, spoke aloud so they'd never turn back, married the king, and ruled the kingdom wisely, with those seven swans forever in the palace ponds, their wings clipped.

'Albertine.' We've started sharing this duty in recent days. 'Who taught you to tell stories this way?'

I'd noted it before, but not thought to pursue it. The hand gestures, the facial expressions, the vocal changes and tones, all designed to draw a listener in. Mother instructed me – just as her mother had her – when the mood took, and back and back and back through all the tellers from first to last. It *might* have been Leonora, but she's not spent much time with them in the last few years, hidden in her rooms, losing her sight, and her interest in Albertine is only a recent thing.

Albertine looks uncomfortable. I smile. 'Was it Miss Beckwith?' Her eyes widen, she looks at her brother, who reddens. 'It's not Connell's fault, I already knew of her – but she's our secret, yes?'

She nods, relieved. 'She was here only a short while, but she taught me the telling. I did like her for that.'

'When she left, did she say where she was going?'

Albertine shakes her head. 'We didn't know she was leaving. Luned said she was gone.'

'No,' says Connell, 'Father did.'

Albertine swallows. 'Luned told me the night before Father did.'

Huh.

'Sarai?' She deigns to look up from where she's been drowsing, curled in a wingback chair that seems set to swallow her. 'Sarai, who taught you about plants and their names?'

'Luned. Her grandmother taught her and she taught me,' she mumbles. I suspect it's only her sleepiness that makes her honest.

Ah, didn't Luned tell me her nan had been a cunning woman when she came for help that evening? I think of the chain of red flowers I took from Sarai in the churchyard that afternoon, and how I'd experimented with it, crushing a few petals to mix with cheese in the mousetraps. Finding the mice stiff and cold in the morning. I might ask other questions, but I don't think I need to.

'Thank you, children. Albertine, please finish your tale, my dear, then we all must sleep.'

* * *

It's cold in the woods, the wind picking its way right through my thick coat and gloves. At the Lewises' cottage, Eirlys gave me directions and I've become more confident about navigating the estate, but I wonder how long I've got this afternoon before the sun begins to set, unwilling as it is to remain long during these winter days. Eventually I hear the sound of axes biting into trees, ringing with that peculiarly sharp echo that travels best through icy air.

Thomas Lewis is working further afield today. He's stripped to the waist, sweating despite the season, but the two young men with him – other tenants' sons, Tib's I think – still have their sweaters on. Thomas sees me and grins, waves. I hear him tell the lads to take a break and the relief on their faces is clear; even with a couple of decades on them, he still sets a blistering work pace. Any trace of his earlier illness is gone.

'Asher,' he says, crossing the clearing, hand out for me to take.

'Thomas. Are you well?'

'Fit as a fiddle.' Arms spread wide, muscles flexed. 'What can I do for you today? Can't imagine you've come out here for the good of your health.'

I smile. 'I have some questions.'

'Come and have a sit. I could do with a rest myself but don't tell that pair.' He jerks his head in the direction of his assistants. 'If they ask, I'll say you were feeling faint.'

We settle on a felled trunk, protected from the wind by a brace of trees. In the sun it would be quite pleasant, but the sky's grey, threatening the snow that will soon blanket Morwood and the Tarn. I pick at the fingers of my gloves, but don't remove them. All the way over I tried to work out how to say what I want to say; the perfect words are still not there, so I must use the imperfect ones. 'Thomas, I must ask something in confidence and rest assured I will never share what you tell me.'

'That sounds serious.' He laughs, but there's a nervousness to it. It makes me suspect this ordinary man has only one secret, and now I shall demand it of him. 'I might not answer.'

'You will,' I say, and I touch his arm with my gloved hand. 'You'll answer because I saved you and your family when someone wished you ill. And I think they tried to hurt you for what you knew.'

'I know nothing, Asher Todd, what secrets would a coppice-worker have?'

323

'Thomas.' I stare at him, keeping my hand in place.

Eventually he shakes his head, looks away from me, over to the lads, then back at me. 'Go on then. Get it over with.'

'There was a young woman who came to Morwood before me. A governess, and she wasn't here long. Her name was Hilarie Beckwith. She did not leave of her own volition. Where is she, Thomas?'

He stares at his large hands, at the callouses and lines, the valleys and troughs of his life. He stares for so long I think he might not answer, but I am good at waiting. 'Didn't know her name. Mr Morwood brought her to me very early one morning, sun hadn't even risen. Had her wrapped in a blanket and draped over a horse.' He clears his throat, licks his lips. 'Said there'd been an accident and I couldn't tell anyone. If I did I'd be out of my living and me and my family turned off the estate to starve.'

'Ah.' I think about how belonging to a place like this is life and death to some. Community, family, safety and support. How the threat of losing it would be enough to make a man lie, hide a crime, hush his conscience. After all, he didn't know Hilarie Beckwith; she wasn't of the Tarn. Luther could hold a sword above his head, and Thomas had worked with the master of Morwood long enough to know he'd make good on his threats.

'And I thought "She's already dead, there's naught to be done." And so I took her.' He rubs his face. 'But sometimes I think I hear a girl's voice singing in some parts, always somewhere close by, but I can never see her.'

'How had she been killed?'

He shrugs but says, 'There were marks on her throat.'

'Did you tell your wife? Or Heledd?'

He shakes his head. 'Bad enough I've got to carry it.'

'Where is she, Thomas?' I switch my grip, take his fingers in mine. Part of me wants to snap them – for his weakness, his cowardice – but I'm not really in a position to judge anyone, am I? Instead I'm gentle, transmitting the warmth of my gloved hand to his rapidly cooling digits.

'The quarry.' His head bows. Tears make marks on the doeskin of his breeches. 'I chained her to a block and sank her.'

'Did Mr Morwood say what had happened to her? This "accident"?'

'No. Just that it was one.'

I rise. He remains seated, looks smaller, but relieved.

'Thank you, Thomas, for telling me.'

'I'm sorry, Asher.'

I pat his shoulder, but I don't tell him it's alright.

* * *

I think of that day when Eli took us home via the quarry, of seeing a flash of white across the gaping mouth of the pit, over amongst the trees. I think of the early morning I went there on my own to find the kaolinite clay needed for filters to clean the well at the Lewises' cottage. I think of the mist that gathered so quickly even as it should have been burning up in the sunlight. How I lost my bearings, of the thing with an indistinct face that dived at me, made me fall. How I ran back to Morwood and have refused to think of it ever since because I had enough haunts of my own. I wonder that I've never heard her singing like Thomas Lewis has, but then she's not my ghost, is she? I think of the tugging on my coat as the fog swirled around me like a snowstorm.

I wonder if she knew why I'd come? That her aunt had sent someone to look for her. I wonder if she knew how long I took to do anything? As I approach the path that leads down to the water of the quarry, I wonder if she's angry.

I have three bundles of lavender and sage in my pocket. I thought perhaps I'd need to plant it somewhere, to grow in spring, but I'd never thought what to do if she'd been put in water. I step onto the firm damp loam. There's no trace of any mist today, not when I'm near the path, but as I get closer to where the brown liquid laps the shore, white fog steams up from the ground. Soon I'm surrounded but I keep going, counting my steps until I know I'm close to the place where dirt becomes fluid. The mist swirls, parts, shows me I'm right. I wait a while longer, think I feel someone watching me from somewhere in the whiteness. Wait until I feel that tug on my coat again.

'Hilarie Beckwith,' I say and the tugging stops, but the weight of a hand remains there – interesting that she has some force still. 'Your aunt, Phoebe Hardgrace, sent me to find you.' A small pull once more. 'I cannot see you brought from the depths, but I will make sure your aunt knows where you lie.' Another tug. 'I'm sorry this happened to you.'

I turn around, thinking to get a glimpse of her, to ask her one question to confirm my suspicions, and there she is. So very close to me, and I can't believe I've only just smelled the decay of her, dripping wet, shreds of a nightgown clinging to her, all that beauty gone. Lips chewed away, exposing teeth, eyes picked out by fishes in tiny mouthfuls, empty sockets green with algae. Those teeth part and she screams so loudly my ears ache. I can hardly believe it won't bring everyone running from across the estate –

but I know it won't. I'm alone with this thing, this heavy ghost, so different from my mother, a creature whose rage is giving her heft. The stinking breath pushes at me, I stumble backwards, hearing as much as feeling my heels go into the water, tipping and tilting because the gentle slope of the bank sharply drops off somewhere close by. I fear if I go in, I'll never come out. That Hilarie Beckwith will drag me a'down for company.

I throw myself forward, stumble, yet don't fall. Stagger into the apparition, the ghostly governess, and feel as if I've walked through a spider's web, through slime, through something truly unpleasant. She's not solid; she gives a gurgle. She might have no ill-will towards me, but I'm not prepared to give her the benefit of the doubt. I dig the bundles from my pocket and turn, hurling them into the mist. I hear three splashes, whisper *Depart*, and the mist clears almost immediately as if it had never been.

Hilarie Beckwith is gone too.

34

My mind runs from thought to thought as I return home.

What if Luther cared enough for someone to cover up a murder? What if someone knew enough of his secrets to blackmail him? Then why wouldn't he just dispose of them? Because he's many things but he's not a murderer. Or did he simply do it to cover up a scandal? It's one thing to sow a field of bastard children – that's expected of a lord of the manor – but a murder within your very walls. What sort of a man can't control his own household?

There are just the last skerricks of daylight when I get back. I kick my muddy boots off at the front and sneak in. No one sees me – I'm good at not being seen – and I take the stairs up to the attic, knock softly on Luned's door. There's no answer and I did not expect there to be: she'll be looking after Connell and Sarai in the kitchen while Tib Postlethwaite watches on with equal parts irritation and amusement. I'm careful and quick, checking the chest of drawers, desk and bedside table to no avail. I get down on my hands and knees, peer under the bed. There's a box, roughly the width of both my hands stretched out; I pull it out. It's clean, no trace of dust, so it's not sat there untouched for long periods of time. The wood is old and split in places, the mother-of-pearl inlay is discoloured. Something passed down, I think.

There's no lock, just a simple bolt and latch. I open it.

Inside: a small notebook, well-thumbed, recipes (spells) scrawled in a barely legible script; a shrivelled paw of something; a calico bag of dried silphium. Then: three small blue bottles, all empty, but the same sort as the one left with the Lewis family; a sachet almost empty, but with a trace of red powder inside, crushed flowers, an identical shade to the blood-bells from the churchyard.

I sit back on the floor, staring into the box. Luned and her cunning woman grandmother. Luned and her desperation to find a way out. Luned saying, *You've got to protect what little chance you've got in the world.*

And I think of Miss Hilarie Beckwith and how very beautiful she was. How Luther's eye would have turned towards her so quickly, whether she was interested or not. And Luned, like Jessamine, watching Luther pursue a new plaything; but Luned, unlike Jessamine, caring whether Luther turned away from her. Luned with so many hopes of getting out, away, all of them strung on the strands from Luther's purse. Luned, thinking she had so much at stake, when there was never anything at all.

You've got to protect what little chance you've got in the world.

Luned winding her strong and sturdy little hands around Hilarie Beckwith's slender neck and squeezing. Telling Luther or him discovering it, then covering for her from guilt or shame or genuine care. Luther, involving Thomas Lewis because he was too lazy to dispose of a body on his own, and Luned having no faith that the coppicer would keep the secret. A panicked plan on her part, not much thought involved, sloppily mixed blood-bell poison thrown in the well, then brought as "medicine from Luther" when they failed to die soon enough.

And then… then perhaps giving up at that second failure?

You've got to protect what little chance you've got in the world.

Oh, Luned.

I close the box and slide it carefully back beneath the bed. Looking around the little room I make sure nothing is out of place.

Luned has to go.

Why am I trying to help her?

Save her?

Am I?

Do I see myself in her? Trapped and lost and wanting something else? Something more? Something different?

Or is this my mother all over again? Have I been trained to react to broken wicked things? To try and help them in the hope they will be fixed? In the hope of kindness, affection, gratitude?

How broken am I that I keep doing this?

* * *

'Come to me tonight,' Eli murmurs in my ear. I'm tidying the folded washing in the laundry room, making it uniform the way Mrs Charlton likes it. When she returns I don't want her thinking I've let this house go to wrack and ruin in her absence. The Binions never make sure the edges all line up properly because the young are too lazy to bother. I take pride in this place as if it is mine. As if I belong. As if I'll stay. It's just to keep my mind away from the things that will consume me.

I shake my head. 'Tomorrow,' I promise, and he doesn't insist. He's learned enough about me to know that won't help. He disappears with a last soft kiss on the back of my neck and I spend another half an hour bustling about the kitchen and the rest of the downstairs area, making sure all is in order. Tib always goes home straight after she's finished cooking the evening meal. Burdon is in the hallway when I go into the library to check the fire's been banked.

'Miss Todd?'

'Yes, Burdon.'

'Have you… it's a strange question, I know, but have you noticed a change in Master Luther?'

'Honestly, I don't think I've spent enough time with him to make such a judgement,' I demur.

'Don't be wriggly, Miss Todd, you see plenty around here with those big eyes eating it up, storing it away. Don't think I don't notice.' He waves a finger at me.

'You're far more imaginative than I'd given you credit for, Burdon,' I tease. 'But you might be right. He does seem… happier. He's certainly better with the children. Perhaps the time away has given him the opportunity to consider and count his blessings.'

He grumbles, unsatisfied.

'Sleep well, Burdon. I'll put out the lamps.' I watch his light move up the stairs into the blackness of the upper reaches, up, up, up until even the glow is gone. I finish my tidying – fidgeting – and follow him.

* * *

I dream that I've found the door to the Witches' vault once again, and I'm descending into a darkness that grows thicker and thicker, until it swallows the flame of my lantern and begins to feel like soil covering my feet, then rising, rising, rising, until I'm buried and can no longer breathe. There's a weight on my chest, the heaviness of being in this house of secrets and lies – the ones that reside here and the ones I brought with me.

And I realise it's not a dream and I truly cannot breathe.

A pillow is being pressed down on my face. So very hard. My lungs are aching. I hook one hand around a wrist that's holding the pillow and I tear at the skin, feel it come up in furrows beneath my nails. There's a cry and a curse and the pressure lessens. I take the opportunity to grab at the fabric and push it away. My assailant off-balance, I sit up and swing wildly, my fist connecting with a face, a nose, the crunch of cartilage. A beam of light from a hooded lantern on the dresser shows blonde dishevelled hair, a white nightgown. *Luned*.

'What were you doing in my room?'

'How did you—' almost breathless, I blurt before I think better of it.

'Saw you coming down the stairs, didn't I? No other reason you'd be up there unless you're doing favours for Burdon.' Her nose is bleeding, so's her bottom lip, already swelling. She puts her back to the door and slides down it to sit on the floor. 'You hit like a man.'

I shrug, get out of bed. Take two steps and my knees go from under me, a sudden weakness. Breathing hard, drawing in cold air that tastes like nectar after the bleak blackness of near-suffocation. Now we're sitting a few yards apart, staring at each other. I gesture at the discarded pillow. 'Why did you—'

'Tib's boys said you'd been talking to Thomas Lewis and you made him cry. Then I saw your boots by the door – that clay mud from the quarry. Then seeing you come down from the attic, I figured…'

'You're smarter than I thought.'

'And you're dumber than I thought.'

I can't fault her on that. Clearing my throat, I say, 'Her name was Hilarie Beckwith. I don't really know what she was like, but her aunt misses her. She did not leave here. She's in the quarry – does she sing to you sometimes? Do you hear her?'

She begins to cry, nodding, palming tears and snot and blood away but just spreading it further over her face.

'Luther told you he'd had Thomas dispose of her, but you feared he'd betray you. That his fear of Luther wasn't enough. Two attempts at poisoning, Luned, both quite poor. Trying to murder a whole family. Then you gave up – why?'

'It's not easy to kill someone, you know. Hard up close, less so at a distance. But still, you imagine it. Imagine how they suffer. After the second time… it didn't seem to matter. I thought they'd keep their mouths shut.'

I shake my head. 'But why did you kill Hilarie Beckwith?'

'Because of how he looked at her! It was only a matter of time before he set me aside.'

You've got to protect what little chance you've got in the world.

I shake my head. 'No. There'd have been nothing on her side of it. She wasn't interested in men. She'd have been more interested in you than Luther.'

Luned starts to cry harder. She tries to get something out, however I can't understand. 'Say again?'

'I said, *I can't take a fucking step but I land on a thorn.*'

She stares at me, shakes her head. I could turn her in – or try. Who knows what the constable in the Tarn would do? Nothing much, I suspect, if Luther threatened his position or looked at him sideways. But if Luther didn't intervene? My mother didn't intervene? Who'd believe Luned was helped by the lord of the

333

manor? Nothing would touch Luther, only Luned would be punished. She's no less guilty, but somehow I can't bring myself to... *She was trying to smother you*, I remind myself. *It was a pretty half-hearted effort*, I reply. I think about all the dreadful things I have done and know I'm in no position to judge her.

'Have you ever heard the story? About the path of thorns?' She grins in a fractured fashion through her tears and that looks like it hurts.

'No. Not that one.'

'My nan used to tell me. Over and over and I could never work out *why*. Didn't tell the others, just me. Why she'd keep saying the same thing and looking at me as if I was an idiot. She'd say, "D'you see? D'you see, girl?" and I'd say *yes* but she knew I didn't.' Luned shakes her head, shrugs. 'You're clever. You might get it faster.'

'Try me,' I say and think about the ridiculousness of the pair of us sitting on this floor, on this pretty rug, her with her broken nose and me with my knuckles aching and grazed from when I punched her and caught her teeth. Telling stories in the cold hours of the night, no one to save us.

'Before the beginning of everything, there was a girl whose feet hurt.'

'Good start.'

'Do you want to hear it or not?'

I nod.

'Then shut up.' She takes a breath. 'Before the beginning of everything, there was a girl whose feet hurt. She went to her mother and said, "Mam, my feet hurt." And her mother said *Yes*. The girl then went to her grandmother and said, "Nan, my feet hurt." And

334

the grandmother said *Yes*. The girl went to every woman in her family, in her village. To each and every one she said, "My feet hurt." They all said *Yes*. And the girl's feet hurt forever.' Luned leans her head back against the door, her neck arched like a swan's, presented like a sacrifice. 'So, what do you think?'

'Life. A woman's life is the path of thorns,' I say. 'We walk through it, our feet will always hurt.'

'I knew you were smart.' She presses her lips together, calls me by my name for the first time. 'Asher? My feet hurt.'

I say, 'Yes.'

And we both begin to cry.

* * *

It's desperately cold in the darkness of the stables. Outside the snow has finally begun to fall. My fingers falter as I saddle the brown horse Archie left behind. It's a good enough beast, not the best, but good enough. Someone saw him coming when they sold it to him, but they didn't rob him completely. I lead him out of the stall and apologise for sending him into the maw of winter. Luned, dressed in thick trousers, two cable-knit jumpers, a scarf, boots, a woollen cap and a thick coat looks at the animal with suspicion.

'You can ride, can't you?'

She nods. 'Doesn't mean I like it.'

'Ride south for an hour – it's not hard; follow the road, and you'll come to Tyler's Burren.'

'I know what's around here,' she snaps. I cut her hair close to the scalp and she looks like a hard pretty boy.

'There's an inn. Only spend one night there. No one will be looking for you, at least not for a day or two.'

'You won't tell them?' She fidgets with the strap of the satchel across her back. It contains whatever items of her life she thought worth saving and a purse with some of the Witches' coins in it. It's the closest I can give her to a new start. To saving her. Whatever she does now is her choice.

'I'll never tell them, Luned.' I touch her shoulder and she does not move away. 'Tomorrow morning, take the road for St Sinwin's. From there take a ship. Go where you will. Stay safe, do no ill, help where you can – this is the price of my aid. Only you will know if you pay it or not.'

She stares at me for a moment, then throws her arms around me. We stay like that for long breaths, until she says, 'You're the best friend I've ever had, and that's the worst thing in the world.'

'I'd also suggest you work on your compliments.' I pull away, bend, and clasp my hands for her foot. With a boost, she scrambles into the saddle. 'Look after yourself, Luned.'

She urges the horse forward, then reins him in; looking back over her shoulder at me she says, 'Will I see you again?'

'Not if you're lucky.'

We both snort, then she says, 'Whatever you're doing here, Asher Todd, I hope it's worth it. I shouldn't but I hope you succeed.'

And then she's gone, the snow muffling the footfalls of Archie's mount.

35

'Asher, you look terrible. You really must get some more sleep,' says Leonora, buttering a slice of toast. The sunlight streams in the window behind her, creating a halo of her hair. 'Tell Eli Bligh to keep his hands to himself.'

I don't react, just sip my coffee. The children stare at me, wide-eyed. At the other end of the breakfast table, Heloise-Luther raises an eyebrow – apparently the only four people who didn't know my nocturnal habits. I'd have preferred it to remain that way; it's never paid for Mother to have my secrets.

'Really, Miss Todd?' asks Heloise-Luther, leaning forward as if to gossip; a very un-Lutherish thing to do. 'Do tell: will there be wedding bells?'

'Don't be ridiculous, M-Mr Morwood.' I don't manage to moderate my tone, only to change the words that tumble out. Leonora's brows shoot towards her hairline, but Mother merely smiles. It will amuse her to score a hit so easily.

I wonder what they would both do if I removed the mourning ring, sat here eating breakfast with my own face. Tell my grandmother what I have done, who is really sitting at the table with her. Would the shock cause Leonora to keel over? I think not, she's tougher than that. What would bother her more? The witchcraft or the sight of her long-lost daughter's face? The return of that daughter and the granddaughter she never knew. What if I were to tell her that I've already done to her children what she wants me to do to her? That I won't – can't – do it again, not for anything in the world.

What if I stood and left her and her daughter-son to talk after all this time?

'Where is Luned?' Leonora snaps. 'Honestly, that girl.'

I shrug, don't ask what she wants, don't offer aid. A quick bored glance at my mother-uncle and I look away. But Leonora is off on another tangent, snapping at poor Albertine. 'Don't put so much cream on your porridge, child. It will spoil your complexion.'

Her tone's proprietorial; already she's regarding the child as an asset she owns. That she hopes to possess in more ways than one. Albertine ducks her head, puts the jug back on the table. I shudder; it sounded like my mother talking to me.

'Whatever's the matter, Asher? Are you getting ill?' Leonora sounds more irritated than concerned. As if it might inconvenience her.

'No, Mrs Morwood, just a little cold.'

The door opens and one of the Binions enters carrying a fresh pot of coffee and a tray of bacon. I give her a nod and she blinks in return – the biggest reaction one ever receives from them. She sets her burdens on the sideboard, then turns quickly and exits, leaving the door a little ajar. I don't know if they keep forgetting to serve the food, or simply have too strong a desire to get out of the room and the gaze of Leonora, the indifference of Luther.

'Luned—' I think Leonora chooses that name because she can never remember the Binions' '—close the… oh, damnation.'

'I'll do it, Grandmother.' Connell leaps up from his seat.

I smile. 'Thank you, Connell.'

'Quite the gentleman, my boy,' Heloise-Luther says with a broad grin, that his son tentatively returns. Leonora does not acknowledge the lad. Heloise-Luther has been different, kinder and gentler with the children, and Connell doesn't know what to make of it. I asked him yesterday if his father had ever been kind and he replied that he did not recall so. The poor boy must think it a trap; I can't say I am completely sure it isn't.

Leonora changes directions, charges: 'Asher, be so kind as to go into the Tarn after lunch and see if Zaria has done her work.'

'It's not even been a week,' I say. I take a sip of coffee in the hope it will make my headache go away. 'Besides, the surgery is open this afternoon.'

'Then go this morning.'

'Mrs Morwood—'

'I was not asking, Asher Todd! The children will not die for lack of a day's education.'

Recklessness burns through me. 'If that's your attitude then I fail to understand why you bothered to hire me.'

There is the sharpest silence in the room that I've ever heard. Almost like the sort that comes after a slap to the face. The moment of disbelief when time and even breath stop. Just that sliver of a moment before all hell breaks loose. Then: rescue from an unexpected source.

'Mother, Miss Todd is clearly unwell. Look, she is pale and her hands are shaking. I suggest she spends the morning resting. Folk will expect her help in the afternoon. The poor girl is exhausted, expending so much of her energy caring for others. I shall entertain the children – perhaps a ride around the estate?' Heloise-Luther smiles and speaks in a low, soothing tone; the voice of reason. I don't know if it's the content of his comment or simply the fact she's never seen him act as a peacemaker before, but Leonora is surprised enough to not contradict him.

'Alright. Rest for today, Asher, but I expect you to see Zaria tomorrow morning.'

'Yes, Mrs Morwood,' I say, but my throat is raw and rough and I sound as if I'm about to cry. Perhaps I am.

* * *

I spend the rest of the day avoiding my mother. It's not hard as she does not seek me out, and I notice her riding off again after lunch. I wonder that she still has places to visit. Then again, this was her home and she has been in exile for a long time.

Her lies need to be addressed. Or do they? Do I ignore them? Simply prepare to leave. What point is there in confronting her? There will just be more lies.

I think about Luned gaining the freedom I've wanted for myself.

I think about the children, suspended in the toxic air of this house.

I think about Leonora and what she might do if I am gone; will she try to find another such as me? Even if she fails, how will she shape Albertine? When Jessamine returns, will she be able to stand against the old woman?

And when Jessamine returns, what will Heloise-Luther do? Does my mother remember what her own ghost tried to do to her brother's wife? What memory does a spectre have for the things it did after death?

I feel like a ghost, like a thing made of mist, shreds of me taken away each time there is a fresh breeze, stripping me away until there will be nothing left. Everything is shaken, destabilised – just as I came to break this house, so too I'm breaking. The fault lines that run through me are growing wider and wider.

I must leave before I'm entirely sundered.

* * *

The next day I take a healthful walk into the Tarn. I have morning tea at the coffeehouse, I listen to the gossip about the still-missing priest and wonder again when someone will decide to write to Lodellan for a replacement. I do not go and see Zaria Taverell. How long before Leonora decides to go into the village herself? How many days will I be gone when she does? What will happen when she discovers my deceit? How long before she begins the process again of removing Heloise-Luther from her position? How long before my mother finds out and retaliates?

I think about Luned, try to calculate how far away she will be by now – perhaps a quarter of the way to St Sinwin's Harbour? I should have gone with her. I thought it as I watched her disappear into the icy black of last night. I should have gone, I've done what I must – what I promised. What am I waiting for? What is holding me, really?

Eli?

It means nothing. Have I said that enough times to make it true? *Turn from that, Asher, do not examine it too closely.*

The children; what will happen to them if left here with their grandmother and a father who's both more and less than he was? What will happen when Jessamine comes home and finds… what has replaced Luther? All these things I so adamantly avoided considering before – how else would I have been able to do what I had to? – all these thoughts come rushing in now there's no seawall to hold them back.

My musings are interrupted when I reach the outskirts of the manor garden, and I come across Burdon, sitting quietly on a tree stump, smoking a pipe. He clearly did not expect to be found.

I grin. 'I've never seen you out here before.'

He shakes his head. 'I seldom come. But… that house feels strange.' He examines the toes of his shoes, then says wistfully, 'When do you think Mrs Charlton will be home?'

'Missing her?' I ask.

'I'm just used to her being around. Nothing's felt right since she went away. And the young mistress. She's kind.'

I could tell him that the house was strange before that, since I arrived in fact. 'Burdon?'

'Hmm?'

'May I ask you something?'

'Just did.'

'Very funny. You've been here a long time?'

He nods. 'Man and boy, been in service to the Morwoods.'

'I saw Mrs Morwood with a painting some days ago – a young woman, beautiful, with red hair and blue eyes.' He's gone still, but I press on as if I know no better. 'She said it was her daughter.'

He puffs on the pipe in perturbation.

'She seemed rather sad.'

More puffs, no answers.

'I'm going to keep asking, Burdon.'

He removes the pipe, sighs, and smoke envelops his head for

342

a moment before the wind whips it away. Burdon looks at me as if assessing my trustworthiness or otherwise. Here, at the end, I feel I can ask such things. Who else in my life ever knew my mother *before*? Before she had me. Before *everything* happened.

'Burdon?'

'I'm getting to it,' he snaps. Shakes his head, slants his eyes at me sideways. 'Miss Heloise was the eldest, Master Luther a year or so younger. Not much between them, but the mistress preferred Heloise, and the master the lad. Never have I seen a more spoiled pair of brats, the parents competing to see who could spoil them more.'

I laugh out loud, surprised; the idea of them as mere *brats* pushed the sound from me. But Burdon's face remains dour.

'It's not a joke, missy. They were friends, I suppose, didn't fight all the time, sometimes got along better than well. But there was always the fact that the mistress was determined Heloise would inherit the estate, the lad would be nothing. He'd draw an allowance like some... spinster sister.' He shakes his head. 'His mother never gave him anything to be proud of – is it any wonder he disgraced himself?'

'Oh.' I examine his expression carefully. In all of Heloise's tales, she was more sinned against than sinning. Still and all, it's a long bow to blame everything on Luther. 'And you don't think...'

'Girls don't need to inherit, not if there's a perfectly serviceable son about.' He puffs on his pipe again as if drawing in fuel to fire his outrage at women who don't know their place.

'Ah,' I say. He'll be *delighted* to hear about Albertine then. Poor Luther deprived once again.

'What happened to her?' I ask. 'To Miss Heloise?'

343

'Sent away. Finally got herself into trouble, silly little trollop, and the old mistress couldn't bear it. Couldn't bear to think of all her plans brought down because the stupid girl couldn't keep her legs together.' He puffs on the pipe again. 'I don't know what happened to her. Or the baby. I wonder about the baby sometimes, though. What happened to it. It's strange to think of all that vibrant, difficult life dead in a ditch somewhere.'

'Thank you, Burdon. That was a horrible story,' is what I manage to get out past the lump in my throat. I change the subject. 'Will you ever leave Morwood, do you think? Retire?'

He looks at me like I'm a fool. 'It's my home, Miss Todd.'

And I realise that most people will remain somewhere as long as they can no matter that it's no good for them. Home might be a pile of shit, but they'll stay because it's warm and the smell is familiar and they'll cling to that. They'll cling to it because leaving, walking into the rain to be washed clean would mean being cold and wet, walking away from what you know will mean being lost. No matter that you will make a new way, a new path – the majority of folk don't get beyond their fear of change.

What would happen if I told him everything? Secrets do not stay in the dark where we put them. Some lie dormant, but others slither beneath doors, over windowsills, through the cracks in walls, out into the light where everyone can see them, poke at them, know them. Sometimes they burst from us when we least expect them. I feel as if I've held these ones for too long; I'm no longer the vault I once was.

Burdon rises. 'Coming in, Miss Todd? Getting cold.'

I shake my head, force a smile. 'I think I'll stay out a while longer. It's refreshing. Thank you, Burdon.'

I watch the butler go, walking briskly with a slight hitch in his step. An old man's gait.

When he's gone from my sight, I vomit until there's nothing left in my stomach but a pale thin yellow fluid.

36

I walk back towards the house.

It looms, looking perfectly stable, solid, a thing that will stand for another hundred years. But I know it's rotting. A leviathan decaying on its foundations. Dying slowly, still living, shifting, moving, its death throes sending vibrations through the earth. Inhabited by prey and predators. Liars and thieves and cheats and murderers. And I'm one of them, it cannot be denied; one of them by blood and acts.

As I approach the kitchen garden, I see my mother-uncle crossing the lawn heading in the direction of my surgery. He sees me and changes course, smiling. I do not return it. I try to walk past him, but he catches at my hand, pulls me to a halt.

'Asher, my Asher! So bleak an expression. What's wrong, my girl?'

'You lied to me,' I say flatly.

'I'm afraid you'll need to be more specific. In relation to what?' Her tone is cool; she never liked being called a liar even when she was caught in the middle of one.

'When I asked if Luther had killed Hilarie Beckwith you said no, but I asked the wrong question, didn't I?' I take a shaking

346

breath, uncertain if my anger comes from weariness or distress. 'You didn't tell me Luther knew Luned had done it.'

'Of course I didn't tell you. I knew how you'd react, my little silly. Always so upright about these things.' She touches my face and it's all I can do not to scream; I pull away as if scalded.

'*Upright?* Do you have any idea what I've done? The lies I've told, the things I've stolen, the blood I've spilled?'

'And you have done those things for *me* because you're my good daughter, Asher Todd. Asher Morwood. Shall we call you that? Shall we acknowledge you as mine? Luther's scattered so many bastards around here, why not another? Show your glorious face, give you another name. No one would ever know – Asher Todd would leave, and you would arrive, seeking your father. And when the time comes, Morwood could be yours. Wouldn't you like that, my dove?'

I can't think of anything worse. 'More lies.'

'What's one more?' She laughs.

What's one more indeed? *One more stone in the pocket as you wade into the river, Asher.* Just one more.

Mother examines her nails – her brother's nails – as if she's sitting at a mirror, making herself ready for a lover. 'I don't suppose you know where Luned is, do you, darling girl? I did go looking for her last night in hopes of a chat, but she was nowhere to be found.'

I stare at my mother-uncle.

'Only,' she continues, 'I'd hate to think you lost your temper and did something rash? Before I was ready to let her go…'

'I have no idea where she is, Mother.' I think my contempt

347

burns away any trace of the lie. It's not entirely a lie; I know where she's going, I don't know precisely where she is.

Her voice softens. 'Everybody lies, Asher, don't be so foolish. You're no longer a child.' She – he – wraps both hands around my head, cupping my face tightly. 'This is what we've worked towards. Everything. Here. In my grasp.'

'Yes,' I mumble between compressed lips. 'Everything you wanted.'

And lied for. My mother couldn't have known what I'd become when I was small. No, but she saw soon enough. Saw that I was clever, that something strange ran through my veins. And she broke me so she could put me back together in the best way to serve her.

'Aren't you happy, Asher? You've made Mama so happy.'

'Leave me be, Mother.'

I pull away and turn from her.

'Oh, Asher?'

In spite of myself, I stop, arrested by a voice that's both hers and not. I don't look at her, though.

'I don't suppose you know where the god-hound has gone, my dove? Only I went looking for him yesterday, took a ride to the church at last, where he and I would meet. Where we made you. But it seems he's disappeared. I was rather hoping to have a friendly catch-up with your father.' There's a tremor of rage in her tone, as if she knows. But she can't. She can only suspect. 'I *don't suppose* you have any inkling?'

'No, Mother. I do not. I am not responsible for the disappearance of everyone in the Tarn.' *Only some of them.*

* * *

348

I've barely set foot inside when Leonora calls for me as I pass the library door.

She's sitting at the desk, account books open in front of her. She says to her granddaughter beside her, 'Go. We are done for the day.'

Albertine is quick to rise, quick to leave. She gives me a tremulous smile as we pass, and I touch her arm briefly. I imagine Leonora's temper has been foul today. The woman in question raises her eyes to my face, returns them to the page of numbers.

'Are you still unwell. You're very pale.'

'I am well enough.'

'Good. Have you seen Luned?'

'Not today.' Honestly, this is the most in-demand the maid has ever been. They've never paid such attention to her presence or absence before; she would probably find bitter humour in it. For a moment I imagine us laughing over it.

'Where could that child be?'

'She was not in her room this morning when I checked. Perhaps I should have asked at the inn when I was in the village.'

'Yes.' She looks at me at last. 'I don't like waiting, Asher Todd.'

'What do you need her for, Mrs Morwood?'

'Fetching and carrying. Looking after those children when you're running errands for me.' Everyone is Leonora's errand boy. 'I do not like waiting.'

'You do not have a large enough staff for that, I'm afraid,' I say mildly.

'I do not like waiting for *anything*, Asher Todd.' And the look she gives me is to tell me she means something very specific.

'You must be patient. There are ingredients I require and they are not easy to come by. The apothecary is gathering some – those he can be trusted not to gape at – and there are others I must gather myself.' Then a thought comes to me and it's brilliant and I can't believe it's only just appeared. 'Things you do not want to take from the people of the Tarn because you do not want them hunting for what they will think has come to their village.' I hold her gaze. 'You do not want them turning their eyes towards this house and thinking that anything other than a normal family lives here.'

'As if I care what anyone thinks.' She makes a noise almost like a spit. *You did once*, I think, *so much that you threw my mother out. Or perhaps that was as much hurt pride and disappointment, bitter revenge for all your fine plans being destroyed by Heloise's carnal wishes. And you care that they see you ageing. You care that your beauty had almost fled.*

Perhaps in response to my thoughts she touches her face, fingers exploring the skin that looks much better than it did, but not as good as she wants it to be. She wants her granddaughter's youth, firm and pliable flesh, bright eyes, soft shiny hair. She wants another life; how interesting that she and her daughter have wanted the same thing.

'Can you blame me for my impatience? I feel my years heavier each day. The mirror tells me how close I am to death, my bones weigh more than they should. Don't make me wait too long, Asher Todd.'

'The acquisition of certain items would cause my death if anyone were to find me out. And I imagine my burning or drowning or hanging would be counter-intuitive to your wishes.' I shrug. 'It will be done when I am able.'

She sits back in her chair, clenches her jaw, breathes heavily through her nostrils like a bull considering its next charge. 'Asher Todd?'

'Yes, Mrs Morwood?'

'A word of warning: my son has only a brief attention span.'

'Oh.' It takes a moment before I get her meaning. 'That's not a consideration, Mrs Morwood. Your son or his whims.'

'I saw you in the garden before, speaking with him rather intimately.' Ha! If she'd only heard the conversation she'd know there's greater matters to worry about. She waves a finger. 'Eli Bligh is no proof against whatever Luther wants.'

'Mrs Morwood. I have no doubt your son considers the wishes of women as irrelevant. But I have no interest in his desires. Looks can be deceiving and what you saw was not what you think. Now, I shall go and relieve Tib of the children.'

When I am not here…

When I'm not here, the threat to Albertine will be gone.

Leonora isn't mad enough to try and do what she wants me to do.

When I am gone Albertine will be safe.

I will leave the night after tomorrow.

* * *

Eli is warm and solid beside me. I roll into him, trying to get closer still, to meld with him as if our skins and bones and flesh might become one, something stronger and stranger than the world can break apart. The only stable thing I've known in such a long time. Ever.

Outside the window, the moon is full. We're both awake. He says, 'It's a wolf wife's moon.'

'When desperate women seek husbands among the four-legged? Waiting by a pond at midnight?'

He laughs softly into my hair. 'Some of them. Not necessarily all desperate but seeking different qualities in a mate. Women whose husbands understand that though they roam, they will return.'

'Would you leave?' I blurt it out before my brain can even consider not saying it.

'What?'

'Would you leave Morwood? Ever?'

'Why would I?' He looks down at me. 'I'm not saying *no*, but what's my good reason?'

If I asked you.

But I can't say that. Can't risk that. It would be too hard to hear *no*.

'Just if. Just wondering,' I finish weakly, trying to roll away, suddenly feeling stiff and lonely. He doesn't let me go, his long arms tighten around me, but I'm no longer as warm as I was, knowing I'll leave him behind.

37

The next day passes in a blur. I pay little attention to what's said to me, to what I do or say. I smile and nod while my mind picks at the knots I must undo to untether myself from Morwood. Before I go to bed that night, I rationalise my possessions. What can I possibly do without, what must I take with me. In the end it's very little. Just what I can fit in the carpet bag and the satchel. The trunk must remain, and there's nothing in it that I can't shed like a spare skin. I'll dress in my trousers and boots, coat and one of the jumpers I've stolen from Eli. After midnight, I'll take Luther's black stallion from the stables and disappear into the blackness like Luned. I might even take the same path as her, to St Sinwin's and out to sea. Or Breakwater if I feel brave, though I've heard it's anarchy there since the death of the Queen of Thieves.

* * *

'Did you make Luned go away like you made Mama go away?'

I'm not prepared for Sarai's question as we file into the classroom the next morning, although perhaps, all things considered, I should be. She was so quiet at breakfast, neither Luther nor Leonora in attendance. I almost admire her concerted dislike of me. I sigh and lie. 'No, Sarai. I didn't make either of them go away.'

I pick through the pieces of chalk in the box on the little desk, searching for I don't know what. None of the colours make sense to me. 'Your mother will return soon.'

'What about Luned?' she pursues. *Luned*, I think, *thought not one moment about leaving you behind.*

'Sarai,' says Albertine. 'Stop being so rude to Miss Asher.'

'You're being mean, Sarai,' says Connell.

They're both so wrong and I do love them for it. Such kind children in spite of everything: a cruel father, a distant grandmother. But they have a mother who loves them, a mother who only left them because I promised I would look after them. And I have done to the best of my ability.

'It's alright,' I say. 'Sarai is missing her mother, and her friend. I understand.'

I finally choose a blueish-white stick and write mathematics questions on the board. I tell them to first of all write out the times tables from 1 to 10 in their books, then answer the questions when they are done.

I take Sarai a fresh notebook and some new watercolours and lean down to put them in front of her. She whispers, 'You said you would go.'

I nod, whisper back, 'And so I shall, very soon.'

I promised Jessamine I would watch over them. Watch over them in the mess I have created, all at my mother's behest. But as long as I'm here, the danger to Albertine remains. When I am gone—

The door opens, and Burdon pops his head in. 'Miss Todd, Mrs Morwood would like a word. She is in her rooms. Now.'

I nod, suppress a sigh, and instruct Albertine and Connell to keep on with their work, tell Sarai not to make a mess, and pick my way up to Leonora's suite. I knock, hear her curt permission, and go in. She's standing by the window, rather like the first time I saw her, the corona of bright morning light making of her a silhouette. Except this time, when she steps closer to me, I can see she's wearing a winter-weight riding habit I've not seen before. She's been out; she's shaking.

'Mrs Morwood, are you well? Have you been in the cold? Have you caught a chill?'

'I have been into the Tarn, Asher Todd, and seen Zaria Taverell. Who has seen neither hide nor hair of you in days and days, which is curious as you told me you had delivered my instructions to her some while ago.'

Of all the times for her to decide to undertake her own errands. What to say, what to do?

'Mrs Morwood—'

'It's my son, isn't it?'

'Mrs Morwood—'

'He's turned your head. Turned your heart against me. What has he promised?' The colour in her cheeks is very high, but her lips are pale and bloodless. Her voice is rising. 'What have you agreed to, your perfidious whore?'

'Nothing has been agreed upon—'

'Oh, so you have discussed the matter!?'

'No!'

'And this ritual you promised me, this renewal – lies, no doubt. Some little tricks to string me along like a fool, like I'm as stupid as that doctor-professor! Promising me Albertine's body, my time over again!' Yelling so I wonder who else might hear everything she says.

'No, Mrs Morwood—' *No, you demanding it.*

In a few long strides she's in front of me and her hand whips up to slap my cheek, once, twice. Then a barrage of blows that make my brain rattle and my face burn as much with humiliation as with injury. And she's shouting. Shouting how she never should have trusted me, that I'm a charlatan and a thief, an evil influence, that I never intended to help her and she will see me hanged for the murder of Archie O'Sullivan, or better still burned for witchcraft. How she will make me pay.

She's stronger than I'd have thought, and her anger gives extra force to the hits. I raise my hands to try and protect myself but she's now pushing, and I fall over a footstool. Then she starts kicking in earnest, my legs, stomach, working her way up to my ribs and aiming at my head. The last time I was attacked like this I was thirteen and it was Heloise delivering the beating for some offence or other. I cringe and curl into a ball for cover.

Then the kicks are suddenly gone. I unfurl slowly in case she's trying to lull me into a false sense of security, peek between my arms, and see a man's shoes. And several inches above the floor, a woman's riding boots, shiny and black, doing an unhappy little jig, a sort of circular motion that loses its force, gets slower and slower, the rotations sloppier and sloppier.

I look up and see my mother-uncle's face, red with rage and very like Leonora's was only moments ago. Her large man's hands are around her mother's throat, throttling like she's a chicken for Sunday lunch. Soon, Leonora's feet swing gently from side to side.

'Mother! Mother! Mother!' I say and realise that I'm not the only one saying it.

Heloise-Luther's lips keep moving, and her hands keep squeezing.

I scramble to my feet, pull at her arms, but they're stiff and strong and steel, her grip on Leonora inexorable. The old woman's head is tilted to the side, eyes and tongue bulging, lips blue, cyanotic, elegant hairstyle falling loose of its pins and tumbling down her shoulders.

She dies without ever knowing who I am. I'm uncertain whether that's a cause for sadness or relief.

'Mother. Mother, you must let her go.' I pry at her trap of fingers. 'Mother, please. Mother, she's gone. Leonora is gone.'

And all of a sudden, Heloise releases the old woman, who drops like a stone and hits the carpeted floor with that strange heft of the dead, as if their weight has suddenly increased with the loss of their soul. My mother stumbles back, falls into a chair, staring at her own mother's body. I kneel and touch Leonora's throat. The skin's still warm, but there's no pulse, and she's staring at me, as if to remind me even in her death what a liar I am. As if she knows, now, what I've done.

'Oh, Mother,' I say. 'What have you done?'

'She was hurting you,' she says in a hoarse voice. I cannot tell if my salvation came from genuine care or a sense of ownership – that she was the only one who might treat me like a possession. Perhaps I was simply something her mother was interfering with, and all these years of resentment were simply a powder keg waiting for a spark.

'Oh, Mother.' I sit back on the floor, holding my head in my hands.

'The quarry. Like that girl. We'll drop her in the water, weigh the body down.' She doesn't even bother to remember the name.

'No, Mother. No. Leonora cannot disappear. She will be missed, there will be a search. She isn't a person of no consequence; you cannot murder her so easily.'

Heloise-Luther stares at me, then nods. She rises and I feel a wave of dread. Stooping, she picks up her mother as if she is nothing more than a sack and carries her from the room. I scramble to my feet, muttering *Mother, Mother, Mother* like a desperate prayer, but she doesn't answer. I make it into the corridor, limp along to the stairwell just in time to see *my* mother heft *her* mother over the banister. I scream – as if this is the worst thing I've seen!

The sound of Leonora hitting the marble floor in the foyer below is sickeningly loud even two storeys up. I run over to join Heloise-Luther at the railing.

'She appeared to grow faint, she lost her balance as we watched. We were too far away to help. There was nothing we could do,' Mother says coldly, quickly.

I stare at her. How deep a hole will she dig for me? How long will I allow her to do so? How long will I let her wield the shovel?

From below come shouts and shrieks: Burdon and one or more of the Binions. Luther and I rush down the stairs. He kneels by his mother's body, gathers her up and howls. I stammer out the tale he's concocted; there are tears on my cheeks and they are genuine.

* * *

Later, much later:

Leonora is laid out on her counterpane, the terrible head wounds cleaned and bandaged so her skull stays in place (and I have dressed her in a high-necked dress to cover her son's fingermarks).

The children are put to bed with gentle explanations and sleeping draughts.

Eli sent into the Tarn to order a coffin swiftly made.

A letter written by Heloise-Luther to Zaria Taverell to advise that his mother's last executed will is to stand.

Heloise-Luther and I sit by Leonora's bedside, one to the left, one to the right. This death-watch being done by her closest family though she did not truly know it. Part of me wonders if, when they bury her, they might discover my father's remains. The winter chill will have slowed his decay; surely the stink will be no more than one would expect in a closed tomb.

'Who will conduct the funeral?' I ask, as much to hear a voice as out of curiosity.

My mother shrugs. 'I'll say the words. We can do something proper when a new one is sent.'

'I don't know if she'd decided to report his disappearance to the authorities in Lodellan or if she was waiting to see if he came back.' I clear my throat. 'You should do that.'

'You can do that for me, my Asher. You're so good at arranging things.' She smiles at me from across the bed. 'I'll need your help in running things here.'

I close my eyes, drop my head backwards to stretch my neck, roll my shoulders, pray to sleep forever. 'Mother—'

'I will need you, Asher, at my right hand. And I will most certainly need you when I tire of this body and wish to migrate to Albertine's. What a cunning old bitch my mother was.'

Leonora and her shouting, her very loud voice. My mother and her tendency to listen at doors, to harvest secrets that she might use. A sliver of ice slips into my heart and I freeze. Cold, cold, so cold.

She continues, 'Should have thought of it myself. I mean, I've had fun in this body – and will have more besides – but what an ingenious idea. A while longer of this, then I can be a girl again. Imagine, all my chances anew, to be a rich heiress, owner of this place, a husband of my choosing, children that I wanted!'

And, oh how that hurts. Even after everything that's happened, that still rips and tears and stabs at the heart of me. It will forever, I suppose; that mother-wound will always be raw.

'No, Mother. No more. I'll not do this again. You have what I promised you: another opportunity. Your brother's life in return for everything he stole from you. Let that be enough.'

She shakes her head. 'No. Not enough. Not ever. But you will obey me or I will shake the boy and the littlest girl. I know you're fond of them. You're soft and you won't want to hold their still little bodies, not when you can save them so easily. You will do as you're bid, Asher, my Asher, you will stay with your mother and help me. And so, you will unpack that bag you've hidden in your room because you are not going anywhere.'

38

Once upon a time, there was a stupid little girl who thought if she could just try hard enough, her mother would be happy. Would be pleased. Would be good. Would love her all the time, not just when she was in the right mood.

Once upon a time, there was a stupid little girl who obeyed over and over, even though the voice in her head said she wasn't doing the right thing. But she ignored the voice and became so used to dark things that eventually she had trouble telling the shadows from the light.

Once upon a time, there was a stupid little girl who said *Yes* to every demand her mother made. But then, at last, that little girl decided to say *No. No more*.

And then things got *really* bad.

Because I wouldn't say the words, make the promise, because she didn't trust me anymore – seemed to realise that I was no longer under her thumb – Heloise-Luther dragged me from Leonora's suite and locked me in her own old room (not mine, too many things there, she said, with which to make mischief). She'd come to understand, she said, even her threats to the children would not work, not on their own – that I would find my way to defying her – so I had to be punished until I was broken once more.

Night has passed by twice, and I believe it will fall again soon. I've had no food, and only slightly brackish water from the tap in the small bathroom. The windows will not open; I have stood here during the day but no one who's passed by in the garden below has looked up at my tapping on the glass – I do not shout for fear it will bring my mother. At night, when Eli might peer from his cottage, I have no light with which to signal. The bruises and cuts Leonora gave me ache without any sort of salve. My scalp itches and hurts where my mother dragged me along, Luther's strength far beyond what her own had been.

I wonder what Luther has told them about me? About where I am? Or has he said that I am already gone? Asher Todd has disappeared, and when I'm next seen by the Morwoods my mother-uncle will have pulled the mourning ring from my finger. The Asher they know will never be seen again.

But for the moment I wait here where Heloise once sat with the door locked against her, waiting to hear her mother's verdict, the pronouncement of her fate. Where Heloise's ghost sat, waiting to be released. I sit here, instructed to think about what I've done and what I've refused to do. And I'm to think about what might happen to the children if I don't do what my mother wants.

Think of Albertine, she said, *as the price of the other two. Besides, it wouldn't be for another year or three, and the girl would have a lovely life in that time.* Heloise-Luther would see to that. *How could you even think of leaving me* now *when we have everything? What sort of a daughter are you, Asher Morwood?*

Think on that, Asher, just think.

But I don't think on it because I'm so hungry it makes me feel

362

ill and dizzy. I curl in the middle of the dusty mattress, around my stomach as if to comfort it, as if it won't cramp so much. The room is freezing to boot and I shiver so hard my teeth rattle. I might set a little fire, turn the mattress to a pyre… but how to keep it from spreading? How many might I turn to cinders along with myself?

Sometimes I've seen Leonora moving around the room, but I don't know if that's just hallucinations from the kicks to the head and the hunger. She never stops and pays attention to me – not a proper haunting then. Sometimes I've told her fairy tales: the priest who was eaten by the good wolf of the woods; the maid who escaped a terrible life aided by the worst best friend in the world; the woman whose daughter put her into another's body so she might do whatever she wanted.

I think I tell her these things. After a while I'm not sure the voice I hear is my own, or if it's in or outside of my head. I'm fairly sure I tell her the tale of the mother wolf that I came across in my reading, that I held back to share with Eli but never got around to doing.

So long ago that we are not sure when, there was a mother wolf. She was not like others of her kind. She was very large and could speak. She knew the secrets of plants and herbs and healing. She birthed grand litters, perhaps twenty cubs at a time, and she sent them on their way to all the distant lands, so her blood might flow as far as the eye could see, and ever beyond.

Not only animals came to beg her wisdom, but also the people of the village deep in the forest where the mother wolf lived. When the harshest winter to ever be felt arrived, when the folk realised their stores would not be enough, they went to the mother wolf

and begged her help. She thought long and hard about what she
might do, and she warned them, 'I can provide succour but you
will be changed.' They answered, 'We don't care, only save us and
our little ones.'

So, the mother wolf suckled every villager willing to take
her milk. She did so throughout the season, that terrible winter,
and by snows' end the villagers had indeed been changed. They
no longer walked only the path of two legs, but that of four,
transforming at first on the full moon, and then gradually, as they
grew more used to their new selves, whenever they wished it. The
blood of the wolf ran through those people, and through their
offspring, and their offspring's get. They went out into the world,
where sometimes they trod with two feet, sometimes with four.

I look towards the window, to the blue-black of the sky, the
pinpoints of stars. I think about Eli and his blood, how he's like
one of those pinpoints, all those years of the mother wolf's children
narrowed down to one single locus.

I think on my blood and all I have done. I imagine a life in
which I'm born to a family with the kindness of a mother wolf.
I imagine a life in which I continue to obey my mother. I imagine
myself making promises to my conscience, to the guilt that will
surely whittle me away to thinness in years to come even though
I might smile and laugh again.

I imagine Albertine, but not. Not that sweet, clever girl. Heloise-
Albertine, a new mistress to order me about, a new body, but the
same shifting spirit.

I imagine something happening to Albertine, some infirmity or
illness, and Heloise turning her gleaming eyes towards Sarai.

I imagine her ordering me to find the means to jump myself into that child so I might forever be there to perform this service over and over. To rehouse her into any child that might be had, the bloodline advancing, but the soul unchanging.

I imagine making promises to myself that one day I will kill her and end it all.

I imagine myself being too weak and scared, too beaten and broken to ever take that step.

I imagine losing everyone I care for all to salve that mother wound that gapes in me.

I imagine telling the children what I have done. Telling Eli, perhaps Zaria and Heledd. Telling them everything but then I know I will burn. Worse, I'll see their faces when they realise what I am. I will see their faces and know what they think of me, and I couldn't bear that. It is my secret and mine alone, to bear and to burn with.

I have been telling myself that if I am not here, the children are not in danger. But if I am not here, what's to stop Heloise treating Albertine, Connell and Sarai as she did me? What might she make and remake of them once she's shattered them? Why would I sow a field of such misery as I myself grew in? How could I do that, knowing what it did to me?

I must have fallen asleep at some point though I don't recall drifting off. But a noise rouses me and I open my eyes, still to the blue-black of night. This same night? Or another? How long have I slept? I close my eyes again.

'Asher Todd?' A whisper, a hiss. I'm dreaming still. There's no sound here where I am. This room swallows it. 'Asher Todd!'

I'm being pulled at, tugged to the edge of the bed. A hand slaps my cheek lightly, but it still stings over the top of Leonora's blows.

Opening my eyes I find Tib Postlethwaite staring at me, the Binions either side of her. The older woman's expression says she's got no time for my self-pity, thank you very much.

'Asher Todd, get up and get out.'

'What's happened.'

'Master Luther said you'd left. Gone back to Whitebarrow. You weren't needed anymore. But the girls here have been snooping – Solenn saw you at the window yesterday.'

I look at the twin she indicates, who grins. Smart enough not to draw attention, there's me thinking myself unnoticed. 'Thank you. All of you.'

'He's been drinking since his mother died. Hasn't stopped. We've had to wait this long to come and find you – he's passed out in the library. I don't know how long we've got, but you must leave. Whatever is happening, it's not good.'

'Where are the children? Are they alright?' I grip her arm when she looks away.

'The boy… Luther beat Connell when he kept asking where you were.' She sees my expression and hastens to add, 'The lad's bruised, but he'll recover well enough. Burdon pulled Luther off him.'

'And where is Burdon now?'

'Drunk, of course – how else is Burdon each night? How else does he sleep? Come along, you must leave.'

I shake my head, but I stand, shakily. 'Tib, you and the girls must go. Take the children to the Lewises deep in the woods. Can you find your way there in the dark?'

'Of course. But what about you? Eli won't—'

'You must send Eli to St Dane's. He must bring Jessamine

home. Tell him he must go now. I will explain everything when he returns, but the children's mother must come home now. First, have him go to Zaria Taverell and tell her that Luther murdered his mother.' The Binions gasp but Tib remains silently unsurprised – it's hard to fool old women. Zaria would rouse the constable, the constable would argue for a while, which would give me the time I needed.

'And what about you, Asher Todd? What will you do?' Tib stares at me coldly.

'Finish what I started.'

39

From my bedroom, chewing on a hunk of bread to quiet my stomach and give me strength, I watch the scene below, or as much of it as I can in the darkness. Lanterns moving to and fro as Tib and the twins herd the children out, all of them hastily wrapped in coats and scarves. Tib stops at Eli's cottage, rouses him, gives him his marching orders. His head shakes but the older woman insists, a finger in his face until his shoulders slump. He spares my window a glance, but I've no candles and he won't be able to see me. He'll be obedient, to his aunt and to my word. I'm relying on it.

He ducks inside, comes back out shrugging on a coat and a hat, heads towards the stables. Tib and her little band scurry into the woods like hounds released on the scent of a fox. Except they're more like foxes fleeing hounds. To the right, Eli reappears leading one of the bays; he mounts, digs his heels into its flanks and they're away into the night.

That's it then, Asher Todd.

I rest both hands on the sill, feel its solidity, the dips and nicks in the wooden surface. It's grounding. Taking a deep breath, I turn and force myself from the room, barefoot and silent. One, two, three. I stop, legs frozen. *Move.* My feet shake, toes curling, but I force them: right up, right down, left up, left down. *Move.*

Clean up the mess you made, Asher Todd.

Hurry before the master of the house rouses from her stupor. Decides she wants something, realises there's no one else about. No one here but Mother and me.

Move, Asher Morwood.

Luther's in the library. Heloise is in the library. I tiptoe out the kitchen door, go to the surgery, snow freezing my feet. Once there, I make what preparations I can; ensure the hearth is full of kindling. When I take another deep, deep breath it feels as if it's the first in a long time. A few more glances around but there's nothing more I can do. I do not have the time to waste.

I creep to the windows of the library. Normally, the curtains would have been drawn by now against the cold and the darkness. But there are no staff to take care of Heloise-Luther's comforts, are there? I've been locked away two, three days and the household has already fallen apart. I peer through the glass: there is my mother, my uncle, sprawled in a chair in front of the desk, a carafe of wine and a volume open in front of her – perhaps the account book Leonora was reading. Heloise is probably getting her head around what the estate is worth, how it functions; though she can access Luther's memories, whether she will pay attention is another matter. She'll make bad decisions all on her own.

I raise my hand and tap on the window. She doesn't stir. I do it again, harder, louder. Still nothing. Swearing, I go back inside.

In the library now, I can hear her snoring like a sot. I raise the carafe and pour the red wine over my mother-uncle's face. It's a moment before she starts sputtering, but as soon as she's sitting up, I drop the container, let it smash, and dance back to the doorway.

'Mother.'

It's all I need to say. She's on her feet and I'm haring away along the corridor, towards the kitchen door. I wonder if she's pulled up Luther's memory of this very chase? When I led him to the surgery and brought my mother back? Perhaps it's not foremost in her mind at this point; drunk and sleepy, those befuddling factors will work in my favour, I hope. And I did not wear this face then, but my own.

I bang through the kitchen door, then across the flagged floor and out into the potager. Around the corner and across the lawn towards the merry little light of the surgery, that single candle burning to guide me home. But I'd not banked on Heloise being so fleet of foot: she's gotten full control of her new body, even inebriated, knows Luther in and out and is using him to her best advantage. She takes me down a few paces from the open door.

The ground is hard and cold, painful on my exposed face. My mother-uncle's weight grinds me into the earth as if she'll bury me, then she rears back, flips me over to face the sky and her. I kick up at the same time, catching the soft flesh between his legs. A pain she never expected to feel, I suspect.

A howl, such a terrible howl he – she – gives but there's no one around to hear it. She falls away, curling around her aching balls. It wins me the time to scramble backwards on my behind, roll over to hands and knees and rise. I'm in the door before Heloise-Luther comes after me, stumbling over the threshold. She kicks the door shut behind her, thinking my aim is to escape – as if I didn't recall the other door, the one leading to the stream. But I'm not going anywhere.

'Asher! I will make you regret you were ever born!' Mother roars, that terrifying mix of her voice and her brother's but I think hers is worse. It doesn't matter anymore.

'Oh, Mother. You've done that so many times. Aren't you tired of it? I know I am.'

Only then does Luther's nose begin to twitch. He's finally caught the whiff of it, the white spirit I spilled before I left, over the wood in the hearth, the curtains. I knock over the single candle, hear the breath of the air as the flame and alcohol meet, the *whump!* as sparks shoot out, onto the floor where I made the pattern of a great circle with a star in it, and inside which my mother and I now stand.

I flick my fingers, *wish*, and the flames leap higher and Heloise-Luther turns her back to me, panicking, tries to cross that line of fire, to get out of the circle, to the door, but the burning boundary won't let her go – she's a creature of magic, has been since I put her in her brother's body. She's ruled by different laws. I pull the scalpel from my pocket, the one Leonora used on Archie, the one with which I threatened Luther when he was no more than himself.

He's very tall, is Heloise-Luther, so I slip the scalpel into his back, into one kidney, quickly, then the other before he's got the wit to turn on me. When he does swivel around, I slice his throat, the blade a swift silver arc. Slowly, my mother-uncle falls, grasping at my skirts as she sinks.

I take Meliora's ring from my finger and toss it into the hearth; I'll die with my own face on. The hair hanging over my shoulders turns from dull brown to fox red. I see my mother staring up at me, at her own face. Perhaps if I'd looked less like her she'd have been able to distinguish better between the two of us. Perhaps she'd have thought of me as a separate thing and not merely a tool to put her will in train. Then again, if Heloise had been less herself, none of this would have happened.

The smoke is getting thicker as the building catches fire properly. I sit down, coughing, and gather my mother into my arms. Hold her as she bleeds and dies in a body not her own; her second death, no better than the previous one. I tell her in a voice I'm unsure she can hear above the roar of the flames that this is for the best. That all will be well. That she's on the path she should have taken with her first death. That we will go together.

I begin to cough, feel the life seep out of me as the smoke pushes its way in, tries to fill me. The orange-gold of the fire creeps closer. Soon, the grey turns to black.

40

I wake when I do not expect to, coughing, lungs aching, and my skin feels unbearably hot. The ground beneath me is hard but the cold of it is welcome; above is a black sky from which falls a mix of cinders and snow. I turn my head to the side and see my own red hair: with the mourning ring gone into the flames my camouflage is no more. Eli Bligh is staring at me like he's never seen the like.

I say his name, rough and low in a dry throat. He doesn't respond. I say it again, louder. 'Eli.'

'Who are you? Where's Asher?' He looks towards the pyre of the surgery, gaze desperate. He's a man who thinks he saved the wrong woman; that Asher Todd is turning into embers and ash in that little building. He's not entirely wrong.

'It's me,' I say. 'I'm Asher Todd.'

'You're not. I don't know who you are. Asher Todd's got dark hair and dark eyes, a gentle face…'

But he's staring at me properly now and experiencing, I think, the same moment that Archie did when he first saw me with a changed face. That moment of some sort of recognition when you realise that all is not as it seems, that a concentrated gaze will show more than a cursory glance. That somewhere in the architecture of features there is a familiarity.

'I know, Eli Bligh, that you sometimes go on two feet, sometimes on four. How many can say that? I know every mark on your body, but perhaps I'll spare us both your blushes. I know the scar I put there. I know your blood runs from the mother wolf.'

'How?' He gestures to his own features as if they're the ones in question.

'By ways and means, Eli Bligh, that you don't need to know.' I sit up, slowly, sighing as my ribs ache – as everything aches. 'You shouldn't be here. I sent you away, saw you ride off.'

'And I turned around again as soon as I spoke with Zaria.'

'Disobedient. Coming to the rescue. You should be on your way to St Dane's.' *While I become nothing more than particles on the winter wind.*

'If I'd known it would displease you so, I'd have taken more time.'

We look at each other, burst out laughing for all it's no laughing matter.

He comes to kneel beside me, touches my face, pushes back the red knots of hair, runs a finger down the bruises left by Leonora's attack those days ago.

'You should not have brought me forth.' I wipe at the smears of soot on his chest. 'I cannot remain here, Eli Bligh.'

'You can't leave me.'

'Oh, didn't your aunt say I'd hurt you?' Our foreheads meet, then lips. I pull away. 'Tell them I died. Tell them Luther killed Leonora. That's the truth or the best of it. Tell them I burned with Luther in there – they'll be hard pressed to find even him when that heat's done. No one knows this face, not on me.' *Burdon might.*

Tib might. All the more reason to leave now. 'For all intents and purposes Miss Todd is gone.'

'What's your name? Tell me that at least.'

'What I told you. That much is right, after all.'

He picks at pieces of frosted grass. 'Where will you go?'

I think of Whitebarrow. I think of the Witches waiting beneath the university. I think of the house Archie left behind. He had no family; it will still be waiting. I lived there for nigh on two years, no one will think it strange if I return and take up residence once more. I will tell anyone who asks that I'm waiting for him to come home. I'm its custodian. Stay there for a year until I know what more I want to do. Until I can settle on a direction. In Leonora's rooms there's a legion of jewellery she left behind. Any number of pieces could keep me for years. Sell them, invest the money, buy a little store somewhere, make medicines, help. Live. Do something for myself.

Or stay?

Move into the Tarn with my new face, take a new name, be their doctor. Share Eli's bed. Watch the Morwood children grow though they'll never know who I was. What I did. What I might have done. How I put them at risk. How I saved them.

Would it be so much to ask? A quiet life lived only for myself.

And what of Eli, who knows both my faces but cannot know everything I've done. I'm not ready to trust anyone with that – cannot imagine that I will ever be. And would I want him to know everything? Anything more? And if I am with him will he be content not to ask? I doubt it. Perhaps it will lie quiet between us for a year or two, perhaps more, but eventually his questions will begin and I will refuse to tell (I think he knows this too), and it will become bitter fruit.

'Where will you go?' he asks again.

'I don't know,' I say.

'Stay.'

I don't answer. He holds me.

We go to the manor. We wash the dirt and soot and blood from each other. We make love in my bed, then I tell him he must go and collect Tib and the children from the Lewises, bring them home. I write a letter to Jessamine at St Dane's telling her the house is safe and she must return and care for her little ones.

When daylight is breaking and Eli is gone, I dress. I go to Leonora's suite and pocket ten necklaces, five bracelets and eight rings. From the lockbox in Luther's office I take a pouch filled with gold coins; the Witches' bounty won't last forever and this is the only inheritance I'm ever likely to receive from Morwood. I gather my already packed carpet bag and satchel and then I go to the stables.

I saddle Luther's new black stallion. I lash my bag down, then I mount. I've got a full day and can get quite far away, even staying off the beaten paths. It will be a long trip to Whitebarrow, but I cannot get the idea of the Witches out of my mind, and all they might have to teach me – if only I can find my way back to them. Surely I can find the path one more time?

I will tell Mater Hardgrace what happened to her poor niece, and I will lie and tell her that justice was done.

Eli won't be surprised when he returns and finds me gone, I think. But he knows my true face; if he chooses to seek me – his wolf's wife – he will know me when he sees me. He might sniff me out in the city of my birth. Or he might remain here where he can stalk on two legs or four as it pleases him.

I urge the horse to a trot and we take the winding driveway up the incline, into the woods, towards where the great black metal gates of Morwood spill out onto the road and back to the wide, wide world.

AUTHOR'S NOTE

Welcome back to the world of Sourdough.

The Path of Thorns was inspired by a combination of things: seeing a piece of artwork by the amazing Ruth Sanderson at World Fantasy in 2014, and then thinking about the question 'What would happen if Jane Eyre met Frankenstein?' (That's Dr Frankenstein, not his monster.) That set me off on a rollercoaster ride of weird family dynamics, manipulation and lies, false faces, lost families and found, terrible acts and the potential for redemption. So, the usual really.

As always, the Sourdough world isn't the real world. It's not an historical world. It's the place that lives inside my head, a mix of fairytales and different time periods (mainly Victorian, Renaissance and Medieval). The religion looks a bit like a Judeo-Christian mash-up – which is precisely what it is. But it's not anywhere that's ever existed, so looking for historical accuracy will make your brain explode, and we don't want that.

And once again, I've taken the opportunity to pepper this story with something old and something new. The story excerpt Asher reads to Leonora from *Murcianus' Books of Curses* originally appeared in *Sourdough and Other Stories* (Tartarus Press, 2010) as 'The Bones Remember Everything'. The story Asher tells

Jessamine is a version of 'Gallowberries', also from *Sourdough and Other Stories*. The version of 'Little Red Riding Hood' that Leonora tells Asher was originally published as 'Red Skein' in Walking Bones Magazine (Fall 2006). *Deor's Art of War* is a book mentioned in *The Bitterwood Bible and Other Recountings*. 'The Wolf's Wife', 'The Mother Wolf', 'The Wolf's Children' and 'The Seven Swans' are new to this novel.

ACKNOWLEDGEMENTS

With gratitude as always to Mum and Dad, Ron and Stephen, my agent Meg Davis, the Infamous Write Club (Pete, Kathleen and Jo), Jodi Cleghorn (for the phrase "outrage unstrung"), to Mary Shelley and Charlotte Brontë for the inspiration and the nightmares, and to my wonderful editor Cath, to Hayley for copyediting above and beyond, to Julia for the gorgeous cover, and the team at Titan for making all the words stick together in roughly all the right places.

ABOUT THE AUTHOR

Angela Slatter is the author of the supernatural crime novels *Vigil*, *Corpselight* and *Restoration* (Jo Fletcher Books), the novellas *Of Sorrow and Such* and *Ripper*, as well as eleven short story collections, including *The Girl with No Hands and Other Tales*, *Sourdough and Other Stories*, *The Bitterwood Bible and Other Recountings*, and *A Feast of Sorrows: Stories*. *Vigil* was nominated for the Dublin Literary Award in 2018 and *All the Murmuring Bones* was a finalist for the Queensland Literary Awards Book of the Year in 2021. She has won a World Fantasy Award, a British Fantasy Award, a Ditmar, two Australian Shadows Award and seven Aurealis Awards.

Her work has been translated into Bulgarian, Chinese, Russian, Italian, Spanish, Japanese, Polish, Czechoslovakian, French, Hungarian, Turkish and Romanian. She has an MA and a PhD in Creative Writing, is a graduate of Clarion South 2009 and the Tin House Summer Writers Workshop 2006, and in 2013 she was awarded one of the inaugural Queensland Writers Fellowships. When she's not writing, she teaches for the Australian Writers' Centre. Follow her on Twitter and Instagram @AngelaSlatter.

For more fantastic fiction, author events,
exclusive excerpts, competitions, limited editions and more

VISIT OUR WEBSITE
titanbooks.com

LIKE US ON FACEBOOK
facebook.com/titanbooks

FOLLOW US ON TWITTER AND INSTAGRAM
@TitanBooks

EMAIL US
readerfeedback@titanemail.com